Wireless

continued . . .

"Unlike some, [Stross is] equally adept at both long and short form . . . This collection of stories both shows off his talent and lets us look at the themes he embraces. The future isn't so much dark or bright but made up of the present, and to Stross, that's often a mutable base to start with."
—*SFRevu*

"These aren't just short stories; they're real worlds for you to visit."
—*The Agony Column*

"[Stross] is wonderfully fun to read, and I highly recommend this collection."
—*Grasping for the Wind*

"A selection of a number of Stross's best short stories written over a number of years, allowing you to see why this author has become a firm fan favorite over the years. Thought of [by] some as the Morrissey of sci-fi, you can't help but appreciate the pure genius of his writing within each tale. Even the collaborations of the tales within have his fingerprints all over and demonstrate how he not only honed his skill but brought fans back to the hard-sci-fi fold as he reenergized it with this offering."
—*Falcata Times*

Saturn's Children

"Good fun, and a rare enough book that I'd buy it again. Yes, Heinlein himself would've liked this."
—*The San Diego Union-Tribune*

"Sex oozes from every page of this erotic futuristic thriller."
—*Publishers Weekly*

"Freya is a bot Lara Croft, a strong-willed, skilled beauty who uses brain and some brawn to think her way out of danger. Charles Stross answers the Philip K. Dick philosophical question *Do Androids Dream of Electric Sheep?* with this original look at a mirror humanoid culture."
—*Midwest Book Review*

"[Stross] always brings a fresh perspective to the genre, reinventing the future in bold new ways. Part space opera, [and] part homage to late SF grand masters Robert Heinlein and Isaac Asimov."
—*Library Journal*

"*Saturn's Children* is what happens when Charles Stross, already one of the most imaginative, cutting-edge science fiction authors out there, mixes up some James Bond and Honey West, and filters the whole thing through Robert Heinlein's *Friday*. Stross paints an interesting picture of a future where androids have inherited the solar system . . . It's as thoughtful, complex, and bizarre as any of his works. He's outdone himself with this one. It's friendly and inviting, but once it's pulled you in, it starts to really play with your perceptions . . . He's done a superb job at telling an exciting story that makes you think afterwards. It's a sexy, strange space opera/spy thriller that delivers a kick, and Stross is definitely at the top of his game here."   —*SF Site*

"Stross has created a fun, thoughtful read that will delight Asimov fans as it makes grand use of his Three Laws of Robotics. The inventive story line and strong character development along with Freya's dynamite personality make for a sound pulp-fiction read. Stross writes with a dry wit and fleshes out his characters with little details . . . that are sure to amuse."   —*Monsters and Critics*

"A good, fun read—you'll enjoy it."   —*SFRevu*

"A tremendously imagined milieu, with imagery often deeply haunting . . . I drank these environments in lustily. It's a lucid, textured, *breathing* artificial future that often utterly hypnotized me, and the sort of thing I wish more authors had the imagination to bring to their own space operas."
          —SF Reviews.net

"Intriguing . . . [It] looks to be another solid entry in Stross's quickly increasing bibliography."   —SFFWorld.com

"Charmingly weird . . . a fast-paced thriller . . . There's a lot to enjoy (and mull over) in this often-satirical novel . . . So you'll want to come to this space thriller for hard-science fun and a little sexy time, but you'll stay because Stross always raises interesting philosophical questions that stick around in your brain."   —*io9*

Ace Books by Charles Stross

Wireless

CHARLES STROSS

ACE BOOKS, NEW YORK

THE BERKLEY PUBLISHING GROUP
Published by the Penguin Group
Penguin Group (USA) Inc.
375 Hudson Street, New York, New York 10014, USA

Penguin Group (Canada), 90 Eglinton Avenue East, Suite 700, Toronto, Ontario M4P 2Y3, Canada
(a division of Pearson Penguin Canada Inc.)
Penguin Books Ltd., 80 Strand, London WC2R 0RL, England
Penguin Group Ireland, 25 St. Stephen's Green, Dublin 2, Ireland (a division of Penguin Books Ltd.)
Penguin Group (Australia), 250 Camberwell Road, Camberwell, Victoria 3124, Australia
(a division of Pearson Australia Group Pty. Ltd.)
Penguin Books India Pvt. Ltd., 11 Community Centre, Panchsheel Park, New Delhi—110 017, India
Penguin Group (NZ), 67 Apollo Drive, Rosedale, North Shore 0632, New Zealand
(a division of Pearson New Zealand Ltd.)
Penguin Books (South Africa) (Pty.) Ltd., 24 Sturdee Avenue, Rosebank, Johannesburg 2196,
South Africa

Penguin Books Ltd., Registered Offices: 80 Strand, London WC2R 0RL, England

This is a work of fiction. Names, characters, places, and incidents either are the product of the author's imagination or are used fictitiously, and any resemblance to actual persons, living or dead, business establishments, events, or locales is entirely coincidental. The publisher does not have any control over and does not assume any responsibility for author or third-party websites or their content.

WIRELESS

An Ace Book / published by arrangement with the author

PRINTING HISTORY
Ace hardcover edition / July 2009
Ace mass-market edition / July 2010

Copyright © 2009 by Charles Stross.
Previous publication information can be found on page 319.
Cover art by S. Miroque.
Cover design by Rita Frangie.
Interior text design by Tiffany Estreicher.

ISBN: 978-0-441-01893-2

ACE
Ace Books are published by The Berkley Publishing Group,
a division of Penguin Group (USA) Inc.,
375 Hudson Street, New York, New York 10014.
ACE and the "A" design are trademarks of Penguin Group (USA) Inc.

PRINTED IN THE UNITED STATES OF AMERICA

10 9 8 7 6 5 4 3 2 1

For David Pringle, Gardner Dozois,
and Sheila Williams

Contents

Contents

Introduction

Hello, and welcome to *Wireless*.

This is not a novel. This is a short-story collection. This is not a short story. This is the introduction to a short-story collection. This is not fiction. This is a sequence of concepts that I am transferring into your conscious awareness via the medium of words, some of which may be false. *Danger: here be epistemological dragons . . .*

I'm Charlie Stross, and I have a vice I indulge in from time to time: I write short fiction. I've been writing short stories (in various length factors) and getting them published in magazines for a long time—my first short story in the British SF magazine *Interzone* came out in 1986—and although I don't make much money at it, I still keep doing it, even though these days I write full-time for my living.

Short stories are a famously dead format in most genres of written fiction. Back in the 1950s, there was a plethora of fiction magazines on the shelves of every newsagent: but changes in the structure of the magazine-publishing business killed the fiction markets, and what had once been a major source of income for many writers turned into a desert. Even science fiction—which has a long tradition of short stories as a major subfield, going back to the 1920s and the pages of *Astounding*

Science Fiction, and which has fared better than other genres in terms of the survival of the monthly magazines—isn't a terribly fertile field to plow. Because of the way the publishing industry has evolved, if you want to earn a living, you really need to write novels: short-fiction outlets, with a very few exceptions, pay abysmally.

It wasn't always thus. The science fiction novel was itself something of a novelty until the 1950s; the famous names of the early-SF literary canon—Isaac Asimov, Robert Heinlein, Arthur C. Clarke, and less-well-remembered names such as Fredric Brown and Cyril Kornbluth and Alfred Bester—were primarily short-fiction writers. With dozens of monthly newsstand pulp-fiction magazines demanding to be fed, and a public not yet weaned to the glass teat of television, the field was huge. Video didn't so much kill the radio star as it did for the short-fiction markets, providing an alternative distraction on demand for tired workers to chill out with.

But the SF short-story field survives to this day. It's in much better shape, paradoxically, than other genres, where the form has all but died. It would be hard to describe it as thriving, at least compared to the golden age of pulps—but science fiction readers are traditionalists, and those of us who write short fiction aren't primarily in it for the money: we've got other, less obvious, incentives.

(Actually, I'm not sure I know anyone who writes fiction at *any* length solely for money. If you've got the skill to string words into sentences, there are any number of ways to earn a living, most of which are far less precarious than the life of a freelance fiction writer. At the risk of overgeneralizing, it's one of those occupations you go into because you can't *not* do it, and any attempts to justify it by pointing to commercial success are, at best, special pleading. If Stephen King had failed to get his big break with *Carrie*, if J. K. Rowling's first Harry Potter book had sold out its first thousand-copy print run and thereafter gone out of print, I'm willing to bet that they'd have kept on writing regardless.)

Speaking for myself, I'm an obsessive fiction writer. I write because I've got a cloud of really neat ideas buzzing around my brain, and I need to let them out lest my head explode. But having ideas is only part of the reason I write—otherwise, I could just keep a private journal. The other monkey riding my back is the urge to communicate, to reach out and touch someone. (Or to lift the lid on their brainpan, sprinkle some cognitive dissonance inside, stir briskly, then tiptoe away with a deranged titter.) Everyone I know who does this job has got the same monkey on their shoulders, urging them on, inciting them to publish or be damned, communicate or die.

If you're a compulsive communicator, nothing gets your attention like feedback from the public—a signal saying "message received." To many writers, money is one kind of feedback; nothing says "message received" quite like the first royalty check after your book earns out the advance. It tells you that people actually went out and *bought it.* (And it pays the grocery bills.) Then there are the reviews, be they brilliant or misguided, or occasionally brilliant *and* misguided, which tell you a little bit about how the message was received or misunderstood. They don't pay the grocery bills, but they still matter to us.

But the feedback from a novel is slow to arrive, and thin beer indeed after the amount of effort that went into fermenting the brew.

Imagine you've got an office job. You go to work every day, and there's a perk: the office is about ten feet from your bedroom door. (No lengthy commute!) You sit in that office—alone, for the most part—and write, hopefully without interruption or human companionship. Sometimes you get bored and take a day or two off, or go do the housework, or go shopping. And sometimes you find yourself working there at 10 p.m. on a Saturday night because you took Friday off, and Thursday before it, and your demon conscience is whispering in your ear, reminding you to put in the hours. You're almost always on your own.

You'll find it generally takes somewhere between a month and a year to write a novel—sometimes more, sometimes less. And once it's written, you deliver it to your agent or editor, and it disappears for a couple of months. Then it reappears as a job in the publisher's production queue, moving in lockstep through a series of well-defined processes on its way to being turned into cartons of finished books. There's a little wiggle room, but in general if you turn in a book, it will take a year to show up in hardcover (and then another year before it's reprinted in paperback).

So: once a year, you get the fanfare and fireworks show of a new book coming into print. And then the reviews and reader comments trickle in, usually over a period of a couple of months. Then the long silence resumes, punctuated by the odd piece of fan mail (a surprising proportion of which is concerned with pointing out the same hugely significant typo on page seven—that escaped both you and your editors—as the previous sixteen e-mails) . . .

Short stories are different: they push the reward-feedback button much more frequently than novels. (And that's why a lot of us start out writing short stories before we tackle novels.) There's an addictive quality to writing short stories, like being a rat in a behavioral-science experiment that rewards correct performance of some complex task with a little electric shock to the medial forebrain bundle. Not only do they not take months or years to write (when things are going well, it's more like hours or days), but you can send them out to a magazine or anthology editor with some hope of hearing back within a couple of months. Better still, if a magazine decides to buy your story, it can be in print in a couple of months. Push the button harder, rat! It's great training for acquiring the motivation to engage with the bigger, slower job of writing a novel.

The speed of the short-story publication cycle brings me to the second reason I write them: I get to play with new ideas in a way I can't manage at novel length. Novels are huge, cumbersome projects that take a long time to bolt together; in contrast, short stories are a quick vehicle for trying out something new, the fiction writer's experimental workbench. I can focus on a particular idea or technique to the exclusion of everything else—which brings it into focus and lets me explore it to the full without worrying about whether it unbalances the plot development or fits with the protagonist's motivations or whatever.

The lack of money also means there's less at stake. If I'm working on a novel, I can't afford to try out an untested new writing technique in it. At worst, I might end up having to throw six months' writing in the trash when it proves unfixable: a mess in any situation, and potentially catastrophic if you're self-employed and working to deadline. But I can take a day or two off to write a short story and see if it works: throw it at a magazine, put it out in public, and see if my readers throw rotten tomatoes or gold sovereigns. Or, for a bigger idea—a new stylistic experiment, for example—I can treat it as a pilot project for a novel: take a month, write a couple of novelettes or a novella, find a home for them in an anthology or a magazine.

Anyway: here's *Wireless*.

I wrote the stories in this collection between 1998 and 2008. Some of them were purportedly written for money—at least, an editor approached me, and said, "Would you like to write me a story about Subject X? I'll pay!"—but none of them was cost-effective; the money was just the excuse. They span the spectrum from the short-short "MAXOS" all the way up to "Palimpsest" and "Missile Gap," novellas that bump up close to the complexity and depth associated with novels. Some of them were written in response to a specific challenge from an editor ("Unwirer," for example, had to fit a theme anthology's remit—tales in which the developmental history of science and technology had followed a different path) while some were written in response to challenges from within ("Snowball's Chance" because an imp of the perverse taunted me to write a traditional Pact with the Devil story). Some were stylistic experiments ("Trunk and Disorderly" might, had things gone differently, become the opening of a novel; instead, I settled for the easier technique of *Saturn's Children*) while others were exercises in a familiar key ("Down on the Farm," for example, is one of a piece with my other Laundry stories, collected in *The Atrocity Archives* and *The Jennifer Morgue*).

What they've all got in common, however, is that they're a communication channel. Hello, are you receiving? Over.

Missile Gap

● BOMB SCARE

Gregor is feeding pigeons down in the park when the sirens go off.

A stoop-shouldered fortysomething male in a dark suit, pale-skinned and thin, he pays no attention at first: the birds hold his attention. He stands at the side of a tarmac path, surrounded by damp grass that appears to have been sprayed with concrete dust, and digs into the outer pocket of his raincoat for a final handful of stale bread crumbs. Filthy, soot-blackened city pigeons with malformed feet jostle with plump white-collared wood pigeons, pecking and lunging for morsels. Gregor doesn't smile. What to him is a handful of stale bread is a deadly business for the birds: a matter of survival. The avian struggle for survival runs parallel to the human condition, he thinks. It's all a matter of limited resources and critical positioning. Of intervention by agencies beyond their bird-brained understanding, dropping treats for them to fight over. Then the air-raid sirens start up.

The pigeons scatter for the treetops with a clatter of wings. Gregor straightens and looks round. It's not just one siren, and not just a test: a policeman is pedaling his bicycle along the path toward him, waving one-handed. "You there! Take cover!"

Gregor turns and presents his identity card. "Where is the nearest shelter?"

The constable points toward a public convenience thirty yards away. "The basement there. If you can't make it inside, you'll have to take cover behind the east wall—if you're caught in the open, just duck and cover in the nearest low spot. Now, go!" The cop hops back on his black boneshaker and is off down the footpath before Gregor can frame a reply. Shaking his head, he walks toward the public toilet and goes inside.

It's early spring, a weekday morning, and the toilet attendant seems to be taking the emergency as a personal comment on the cleanliness of his porcelain. He jumps up and down agitatedly as he shoves Gregor down the spiral staircase into the shelter, like a short troll in a blue uniform stocking his larder. "Three minutes!" shouts the troll. "Hold fast in three minutes!" So many people in London are wearing uniforms these days, Gregor reflects; it's almost as if they believe that if they play their wartime role properly, the ineffable will constrain itself to their expectations of a humanly comprehensible enemy.

A double bang splits the air above the park and echoes down the stairwell. It'll be RAF or USAF interceptors outbound from the big fighter base near Hanworth. Gregor glances round: a couple of oafish gardeners sit on the wooden benches inside the concrete tunnel of the shelter, and a louche City type in a suit leans against the wall, irritably fiddling with an unlit cigarette and glaring at the NO SMOKING signs. "Bloody nuisance, eh?" he snarls in Gregor's direction.

Gregor composes his face in a thin smile. "I couldn't possibly comment," he says, his Hungarian accent betraying his status as a refugee. (Another sonic boom rattles the urinals, signaling the passage of yet more fighters.) The louche businessman will be his contact, Goldsmith. He glances at the shelter's counter. Its dial is twirling slowly, signaling the marked absence of radon and fallout. Time to make small talk, verbal primate grooming: "Does it happen often?"

The corporate tough relaxes. He chuckles to himself. He'll

have pegged Gregor as a visitor from stranger shores, the new NATO dominions overseas where they settled the latest wave of refugees ejected by the communists. Taking in the copy of the *Telegraph* and the pattern of stripes on Gregor's tie, he'll have realized what else Gregor is to him. "You should know, you took your time getting down here. Do you come here often to visit the front line, eh?"

"I am here in this bunker with you." Gregor shrugs. "There is no front line on a circular surface." He sits down gingerly on the bench opposite the businessman. "Cigarette?"

"Don't mind if I do." The businessman borrows Gregor's cigarette case with a flourish: the symbolic peace offering accepted, they sit in silence for a couple of minutes, waiting to find out if it's the curtain call for World War IV, or just a trailer.

A different note drifts down the staircase, the warbling tone that indicates the all clear these days. The Soviet bombers have turned for home, the ragged lion's stumpy tail tickled yet again. The toilet troll dashes down the staircase and windmills his arms at them: "No smoking in the nuclear bunker!" he screams. "*Get out!* Out, I say!"

Gregor walks back into Regent's Park, to finish disposing of his stale bread crumbs and ferry the contents of his cigarette case back to the office. The businessman doesn't know it yet, but he's going to be arrested, and his English nationalist/neutralist cabal interned: meanwhile, Gregor is being recalled to Washington DC. This is his last visit, at least on this particular assignment. There are thin times ahead for the wood pigeons.

● VOYAGE

It's a moonless night, and the huge reddened whirlpool of the Milky Way lies below the horizon. With only the blue-white pinprick glare of Lucifer for illumination, it's too dark to read a newspaper.

Maddy is old enough to remember a time when night was something else: when darkness stalked the heavens, the Milky Way a faded tatter spun across half the sky. A time when ominous Soviet spheres bleeped and hummed their way across a horizon that curved, when geometry was dominated by pi, astronomy made sense, and serious men with horn-rimmed glasses and German accents were going to the moon. October 2, 1962: that's when it all changed. That's when life stopped making sense. (Of course, it first stopped making sense a few days earlier, with the U-2 flights over the concrete emplacements in Cuba, but there was a difference between the lunacy of brinksmanship—Khrushchev's shoe banging on the table at the UN as he shouted, "We will bury you!"—and the flat-Earth daydream that followed, shattering history and plunging them all into this nightmare of revisionist geography.)

But back to the here and now: she's sitting on the deck of an elderly ocean liner on her way from somewhere to nowhere, and she's annoyed because Bob is getting drunk with the F-deck boys again and eating into their precious grubstake. It's too dark to read the ship's daily news sheet (mimeographed blurry headlines from a world already fading into the ship's wake), it'll be at least two weeks before their next landfall (a refueling depot somewhere in what the National Oceanic and Atmospheric Administration surveyors—in a fit of uncharacteristic wit—named the Nether Ocean), and she's half out of her skull with boredom.

When they signed up for the emigration-board tickets, Bob had joked: "A six-month cruise? After a vacation like that we'll be happy to get back to work!" But somehow the sheer immensity of it all didn't sink in until the fourth week out of sight of land. In those four weeks they'd crawled an expanse of ocean wider than the Pacific, pausing to refuel twice from huge rust-colored barges: and still they were only a sixth of the way to Continent F-204, New Iowa, immersed like the ultimate non sequitur in the ocean that replaced the world's horizons on October 2, 1962. Two weeks later they passed The Radiators. The Radiators thrust from the oceanic depths to the stratosphere, Everest-high black fins finger-combing the watery currents. Beyond them the tropical heat of the Pacific gave way to the subarctic chill of the Nether Ocean. Sailing between them, the ship was reduced to the proportions of a cockroach crawling along a canyon between skyscrapers. Maddy had taken one look at these guardians of the interplanetary ocean, shuddered, and retreated into their cramped room for the two days it took to sail out from between the slabs.

Bob kept going on about how materials scientists from NOAA and the National Institutes were still trying to understand what they were made of, until Maddy snapped at him. He didn't seem to understand that they were the bars on a prison cell. He seemed to see a waterway as wide as the English Channel, and a gateway to the future: but Maddy saw them as a sign that her old life was over.

If only Bob and her father hadn't argued; or if Mum hadn't tried to pick a fight with her over Bob—Maddy leans on the railing and sighs, and a moment later nearly jumps out of her skin as a strange man clears his throat behind her.

"Excuse me, I didn't mean to disturb you."

"That's all right," Maddy replies, irritated and trying to conceal it. "I was just going in."

"A shame: it's a beautiful night," says the stranger. He turns and puts down a large briefcase next to the railing, fiddling with the latches. "Not a cloud in sight, just right for stargazing." She focuses on him, seeing short hair, a small paunch, and a worried thirtysomething face. He doesn't look back, being preoccupied with something that resembles a photographer's tripod.

"Is that a telescope?" she asks, eyeing the stubby cylindrical gadget in his case.

"Yes." An awkward pause. "Name's John Martin. Yourself?"

"Maddy Holbright." Something about his diffident manner puts her at ease. "Are you settling? I haven't seen you around."

He straightens up and tightens joints on the tripod's legs, screwing them into place. "I'm not a settler; I'm a researcher. Five years, all expenses paid, to go and explore a new continent." He carefully lifts the telescope body up and lowers it onto the platform, then begins tightening screws. "And I'm supposed to point this thing at the sky and make regular observations. I'm actually an entomologist, but there are so many things to do that they want me to be a jack-of-all-trades, I guess."

"So they've got you to carry a telescope, huh? I don't think I've ever met an entomologist before."

"A bug-hunter with a telescope," he agrees: "kind of unexpected."

Intrigued, Maddy watches as he screws the viewfinder into place, then pulls out a notebook and jots something down. "What are you looking at?"

He shrugs. "There's a good view of S Doradus from here," he says. "You know, Satan? And his two little angels."

Maddy glances up at the violent pinprick of light, then looks away before it can burn her eyes. It's a star, but bright enough to cast shadows from half a light-year's distance. "The disks?"

"Them." There's a camera body in his bag, a chunky old Bronica from back before the Soviets swallowed Switzerland and Germany whole. He carefully screws it onto the telescope's viewfinder. "The Institute wants me to take a series of photographs of them—nothing fancy, just the best this eight-inch reflector can do—over six months. Plot the ship's position on a map. There's a bigger telescope in the hold, for when I arrive, and they're talking about sending a real astronomer one of these days, but in the meantime they want photographs from sixty thousand miles out across the disk. For parallax, so they can work out how fast the other disks are moving."

"Disks." They seem like distant abstractions to her, but John's enthusiasm is hard to ignore. "Do you suppose they're like, uh, here?" She doesn't say like Earth—everybody knows this isn't Earth anymore. Not the way it used to be.

"Maybe." He busies himself for a minute with a chunky film cartridge. "They've got oxygen in their atmospheres, we know that. And they're big enough. But they're most of a light-year away—far closer than the stars, but still too far for telescopes."

"Or moon rockets," she says, slightly wistfully. "Or sputniks."

"If those things worked anymore." The film is in: he leans over the scope and brings it round to bear on the first of the disks, a couple of degrees off from Satan. (The disks are invisible to the naked eye; it takes a telescope to see their reflected light.) He glances up at her. "Do you remember the moon?"

Maddy shrugs. "I was just a kid when it happened. But I saw the moon, some nights. During the day, too."

He nods. "Not like some of the kids these days. Tell them we used to live on a big spinning sphere, and they look at you like you're mad."

"What do they think the speed of the disks will tell them?" she asks.

"Whether they're all as massive as this one. What they could be made of. What that tells us about who it was that made them." He shrugs. "Don't ask me, I'm just a bug-hunter. This stuff is big, bigger than bugs." He chuckles. "It's a new world out here."

She nods very seriously, then actually sees him for the first time: "I guess it is."

◉ BOLDLY GO

"So tell me, Comrade Colonel, how did it really feel?"

The comrade colonel laughs uneasily. He's forty-three and still slim and boyish-looking, but carries a quiet melancholy around with him like his own personal storm cloud. "I was very busy all the time," he says with a self-deprecating little shrug. "I didn't have time to pay attention to myself. One orbit, it only lasted ninety minutes; what did you expect? If you really want to know, Gherman's the man to ask. He had more time."

"Time." His interrogator sighs and leans his chair back on two legs. It's a horribly old, rather precious Queen Anne original, a gift to some tsar or other, many years before the October Revolution. "What a joke. Ninety minutes, two days, that's all we got before they changed the rules on us."

"'They,' Comrade Chairman?" The colonel looked puzzled.

"Whoever." The chairman's vague wave takes in half the horizon of the richly paneled Kremlin office. "What a joke. Whoever they were, at least they saved us from a pasting in Cuba because of that louse Nikita." He pauses for a moment, then toys with the wineglass that sits, half-empty, before him. The colonel has a glass, too, but his is full of grape juice, out of consideration for his past difficulties. "The 'whoever' I speak of are, of course, the brother socialists from the stars who brought us here." He grins humorlessly, face creasing like the muzzle of a shark that smells blood in the water.

"Brother socialists." The colonel smiles hesitantly, wondering if it's a joke, and if so, whether he's allowed to share it. He's still unsure why he's being interviewed by the premier—in his private office, at that. "Do we know anything of them, sir? That is, am I supposed to—"

"Never mind." Aleksey sniffs, dismissing the colonel's worries. "Yes, you're cleared to know everything on this topic. The trouble is there is nothing to know, and this troubles me, Yuri Alexeyevich. We infer purpose, the engine of a greater history at work—but the dialectic is silent on this matter. I have consulted the experts, asked them to read the chicken entrails, but none of them can do anything other than parrot pre-event dogma: 'Any species advanced enough to do to us what happened that day must of course have evolved true Communism, Comrade Premier! Look what they did for us!' (That was Shchlovskii, by the way.) And yes, I look and I see six cities that nobody can live in, spaceships that refuse to stick to the sky, and a landscape that Sakharov and that bunch of double domes are at a loss to explain. There are fucking miracles and wonders and portents in the sky, like a galaxy we were supposed to be part of that is now a million years too old and shows extensive signs of construction. There's no room for miracles and wonders in our rational world, and it's giving the comrade general secretary, Yuri, the *comrade general secretary*, stomach ulcers; did you know that?"

The colonel sits up straight, anticipating the punch line: it's a well-known fact throughout the USSR that when Brezhnev says "frog," the premier croaks. And here he is in the premier's office, watching that very man, Aleksey Kosygin, chairman of the Council of Ministers, third most powerful man in the Soviet Union, taking a deep breath.

"Yuri Alexeyevich, I have brought you here today because I want you to help set Leonid Illich's stomach at rest. You're an aviator and a hero of the Soviet Union, and more importantly, you're smart enough to do the job and young enough to see it through, not like the old farts cluttering up Stavka. (It's going to take most of a lifetime to sort out, you mark my words.) You're also—you will pardon the bluntness—about as much use as a fifth wheel in your current posting right now: we have to face facts, and the sad reality is that none of Korolev's birds will ever fly again, not even with the atomic bomb pusher-thing they've been working on." Kosygin sighs and shuffles upright in his chair. "There is simply no point in maintaining the Cosmonaut Training Center. A decree has been drafted and will be approved next week: the manned-rocket program is going to be wound up and the Cosmonaut Corps reassigned to other duties."

The colonel flinches. "Is that absolutely necessary, Comrade Chairman?"

Kosygin drains his wineglass, decides to ignore the implied criticism. "We don't have the resources to waste. But, Yuri Alexeyevich, all that training is not lost." He grins wolfishly. "I have new worlds for you to explore and a new ship for you to do it in."

"A new ship." The colonel nods, then does a double take, punch-drunk. "A ship?"

"Well, it isn't a fucking horse," says Kosygin. He slides a big glossy photograph across his blotter toward the colonel. "Times have moved on." The colonel blinks in confusion as he tries to make sense of the thing at the center of the photograph. The premier watches his face, secretly amused: confusion is everybody's first reaction to the thing in the photograph.

"I'm not sure I understand, sir—"

"It's quite simple: you trained to explore new worlds. You can't, not using the rockets. The rockets won't ever make orbit. I've had astronomers having nervous breakdowns trying to explain why, but they all agree on the key point: rockets won't do it for us here. Something wrong with the gravity, they say it even crushes falling starlight." The chairman taps a fat finger on the photograph. "But you can do it using this. We invented it, and the bloody Americans didn't. It's called an ekranoplan, and you rocket boys are going to stop being grounded cosmonauts and learn how to fly it. What do you think, Colonel Gagarin?"

The colonel whistles tunelessly through his teeth: he's finally worked out the scale. It looks like a flying boat with clipped wings, jet engines clustered by the sides of its cockpit—but no flying boat ever carried a runway with a brace of MiG-21s on its back. "It's bigger than a cruiser! Is it nuclear-powered?"

"Of course." The chairman's grin slips. "It cost as much as those moon rockets of Sergei's, *Colonel-General*. Try not to drop it."

Gagarin glances up, surprise and awe visible on his face. "Sir, I'm honored, but—"

"Don't be." The chairman cuts him off. "The promotion was coming your way anyway. The posting that comes with it will earn you as much honor as that first orbit. A second chance at space, if you like. But you can't fail: the cost is unthinkable. It's not your skin that will pay the toll; it's our entire rationalist civilization." Kosygin leans forward intently.

"Somewhere out there are beings so advanced that they skinned the Earth like a grape and plated it onto this disk—or worse, copied us all right down to the atomic level and duplicated us like one of those American Xerox machines. It's not just us, though. You are aware of the other continents in the oceans. We think some of them may be inhabited, too—nothing else makes sense. Your task is to take the *Sergei Korolev*, the first ship of its class, on an historic five-year cruise. You will boldly go where no Soviet man has gone before, explore new worlds and look for new peoples, and establish fraternal socialist relations with them. But your primary objective is to discover who built this giant mousetrap of a world, and why they brought us to it, and to report back to us—before the Americans find out."

● COMMITTEE PROCESS

The cherry trees are in bloom in Washington DC, and Gregor perspires in the summer heat. He has grown used to the relative cool of London, and this unaccustomed change of climate has disoriented him. Jet lag is a thing of the past—a small mercy—but there are still adjustments to make. Because the disk is flat, the daylight source—polar flares from an accretion disk inside the axial hole, the scientists call it, which signifies nothing to most people—grows and shrinks the same wherever you stand.

There's a concrete sixties-vintage office block with a conference suite furnished in burnt umber and orange, chromed chairs and Kandinsky prints on the walls: all very seventies. Gregor waits outside the suite until the buzzer sounds and the receptionist looks up from behind her IBM typewriter and says, "You can go in now; they're expecting you."

Gregor goes in. It's an occupational hazard, but by no means the worst, in his line of work.

"Have a seat." It's Seth Brundle, Gregor's divisional head—a grey-looking functionary, more adept at office back-stabbing than field-expedient assassinations. His cover, like Gregor's, is an innocuous-sounding post in the Office of Technology Assessment. In fact, both he and Gregor work for a different government agency, although the notional task is the same: identify technological threats and stamp on them before they emerge.

Brundle is not alone in the room. He proceeds with the introductions: "Greg Samsa is our London station chief and specialist in scientific intelligence. Greg, this is Marcus." The bald, thin-faced German in the smart suit bobs his head and smiles behind his horn-rimmed glasses. "Civilian consultant." Gregor mistrusts him on sight. Marcus is a defector—a former Stasi spook, from back before the Brezhnev purges of the mid-sixties. Which puts an interesting complexion on this meeting.

"Murray Fox, from Langley."

"Hi," says Gregor, wondering just what kind of insane political critical mass Stone is trying to assemble: Langley and Brundle's parent outfit aren't even on speaking terms, to say the least.

"And another civilian specialist, Dr. Sagan." Greg nods at the doctor, a thin guy with sparkling brown eyes and hippyish long hair. "Greg's got something to tell us in person," says Brundle. "Something very interesting he picked up in London. No sources please, Greg."

"No sources," Gregor echoes. He pulls out a chair and sits down. Now that he's here, he supposes he'll just have to play

the role Brundle assigned to him in the confidential briefing he read on the long flight home. "We have word from an
unimpeachable HUMINT resource that the Russians have—"
He coughs into his fist. "Excuse me." He glances at Brundle.
"Okay to talk about COLLECTION RUBY?"

"They're all cleared," Brundle says dryly. "That's why it
says 'joint committee' on the letterhead."

"I see. My invitation was somewhat terse." Gregor stifles
a sigh that seems to say, *All I get is a most urgent recall; how
am I meant to know what's going on and who knows what?*
"So why are we here?"

"Think of it as another collective analysis board," says
Fox, the man from the CIA. He doesn't look enthused.

"We're here to find out what's going on, with the benefit of some intelligence resources from the other side of the
curtain."

Dr. Sagan, who has been listening silently with his head
cocked to one side like a very intelligent blackbird, raises an
eyebrow.

"Yes?" asks Brundle.

"I, uh—would you mind explaining that to me? I haven't
been on one of these committees before."

No indeed, thinks Gregor. It's a miracle Sagan ever passed
his political vetting: he's too friendly by far with some of
those Russian astronomer guys who are clearly under the
thumb of the KGB's First Department. And he's expressed
doubts—muted, of course—about the thrust of current foreign policy, which is a serious no-no under the McNamara
administration.

"A CAB is a joint committee feeding into the Central
Office of Information's external bureaus on behalf of a blue-
ribbon panel of experts assembled from the intelligence community," Gregor recites in a bored tone of voice. "Stripped of
the bullshit, we're a board of wise men who're meant to rise
above narrow bureaucratic lines of engagement and prepare a
report for the Office of Technology Assessment to pass on to
the director of Central Intelligence. It's not meant to reflect
the agenda of any one department, but to be a Delphi board
synergizing our lateralities. Set up after the Cuban fiasco to
make sure that we never again get backed into that kind of

corner by accidental groupthink. One of the rules of the CAB process is that it has to include at least one dissident: unlike the commies, we know we're not perfect." Gregor glances pointedly at Fox, who has the good sense to stay silent.

"Oh, I see," Sagan says hesitantly. With more force: "So that's why I'm here? Is that the only reason you've dragged me away from Cornell?"

"Of course not, Doctor," oozes Brundle, casting Gregor a dirty look. The East German defector, Wolff, maintains a smug silence: *I am above all this.* "We're here to come up with policy recommendations for dealing with the bigger picture. The *much*-bigger picture."

"The Builders," says Fox. "We're here to determine what our options look like if and when they show up, and to make recommendations about the appropriate course of action. Your background in, uh, SETI recommended you."

Sagan looks at him in disbelief. "I'd have thought that was obvious," he says.

"Eh?"

"We won't have any choice," the young professor explains with a wry smile. "Does a termite mound negotiate with a nuclear superpower?"

Brundle leans forward. "That's a rather radical position, isn't it? Surely there'll be some room for maneuver? We know this is an artificial construct, but presumably the builders are still living people. Even if they've got green skin and six eyes."

"Oh. My. God." Sagan leans forward, his face in his hands. After a moment, Gregor realizes that he's laughing.

"Excuse me." Gregor glances round. It's the German defector, Wolff, or whatever he's called. "Herr Professor, would you care to explain what you find so funny?"

After a moment Sagan leans back, looks at the ceiling, and sighs. "Imagine a single, a forty-five rpm record with a center hole punched out. The inner hole is half an astronomical unit—46 million miles—in radius. The outer edge is of unknown radius, but probably about two and a half AUs—245 million miles. The disk's thickness is unknown—seismic waves are reflected off a mirrorlike rigid layer eight hundred miles down—but we can estimate it at eight thousand miles, if its density averages out at the same as Earth's. Surface gravity is the same as our original planet, and since we've been transplanted here and survived we have learned that it's a remarkably hospitable environment for our kind of life; only on the large scale does it seem different."

The astronomer sits up. "Do any of you gentlemen have any idea just how preposterously powerful whoever built this structure is?"

"How do you mean, 'preposterously powerful'?" asks Brundle, looking more interested than annoyed.

"A colleague of mine, Dan Alderson, did the first analysis. I think you might have done better to pull him in, frankly. Anyway, let me itemize: item number one is escape velocity." Sagan holds up a bony finger. "Gravity on a disk does not diminish in accordance with the inverse square law, the way it does on a spherical object like the planet we came from. We have roughly Earth-like gravity, but to escape, or to reach orbit, takes tremendously more speed. Roughly two hundred times more, in fact. Rockets that from Earth could reach the moon just fall out of the sky after running out of fuel. Next item"—another finger—"the area and mass of the disk. If it's double-sided, it has a surface area equal to billions and billions of Earths. We're stuck in the middle of an ocean full of alien continents, but we have no guarantee that this hospitable environment is anything other than a tiny oasis in a world of strangeness."

The astronomer pauses to pour himself a glass of water, then glances round the table. "To put it in perspective, gentlemen, this world is so big that, if one in every hundred stars had an Earth-like planet, this single structure could support the population of our *entire home galaxy*. As for the mass—this structure is as massive as fifty thousand suns. It is, quite bluntly, impossible: as-yet-unknown physical forces must be at work to keep it from rapidly collapsing in on itself and creating a black hole. The repulsive force, whatever it is, is strong enough to hold the weight of fifty thousand suns: think about that for a moment, gentlemen."

At that point Sagan looks around and notices the blank stares. He chuckles ruefully.

"What I mean to say is, this structure is not permitted by

the laws of physics as we understand them. Because it clearly *does* exist, we can draw some conclusions, starting with the fact that our understanding of physics is incomplete. Well, that isn't news: we know we don't have a unified theory of everything. Einstein spent thirty years looking for one, and didn't come up with it.

"But, secondly." He looks tired for a moment, aged beyond his years. "We used to think that any extraterrestrial beings we might communicate with would be fundamentally comprehensible: folks like us, albeit with better technology. I think that's the frame of mind you're still working in. Back in 'sixty-one we had a brainstorming session at a conference, trying to work out just how big an engineering project a spacefaring civilization might come up with. Freeman Dyson, from Princeton, came up with about the biggest thing any of us could imagine: something that required us to imagine dismantling Jupiter and turning it into habitable real estate.

"This disk is about a hundred million times bigger than Dyson's sphere. And that's before we take into account the time factor."

"Time?" echoes Fox from Langley, sounding confused.

"Time." Sagan smiles in a vaguely disconnected way. "We're nowhere near our original galactic neighborhood and whoever moved us here, they didn't bend the laws of physics far enough to violate the speed limit. It takes light about 160,000 years to cross the distance between where we used to live, and our new stellar neighborhood, the Lesser Magellanic Cloud. Which we have fixed, incidentally, by measuring the distance to known Cepheid variables, once we were able to take into account the measurable blue shift of infalling light and the fact that some of them were changing frequency slowly and seem to have changed rather a lot. Our best estimate is eight hundred thousand years, plus or minus two hundred thousand. That's about four times as long as our species has existed, gentlemen. We're fossils, an archaeology experiment or something. Our relevance to our abductors is not as equals, but as subjects in some kind of vast experiment. And what the purpose of the experiment is, I can't tell you. I've got some guesses, but . . ."

Sagan shrugs, then lapses into silence. Gregor catches

Brundle's eye, and Brundle shakes his head very slightly. *Don't spill the beans.* Gregor nods. Sagan may realize he's in a room with a CIA spook and an East German defector, but he doesn't need to know about the Alienation Service yet.

"Well, that's as may be," says Fox, dropping words like stones into the hollow silence at the table. "But it begs the question: what are we going to tell the DCI?"

"I suggest," says Gregor, "that we start by reviewing COLLECTION RUBY." He nods at Sagan. "Then, maybe when we're all up to speed on *that*, we'll have a better idea of whether there's anything useful we can tell the DCI."

● CANNON FODDER

Madeleine and Robert Holbright are among the last of the immigrants to disembark on the new world. As she glances back at the brilliant white side of the liner, the horizon seems to roll around her head, settling into a strange new stasis that feels unnatural after almost six months at sea.

New Iowa isn't flat and it isn't new: rampart cliffs loom to either side of the unnaturally deep harbor (gouged out of bedrock courtesy of General Atomics). A cog-driven funicular railway hauls Maddy and Robert and their four shipping trunks up the thousand-foot climb to the plateau and the port city of Fort Eisenhower—and then to the arrival and orientation camp.

Maddy is quiet and withdrawn, but Bob, oblivious, natters constantly about opportunities and jobs and grabbing a plot of land to build a house on. "It's the new world," he says at one point. "Why aren't you excited?"

"The new world," Maddy echoes, biting back the urge to say something cutting. She looks out the window as the train climbs the cliff face and brings them into sight of the city. City is the wrong word: it implies solidity, permanence. Fort Eisenhower is less than five years old, a leukemic gash inflicted on the landscape by the Corps of Engineers. The tallest building is the governor's mansion, at three stories. Architecturally, the tone is Wild West meets the Radar Age, raw pine houses contrasting with big grey concrete boxes full of seaward-pointing Patriot missiles to deter the inevitable encroachment of the communist hordes. "It's so *flat.*"

"The nearest hills are two hundred miles away, past the coastal plain—didn't you read the map?"

She ignores his little dig as the train squeals and clanks up the side of the cliff. It wheezes asthmatically to a stop beside a wooden platform and expires in a belch of saturated steam. An hour later they're weary and sweated-up in the lobby of an unprepossessing barrack hall made of raw plywood. There's a large hall and a row of tables and a bunch of bored-looking colonial service types, and people are walking from one position to another with bundles of papers, answering questions in low voices and receiving official stamps. The would-be colonists mill around like disturbed livestock among the piles of luggage at the back of the room. Maddy and Robert queue uneasily in the damp afternoon heat, overhearing snippets of conversation. "Country of origin? Educational qualifications? Yes, but what was your last job?" Religion and race—almost a quarter of the people in the hall are refugees from India or Pakistan or somewhere lost to the mysterious east forever— seem to obsess the officials. "Robert?" she whispers.

"It'll be all right," he says with false certainty. Taking after his dad already, trying to pretend he's the solid family man. Her sidelong glance at him steals any residual confidence. Then it's their turn.

"Names, passports, country of origin?" The guy with the moustache is brusque and bored, irritated by the heat.

Robert smiles at him. "Robert and Madeleine Holbright, from Canada?" He offers their passports.

"Uh-huh." The official gives the documents a very American going-over. "What schooling have you done? What was your last job?"

"I've, uh, I was working part-time in a garage. On my way through college—I was final year at Toronto, studying structural engineering, but I haven't sat the finals. Maddy— Maddy's a qualified paramedic."

The officer fixes her with a stare. "Worked at it?"

"What? Uh, no—I'm freshly qualified." His abrupt questioning flusters her.

"Huh." He makes a cryptic notation against their names

on a long list, a list that spills over the edge of his desk and trails toward the rough floor. "Next." He hands the passports back, and a couple of cards, and points them along to the row of desks.

Someone is already stepping up behind them when Maddy manages to read the tickets. Hers says TRAINEE NURSE. Robert is staring at his and saying, "No, this is wrong."

"What is it, Bob?" She looks over his shoulder as someone jostles him sideways. His card reads LABORER (UNSKILLED); but she doesn't have time to read the rest.

● CAPTAIN'S LOG

Yuri Gagarin kicks his shoes off, loosens his tie, and leans back in his chair. "It's hotter than fucking Cuba!" he complains.

"You visited Cuba, didn't you, boss?" His companion, still standing, pours a glass of iced tea and passes it to the young colonel-general before drawing one for himself.

"Yeah, thanks, Misha." The former first cosmonaut smiles tiredly. "Back before the invasion. Have a seat."

Misha Gorodin is the only man on the ship who doesn't have to give a shit whether the captain offers him a seat, but he's grateful all the same: a little respect goes a long way, and Gagarin's sunny disposition and friendly attitude are a far cry from some of the fuckheads Misha's been stuck with in the past. There's a class of officer who thinks that because you're a *zampolit* you're somehow below them, but Yuri doesn't do that: in some ways he's the ideal New Soviet Man, progress personified. Which makes life a lot easier, because Yuri is one of the very few naval commanders who doesn't have to give a shit what his political officer thinks, and life would be an awful lot stickier without that grease of respect to make the wheels go round. Mind you, Yuri is also commander of the only naval warship operated by the Cosmonaut Corps, which is a branch of the Strategic Rocket Forces, another howling exception to the usual military protocol. Somehow this posting seems to be breaking all the rules . . .

"What was it like, boss?"

"Hot as hell. Humid, like this. Beautiful women, but lots of dark-skinned comrades who didn't bathe often enough—all very jolly, but you couldn't help looking out to sea, over your shoulder. You know there was an American base there, even then? Guantanamo. They don't have the base now, but they've got all the rubble." For a moment Gagarin looks morose. "Bastards."

"The Americans."

"Yes. Shitting on a small defenseless island like that, just because they couldn't get to us anymore. You remember when they had to hand out iodine tablets to all the kids? That wasn't Leningrad or Gorky, the fallout plume: it was Havana. I don't think they wanted to admit just how bad it was."

Misha sips his tea. "We had a lucky escape." Morale be damned, it's acceptable to admit at least that much in front of the CO, in private. Misha's seen some of the KGB reports on the US nuclear capabilities back then, and his blood runs cold; while Nikita had been wildly bluffing about the Rodina's nuclear defenses, the Americans had been hiding the true scale of their own arsenal. From themselves as much as the rest of the world.

"Yes. Things were going to the devil back then, no question: if we hadn't woken up over here, who knows what would have happened? They outgunned us back then. I don't think they realized." Gagarin's dark expression lifts: he glances out of the open porthole—the only one in a private cabin that opens—and smiles. "This isn't Cuba, though." The headland rising above the bay tells him that much: no tropical island on Earth supported such weird vegetation. Or such ruins.

"Indeed not. But, what about the ruins?" asks Misha, putting his tea glass down on the map table.

"Yes." Gagarin leans forward: "I was meaning to talk to you about that. Exploration is certainly in line with our orders, but we are a trifle short of trained archaeologists, aren't we? Let's see: we're 470,000 kilometers from home, six major climatic zones, five continents—it'll be a long time before we get any settlers out here, won't it?" He pauses delicately. "Even if the rumors about reform of the penal system are true."

"It is certainly a dilemma," Misha agrees amiably, deliberately ignoring the skipper's last comment. "But we can take some time over it. There's nobody out here, at least not within range of yesterday's reconnaissance flight. I'll vouch for Lieutenant Chekhov's soundness: he has a solid attitude, that one."

"I don't see how we can leave without examining the ruins, but we've got limited resources, and in any case, I don't want to do anything that might get the Academy to slap our wrists. No digging for treasure until the eggheads get here." Gagarin hums tunelessly for a moment, then slaps his hand on his thigh: "I think we'll shoot some film for the comrade general secretary's birthday party. First we'll secure a perimeter around the beach, give those damned *spetsnaz* a chance to earn all the vodka they've been drinking. Then you and I, we can take Primary Science Party Two into the nearest ruins with lights and cameras. Make a visual record, leave the double domes back in Moscow to figure out what we're looking at and whether it's worth coming back later with a bunch of archaeologists. What do you say, Misha?"

"I say that's entirely logical, Comrade General," says the political officer, nodding to himself.

"That's so ordered, then. We'll play it safe, though. Just because we haven't seen any active settlement patterns doesn't mean there're no aborigines lurking in the forest."

"Like that last bunch of lizards." Misha frowns. "Little purple bastards!"

"We'll make good communists out of them eventually," Yuri insists. "A toast! To making good communists out of little purple lizard-bastards with blowpipes who shoot political officers in the arse!"

Gagarin grins wickedly, and Gorodin knows when he's being wound up on purpose and summons a twinkle to his eye as he raises his glass: "And to poisons that don't work on human beings."

● DISCOGRAPHY

WARNING:

The following briefing film is classified COLLECTION RUBY. If you do not possess both COLLECTION and RUBY clearances, leave the auditorium and report to the screening security officer immediately. Disclosure to unauthorized personnel is a federal offense punishable by a fine of up to ten thousand dollars and/or imprisonment for up to twenty years. You have thirty seconds to clear the auditorium and report to the screening security officer.

VOICE-OVER:

Ocean—the final frontier. For twelve years, since the momentous day when we discovered that we had been removed to this planar world, we have been confronted by the immensity of an ocean that goes on as far as we can see. Confronted also by the prospect of the spread of Communism to uncharted new continents, we have committed ourselves to a strategy of exploration and containment.

FILM CLIP:

An Atlas rocket on the launchpad rises slowly, flames jetting from its tail: it surges past the gantry and disappears into the sky.

CUT TO:

A camera mounted in the nose, pointing back along the flank of the rocket. The ground falls behind, blurring into blue distance. Slowly, the sky behind the rocket is turning black: but the land still occupies much of the fish-eye view. The first-stage engine ring tumbles away, leaving the core engine burning with a pale blue flame: now the outline of the California coastline is recognizable. North America shrinks visibly: eventually another, strange outline swims into view, like a cipher in an alien script. The booster burns out and falls behind, and the tumbling camera catches sunlight glinting off the upper-stage Centaur rocket as its engine ignites, thrusting it higher and faster.

VOICE-OVER:

We cannot escape.

CUT TO:

A meteor streaking across the empty blue bowl of the sky; slowing, deploying parachutes.

VOICE-OVER:

In 1962, this rocket would have blasted a two-ton payload all the way into outer space. That was when we lived on a planet that was an oblate sphere. Life on a dinner plate seems to be different: while the gravitational attraction anywhere on the surface is a constant, we can't get away from it. In fact, anything we fire straight up will come back down again. Not even a nuclear rocket can escape: according to JPL scientist Dan Alderson, escape from a Magellanic disk would require a speed of over one thousand six hundred miles per second. That is because this disk masses many times more than a star—in fact, it has a mass fifty thousand times greater than our own sun.

What stops it collapsing into a sphere? Nobody knows. Physicists speculate that a fifth force that drove the early expansion of the universe—they call it "quintessence"— has been harnessed by the makers of the disk. But the blunt truth is, nobody knows for sure. Nor do we understand how we came here—how, in the blink of an eye, something beyond our comprehension peeled the Earth's continents and oceans like a grape and plated them across this alien disk.

CUT TO:

A map. The continents of earth are laid out—Americas at one side, Europe and Asia and Africa to their east. Beyond the Indonesian island chain Australia and New Zealand hang lonely on the edge of an abyss of ocean.

The map pans right: strange new continents swim into view, ragged-edged and huge. A few of them are larger than Asia and Africa combined; most of them are smaller.

VOICE-OVER:

Geopolitics was changed forever by the Move. While the surface topography of our continents was largely preserved, wedges of foreign material were introduced below the Mohorovicic discontinuity—below the crust—and in the deep ocean floor, to act as spacers. The distances between points separated by deep ocean were, of necessity, changed, and not in our geopolitical favor. While the tactical balance of power after the Move was much as it had been before, the great circle flight paths our strategic missiles were designed for—over the polar ice cap and down into the communist empire—were distorted and stretched, placing the enemy targets outside their range. Meanwhile, although our manned bombers could still reach Moscow with in-flight refueling, the changed map would have forced them to traverse thousands of miles of hostile airspace en route. The Move rendered most of our strategic preparations useless. If the British had been willing to stand firm, we might have prevailed—but in retrospect, what went for us also went for the Soviets, and it is hard to condemn the British for being unwilling to take the full force of the inevitable Soviet bombardment alone.

In retrospect the only reason this was not a complete disaster for us is that the Soviets were caught in the same disarray as ourselves. But the specter of Communism now dominates Western Europe: the supposedly independent nations of the European Union are as much in thrall to Moscow as the client states of the Warsaw Pact. Only the ongoing British State of Emergency offers us any residual geopolitical traction on the red continent, and in the long term we must anticipate that the British, too, will be driven to reach an accommodation with the Soviet Union.

CUT TO:

A silvery delta-winged aircraft in flight. Stub wings, pointed nose, and a shortage of windows proclaim it to be an unmanned drone: a single large engine in its tail thrusts it along, exhaust nozzle glowing cherry red. Trackless wastes unwind below it as the viewpoint—a chase plane—carefully climbs over the drone to capture a clear view of the upper fuselage.

VOICE-OVER:

The disk is vast—so huge that it defies sanity. Some estimates give it the surface area of more than a billion Earths. Exploration by conventional means is futile: hence the deployment of the NP-101 Persephone drone, here seen making a proving flight over landmass F-42. The NP-101 is a reconnaissance derivative of the nuclear-powered D-SLAM Pluto missile that forms the backbone of our post-Move deterrent force. It is slower than a strategic D-SLAM, but much more reliable: while D-SLAM is designed for a quick, fiery dash into Soviet territory, the NP-101 is designed to fly long-duration missions that map entire continents. On a typical deployment the NP-101 flies outward at thrice the speed of sound for nearly a month: traveling fifty thousand miles a day, it penetrates a million miles into the unknown before it turns and flies homeward. Its huge mapping cameras record two images every thousand seconds, and its sophisticated digital computer records a variety of data from its sensor suite, allowing us to build up a picture of parts of the disk that our ships would take years or decades to reach. With resolution down to the level of a single nautical mile, the NP-101 program has been a resounding success, allowing us to map whole new worlds that it would take us years to visit in person.

At the end of its mission, the NP-101 drops its final film capsule and flies out into the middle of an uninhabited ocean, to ditch its spent nuclear reactor safely far from home.

CUT TO:

A bull's-eye diagram. The center is a black circle with a star at its heart; around it is a circular platter, of roughly the same proportions as a 45 rpm single.

VOICE-OVER:

A rough map of the disk. Here is the area we have explored to date, using the NP-101 program.

(A dot little larger than a sand grain lights up on the face of the single.)

That dot of light is a million kilometers in radius—five times the distance that used to separate our old Earth from its moon. To cross the radius of the disk, an NP-101 would have to fly at Mach 3 for almost ten years. We aren't even sure exactly where the center of that dot lies on the disk: our highest sounding rocket, the Nova-Orion block two, can barely rise two degrees above the plane of the disk before crashing back again. Here is the scope of our knowledge of our surroundings, derived from the continental-scale mapping cameras carried by Project Orion:

(A salmon pink area almost half an inch in diameter lights up around the red sand grain on the face of the single.)

Of course, cameras at an altitude of a hundred thousand miles can't look down on new continents and discern signs of communist infiltration; at best they can listen for radio transmissions and perform spectroscopic analyses of the atmospheric gases above distant lands, looking for contaminants characteristic of industrial development such as chlorofluorocarbons and nitrogen oxides.

This leaves us vulnerable to unpleasant surprises. Our long-term strategic analyses imply that we are almost certainly not alone on the disk. In addition to the communists, we must consider the possibility that whoever built this monstrous structure—clearly one of the wonders of the universe—might also live here. We must contemplate their motives for bringing us to this place. And then there are the aboriginal cultures discovered on continents F-29 and F-364, both now placed under quarantine. If some landmasses bear aboriginal inhabitants, we may speculate that they, too, have been transported to the disk in the same manner as ourselves, for some as-yet-unknown purpose. It is possible that they are genuine Stone Age dwellers—or that they are the survivors of advanced civilizations that did not survive the transition to this environment. What is the possibility that there exists on the disk one or more advanced alien civilizations that are larger and more powerful than our own? And would we recognize them as such if we saw them? How can we go about estimating the risk of our encountering hostile Little Green Men—now that other worlds are in range of even a well-equipped sailboat, much less the Savannah-class nuclear-powered exploration ships?

Astronomers Carl Sagan and Daniel Drake estimate the probability as high—so high, in fact, that they believe there are several such civilizations out there.

We are not alone. We can only speculate about why we might have been brought here by the abductors, but we can be certain that it is only a matter of time before we encounter an advanced alien civilization that may well be hostile to us. This briefing film will now continue with an overview of our strategic preparations for first contact, and the scenarios within which we envisage this contingency arising, with specific reference to the Soviet Union as an example of an unfriendly ideological superpower . . .

⊙ TENURE TRACK

After two weeks, Maddy is sure she's going mad.

She and Bob have been assigned a small prefabricated house (not much more than a shack, although it has electricity and running water) on the edge of town. He's been drafted into residential works, put to work erecting more buildings: and this is the nearest thing to a success they've had, because after a carefully controlled protest his status has been corrected, from just another set of unskilled hands to trainee surveyor. A promotion of which he is terribly proud, evidently taking it as confirmation that they've made the right move by coming here.

Maddy, meanwhile, has a harder time finding work. The district hospital is fully staffed. They don't need her, won't need her until the next shipload of settlers arrives, unless she wants to pack up her bags and go tramping around isolated ranch settlements in the outback. In a year's time the governor has decreed they'll establish another town-scale settlement, inland near the mining encampments on the edge of the Hoover Desert. Then they'll need medics to staff the new hospital: but for now, she's a spare wheel. Because Maddy is a city girl by upbringing and disposition, and not inclined to take a job hiking around the bush if she can avoid it.

She spends the first week and then much of the second mooching around town, trying to find out what she can do.

She's not the only young woman in this predicament. While there's officially no unemployment, and the colony's dirigiste administration finds plenty of hard work for idle hands, there's also a lack of openings for ambulance crew, or indeed much of anything else she can do. Careerwise it's like a trip into the 1950s. Young, female, and ambitious? Lots of occupations simply don't exist out here on the fringe, and many others are closed or inaccessible. Everywhere she looks she sees mothers shepherding implausibly large flocks of toddlers, their guardians pinch-faced from worry and exhaustion. Bob wants kids, although Maddy's not ready for that yet. But the alternatives on offer are limited.

Eventually Maddy takes to going through the "help wanted" ads on the bulletin board outside city hall. Some of them are legit: and at least a few are downright peculiar. One catches her eye: field assistant wanted for biological research. *I wonder?* she thinks, and goes in search of a door to bang on.

When she finds the door—raw wood, just beginning to bleach in the strong colonial sunlight—and bangs on it, John Martin opens it and blinks quizzically into the light. "Hello?" he asks.

"You were advertising for a field assistant?" She stares at him. He's the entomologist, right? She remembers his hands on the telescope on the deck of the ship. The voyage itself is already taking on the false patina of romance in her memories compared to the dusty present it has delivered her to.

"I was? Oh—yes, yes. Do come in." He backs into the house—another of these identikit shacks, *colonial, family, for the use of*—and offers her a seat in what used to be the living room. It's almost completely filled by a worktable and a desk and a tall wooden chest of sample drawers. There's an odd, musty smell, like old cobwebs and leaky demijohns of formalin. John shuffles around his den, vaguely disordered by the unexpected shock of company. There's something touchingly cute about him, like the subjects of his studies, Maddy thinks. "Sorry about the mess. I don't get many visitors. So, um, do you have any relevant experience?"

She doesn't hesitate: "None whatsoever, but I'd like to learn." She leans forward. "I qualified as a paramedic before we left. At college I was studying biology, but I had to drop out midway through my second year: I was thinking about going to medical school later, but I guess that's not going to happen here. Anyway, the hospital here has no vacancies, so I need to find something else to do. What exactly does a field assistant get up to?"

"Get sore feet." He grins lopsidedly. "Did you do any lab time? Fieldwork?" Maddy nods hesitantly so he drags her meager college experiences out of her before he continues. "I've got a whole continent to explore and only one set of hands: we're spread thin out here. Luckily NSF budgeted to hire me an assistant. The assistant's job is to be my Man Friday; to help me cart equipment about, take samples, help with basic lab work—very basic—and so on. Oh, and if they're interested in entomology, botany, or anything else remotely relevant, that's a plus. There aren't many unemployed life sciences people around here, funnily enough: have you had any chemistry?"

"Some," Maddy says cautiously; "I'm no biochemist." She glances round the crowded office curiously. "What are you meant to be doing?"

He sighs. "A primary survey of an entire continent. Nobody, but nobody, even bothered looking into the local insect ecology here. There're virtually no vertebrates, birds, lizards, what have you—but back home there are more species of beetle than everything else put together, and this place is no different. Did you know nobody has even sampled the outback fifty miles inland of here? We're doing nothing but throwing up shacks along the coastline and opencast quarries a few miles inland. There could be anything in the interior, absolutely anything." When he gets excited he starts gesticulating, Maddy notices, waving his hands around enthusiastically. She nods and smiles, trying to encourage him.

"A lot of what I'm doing is the sort of thing they were doing in the eighteenth and nineteenth centuries. Take samples, draw them, log their habitat and dietary habits, see if I can figure out their life cycle, try and work out who's kissing cousins with what. Build a family tree. Oh, I also need to do the same with the vegetation, you know? And they want me to keep close watch on the other disks around Lucifer. 'Keep an eye out for signs of sapience,' whatever that means: I figure there's a bunch of leftovers in the astronomical community who feel downright insulted that whoever built this disk and brought us here didn't land on the White House lawn and introduce themselves. I'd better tell you right now, there's enough work here to occupy an army of zoologists and botanists for a century; you can get started on a PhD right here and now if you want. I'm only here for five years, but my successor should be okay about taking on an experienced RA . . . The hard bit is going to be maintaining focus. Uh, I can sort you out a subsistence grant from the governor-general's discretionary fund and get NSF to reimburse him, but it won't be huge. Would twenty Truman dollars a week be enough?"

Maddy thinks for a moment. Truman dollars—the local scrip—aren't worth a whole lot, but there's not much to spend them on. And Bob's earning for both of them anyway. And a PhD . . . *That could be my ticket back to civilization, couldn't it?* "I guess so," she says, feeling a sense of vast relief: so there's something she's useful for besides raising the next generation, after all. She tries to set aside the visions of herself, distinguished and not too much older, gratefully accepting a professor's chair at an Ivy League university. "When do I start?"

○ ON THE BEACH

Misha's first impressions of the disturbingly familiar alien continent are of an oppressively humid heat and the stench of decaying jellyfish.

The *Sergei Korolev* floats at anchor in the river estuary, a huge streamlined visitor from another world. Stubby fins stick out near the waterline, like a seaplane with clipped wings: gigantic Kuznetsov atomic turbines in pods ride on booms to either side of its high-ridged back, either side of the launch/recovery catapults for its parasite MiG fighter-bombers, aft of the broad curve of the ekranoplan's bridge. Near the waterline, a boat bay is open: a naval *spetsnaz* team is busy loading their kit into the landing craft that will ferry them to the small camp on the beach. Misha, who stands just above the waterline, turns away from the giant ground-effect ship and watches his commander, who is staring inland with a faint expression of worry. "Those trees—awfully close, aren't they?" Gagarin says, with the carefully studied stupidity that saw him through the first dangerous years after his patron Khrushchev's fall.

"That is indeed what Captain Kirov is taking care of," replies Gorodin, playing his role of foil to the colonel-general's sardonic humor. And indeed, shadowy figures in olive green battle dress are stalking in and out of the trees, carefully laying trip wires and screamers in an arc around the beachhead. He glances to the left, where a couple of sailors with assault rifles stand guard, eyes scanning the jungle. "I wouldn't worry unduly, sir."

"I'll still be happier when the outer perimeter is secure. And when I've got a sane explanation of this for the comrade general secretary." Gagarin's humor evaporates: he turns and walks along the beach, toward the large tent that's already gone up to provide shelter from the heat of noon. The bar of solid sunlight—what passes for sunlight here—is already at maximum length, glaring like a rod of white-hot steel that impales the disk. (Some of the more superstitious call it the axle of heaven. Part of Gorodin's job is to discourage such nonmaterialist backsliding.)

The tent awning is pegged back: inside it, Gagarin and Misha find Major Suvurov and Academician Borisovitch leaning over a map. Already the scientific film crew—a bunch of dubious civilians from TASS—is busy in a corner, preparing cans for shooting. "Ah, Oleg, Mikhail." Gagarin summons up a professionally photogenic smile. "Getting anywhere?"

Borisovitch, a slight, stoop-shouldered type who looks more like a janitor than a world-famous scientist, shrugs. "We were just talking about going along to the archaeological site, General. Perhaps you'd like to come, too?"

Misha looks over his shoulder at the map: it's drawn in pencil, and there's an awful lot of white space on it, but what they've surveyed so far is disturbingly familiar in outline—familiar enough to have given them all a number of sleepless nights even before they came ashore. Someone has scribbled a dragon coiling in a particularly empty corner of the void.

"How large is the site?" asks Yuri.

"Don't know, sir." Major Suvurov grumps audibly, as if the lack of concrete intelligence on the alien ruins is a personal affront. "We haven't found the end of it yet. But it matches what we know already."

"The aerial survey—" Mikhail coughs, delicately. "If you'd let me have another flight, I could tell you more, General. I believe it may be possible to define the city limits narrowly, but the trees make it hard to tell."

"I'd give you the flight if only I had the aviation fuel," Gagarin explains patiently. "A chopper can burn its own weight in fuel in a day of surveying, and we have to haul everything out here from Archangelsk. In fact, when we go home we're leaving most of our flight-ready aircraft behind, just so that on the next trip out we can carry more fuel."

"I understand." Mikhail doesn't look happy. "As Oleg Ivanovitch says, we don't know how far it reaches. But I think when you see the ruins you'll understand why we need to come back here. Nobody's found anything like this before."

"Old Capitalist Man." Misha smiles thinly. "I suppose."

"Presumably." Borisovitch shrugs. "Whatever, we need to bring archaeologists. And a mass spectroscope for carbon dating. And other stuff." His face wrinkles unhappily. "They were here back when we would still have been living in caves!"

"Except we weren't," Gagarin says under his breath. Misha pretends not to notice.

By the time they leave the tent, the marines have gotten the Korolev's two BRDMs ashore. The big balloon-tired armored cars sit on the beach like monstrous amphibians freshly emerged from some primeval sea. Gagarin and Gorodin sit in the back of the second vehicle with the academician and the film crew: the lead BRDM carries their *spetsnaz* escort team. They maintain a dignified silence as the convoy rumbles and squeaks across the beach, up the gently sloping hillside, then down toward the valley with the ruins.

The armored cars stop, and doors open. Everyone is relieved by the faint breeze that cracks the oven heat of the interior. Gagarin walks over to the nearest ruin—remnants of a wall, waist high—and stands, hands on hips, looking across the wasteland.

"Concrete," says Borisovitch, holding up a lump of crumbled not-stone from the foot of the wall for Yuri to see.

"Indeed." Gagarin nods. "Any idea what this was?"

"Not yet." The camera crew is already filming, heading down a broad boulevard between rows of crumbling foundations. "Only the concrete has survived, and it's mostly turned to limestone. This is *old.*"

"Hmm." The first cosmonaut walks round the stump of wall and steps down to the foundation layer behind it, looking around with interest. "Interior column here, four walls—they're worn down, aren't they? This stuff that looks like a red stain. Rebar? Found any intact ones?"

"Again, not yet, sir," says Borisovitch. "We haven't looked everywhere yet, but . . ."

"Indeed." Gagarin scratches his chin idly. "Am I imagining it, or are the walls all lower on that side?" He points north, deeper into the sprawling maze of overgrown rubble.

"You're right, sir. No theory for it, though."

"You don't say." Gagarin walks north from the five-sided building's ruin, looks around. "This was a road?"

"Once, sir. It was nine meters wide—there seems to have been derelict ground between the houses, if that's what they were, and the road itself."

"Nine meters, you say." Gorodin and the academician hurry to follow him as he strikes off, up the road. "Interesting stonework here, don't you think, Misha?"

"Yes, sir. Interesting stonework."

Gagarin stops abruptly and kneels. "Why is it cracked like this? Hey, there's sand down there. And, um, glass? Looks like it's melted. Ah, trinitite."

"Sir?"

Borisovitch leans forward. "That's odd."

"What is?" asks Misha, but before he gets a reply both Gagarin and the researcher are up again and off toward another building.

"Look. The north wall." Gagarin's found another chunk of wall, this one a worn stump that's more than a meter high: he looks unhappy.

"Sir? Are you all right?" Misha stares at him. Then he

notices the academician is also silent, and looking deeply perturbed. "What's wrong?"

Gagarin extends a finger, points at the wall. "You can just see him if you look close enough. How long would it take to fade, Mikhail? How many years have we missed them by?"

The academician licks his lips: "At least two thousand years, sir. Concrete cures over time, but it takes a very long time indeed to turn all the way to limestone. And then there's the weathering process to take account of. But the surface erosion . . . Yes, that could fix the image from the flash. Perhaps. I'd need to ask a few colleagues back home."

"What's wrong?" the political officer repeats, puzzled.

The first cosmonaut grins humorlessly. "Better get your Geiger counter, Misha, and see if the ruins are still hot. Looks like we're not the only people on the disk with a geopolitical problem . . ."

◉ BEEN HERE BEFORE

Brundle has finally taken the time to pull Gregor aside and explain what's going on; Gregor is not amused.

"Sorry you walked into it cold," says Brundle. "But I figured it would be best for you to see for yourself." He speaks with a Midwestern twang, and a flatness of affect that his colleagues sometimes mistake for signs of an underlying psychopathology.

"See what, in particular?" Gregor asks sharply. "What, in particular?" Gregor tends to repeat himself, changing only the intonation, when he's disturbed. He's human enough to recognize it as a bad habit but still finds it difficult to suppress the reflex.

Brundle pauses on the footpath, looks around to make sure there's nobody within earshot. The Mall is nearly empty today, and only a humid breeze stirs the waters on the pool. "Tell me what you think."

Gregor thinks for a moment, then summons up his full command of the local language: it's good practice. "The boys in the big house are asking for a CAB. It means someone's pulled his head out of his ass for long enough to realize they've got worse things to worry about than being shafted by the Soviets. Something's happened to make them realize they need a policy for dealing with the abductors. This is against doctrine; we need to do something about it fast before they start asking the right questions. Something's shaken them up, something secret, some HUMINT source from the wrong side of the Curtain, perhaps. Could it be that man Gordievsky? But they haven't quite figured out what being here means. Sagan—does his presence mean what I think it does?"

"Yes," Brundle says tersely.

"Oh dear." A reflex trips, and Gregor takes off his spectacles and polishes them nervously on his tie before replacing them. "Is it just him, or does it go further?" He leaves the rest of the sentence unspoken by convention—*Is it just him you think we'll have to silence?*

"Further." Brundle tends to talk out of the side of his mouth when he's agitated, and from his current expression Gregor figures he's really upset. "Sagan and his friends at Cornell have been using the Arecibo dish to listen to the neighbors. This wasn't anticipated. Now they're asking for permission to beam a signal at the nearest of the other disks. Straight up, more or less; 'Talk to us.' Unfortunately, Sagan is well-known, which is why he caught the attention of our nominal superiors. Meanwhile, the Soviets have found something that scared them. CIA didn't hear about it through the usual assets—they contacted the State Department via the embassy; they're that scared." Brundle pauses a moment. "Sagan and his buddies don't know about that, of course."

"Why has nobody shot them already?" Gregor asks coldly.

Brundle shrugs. "We pulled the plug on their funding just in time. If we shot them as well, someone might notice. Everything could go nonlinear while we were trying to cover it up. You know the problem; this is a semiopen society, inadequately controlled. A bunch of astronomers get together on their own initiative—academic conference, whatever—and decide to spend a couple of thousand bucks of research grant money from NIST to establish communications with the nearest disk. How are we supposed to police that kind of thing?"

"Shut down all their radio telescopes. At gunpoint, if necessary, but I figure a power cut or a congressional committee would be just as effective as leverage."

"Perhaps, but we don't have the Soviets' resources to work with. Anyway, that's why I dragged Sagan in for the CAB. It's a Potemkin village, you understand, to convince everybody he contacted that something is being done, but we're going to have to figure out how to shut him up."

"Sagan is the leader of the 'Talk to us, alien gods' crowd, I take it."

"Yes."

"Well." Gregor considers his next words carefully. "Assuming he's still clean and uncontaminated, we can turn him or we can ice him. If we're going to turn him, we need to do it convincingly—full Tellerization—and we'll need to come up with a convincing rationale. Use him to evangelize the astronomical community into shutting up or haring off in the wrong direction. Like Heisenberg and the Nazi nuclear-weapons program." He snaps his fingers. "Why don't we tell him the truth? At least, something close enough to it to confuse the issue completely?"

"Because he's a member of the Federation of American Scientists, and he won't believe anything we tell him without independent confirmation," Brundle mutters through one side of his mouth. "That's the trouble with using a government agency as our cover story."

They walk in silence for a minute. "I think it would be very dangerous to underestimate him," says Gregor. "He could be a real asset to us, but uncontrolled he's very dangerous. If we can't silence him, we may have to resort to physical violence. And with the number of colonies they've already seeded, we can't be sure of getting them all."

"Itemize the state of their understanding," Brundle says abruptly. "I want a reality check. I'll tell you what's new after you run down the checklist."

"Okay." Gregor thinks for a minute. "Let us see. What everyone knows is that between zero three fifteen and twelve seconds and thirteen seconds Zulu time, on October second, 'sixty-two, all the clocks stopped, the satellites went away, the star map changed, nineteen airliners and forty-six ships in transit ended up in terminal trouble, and they found themselves transferred from a globe in the Milky Way galaxy to a disk which we figure is somewhere in the Lesser Magellanic Cloud. Meanwhile the Milky Way galaxy—we assume that's what it is—has changed visibly. Lots of metal-depleted stars, signs of macroscopic cosmic engineering, that sort of thing. The public explanation is that the visitors froze time, skinned the Earth, and plated it over the disk. Luckily they're still bickering over whether the explanation is Minsky's copying, uh, hypothesis, or that guy Moravec with his digital-simulation theory."

"Indeed." Brundle kicks at a paving stone idly. "Now. What is your forward analysis?"

"Well, sooner or later they're going to turn dangerous. They have the historic predisposition toward teleological errors, to belief in a giant omnipotent creator and a purpose to their existence. If they start speculating about the intentions of a transcendent intelligence, it's likely they'll eventually ask whether their presence here is symptomatic of God's desire to probe the circumstances of its own birth. After all, we have evidence of how many technological species on the disk, ten million, twelve? Replicated many times, in some cases. They might put it together with their concept of manifest destiny and conclude that they are, in fact, doomed to give birth to God. Which is an entirely undesirable conclusion for them to reach from our point of view. Teleologists being bad neighbors, so to speak."

"Yes indeed," Brundle says thoughtfully, then titters quietly to himself for a moment.

"This isn't the first time they've avoided throwing around H-bombs in bulk. That's unusual for primate civilizations. If they keep doing that, they could be dangerous."

"Dangerous is relative," says Brundle. He titters again. Things move inside his mouth.

"Don't *do* that!" Gregor snaps. He glances round instinctively, but nothing happens.

"You're jumpy." Brundle frowns. "Stop worrying so much. We don't have much longer here."

"Are we being ordered to move? Or to prepare a sterilization strike?"

"Not yet." Brundle shrugs. "We have further research to continue with before a decision is reached. The Soviets have made a discovery. Their crewed-exploration program. The *Korolev* lucked out."

"They—" Gregor tenses. "What did they find?" He knows about the big nuclear-powered ekranoplan, the dragon of the Caspian, searching the seven oceans for new worlds to conquer. He even knows about the small fleet they're trying to build at Archangelsk, the ruinous expense of it. But this is new. "What did they find?"

Brundle grins humorlessly. "They found ruins. Then they spent another eight weeks mapping the coastline. They've confirmed what they found, they sent the State Department photographs, survey details—the lot." Brundle gestures at the Cuban War monument, the huge granite column dominating the Mall, its shadow pointing toward the Capitol. "They found Washington DC in ruins. One hundred and forty thousand miles that way." He points due north. "They're not total idiots, and it's the first time they've found one of their own species-transfer cognates. They might be well on their way to understanding the truth. Luckily our comrades in Moscow have that side of the affair under control, but they communicated their discovery to the CIA before it could be suppressed, which raises certain headaches.

"We must make sure that nobody *here* asks *why*. So I want you to start by dealing with Sagan."

⊙ COLLECTING JAR

It's noon, and the rippling heat haze turns the horizon to fog in the distance. Maddy tries not to move too much: the cycads cast imperfect shadows, and she can feel the Venetian blinds of light burning into her pale skin. She sighs slightly as she hefts the heavy canvas sample bag out of the back of the Land Rover: John will be needing it soon, once he's finished photographing the mock-termite nests. It's their third field trip together, their farthest dash into the outback, and she's already getting used to working with John. He's surprisingly easy to get on with because he's so absorbed in his work that he's refreshingly free of social expectations. If she didn't know better, she could almost let her guard down and start thinking of him as a friend, not an employer.

The heat makes her mind drift: she tries to remember what sparked her most recent quarrel with Bob, but it seems so distant and irrelevant now—like home, like Bob arguing with her father, like their hurried courthouse wedding and furtive emigration-board hearing. All that makes sense now is the stifling heat, the glare of not-sunlight, John working with his camera out in the noonday sun where only mad dogs and Englishmen dare go. Ah, *it was the washing.* Who was going to do the washing while Maddy was away on the two-day field trip? Bob seemed to think he was doing her a favor, cooking for himself and taking his clothes to the single overused public laundry. (Some year real soon now they'd get washing machines, but not yet . . .) Bob seemed to think he was being bighearted, not publicly getting jealous over her having a job that took her away from home with a male superior who was notoriously single. Bob seemed to think he was some kind of progressive liberated man for putting up with a wife who had read Betty Friedan and didn't shave her armpits. *Fuck you, Bob,* she thinks tiredly, and tugs the heavy strap of the sample case over her shoulder and turns to head in John's direction. There'll be time to sort things out with Bob later. For now, she's got a job to do.

John is leaning over the battered camera, peering through its viewfinder in search of . . . something. "What's up?" she asks.

"Mock-termites are up," he says, very seriously. "See the entrances?" The mock-termites are what they've come to take a look at—nobody's reported on them from close-up, but they're very visible as soon as you venture into the dusty plain. She peers at the foot of the termite mound, a baked-clay hump in the soil that seems to writhe with life. There are little pipelike holes, tunnels almost, emerging from the base of the mound, and little black mock-termites dancing in and out of the holes in never-ending streams. Little is relative—they're almost as large as mice. "Don't touch them," he warns.

"Are they poisonous?" asks Maddy.

"Don't know, don't want to find out this far from the hospital. The fact that there are no vertebrates here—" He shrugs. "We know they're poisonous to other insectoida."

Maddy puts the sample case down. "But nobody's been bitten, or died, or anything."

"Not that we know of." He folds back the lid of the case and she shivers, abruptly cold, imagining bleached bones lying unburied in the long grass of the inland plain, where no humans will live for centuries to come. "It's essential to take care out here. We could be missing for days before anyone noticed, and a search party wouldn't necessarily find us, even with the journey plan we filed."

"Okay." She watches as he takes out an empty sample jar and a label and carefully notes down time and date, distance and direction from the milestone at the heart of Fort Eisenhower. *Thirty-six miles.* They might as well be on another planet. "You're taking samples?"

He glances round. "Of course." Then he reaches into the side pocket of the bag and removes a pair of heavy gloves, which he proceeds to put on, and a trowel. "If you could put the case down over there?"

Maddy glances inside the case as he kneels down by the mock-termite mound. It's full of jars with blank labels, neatly segregated, impassable quarantine zones for improbable species. She looks round. John is busy with the mock-termite mound. He's neatly lopped the top off it: inside, the earth is a squirming mass of—things. Black things, white things like bits of string, and a pulp of half-decayed vegetable matter that smells damply of humus. He probes the mound delicately with the trowel, seeking something. "Look," he calls over his shoulder. "It's a queen!"

Maddy hurries over. "Really?" she asks. Following his gloved finger, she sees something the size of her left forearm, white and glistening. It twitches, expelling something round, and she feels her gorge rise. "Ugh!"

"It's just a happy mother," John says calmly. He lowers the trowel, works it in under the queen, and lifts her—and a collection of hangers-on, courtiers and bodyguards alike—over the jar. He tips, he shakes, and he twists the lid into place. Maddy stares at the chaos within. What is it like to be a mock-termite, suddenly snatched up and transplanted to a mockery of home?

What's it like to see the sun in an electric lightbulb, to go about your business, blindly pumping out eggs and eating and foraging for leaves, under the eyes of inscrutable collectors? She wonders if Bob would understand if she tried to tell him. John stands up and lowers the glass jar into the sample case, then freezes. "Ouch," he says, and pulls his left glove off.

"Ouch." He says it again, more slowly. "I missed a small one. Maddy, medical kit, please. Atropine and neostigmine."

She sees his eyes, pinprick pupils in the noonday glare, and dashes to the Land Rover. The medical kit, olive green with a red cross on a white circle, seems to mock her: she rushes it over to John, who is now sitting calmly on the ground next to the sample case. "What do you need?" she asks.

John tries to point, but his gloved hand is shaking wildly. He tries to pull it off, but the swollen muscles resist attempts to loosen the glove. "Atropine—" A white cylinder, with a red arrow on one side: she quickly reads the label, then pushes it hard against his thigh, feels something spring-loaded explode inside it. John stiffens, then tries to stand up, the automatic syringe still hanging from his leg. He staggers stiff-legged toward the Land Rover and slumps into the passenger seat.

"Wait!" she demands. Tries to feel his wrist. "How many of them bit you?"

His eyes roll. "Just one. Silly of me. No vertebrates." Then he leans back. "I'm going to try and hold on. Your first-aid training."

Maddy gets the glove off, exposing fingers like angry red sausages: but she can't find the wound on his left hand, can't find anything to suck the poison out of. John's breathing is labored and he twitches: he needs the hospital, but it's at least a four-hour drive away and she can't look after him while she drives. So she puts another syringe load of atropine into his leg and waits with him for five minutes while he struggles for breath hoarsely, then follows up with Adrenalin and anything else she can think of that's good for handling anaphylactic shock. "Get us back," he manages to wheeze at her between emphysemic gasps. "Samples, too."

After she gets him into the load bed of the truck, she dashes over to the mock-termite mound with the spare petrol can. She splashes the best part of a gallon of fuel over the heap, coughing with the stink: she caps the jerry can, drags it away from the mound, then strikes a match and throws it flickering at the disordered insect kingdom. There's a soft whump as the igniting gas sets the mound aflame: small shapes writhe and crisp beneath an empty blue sky pierced by the glaring pin-prick of S Doradus. Maddy doesn't stay to watch. She hauls the heavy sample case back to the Land Rover, loads it into the trunk alongside John, and scurries back toward town as fast as she can.

She's almost ten miles away before she remembers the camera, left staring in cyclopean isolation at the scorched remains of the dead colony.

● HOMEWARD-BOUND

The big ground-effect ship rumbles softly as it cruises across the endless expanse of the Dzerzhinsky Ocean at nearly three hundred knots, homeward-bound at last. Misha sits in his cubbyhole—as shipboard political officer he rates an office of his own—and sweats over his report with the aid of a glass of Polish pear schnapps. Radio can't punch through more than a few thousand miles of air directly, however pow-erful the transmitters; on Earth they used to bounce signals off the ionosphere or the moon, but that doesn't work here— the other disks are too far away to use as relays. There's a chain of transceiver buoys marching out across the ocean at two-thousand-kilometer intervals, but the equipment is a pig to maintain, very expensive to build, and nobody is even joking about stringing undersea cables across a million kilo-meters of seafloor. Misha's problem is that the expedition, himself included, is effectively stranded back in the eigh-teenth century, without even the telegraph to tie civilization together—which is a pretty pickle to find yourself in when you're the bearer of news that will make the Politburo shit a brick. He desperately wants to be able to boost this up the ladder a bit, but instead it's going to be his name and his alone on the masthead.

"Bastards. Why couldn't they give us a signal rocket or two?" He gulps back what's left of the schnapps and winds a fresh sandwich of paper and carbon into his top-secret-eyes-only typewriter.

"Because it would weigh too much, Misha," the captain says right behind his left shoulder, causing him to jump and bang his head on the overhead locker.

When Misha stops swearing and Gagarin stops chuckling, the Party man carefully turns his stack of typescript face down on the desk, then politely gestures the captain into his office. "What can I do for you, boss? And what do you mean, they're too heavy?"

Gagarin shrugs. "We looked into it. Sure, we could put a tape recorder and a transmitter into an ICBM and shoot it up to twenty thousand kilometers. Trouble is, it'd fall down again in an hour or so. The fastest we could squirt the message, it would cost about a thousand rubles a character—more to the point, even a lightweight rocket would weigh as much as our entire payload. Maybe in ten years." He sits down. "How are you doing with that report?"

Misha sighs. "How am I going to explain to Brezhnev that the Americans aren't the only mad bastards with hydrogen bombs out here? That we've found the new world and the new world is just like the old world, except it glows in the dark? And the only communists we've found so far are termites with guns?" For a moment he looks haggard. "It's been nice knowing you, Yuri."

"Come on! It can't be that bad—" Gagarin's normally sunny disposition is clouded.

"You try and figure out how to break the news to them." After identifying the first set of ruins, they'd sent one of their MiGs out, loaded with camera pods and fuel: a thousand kilometers inland it had seen the same ominous story of nuclear annihilation visited on an alien civilization: ruins of airports, railroads, cities, factories. A familiar topography in unfamiliar form.

This was New York—once, thousands of years before a giant stamped the bottom of Manhattan Island into the seabed—and that was once Washington DC. Sure, there'd been extra skyscrapers, but they'd hardly needed the subsequent coastal cruise to be sure that what they were looking at was the same continent as the old capitalist enemy, thousands of years and millions of kilometers beyond a nuclear war. "We're running away like a dog that's seen the devil ride out, hoping that he doesn't spot us and follow us home for a new winter hat."

Gagarin frowns. "Excuse me?" He points to the bottle of pear schnapps.

"You are my guest." Misha pours the first cosmonaut a glass, then tops up his own. "It opens certain ideological conflicts, Yuri. And nobody wants to be the bearer of bad news."

"Ideological—such as?"

"Ah." Misha takes a mouthful. "Well, we have so far avoided nuclear annihilation and invasion by the forces of reactionary terror during the Great Patriotic War, but only by the skin of our teeth. Now, doctrine has it that any alien species advanced enough to travel in space is almost certain to have discovered socialism, if not true Communism, no? And that the enemies of socialism wish to destroy socialism and take its resources for themselves. But what we've seen here is evidence of a different sort. This was America. It follows that somewhere nearby there is a continent that was home to another Soviet Union— two thousand years ago. But this America has been wiped out, and our elder Soviet brethren are not in evidence and they have not colonized this other-America—what can this mean?"

Gagarin's brow wrinkled. "They're dead, too? I mean, that the alternate-Americans wiped them out in an act of colonialist imperialist aggression but did not survive their treachery," he adds hastily.

Misha's lips quirk in something approaching a grin: "Better work on getting your terminology right the first time before you see Brezh-nev, comrade," he says. "Yes, you are correct on the facts, but there are matters of *interpretation* to consider. No colonial exploitation has occurred. So either the perpetrators were also wiped out, or perhaps . . . Well, it opens up several very dangerous avenues of thought. Because if New Soviet Man isn't home hereabouts, it implies that something happened to them, doesn't it? Where are all the true communists? If it turns out that they ran into hostile aliens, then . . . Well, theory says that aliens should be good brother socialists. Theory and ten rubles will buy you a bottle of vodka on this one. Something is badly wrong with our understanding of the direction of history."

"I suppose there's no question that there's something we don't know about," Gagarin adds in the ensuing silence, almost as an afterthought.

"Yes. And that's a fig leaf of uncertainty we can hide behind, I hope." Misha puts his glass down and stretches his arms behind his head, fingers interlaced until his knuckles crackle. "Before we left, our agents reported signals picked up in America from—damn, I should not be telling you this without authorization. Pretend I said nothing." His frown returns.

"You sound as if you're having dismal thoughts," Gagarin prods.

"I *am* having dismal thoughts, Comrade Colonel-General, very dismal thoughts indeed. We have been behaving as if this world we occupy is merely a new geopolitical game board, have we not? Secure in the knowledge that brother socialists from beyond the stars brought us here to save us from the folly of the imperialist aggressors, or that anyone else we meet will be either barbarians or good communists, we have fallen into the pattern of an earlier age—expanding in all directions, recognizing no limits, assuming our manifest destiny. But what if there are limits? Not a barbed-wire fence or a line in the sand, but something more subtle. Why does history demand success of us? What we know is the right way for humans on a human world, with an industrial society, to live. But this is not a human world. And what if it's a world in which we're not destined to succeed? Or what if the very circumstances that gave rise to Marxism are themselves transient, in the broader scale? What if there is a—you'll pardon me—a materialist God? We know this is our own far future we are living in. *Why* would any power vast enough to build this disk bring us here?"

Gagarin shakes his head. "There are no limits, my friend," he says, a trifle condescendingly. "If there were, do you think we would have gotten this far?"

Misha thumps his desk angrily. "Why do you think they put us somewhere where your precious rockets don't work?" he demands. "Get up on high, one push of rocket exhaust, and you could be halfway to anywhere! But down here we have to slog through the atmosphere. We can't get away! Does that sound like a gift from one friend to another?"

"The way you are thinking sounds paranoid to me," Gagarin insists. "I'm not saying you're wrong, mind you: only—could you be overwrought? Finding those bombed cities affected us all, I think."

Misha glances out of his airliner-sized porthole: "I fear there's more to it than that. We're not unique, comrade; we've been here before. And we all died. We're a fucking duplicate, Yuri Alexeyevich; there's a larger context to all this. And I'm scared by what the Politburo will decide to do when they see the evidence. Or what the Americans will do . . ."

● LAST SUPPER

Returning to Manhattan is a comfort of sorts for Gregor, after the exposed plazas and paranoid open vistas of the capital. Unfortunately, he won't be here for long—he is, after all, on an assignment from Brundle—but he'll take what comfort he can from the deep stone canyons, the teeming millions scurrying purposefully about at ground level. The Big Apple is a hive of activity, as always, teeming purposeful trails of information leading the busy workers about their tasks. Gregor's nostrils flare as he stands on the sidewalk on Lexington and East 100th. There's an Italian restaurant Brundle recommended when he gave Gregor his briefing papers. "Their *spaghetti con polpette* is to die for," Brundle told him. That's probably true, but what's inarguable is that it's only a couple of blocks away from the offices of the Exobiology Annex to Cornell's New York Campus, where Sagan is head of department.

Gregor opens the door and glances around. A waiter makes eye contact. "Table for one?"

"Two. I'm meeting—ah." Gregor sees Sagan sitting in a booth at the back of the restaurant and waves hesitantly. "He's already here."

Gregor nods and smiles at the astronomer-exobiologist as he sits down opposite the professor. The waiter drifts over and hands him a menu. "Have you ordered?"

"I just got here." Sagan smiles guardedly. "I'm not sure why you wanted this meeting, Mr., uh, Samsa, isn't it?" Clearly he thinks he gets the joke—a typical mistake for a brilliant man to make.

Gregor allows his lower lip to twitch. "Believe me, I'd rather it wasn't necessary," he says, entirely truthfully. "But the climate in DC isn't really conducive to clear thought or long-range planning—I mean, we operate under constraints established by the political process. We're given questions to answer; we're not encouraged to come up with new questions. So what I'd like to do is just have an open-ended informal chat about anything that you think is worth considering. About our situation, I mean. In case you can open up any avenues we ought to be investigating that aren't on the map right now."

Sagan leans forward. "That's all very well," he says agreeably, "but I'm a bit puzzled by the policy process itself. We haven't yet made contact with any nonhuman sapients. I thought your committee was supposed to be assessing our policy options for when contact finally occurs. It sounds to me as if you're telling me that we already have a policy, and you're looking to find out if it's actually a viable one. Is that right?"

Gregor stares at him. "I can neither confirm nor deny that," he says evenly. Which is the truth. "But if you want to take some guesses, I can either discuss things or clam up when you get too close," he adds, the muscles around his eyes crinkling conspiratorially.

"Aha." Sagan grins back at him boyishly. "I get it." His smile vanishes abruptly. "Let me guess. The policy is predicated on MAD, isn't it?"

Gregor shrugs, then glances sideways, warningly: the waiter is approaching. "I'll have a glass of the house red," he says, sending the fellow away as fast as possible. "Deterrence presupposes communication, don't you think?" Gregor asks.

"True." Sagan picks up his bread knife and absentmindedly twirls it between finger and thumb. "But it's how the idiots—excuse me, our elected leaders—treat threats, and I can't see them responding to tool-using nonhumans as anything else." He stares at Gregor. "Let me see if I've got this right. Your committee pulled me in because there has, in fact, been a contact between humans and nonhuman intelligences—or at least some sign that there are NHIs out there. The existing policy for dealing with it was drafted sometime in the sixties under the influence of the hangover left by the Cuban war, and it basically makes the *conservative* assumption that any aliens are green-skinned Soviets and the only language they talk is nuclear annihilation. This policy is now seen to be every bit as bankrupt as it sounds, but nobody knows what to replace it with because there's no data on the NHIs. Am I right?"

"I can neither confirm nor deny that," says Gregor.

Sagan sighs. "Okay, play it your way." He closes his menu. "Ready to order?"

"I believe so." Gregor looks at him. "The *spaghetti con polpette* is really good here," he adds.

"Really?" Sagan smiles. "Then I'll try it."

They order, and Gregor waits for the waiter to depart before he continues. "Suppose there's an alien race out there. More than one. You know about the multiple copies of Earth. The uninhabited ones. We've been here before. Now let's see . . . Suppose the aliens aren't like us. Some of them are recognizable, tribal primates who use tools made out of metal, sea-dwelling ensemble entities who communicate by ultrasound. But others—most of them—are social insects who use amazingly advanced biological engineering to grow what they need. There's some evidence that they've colonized some of the empty Earths. They're aggressive and territorial, and they're so different that . . . Well, for one thing, we think they don't actually have conscious minds except when they need them. They control their own genetic code and build living organisms tailored to whatever tasks they want carried out. There's no evidence that they want to talk to us, and some evidence that they may have emptied some of those empty Earths of their human population. And because of their, um, decentralized ecosystem and biological engineering, conventional policy solutions won't work. The military ones, I mean."

Gregor watches Sagan's face intently as he describes the scenario. There is a slight cooling of the exobiologist's cheeks as his peripheral arteries contract with shock: his pupils dilate and his respiration rate increases. Sour pheromones begin to diffuse from his sweat ducts and organs in Gregor's nasal sinuses respond to them.

"You're kidding?" Sagan half asks. He sounds disappointed about something.

"I wish I were." Gregor generates a faint smile and exhales breath laden with oxytocin and other peptide messengers fine-tuned to human metabolism. In the kitchen, the temporary chef who is standing in for the regular one—off sick, due to a bout of food poisoning—will be preparing Sagan's dish. Humans are creatures of habit: once his meal arrives, the astronomer will eat it, taking solace in good food. (Such a shame about the chef.) "They're not like us. SETI assumes that NHIs are conscious and welcome communication with humans and, in fact, that humans aren't atypical. But let's suppose that humans *are* atypical. The human species has only been around for about a third of a million years, and has only been making metal tools and building settlements for ten thousand. What if the default for sapient species is measured in the millions of years? And they develop strong defense mechanisms to prevent other species moving into their territory?"

"That's incredibly depressing," Sagan admits after a minute's contemplation. "I'm not sure I believe it without seeing some more evidence. That's why we wanted to use the Arecibo dish to send a message, you know. The other disks are far enough away that we're safe, whatever they send back: they can't possibly throw missiles at us, not with a surface escape velocity of twenty thousand miles per second, and if they send unpleasant messages, we can stick our fingers in our ears."

The waiter arrives and slides his entrée in front of Sagan.

"Why do you say that?" asks Gregor.

"Well, for one thing, it doesn't explain the disk. We couldn't make anything like it—I suppose I was hoping we'd have some idea of who did. But from what you're telling me, insect hives with advanced biotechnology . . . That doesn't sound plausible."

"We have some information on that." Gregor smiles reassuringly. "For the time being, the important thing to recognize is that the species who are on the disk are roughly equivalent to ourselves in technological and scientific understanding. Give or take a couple of hundred years."

"Oh." Sagan perks up a bit.

"Yes," Gregor continues. "We have some information—I

can't describe our sources—but anyway. You've seen the changes to the structure of the galaxy we remember. How would you characterize that?"

"Hmm." Sagan is busy with a mouthful of delicious tetrodotoxin-laced meatballs. "It's clearly a Kardashev type-III civilization, harnessing the energy of an entire galaxy. What else?"

Gregor smiles. "Ah, those Russians, obsessed with coal and steel production! This is the information age, Dr. Sagan. What would the informational resources of a galaxy look like if they were put to use? And to what use would an unimaginably advanced civilization put them?"

Sagan looks blank for a moment, his fork pausing halfway to his mouth, laden with a deadly promise. "I don't see—ah!" He smiles, finishes his forkful, and nods. "Do I take it that we're living in a nature reserve? Or perhaps an archaeology experiment?"

Gregor shrugs. "Humans are time-binding animals," he explains. "So are all the other tool-using sentient species we have been able to characterize; it appears to be the one common factor. They like to understand their past as a guide to their future. We have sources that have . . . Think of a game of Chinese whispers. The belief that is most widely held is that the disk was made by the agencies we see at work restructuring the galaxy, to house their, ah, experiments in ontology. To view their own deep past, before they became whatever they are, and to decide whether the path through which they emerged was inevitable or a low-probability outcome. The reverse face of the Drake equation, if you like."

Sagan shivers. "Are you telling me we're just . . . memories? Echoes from the past, reconstituted and replayed some unimaginable time in the future? That this entire monstrous joke of a cosmological experiment is just a sideshow?"

"Yes, Dr. Sagan," Gregor says soothingly. "After all, the disk is not so large compared to an entire galaxy, don't you think? And I would not say the sideshow is unimportant. Do you ever think about your own childhood? And wonder whether the you that sits here in front of me today was the inevitable product of your upbringing? Or could you have become someone completely different—an airline pilot, for example, or a banker? Alternatively, could *someone else* have become *you*? What set of circumstances combine to produce an astronomer and exobiologist? Why should a God not harbor the same curiosity?"

"So you're saying it's introspection, with a purpose. The galactic civilization wants to see its own birth."

"The galactic hive mind," Gregor soothes, amused at how easy it is to deal with Sagan. "Remember, information is key. Why should human-level intelligences be the highest level?" All the while he continues to breathe oxytocin and other peptide neurotransmitters across the table toward Sagan. "Don't let such speculations ruin your meal," he adds, phrasing it as an observation rather than an implicit command.

Sagan nods and returns to using his utensils. "That's very thought-provoking," he says, as he gratefully raises another mouthful to his lips. "If this is based on hard intelligence, it . . . Well, I'm worried. Even if it's inference, I have to do some thinking about this. I hadn't really been thinking along these lines."

"I'm sure if there's an alien menace, we'll defeat it," Gregor assures him, as Sagan masticates and swallows the neurotoxin-laced meatball in tomato sauce. And just for the moment, he is content to relax in the luxury of truth: "Just leave everything to me, and I'll see that your concerns are communicated to the right people. Then we'll do something about your dish, and everything will work out for the best."

● POOR PROGNOSIS

Maddy visits John regularly in hospital. At first it's a combination of natural compassion and edgy guilt; John is pretty much alone on this continent of lies, being both socially and occupationally isolated, and Maddy can convince herself that she's helping him feel in touch, motivating him to recover. Later on it's a necessity of work—she's keeping the lab going, even feeding the squirming white horror in the earth-filled glass jar, in John's absence—and partly boredom. It's not as if Bob's at home much. His work assignments frequently take him to new construction sites up and down the coast. When he is home they frequently argue into the small hours, picking at the scabs on their relationship with the sullen pinch-faced resentment of a couple fifty years gone in despair at the wrongness of their shared direction. So she escapes by visiting John and tells herself that she's doing it to keep his spirits up as he learns to use his prostheses.

"You shouldn't blame yourself," he tells her one afternoon when he notices her staring. "If you hadn't been around, I'd be dead. Neither of us was to know."

"Well." Maddy winces as he sits up, then raises the tongs to his face to nudge the grippers apart before reaching for the water glass. "That won't"—she changes direction in midsentence—"make it easier to cope."

"We're all going to have to cope," he says gnomically, before relaxing back against the stack of pillows. He's a lot better now than he was when he first arrived, delirious with his hand swollen and blackening, but the aftereffects of the mock-termite venom have weakened him in other ways. "I want to know why those things don't live closer to the coast. I mean, if they did, we'd never have bothered with the place. After the first landing, that is." He frowns. "If you can ask at the crown surveyor's office if there are any relevant records, that would help."

"The crown surveyor's not very helpful." That's an understatement. The crown surveyor is some kind of throwback; last time she went to his office to ask about maps of the northeast plateau he'd asked her whether her husband approved of her running around like this. "Maybe when you're out of here." She moves her chair closer to the side of the bed.

"Dr. Smythe says next week, possibly Monday or Tuesday." John sounds frustrated. "The pins and needles are still there." It's not just his right hand, lopped off below the elbow and replaced with a crude affair of padding and spring steel; the venom spread and some of his toes had to be amputated. He was having seizures when Maddy reached the hospital, four hours after he was bitten. She knows she saved his life, that if he'd gone out alone, he'd almost certainly have been killed, so why does she feel so bad about it?

"You're getting better," Maddy insists, covering his left hand with her own. "You'll see." She smiles encouragingly.

"I wish—" For a moment John looks at her; then he shakes his head minutely and sighs. He grips her hand with his fingers. They feel weak, and she can feel them trembling with the effort. "Leave Johnson"—the surveyor—"to me. I need to prepare an urgent report on the mock-termites before anyone else goes poking them."

"How much of a problem do you think they're going to be?"

"Deadly." He closes his eyes for a few seconds, then opens them again. "We've got to map their population distribution. And tell the governor-general's office. I counted twelve mounds in roughly an acre, but that was a rough sample, and you can't extrapolate from it. We also need to learn whether they've got any unusual swarming behaviors—like army ants, for example, or bees. Then we can start investigating whether any of our insecticides work on them. If the governor wants to start spinning out satellite towns next year, he's going to need to know what to expect. Otherwise, people are going to get hurt." *Or killed,* Maddy adds silently.

John is very lucky to be alive: Dr. Smythe compared his condition to a patient he'd once seen who'd been bitten by a rattler, and that was the result of a single bite by a small one. *If the continental interior is full of the things, what are we going to do?* Maddy wonders.

"Have you seen any sign of her majesty feeding?" John asks, breaking into her train of thought.

Maddy shivers. "Turtle tree leaves go down well," she says quietly. "And she's given birth to two workers since we've had her. They chew the leaves to mulch, then regurgitate it for her."

"Oh, really? Do they deliver straight into her mandibles?"

Maddy squeezes her eyes tight. This is the bit she was really hoping John wouldn't ask her about. "No," she says faintly.

"Really?" He sounds curious.

"I think you'd better see for yourself." Because there's no way in hell that Maddy is going to tell him about the crude wooden spoons the mock-termite workers have been crafting from the turtle tree branches, or the feeding ritual, and what they did to the bumbler fly that got into the mock-termite pen through the chicken-wire screen.

He'll just have to see for himself.

○ RUSHMORE

The *Korolev* is huge for a flying machine but pretty small in nautical terms. Yuri is mostly happy about this. He's a fighter jock at heart, and he can't stand Navy bullshit. Still, it's a far cry from the MiG-17s he qualified in. It doesn't have a cockpit, or even a flight deck—it has a *bridge*, like a ship, with the pilots, flight engineers, navigators, and observers sitting in a horseshoe around the captain's chair. When it's thumping across the sea barely ten meters above the wave tops at nearly five hundred kilometers per hour, it rattles and shakes until the crew's vision blurs. The big reactor-powered turbines in the tail pods roar, and the neutron detectors on the turquoise radiation bulkhead behind them tick like demented deathwatch beetles: the rest of the crew are huddled down below in the nose, with as much shielding between them and the engine rooms as possible. It's a white-knuckle ride, and Yuri has difficulty resisting the urge to curl his hands into fists because whenever he loses concentration his gut instincts are telling him to grab the stick and pull up. The ocean is no aviator's friend, and skimming across this infinite grey expanse between planet-sized landmasses forces Gagarin to confront the fact that he is not, by instinct, a sailor.

They're two days outbound from the new-old North America, forty thousand kilometers closer to home and still weeks away even though they're cutting the corner on their parabolic exploration track. The fatigue is getting to him as he takes his seat next to Misha—who is visibly wilting from his twelve-hour shift at the con—and straps himself in. "Anything to report?" he asks.

"I don't like the look of the ocean ahead," says Misha. He nods at the navigation station to Gagarin's left: Shaw, the Irish ensign, sees him and salutes.

"Permission to report, sir?" Gagarin nods. "We're coming

up on a thermocline boundary suggestive of another radiator wall, this time surrounding uncharted seas. Dead reckoning says we're on course for home, but we haven't charted this route, and the surface waters are getting much cooler. Anytime now we should be spotting the radiators, and then we're going to have to start keeping a weather eye out."

Gagarin sighs: exploring new uncharted oceans seemed almost romantic at first, but now it's a dangerous but routine task. "You have kept the towed array at altitude?" he asks.

"Yes, sir," Misha responds. The towed array is basically a kite-borne radar, tugged along behind the *Korolev* on the end of a kilometer of steel cable to give them some warning of obstacles ahead. "Nothing showing—"

Right on cue, one of the radar operators raises a hand and waves three fingers.

"—Correction, radiators ahoy, range three hundred, bearing . . . Okay, let's see it."

"Maintain course," Gagarin announces. "Let's throttle back to two hundred once we clear the radiators, until we know what we're running into." He leans over to his left, watching over Shaw's shoulder.

The next hour is unpleasantly interesting. As they near the radiator fins, the water and the air above it cool down. The denser air helps the *Korolev* generate lift, which is good, but they need it, which is bad. The sky turns grey and murky, and rain falls in continuous sheets that hammer across the armored bridge windows like machine-gun fire. The ride becomes gusty as well as bumpy, until Gagarin orders two of the nose turbines started just in case they hit a downdraft. The big jet engines guzzle fuel and are usually shut down in cruise flight, used only for takeoff runs and extraordinary situations. But punching through a cold front and a winter storm isn't flying as usual as far as Gagarin's concerned, and the one nightmare all ekranoplan drivers face is running into a monster ocean wave nose first at cruise speed.

Presently the navigators identify a path between two radiator fins, and Gagarin authorizes it. He's beginning to relax as the huge monoliths loom out of the grey clouds ahead when one of the sharp-eyed pilots shouts: "Icebergs!"

"Fucking hell." Gagarin sits bolt upright. "Start all boost

engines! Bring up full power on both reactors! Lower flaps to nine degrees and get us the hell out of this!" He turns to Shaw, his face grey. "Bring the towed array aboard, now."

"Shit." Misha starts flipping switches on his console, which doubles as damage control central. *"Icebergs?"*

The huge ground-effect ship lurches and roars as the third pilot starts bleeding hot exhaust gases from the running turbines to start the other twelve engines. They've probably got less than six hours' fuel left, and it takes fifteen minutes on all engines to get off the water, but Gagarin's not going to risk meeting an iceberg head-on in ground-effect. The ekranoplan can function as a huge, lumbering, ungainly seaplane if it has to; but it doesn't have the engine power to do so on reactors alone, or to leapfrog floating mountains of ice. And hitting an iceberg isn't on Gagarin's to-do list.

The rain sluices across the roof of the bridge, and now the sky is louring and dark, the huge walls of the radiator slabs bulking in twilight to either side. The rain is freezing, super-cooled droplets that smear the *Korolev*'s wings with a lethal sheen of ice. "Where are the leading-edge heaters?" Gagarin asks. "Come on!"

"Working, sir," calls the number four pilot. Moments later the treacherous rain turns to hailstones, rattling and booming but fundamentally unlikely to stick to the flight surfaces and build up weight until it flips the ship over. "I think we're going to—"

A white and ghostly wall comes into view in the distance, hammering toward the bridge windows like a runaway freight train. Gagarin's stomach lurches. "Pull up, pull up!" The first and second pilots are struggling with the hydraulically boosted controls as the *Korolev*'s nose pitches up almost ten degrees, right out of ground-effect. "Come on!"

They make it.

The iceberg slams out of the darkness of the storm and the sea like the edge of the world; fifty meters high and as massive as mountains, it has lodged against the aperture between the radiator fins. Billions of tons of pack ice has stopped dead in the water, creaking and groaning with the strain as it butts up against the infinite. The *Korolev* skids over the leading edge of the iceberg, her keel barely clearing it by ten meters, and continues to climb laboriously into the darkening sky. The blazing eyes of her reactors burn slick scars into the ice below. Then they're into the open water beyond the radiator fins, and although the sea below them is an expanse of whiteness, they are also clear of icy mountains.

"Shut down engines three through fourteen," Gagarin orders once he regains enough control to keep the shakes out of his voice. "Take us back down to thirty meters, Lieutenant. Meteorology, what's our situation like?"

"Arctic or worse, Comrade General." The meteorologist, a hatchet-faced woman from Minsk, shakes her head. "Air temperature outside is thirty below, pressure is high." The rain and hail have vanished along with the radiators and the clear seas—and the light, for it is now fading toward nightfall.

"Hah. Misha, what do you think?"

"I think we've found our way into the freezer, sir. Permission to put the towed array back up?"

Gagarin squints into the darkness. "Lieutenant, keep us at two hundred steady. Misha, yes, get the towed array back out again. We need to see where we're going."

The next three hours are simultaneously boring and fraught. It's darker and colder than a Moscow apartment in winter during a power cut; the sea below is ice from horizon to horizon, cracking and groaning and splintering in a vast expanding V-shape behind the *Korolev*'s pressure wake. The spectral ruins of the Milky Way galaxy stretch overhead, reddened and stirred by alien influences. Misha supervises the relaunch of the towed array, then hands over to Major Suvurov before stiffly standing and going below to the unquiet bunk room. Gagarin sticks to a quarter-hourly routine of reports, making sure that he knows what everyone is doing. Bridge crew come and go for their regular station changes. It is routine, and deadly with it. Then:

"Sir, I have a return. Permission to report?"

"Go ahead." Gagarin nods to the navigator. "Where?"

"Bearing zero—it's horizon to horizon—there's a crest rising up to ten meters above the surface. Looks like landfall, range one sixty and closing. Uh, there's a gap and a more distant landfall at thirty-five degrees, peak rising to two hundred meters."

"That's some cliff." Gagarin frowns. He feels drained, his brain hazy with the effort of making continual decisions after six hours in the hot seat and more than two days of this thumping, roaring progression. He glances round. "Major? Please summon Colonel Gorodin. Helm, come about to zero thirty-five. We'll take a look at the gap and see if it's a natural inlet. If this is a continental mass, we might as well take a look before we press on for home."

For the next hour they drive onward into the night, bleeding off speed and painting in the gaps in the radar map of the coastline. It's a bleak frontier, inhumanly cold, with a high interior plateau. There are indeed two headlands, promontories jutting into the coast from either side of a broad, deep bay. Hills rise from one of the promontories and across the bay. Something about it strikes Gagarin as strangely familiar, if only he could place it. Another echo of Earth? But it's too cold by far, a deep Antarctic chill. And he's not familiar with the coastline of Zemlya, the myriad inlets off the northeast passage, where the submarines cruise on eternal vigilant patrols to defend the frontier of the Rodina.

A thin predawn light stains the icy hilltops grey as the Korolev cruises slowly between the headlands—several kilometers apart—and into the wide-open bay beyond. Gagarin raises his binoculars and scans the distant coastline. There are structures, straight lines! "Another ruined civilization?" he asks quietly.

"Maybe, sir. Think anyone could survive in this weather?" The temperature has dropped another ten degrees in the predawn chill, although the ekranoplan is kept warm by the outflow of its two Kuznetsov aviation reactors.

"Hah."

Gagarin begins to sweep the northern coast when Major Suvurov stands up. "Sir! Over there!"

"Where?" Gagarin glances at him. Suvurov is quivering with anger, or shock, or something else. He, too, has his binoculars out.

"Over there! On the southern hillside."

"Where—" He brings his binoculars to bear as the dawnlight spills across the shattered stump of an immense skyscraper.

There is a hillside behind it, a jagged rift where the land has risen up a hundred meters. It reeks of antiquity, emphasized by the carvings in the headland. Here is what the expedition has been looking for all along, the evidence that they are not alone.

"My God." Misha swears, shocked into politically incorrect language.

"Marx," says Gagarin, studying the craggy features of the nearest head. "I've seen this before, this sort of thing. The Americans have a memorial like it. Mount Rushmore, they call it."

"Don't you mean Easter Island?" asks Misha. "Sculptures left by a vanished people . . ."

"Nonsense! Look there, isn't that Lenin? And Stalin, of course." Even though the famous moustache is cracked and half of it has fallen away from the cliff. "But who's that next to them?"

Gagarin brings his binoculars to focus on the fourth head. Somehow it looks far less weathered than the others, as if added as an afterthought, perhaps some kind of insane statement about the mental health of its vanished builders. Both antennae have long since broken off, and one of the mandibles is damaged, but the eyeless face is still recognizably unhuman. The insectile head stares eyelessly out across the frozen ocean, an enigma on the edge of a devastated island continent. "I think we've found the brother socialists," he mutters to Misha, his voice pitched low so that it won't carry over the background noise on the flight deck. "And you know what? Something tells me we didn't want to."

● ANTHROPIC ERROR

As the summer dry season grinds on, Maddy finds herself spending more time at John's home-cum-laboratory, doing the cleaning and cooking for herself in addition to maintaining the lab books and feeding the live specimens. During her afternoons visiting in the hospital she helps him write up his reports. Losing his right hand has hit John hard: he's teaching himself to write again, but his handwriting is slow and childish.

She finds putting in extra hours at the lab preferable to the empty and uncomfortable silences back in the two-bedroom prefab she shares with Bob. Bob is away on field trips to out-lying ranches and quarries half the time and working late the other half. At least, he says he's working late. Maddy has her suspicions. He gets angry if she isn't around to cook, and she gets angry right back at him when he expects her to clean, and they've stopped having sex. Their relationship is in fact going downhill rapidly, drying up and withering away in the arid continental heat, until going to work in John's living room among the cages and glass vivaria and books feels like taking refuge. She has taken to spending more time there, working late for real, and when Bob is away she sleeps on the wicker settee in the dining room.

One day, more than a month later than expected, Dr. Smythe finally decides that John is well enough to go home. Embarrassingly, she's not there on the afternoon when he's finally discharged. Instead, she's in the living room, typing up a report on a subspecies of the turtle tree and its known para-sites, when the screen door bangs and the front door opens. "Maddy?"

She squeaks before she can stop herself. "John?" She's out of the chair to help him with the battered suitcase the cabbie half-helpfully left on the front stoop.

"Maddy." He smiles tiredly. "I've missed being home."

"Come on in." She closes the screen door and carries the suitcase over to the stairs. He's painfully thin now, a far cry from the slightly-too-plump entomologist she'd met on the colony liner. "I've got lots of stuff for you to read—but not until you're stronger. I don't want you overworking and put-ting yourself back in hospital!"

"You're an angel." He stands uncertainly in his own living room, looking around as if he hadn't quite expected to see it again. "I'm looking forward to seeing the termites."

She shivers abruptly. "I'm not. Come on." She climbs the stairs with the suitcase, not looking back. She pushes through the door into the one bedroom that's habitable—he's been using the other one to store samples—and dumps the case on the rough dressing table. She's been up here before, first to collect his clothing while he was in hospital and later to clean and make sure there were no poisonous spiders lurking in the corners. It smells of camphor and dusty memories. She turns to face him. "Welcome home." She smiles experimentally.

He looks around. "You've been cleaning."

"Not much." She feels her face heat.

He shakes his head. "Thank you."

She can't decide what to say. "No, no, it's not like that. If I wasn't here, I'd be . . ."

John shuffles. She blinks at him, feeling stupid and foolish. "Do you have room for a lodger?" she asks.

He looks at her, and she can't maintain eye contact. It's all going wrong, not what she wanted.

"Things going badly?" he asks, cocking his head on one side and staring at her. "Forgive me, I don't mean to pry—"

"No, no, it's quite all right." She sniffs. Takes a breath. "This continent breaks things. Bob hasn't been the same since we arrived, or I, I haven't. I need to put some space between us, for a bit."

"Oh."

"Oh." She's silent for a while. "I can pay rent—"

This is an excuse, a transparent rationalization, and not entirely true, but she's saved from digging herself deeper into a lie because John manages to stumble and reaches out to steady himself with his right arm, which is still not entirely healed, and Maddy finds herself with his weight on her shoulder as he hisses in pain. "Ow! Ow!"

"I'm sorry! I'm sorry!"

"It wasn't you—" They make it to the bed, and she sits him down beside her. "I nearly blacked out then. I feel useless. I'm not half the man I was."

"I don't know about that," she says absently, not quite registering his meaning. She strokes his cheek, feeling it slick with sweat. The pulse in his neck is strong. "You're still recovering. I think they sent you home too early. Let's get you into bed and rest up for a couple of hours, then see about something to eat. What do you say to that?"

"I shouldn't need nursing," he protests faintly, as she bends down and unties his shoelaces. "I don't need . . . nursing." He runs his fingers through her hair.

"This isn't about nursing."

Two hours later, the patient is drifting on the edge of sleep, clearly tired out by his physical therapy and the strain of homecoming. Maddy lies curled up against his shoulder, staring at the ceiling. She feels calm and at peace for the first time since she arrived here. *It's not about Bob anymore, is it?* she asks herself. *It's not about what anybody expects of me. It's about what I want, about finding my place in the universe.* She feels her face relaxing into a smile. Truly, for a moment, it feels as if the entire universe is revolving around her in stately synchrony.

John snuffles slightly, then startles and tenses. She can tell he's come to wakefulness. "Funny," he says quietly, then clears his throat.

"What is?" *Please don't spoil this,* she prays.

"I wasn't expecting this." He moves beside her. "Wasn't expecting much of anything."

"Was it good?" She tenses.

"Do you still want to stay?" he asks hesitantly. "Damn, I didn't mean to sound as if—"

"No, I don't mind—" She rolls toward him, then is brought up short by a quiet, insistent tapping that travels up through the inner wall of the house. "Damn," she says quietly.

"What's that?" He begins to sit up.

"It's the termites."

John listens intently. The tapping continues erratically, on-again, off-again bursts of clattering noise. "What is she doing?"

"They do it about twice a day," Maddy confesses. "I put her in the number two aquarium with a load of soil and leaves and a mesh lid on top. When they start making a racket I feed them."

He looks surprised. "This I've got to see."

The walls are coming back up again. Maddy stifles a sigh: it's not about her anymore; it's about the goddamn mock-termites. Anyone would think they were the center of the universe, and she was just here to feed them. "Let's go look, then." John is already standing up, trying to pick up his discarded shirt with his prosthesis. "Don't bother," she tells him. "Who's going to notice, the insects?"

"I thought—" He glances at her, taken aback. "Sorry. Forget it."

She pads downstairs, pausing momentarily to make sure he's following her safely. The tapping continues, startlingly loud. She opens the door to the utility room in the back and turns on the light. "Look," she says.

The big glass-walled aquarium sits on the worktop. It's lined with rough-tamped earth and on top, there are piles of denuded branches and wood shavings. It's near dusk, and by the light filtering through the windows she can see mock-termites moving across the surface of the muddy dome that bulges above the queen's chamber. A group of them have gathered around a curiously straight branch: as she watches, they throw it against the glass like a battering ram against a castle wall. A pause, then they pick it up and pull back, and throw it again. They're huge for insects, almost two inches long: much bigger than the ones thronging the mounds in the outback. "That's odd." Maddy peers at them. "They've grown since yesterday."

"They? Hang on, did you take workers, or . . . ?"

"No, just the queen. None of these bugs is more than a month old."

The termites have stopped banging on the glass. They form two rows on either side of the stick, pointing their heads up at the huge, monadic mammals beyond the alien barrier. Looking at them closely Maddy notices other signs of morphological change: the increasing complexity of their digits, the bulges at the backs of their heads. *Is the queen changing, too?* she asks herself, briefly troubled by visions of a malignant intelligence rapidly swelling beneath the surface of the vivarium, plotting its escape by moonlight.

John stands behind Maddy and folds his arms around her. She shivers. "I feel as if they're *watching* us."

"But to them it's not about us, is it?" he whispers in her ear. "Come on. All that's happening is you've trained them to ring a bell so the experimenters give them a snack. They think the universe was made for their convenience. Dumb insects, just a bundle of reflexes really. Let's feed them and go back to bed."

The two humans leave and climb the stairs together, arm in arm, leaving the angry aboriginal hive to plot its escape unnoticed.

● IT'S ALWAYS OCTOBER THE FIRST

Gregor sits on a bench on the Esplanade, looking out across the river toward the Statue of Liberty. He's got a bag of stale bread crumbs, and he's ministering to the flock of pigeons that scuttle and peck around his feet. The time is six minutes to three on the afternoon of October the First, and the year is irrelevant. In fact, it's too late. This is how it always ends, although the onshore breeze and the sunlight are unexpected bonus payments.

The pigeons jostle and chase one another as he drops another piece of crust on the pavement. For once he hasn't bothered to soak them overnight in 5 percent warfarin solution. There is such a thing as a free lunch, if you're a pigeon in the wrong place at the wrong time. He's going to be dead soon, and, if any of the pigeons survive, they're welcome to the wreckage.

There aren't many people about, so when the puffing middle-aged guy in the suit comes into view, jogging along as if he's chasing his stolen wallet, Gregor spots him instantly. It's Brundle, looking slightly pathetic when removed from his man-hive. Gregor waves hesitantly, and Brundle alters course.

"Running late," he pants, kicking at the pigeons until they flap away to make space for him at the other end of the bench.

"Really?"

Brundle nods. "They should be coming over the horizon in another five minutes."

"How did you engineer it?" Gregor isn't particularly interested, but technical chitchat serves to pass the remaining seconds.

"Man-in-the-middle, ramified by all their intelligence assessments." Brundle looks self-satisfied. "Understanding their caste specialization makes it easier. Two weeks ago we told the GRU that MacNamara was using the NP-101 program as cover for a preemptive D-SLAM strike. At the same time we got the NOAA to increase their mapping-launch frequency, and pointed the increased level of Soviet activity out to our sources in SAC. It doesn't take much to get the human hives buzzing with positive feedback."

Of course, Brundle and Gregor aren't using words for this incriminating exchange. Their phenotypically human bodies conceal some useful modifications, knobby encapsulated tumors of neuroectoderm that shield the delicate tissues of their designers, neural circuits that have capabilities human geneticists haven't even imagined. A visitor from a more advanced human society might start chattering excitedly about wet-phase nanomachines and neural-directed broadband packet radio, but nobody in New York on a sunny day in 1979 plus one million is thinking in those terms. They still think the universe belongs to their own kind, skull-locked social—but not eusocial—primates. Brundle and Gregor know better. They're workers of a higher order, carefully tailored to the task in hand, and although they look human, there's less to their humanity than meets the eye. Even Gagarin can probably guess better, an individualist trapped in the machinery of a utopian political hive. The termites of New Iowa and a host of other Galapagos continents on the disk are not the future, but they're a superior approximation to anything humans have achieved, even those planetary instantiations that have doctored their own genome in order to successfully implement true eusocial societies. Group minds aren't prone to anthropic errors.

"So it's over, is it?" Gregor asks aloud, in the stilted serial speech to which humans are constrained.

"Yep. Any minute now—"

The air-raid sirens begin to wail. Pigeons spook, exploding outward in a cloud of white panic.

"Oh, look."

The entity behind Gregor's eyes stares out across the river, marking time while his cancers call home. He's always vague about these last hours before the end of a mission—a destructive time, in which information is lost—but at least he remembers the rest. As do the hyphae of the huge rhizome network spreading deep beneath the park, thinking slow vegetable thoughts and relaying his sparky monadic flashes back to his mother by way of the engineered fungal strands that thread the deep ocean floors. The next version of him will be created knowing almost everything: the struggle to contain the annoying, hard-to-domesticate primates with their insistent paranoid individualism, the dismay of having to carefully sterilize the few enlightened ones like Sagan . . .

Humans are not useful. The future belongs to ensemble intelligences, hive minds. Even the mock-termite aboriginals have more to contribute. And Gregor, with his teratomas and his shortage of limbs, has more to contribute than most. The culture that sent him, and a million other anthropomorphic infiltrators, understands this well: he will be rewarded and propagated, his genome and memeome preserved by the collective even as it systematically eliminates yet another outbreak of humanity. The collective is well on its way toward occupying a tenth of the disk, or at least of sweeping it clean of competing life-forms. Eventually it will open negotiations with its neighbors on the other disks, joining the process of forming a distributed consciousness that is a primitive echo of the vast ramified intelligence wheeling across the sky so far away. And this time round, knowing *why* it is being birthed, the new God will have a level of self-understanding denied to its parent.

Gregor anticipates being one of the overmind's memories: it is a fate none of these humans will know save at second-hand, filtered through his eusocial sensibilities. To the extent that he bothers to consider the subject, he thinks it is a disappointment. He may be here to help exterminate them, but it's not a personal grudge: it's more like pouring gasoline on a troublesome ant heap that's settled in the wrong backyard. The necessity irritates him, and he grumbles aloud in Brundle's direction: "If they realized how thoroughly they'd been infiltrated, or how badly their own individuality lets them down—"

Flashes far out over the ocean, ruby glare reflected from the thin tatters of stratospheric cloud.

"—They might learn to cooperate someday. Like us."

More flashes, moving closer now as the nuclear battlefront evolves.

Brundle nods. "But then, they wouldn't be human anymore. And in any case, they're much too late. A million years too late."

A flicker too bright to see, propagating faster than the signaling speed of nerves, punctuates their conversation. Seconds later, the mach wave flushes their cinders from the bleached concrete of the bench. Far out across the disk, the game of ape and ant continues; but in this place and for the present time, the question has been answered. And there are no human winners.

Afterword—"Missile Gap"

In late 2004, Gardner Dozois—then editor of *Asimov's Science Fiction* magazine—asked me if I'd like to write a novella for him. Like many such invitations, it came with strings attached; he was commissioning long stories for an anthology titled *One Million A.D.* I find tales of the very distant future hard to write. How do you find a way to connect with deep time? Few of us have even a tenuous grasp on the meaning of a single century, let alone a century of centuries of centuries! The sum total of recorded human history is less than six thousand years; few of our institutions have lasted even one millennium without major change. A million years is somewhere between four and twenty times the life span of our entire species (the paleontologists are a little vague on precisely when *Homo sapiens sapiens* first showed up on the scene). Given that the focus of almost all fiction is the human condition, and that the human condition doesn't scale well across even centuries (much less deep geological time), I decided to approach the subject indirectly.

Rogue Farm

It was a bright, cool March morning: mare's tails trailed across the southeastern sky toward the rising sun. Joe shivered slightly in the driver's seat as he twisted the starter handle on the old front-loader he used to muck out the barn. Like its owner, the ancient Massey Ferguson had seen better days; but it had survived worse abuse than Joe routinely handed out. The diesel clattered, spat out a gobbet of thick blue smoke, and chattered to itself dyspeptically. His mind as blank as the sky above, Joe slid the tractor into gear, raised the front scoop, and began turning it toward the open doors of the barn—just in time to see an itinerant farm coming down the road.

"Bugger," swore Joe. The tractor engine made a hideous grinding noise and died. He took a second glance, eyes wide, then climbed down from the tractor and trotted over to the kitchen door at the side of the farmhouse. "Maddie!" he called, forgetting the two-way radio clipped to his sweater hem. "Maddie! There's a farm coming!"

"Joe? Is that you? Where are you?" Her voice wafted vaguely from the bowels of the house.

"Where are *you*?" he yelled back.

"I'm in the bathroom."

"Bugger," he said again. "If it's the one we had round the end last month . . ."

The sound of a toilet sluiced through his worry. It was followed by a drumming of feet on the staircase, then Maddie erupted into the kitchen. "Where is it?" she demanded.

"Out front, about a quarter mile up the lane."

"Right." Hair wild and eyes angry about having her morning ablutions cut short, Maddie yanked a heavy green coat on over her shirt. "Opened the cupboard yet?"

"I was thinking you'd want to talk to it first."

"Too right I want to talk to it. If it's that one that's been lurking in the copse near Edgar's pond, I got some *issues* to discuss with it." Joe shook his head at her anger and went to unlock the cupboard in the back room. "You take the shotgun and keep it off our property," she called after him. "I'll be out in a minute."

Joe nodded to himself, then carefully picked out the twelve-gauge and a preloaded magazine. The gun's power-on self-test lights flickered erratically, but it seemed to have a full charge. Slinging it, he locked the cupboard carefully and went back out into the farmyard to warn off their unwelcome visitor.

The farm squatted, buzzing and clicking to itself, in the road outside Armitage End. Joe eyed it warily from behind the wooden gate, shotgun under his arm. It was a medium-sized one, probably with half a dozen human components subsumed into it—a formidable collective. Already it was deep into farm-fugue, no longer relating very clearly to people outside its own communion of mind. Beneath its leathery black skin he could see hints of internal structure, cytocellular macroassemblies flexing and glooping in disturbing motions. Even though it was only a young adolescent, it was already the size of an antique heavy tank, and blocked the road just as efficiently as an Apatosaurus would have. It smelled of yeast and gasoline.

Joe had an uneasy feeling that it was watching him. "Buggerit, I don't have time for this," he muttered. The stable waiting for the small herd of cloned spidercows cluttering up the north paddock was still knee-deep in manure, and the tractor seat wasn't getting any warmer while he shivered out here waiting for Maddie to come and sort this thing out. It wasn't a big herd, but it was as big as his land and his labor could manage—the big biofabricator in the shed could assemble mammalian livestock faster than he could feed them up and sell them with an honest HAND-RAISED NOT VAT-GROWN label. "What do you want with us?" he yelled up at the gently buzzing farm.

"Brains, fresh brains for baby Jesus," crooned the farm in a warm contralto, startling Joe half out of his skin. "Buy my brains!" Half a dozen disturbing cauliflower shapes poked suggestively out of the farm's back, then retracted, coyly.

"Don't want no brains around here," Joe said stubbornly, his fingers whitening on the stock of the shotgun. "Don't want your kind round here, neither. Go away."

"I'm a nine-legged semiautomatic groove machine!" crooned the farm. "I'm on my way to Jupiter on a mission for love! Won't you buy my brains?" Three curious eyes on stalks extruded from its upper glacis.

"Uh—" Joe was saved from having to dream up any more ways of saying *fuck off* by Maddie's arrival. She'd managed to sneak her old battle dress home after a stint keeping the peace in Mesopotamia twenty years ago, and she'd managed to keep herself in shape enough to squeeze inside. Its left knee squealed ominously when she walked it about, which wasn't often, but it still worked well enough to manage its main task—intimidating trespassers.

"You." She raised one translucent arm, pointed at the farm. "Get off my land. *Now.*"

Taking his cue, Joe raised his shotgun and thumbed the selector to full auto. It wasn't a patch on the hardware riding Maddie's shoulders, but it underlined the point. The farm hooted. "Why don't you love me?" it asked plaintively.

"Get orf my land," Maddie amplified, volume cranked up so high that Joe winced. *"Ten seconds! Nine! Eight—"* Thin rings sprang out from the sides of her arms, whining with the stress of long disuse as the Gauss gun powered up.

"I'm going! I'm going!" The farm lifted itself slightly, shuffling backward. "Don't understand. I only wanted to set you free to explore the universe. Nobody wants to buy my fresh fruit and brains. What's wrong with you people?"

They waited until the farm had retreated round the bend at the top of the hill. Maddie was the first to relax, the rings retracting into the arms of her battle dress, which solidified from ethereal translucency to neutral olive drab as it powered down. Joe safed his shotgun. "Bastard," he said.

"Fucking A." Maddie looked haggard. "That was a bold one." Her face was white and pinched-looking, Joe noted: her fists were clenched. She had the shakes, he realized without surprise. Tonight was going to be another major nightmare night, and no mistake.

"The fence." They'd discussed wiring up an outer wire to the CHP baseload from their little methane plant, on again and off again for the past year.

"Maybe this time. Maybe." Maddie wasn't keen on the idea of frying passersby without warning, but if anything might bring her around, it would be the prospect of being squatted by a rogue farm. "Help me out of this, and I'll cook breakfast," she said.

"Got to muck out the barn," Joe protested.

"It can wait on breakfast," Maddie said shakily. "I need you."

"Okay." Joe nodded. She was looking bad; it had been a few years since her last fatal breakdown, but when Maddie said *I need you*, it was a bad idea to ignore her. That way led to backbreaking labor on the biofab and loading her backup tapes into the new body; always a messy business. He took her arm and steered her toward the back porch. They were nearly there when he paused.

"What is it?" asked Maddie.

"Haven't seen Bob for a while," he said slowly. "Sent him to let the cows into the north paddock after milking. Do you think—"

"We can check from the control room," she said tiredly. "Are you really worried . . . ?"

"With that thing blundering around? What do *you* think?"

"He's a good working dog," Maddie said uncertainly. "It won't hurt him. He'll be alright; just you page him."

●

After Joe helped her out of her battle dress, and after Maddie spent a good long while calming down, they breakfasted on eggs from their own hens, homemade cheese, and toasted bread made with rye from the hippie commune on the other side of the valley. The stone-floored kitchen in the dilapidated house they'd rebuilt together over the past twenty years was warm and homely. The only purchase from outside the valley was the coffee, beans from a hardy GM strain that grew like a straggling teenager's beard all along the Cumbrian hilltops. They didn't say much: Joe, because he never did, and Maddie, because there wasn't anything that she wanted to say. Silence kept her personal demons down. They'd known each other for many years, and even when there wasn't anything to say they could cope with each other's silence. The voice radio on the windowsill opposite the cast-iron stove stayed off, along with the TV set hanging on the wall next to the fridge. Breakfast was a quiet time of day.

"Dog's not answering," Joe commented over the dregs of his coffee.

"He's a good dog." Maddie glanced at the yard gate uncertainly. "You afraid he's going to run away to Jupiter?"

"He was with me in the shed." Joe picked up his plate and carried it to the sink, began running hot water onto the dishes. "After I cleaned the lines I told him to go take the herd up the paddock while I did the barn." He glanced up, looking out the window with a worried expression. The Massey Ferguson was parked right in front of the open barn doors, as if to hold at bay the mountain of dung, straw, and silage that mounded up inside like an invading odious enemy, relic of a frosty winter past.

Maddie shoved him aside gently and picked up one of the walkie-talkies from the charge point on the windowsill. It bleeped and chuckled at her. "Bob, come in, over." She frowned. "He's probably lost his headset again."

Joe racked the wet plates to dry. "I'll move the midden. You want to go find him?"

"I'll do that." Maddie's frown promised a talking-to in store for the dog when she caught up with him. Not that Bob would mind: words ran off him like water off a duck's back. "Cameras first." She prodded the battered TV set to life and grainy, bisected views flickered across the screen: garden, yard, dutch barn, north paddock, east paddock, main field, copse. "Hmm."

She was still fiddling with the smallholding surveillance

system when Joe clambered back into the driver's seat of the tractor and fired it up once more. This time there was no cough of black smoke, and as he hauled the mess of manure out of the barn and piled it into a three-meter-high midden, a quarter of a ton at a time, he almost managed to forget about the morning's unwelcome visitor. Almost.

By late morning the midden was humming with flies and producing a remarkable stench, but the barn was clean enough to flush out with a hose and broom. Joe was about to begin hauling the midden over to the fermentation tanks buried round the far side of the house when he saw Maddie coming back up the path, shaking her head. He knew at once what was wrong.

"Bob," he said, expectantly.

"Bob's fine. I left him riding shotgun on the goats." Her expression was peculiar. "But that *farm*—"

"Where?" he asked, hurrying after her.

"Squatting in the woods down by the stream," she said tersely. "Just over our fence."

"It's not trespassing, then."

"It's put down feeder roots! Do you have any idea what that means?"

"I don't—" Joe's face wrinkled in puzzlement. "Oh."

"Yes. *Oh*." She stared back at the outbuildings between their home and the woods at the bottom of their smallholding, and if looks could kill, the intruder would be dead a thousand times over. "It's going to estivate, Joe, then it's going to grow to maturity on our patch. And do you know where it said it was going to go when it finishes growing? Jupiter!"

"Bugger," Joe said faintly, as the true gravity of their situation began to sink in. "We'll have to deal with it first."

"That wasn't what I meant," Maddie finished. But Joe was already on his way out the door. She watched him crossing the yard, then shook her head. "Why am I stuck here?" she asked aloud, but the cooker wasn't answering.

○

The hamlet of Outer Cheswick lay four kilometers down the road from Armitage End, four kilometers past mostly derelict houses and broken-down barns, fields given over to weeds and walls damaged by trees. The second half of the twenty-first century had been cruel years for the British agrobusiness sector; even harsher if taken in combination with the decline in population and the consequent housing surplus. As a result, the dropouts of the forties and fifties were able to take their pick from among the gutted shells of once-fine farmhouses. They chose the best and moved in, squatted in the derelict outbuildings, planted their seeds and tended their flocks and practiced their DIY skills, until a generation later a mansion fit for a squire stood in lonely isolation alongside a decaying road where no cars drove. Or rather, it would have taken a generation had there been any children against whose lives it could be measured; these were the latter decades of the population crash, and what a previous century would have labeled downshifter dink couples were now in the majority, far outnumbering the breeder colonies. In this aspect of their life, Joe and Maddie were boringly conventional. In other respects they weren't: Maddie's nightmares, her aversion to alcohol, and her withdrawal from society were all relics of her time in Peaceforce. As for Joe, he liked it here. Hated cities, hated the net, hated the burn of the new. Anything for a quiet life . . .

The Pig and Pizzle, on the outskirts of Outer Cheswick, was the only pub within about ten kilometers—certainly the only one within staggering distance for Joe when he'd had a skinful of mild—and it was naturally a seething den of local gossip, not least because Ole Brenda refused to allow electricity, much less bandwidth, into the premises. (This was not out of any sense of misplaced technophobia, but a side effect of Brenda's previous life as an attack hacker with the European Defense Forces.)

Joe paused at the bar. "Pint of bitter?" he asked tentatively. Brenda glanced at him and nodded, then went back to loading the antique washing machine. Presently she pulled a clean glass down from the shelf and held it under the tap.

"Heard you've got farm trouble," she said noncommittally as she worked the hand pump on the beer engine.

"Uh-huh." Joe focused on the glass. "Where'd you get that?"

"Never you mind." She put the glass down to give the head time to settle. "You want to talk to Arthur and Wendy the Rat about farms. They had one the other year."

"Happens." Joe took his pint. "Thanks, Brenda. The usual?"

"Yeah." She turned back to the washer. Joe headed over to the far corner, where a pair of huge leather sofas, their arms and backs ripped and scarred by generations of Brenda's semi-feral cats, sat facing each other on either side of a cold hearth. "Art, Rats. What's up?"

"Fine, thanks." Wendy the Rat was well over seventy, one of those older folks who had taken the p53 chromosome hack and seemed to wither into timelessness: white dreadlocks, nose and ear studs dangling loosely from leathery holes, skin like a desert wind. Art had been her boy toy once, back before middle age set its teeth into him. He hadn't had the hack, and looked older than she did. Together they ran a smallholding, mostly pharming vaccine chicks but also doing a brisk trade in high-nitrate fertilizer that came in on the nod and went out in sacks by moonlight.

"Heard you had a spot of bother?"

"'S true." Joe took a cautious mouthful. "Mm, good. You ever had farm trouble?"

"Maybe." Wendy looked at him askance, slitty-eyed. "What kinda trouble you got in mind?"

"Got a farm collective. Says it's going to Jupiter or something. Bastard's homesteading the woods down by old Jack's stream. Listen . . . Jupiter?"

"Aye, well, that's one of the destinations, sure enough." Art nodded wisely, as if he knew anything.

"Naah, that's bad." Wendy the Rat frowned. "Is it growing trees yet, do you know?"

"Trees?" Joe shook his head. "Haven't gone and looked, to tell the truth. What the fuck makes people do that to themselves, anyway?"

"Who the fuck cares?" Wendy's face split in a broad grin. "Such as don't think they're human anymore, meself."

"It tried to sweet-talk us," Joe said.

"Aye, they do that," said Arthur, nodding emphatically. "Read somewhere they're the ones as think we aren't fully human. Tools an' clothes and farmyard machines, like? Sustaining a pre-post-industrial lifestyle instead of updating our genome and living off the land like God intended?"

"'Ow the hell can something with nine legs and eyestalks call itself *human*?" Joe demanded, chugging back half his pint in one angry swallow.

"It used to be, once. Maybe used to be a bunch of people." Wendy got a weird and witchy look in her eye. "'Ad a boyfriend back thirty, forty years ago, joined a Lamarckian clade. Swapping genes an' all, the way you or me'd swap us underwear. Used to be a 'vironmentalist back when antiglobalization was about big corporations pissing on us all for profits. Got into gene hackery and self-sufficiency big-time. I slung his ass when he turned green and started photosynthesizing."

"Bastards," Joe muttered. It was deep green folk like that who'd killed off the agricultural-industrial complex in the early years of the century, turning large portions of the countryside into ecologically devastated wilderness gone to rack and ruin. Bad enough that they'd set millions of countryfolk out of work—but that they'd gone on to turn green, grow extra limbs, and emigrate to the outer solar system was adding insult to injury. And having a good time in the process, by all accounts. "Din't you 'ave a farm problem, coupla years back?"

"Aye, did that," said Art. He clutched his pint mug protectively.

"It went away," Joe mused aloud.

"Yeah, well." Wendy stared at him cautiously.

"No fireworks, like." Joe caught her eye. "And no body. Huh."

"Metabolism," said Wendy, apparently coming to some kind of decision. "That's where it's at."

"Meat—" Joe, no biogeek, rolled the unfamiliar word around his mouth irritably. "I used to be a software dude before I burned, Rats. You'll have to 'splain the jargon fore using it."

"You ever wondered how those farms *get* to Jupiter?" Wendy probed.

"Well." Joe shook his head. "They, like, grow stage trees? Rocket logs? An' then they estivate, and you are fucked if they do it next door, 'cause when those trees go up, they toast about a hundred hectares?"

"Very good," Wendy said heavily. She picked up her mug in both hands and gnawed on the rim, edgily glancing around as if hunting for police gnats. "Let's you and me take a hike."

Pausing at the bar for Ole Brenda to refill her mug, Wendy led Joe out past Spiffy Buerke and her latest femme—a pair of throwbacks in green Wellingtons and Barbour jackets—out into what had once been a car park and was now a tattered wasteground behind the pub. It was dark, and no residual light pollution stained the sky: the Milky Way was visible overhead, along with the pea-sized red cloud of orbitals that had gradually swallowed Jupiter over the past few years. "You wired?" asked Wendy.

"No, why?"

She pulled out a fist-sized box and pushed a button on the side of it, waited for a light on its side to blink green, and nodded. "Fuckin' polis bugs."

"Isn't that a—"

"Ask me no questions, an' I'll tell you no fibs." Wendy grinned.

"Uh-huh." Joe took a deep breath: he'd guessed Wendy had some dodgy connections, and this—a portable local jammer—was proof: any police bugs within two or three meters would be blind and dumb, unable to relay their chat to the keyword-trawling subsentient coppers whose job it was to prevent conspiracy-to-commit offenses before they happened. It was a relic of the Internet age, when enthusiastic legislators had accidentally demolished the right of free speech in public by demanding keyword monitoring of everything within range of a network terminal—not realizing that in another few decades "network terminals" would be self-replicating 'bots the size of fleas and about as common as dirt. (The net itself had collapsed shortly thereafter, under the weight of self-replicating viral libel lawsuits, but the legacy of public surveillance remained.) "Okay. Tell me about meta, metab—"

"Metabolism." Wendy began walking toward the field behind the pub. "And stage trees. Stage trees started out as science fiction, like? Some guy called Niven—anyway. What you do is, you take a pine tree and you hack it. The xylem vessels running up the heartwood, usually they just lignify and die in a normal tree. Stage trees go one better, and before the cells die they *nitrate* the cellulose in their walls. Takes one fuckin' crazy bunch of hacked enzymes to do it, right? And lots of energy, more energy than trees'd normally have to waste. Anyways, by the time the tree's dead it's ninety percent nitrocellulose, plus built-in stiffeners and baffles and microstructures. It's not, like, straight explosive—it detonates cell by cell, and *some* of the xylem tubes are, eh, well, the farm grows custom-hacked fungal hyphae with a depolarizing membrane nicked from human axons down them to trigger the reaction. It's about efficient as 'at old-time satellite-launcher rocket. Not very, but enough."

"Uh." Joe blinked. "That meant to mean something to me?"

"Oh 'eck, Joe." Wendy shook her head. "Think I'd bend your ear if it wasn't?"

"Okay." He nodded, seriously. "What can I do?"

"Well." Wendy stopped and stared at the sky. High above them, a belt of faint light sparkled with a multitude of tiny pinpricks; a deep green wagon train making its orbital transfer window, self-sufficient posthuman Lamarckian colonists, space-adapted, embarking on the long, slow transfer to Jupiter.

"Well?" He waited expectantly.

"You're wondering where all that fertilizer's from," Wendy said elliptically.

"Fertilizer." His mind blanked for a moment.

"Nitrates."

He glanced down, saw her grinning at him. Her perfect fifth set of teeth glowed alarmingly in the greenish overspill from the light on her jammer box.

"Tha' knows it make sense," she added, then cut the jammer.

●

When Joe finally staggered home in the small hours, a thin plume of smoke was rising from Bob's kennel. Joe paused in front of the kitchen door and sniffed anxiously, then relaxed. Letting go of the door handle, he walked over to the kennel

and sat down outside. Bob was most particular about his den—
even his own humans didn't go in there without an invitation.
So Joe waited.

A moment later there was an interrogative cough from
inside. A dark, pointed snout came out, dribbling smoke from
its nostrils like a particularly vulpine dragon. "Rrrrrrr?"

"'S me."

"Uuurgh." A metallic click. "Smoke good smoke joke
cough tickle funny arf arf?"

"Yeah, don't mind if I do."

The snout pulled back into the kennel; a moment later it
reappeared, teeth clutching a length of hose with a mouthpiece
on one end. Joe accepted it graciously, wiped off the mouthpiece, leaned against the side of the kennel, and inhaled. The
weed was potent and smooth: within a few seconds it stilled
the uneasy dialogue in his head.

"Wow, tha's a good turnup."

"Arf-arf-ayup."

Joe felt himself relaxing. Maddie would be upstairs, snoring quietly in their decrepit bed: waiting for him, maybe. But
sometimes a man just had to be alone with his dog and a good
joint, doing man-and-dog stuff. Maddie understood this and
left him his space. Still . . .

"'At farm been buggering around the pond?"

"Growl exclaim fuck-fuck yup! Sheep-shagger."

"If it's been at our lambs—"

"Nawwwwrr. Buggrit."

"So whassup?"

"Grrrr, Maddie yap-yap farmtalk! Sheep-shagger."

"Maddie's been *talking* to it?"

"Grrr yes-yes!"

"Oh shit. Do you remember when she did her last
backup?"

The dog coughed fragrant blue smoke. "Tank thump-
thump full cow moo beef clone."

"Yeah, I think so too. Better muck it out tomorrow. Just
in case."

"Yurrrrrp." But while Joe was wondering whether this was
agreement or just a canine eructation, a lean paw stole out of
the kennel mouth and yanked the hookah back inside. The

resulting slobbering noises and clouds of aromatic blue smoke left Joe feeling a little queasy: so he went inside.

○

The next morning, over breakfast, Maddie was even quieter than usual. Almost meditative.

"Bob said you'd been talking to that farm," Joe commented over his eggs.

"Bob—" Maddie's expression was unreadable. "Bloody dog." She lifted the lid on the Rayburn's hot plate and peered at the toast browning underneath. "Talks too much."

"Did you?"

"Ayup." She turned the toast and put the lid back down on it.

"Said much?"

"It's a farm." She looked out the window. "Not a fuckin' worry in the world 'cept making its launch window for Jupiter."

"It—"

"Him. Her. They." Maddie sat down heavily in the other kitchen chair. "It's a collective. Usedta be six people. Old, young, whatther, they's decided ter go to Jupiter. One of 'em was telling me how it happened. How she'd been an accountant in Bradford, had a nervous breakdown. Wanted *out*. Self-sufficiency." For a moment her expression turned bleak. "Felt herself growing older but not bigger, if you follow."

"So how's turning into a bioborg an improvement?" Joe grunted, forking up the last of his scrambled eggs.

"They're still separate people: bodies are overrated, anyway. Think of the advantages: not growing older, being able to go places and survive anything, never being on your own, not bein' trapped—" Maddie sniffed. "Fuckin' toast's on fire!"

Smoke began to trickle out from under the hot-plate lid. Maddie yanked the wire toasting rack out from under it and dunked it into the sink, waited for waterlogged black crumbs to float to the surface before taking it out, opening it, and loading it with fresh bread.

"Bugger," she remarked.

"You feel trapped?" Joe asked. *Again?* he wondered.

Maddie grunted. "Not your fault, love. Just life."

"Life." Joe sniffed, then sneezed violently as the acrid smoke tickled his nose. "Life!"

"Horizon's closing in," she said quietly. "Need a change of scenery."

"Ayup, well, rust never sleeps, right? Got to clean out the winter stables, haven't I?" said Joe. He grinned uncertainly at her as he turned away. "Got a shipment of fertilizer coming in."

●

In between milking the herd, feeding the sheep, mucking out the winter stables, and surreptitiously EMPing every police 'bot on the farm into the electronic afterlife, it took Joe a couple of days to get round to running up his toy on the household fabricator. It clicked and whirred to itself like a demented knitting machine as it assembled the gadgets he'd ordered—a modified crop sprayer with double-walled tanks and hoses, an air rifle with a dart loaded with a potent cocktail of tubocurarine and etorphine, and a breathing mask with its own oxygen supply.

Maddie made herself scarce, puttering around the control room but mostly disappearing during the daytime, coming back to the house after dark to crawl, exhausted, into bed. She didn't seem to be having nightmares, which was a good sign: Joe kept his questions to himself.

It took another five days for the smallholding's power field to concentrate enough juice to fuel up his murder weapons. During this time, Joe took the house off-net in the most deniable and surreptitiously plausible way, a bastard coincidence of squirrel-induced cable fade and a badly shielded alternator on the backhoe to do for the wireless chitchat. He'd half expected Maddie to complain, but she didn't say anything: just spent more time away in Outer Cheswick or Lower Gruntlingthorpe or wherever she'd taken to going.

Finally, the tank was full. So Joe girded his loins, donned his armor, picked up his weapons, and went to do battle with the dragon by the pond.

The woods around the pond had once been enclosed by a wooden fence, a charming copse of old-growth deciduous trees, elm and oak and beech growing uphill, smaller shrubs nestling at their ankles in a green skirt that reached all the way to the almost-stagnant waters. A little stream fed into it during rainy months, under the feet of a weeping willow; children had once played here, pretending to explore the wilderness beneath the benevolent gaze of their parental-control cameras.

That had been long ago. Today the woods really *were* wild. No kids, no picnicking city folks, no cars. Badgers and wild coypu and small, frightened wallabies roamed the parching English countryside during the summer dry season. The water drew back to expose an apron of cracked mud, planted with abandoned tin cans and a supermarket trolley of Precambrian vintage, its GPS tracker long since shorted out. The bones of the technological epoch, poked from the treacherous surface of the fossil mud bath. And around the edge of the mimsy puddle, the stage trees grew.

Joe switched on his jammer and walked in among the spear-shaped conifers. Their needles were matte black and fuzzy at the edges, fractally divided, the better to soak up all the available light: a network of taproots and lacy black grasslike stuff covered the ground around them. Joe's breath wheezed noisily in his ears, and he sweated into the airtight suit as he worked, pumping a stream of colorless, smoking liquid at the roots of each ballistic trunk. The liquid fizzed and evaporated on contact: it seemed to bleach the wood where it touched. Joe carefully avoided the stream: this stuff made him uneasy. (As did the trees, but liquid nitrogen was about the one thing he'd been able to think of that was guaranteed to kill them stone dead without igniting them. After all, they had cores that were made of gun cotton—highly explosive, liable to go off if you subjected them to a sudden sharp impact or the friction of a chain saw.) The tree he'd hit on creaked ominously, threatening to fall sideways, and Joe stepped round it, efficiently squirting at the remaining roots. Right into the path of the distraught farm.

"My holy garden of earthly delights! My forest of the imaginative future! My delight, my trees, my trees! *My trees!*" Eyestalks shot out and over, blinking down at him in horror as the farm reared up on six or seven legs and pawed the air in front of him. "Destroyer of saplings! Earth mother rapist! Bunny-strangling vivisectionist!"

"Back off," said Joe, dropping his cryogenic squirter as he reached for his air gun.

The farm came down with a ground-shaking thump in front of him and stretched eyes out to glare at him from both sides. They blinked, long black eyelashes fluttering across angry blue irises. "How *dare* you?" demanded the farm. "My treasured treelings!"

"Shut the fuck up," Joe grunted, shouldering his gun. "Think I'd let you burn my holding when tha' rocket launched? Stay the *fuck* away," he added as a tentacle began to extend from the farm's back.

"My crop," it moaned quietly: "My exile! Six more years around the sun chained to this well of sorrowful gravity before next the window opens! No brains for baby Jesus! Defenestrator! We could have been so happy together if you hadn't fucked up! Who set you up to this? Rat Lady?" It began to gather itself, muscles rippling under the leathery mantle atop its leg cluster.

Joe shot it.

Tubocurarine is a muscle relaxant: it paralyzes skeletal muscles, those that connect bones, move limbs, and sustain breathing. Etorphine is a ridiculously strong opiate—twelve hundred times as potent as heroin. Given time, a farm, with its alien adaptive metabolism and consciously controlled proteome might engineer a defense against the etorphine—but Joe dosed his dart with enough to stun a sperm whale, and he had no intention of giving the farm enough time. It shuddered and went down on one knee as he closed in on it, a syrette raised. "Why?" it asked plaintively in a voice that almost made him wish he hadn't pulled the trigger. "We could have gone together!"

"Together?" he asked. Already the eyestalks were drooping; the great lungs wheezed effortfully as it struggled to frame a reply.

"I was going to ask you," said the farm, and half its legs collapsed under it, with a thud like a baby earthquake. "Oh, Joe, if only . . ."

"*Maddie?*" he demanded, nerveless fingers dropping the tranquilizer gun.

A mouth appeared in the farm's front, slurred words at him

from familiar-seeming lips, words about Jupiter and p
ises. Appalled, Joe backed away from the farm. Passing t
first dead tree, he dropped the nitrogen tank: then an impulse
he couldn't articulate made him turn and run, back to the
house, eyes almost blinded by sweat or tears. But he was too
slow, and when he dropped to his knees next to the farm, the
emergency pharmacopoeia clicking and whirring to itself in
his arms, he found it was already dead.

"Bugger," said Joe, and he stood up, shaking his head.
"Bugger." He keyed his walkie-talkie. "Bob, come in, Bob!"

"Rrrrowl?"

"Momma's had another breakdown. Is the tank clean, like
I asked?"

"Yap!"

"Okay. I got 'er backup tapes in t'office safe. Let's get't'ank
warmed up for 'er an' then shift t'tractor down 'ere to muck
out this mess."

◉

That autumn, the weeds grew unnaturally rich and green
down in the north paddock of Armitage End.

A Colder War

● ANALYST

Roger Jourgensen tilts back in his chair, reading.

He's a fair-haired man, in his mid-thirties: hair razor-cropped, skin pallid from too much time spent under artificial lights. Spectacles, short-sleeved white shirt and tie, photographic ID badge on a chain round his neck. He works in an air-conditioned office with no windows.

The file he is reading frightens him.

Once, when Roger was a young boy, his father took him to an open day at Nellis AFB, out in the California desert. Sunlight glared brilliantly from the polished silverplate flanks of the big bombers, sitting in their concrete-lined dispersal bays behind barriers and blinking radiation monitors. The brightly colored streamers flying from their pitot tubes lent them a strange, almost festive appearance. But they were sleeping nightmares: once awakened, nobody—except the flight crew—could come within a mile of the nuclear-powered bombers and live.

Looking at the gleaming, bulging pods slung under their wingtip pylons, Roger had a premature inkling of the fires that waited within, a frigid terror that echoed the siren wail of the air-raid warnings. He'd sucked nervously on his ice cream and gripped his father's hand tightly while the band ripped through a cheerful Sousa march, and only forgot his fear when a flock of Thunderchiefs sliced by overhead and rattled the car windows for miles around.

He has the same feeling now, as an adult reading this intelligence assessment, that he had as a child, watching the nuclear-powered bombers sleeping in their concrete beds.

There's a blurry photograph of a concrete box inside the file, snapped from above by a high-flying U-2 during the autumn of '61. Three coffin-shaped lakes, bulking dark and gloomy beneath the arctic sun; a canal heading west, deep in the Soviet heartland, surrounded by warning trefoils and armed guards. Deep waters saturated with calcium salts, concrete cofferdams lined with gold and lead. A sleeping giant pointed at NATO, more terrifying than any nuclear weapon.

Project Koschei.

O RED SQUARE REDUX

WARNING:

The following briefing film is classified SECRET GOLD JULY BOOJUM. If you do not have SECRET GOLD JULY BOOJUM clearance, leave the auditorium *now* and report to your unit security officer for debriefing. Failing to observe this notice is an imprisonable offense.

You have sixty seconds to comply.

VIDEO CLIP:

Red Square in springtime. The sky overhead is clear and blue; there's a little wispy cirrus at high altitude. It forms a brilliant backdrop for flight after flight of four-engined bombers that thunder across the horizon and drop behind the Kremlin's high walls.

VOICE-OVER:

Red Square, the May Day parade, 1962. This is the first time that the Soviet Union has publicly displayed weapons classified GOLD JULY BOOJUM. Here they are:

VIDEO CLIP:

Later in the same day. A seemingly endless stream of armor and soldiers marches across the square, turning the air grey with diesel fumes. The trucks roll in line eight abreast, with soldiers sitting erect in the back. Behind them rumble a battalion of T-56s, their commanders standing at attention in their cupolas, saluting the stand. Jets race low and loud overhead, squadrons of MiG-17 fighters.

Behind the tanks sprawl a formation of four low-loaders: huge tractors towing low-slung trailers, their load beds strapped down under olive drab tarpaulins. Whatever is under them is uneven, a bit like a loaf of bread the size of a small house. The trucks have an escort of jeeplike vehicles on each side, armed soldiers sitting at attention in their backs.

There are big five-pointed symbols painted in silver on each tarpaulin, like pentacles. Each star is surrounded by a stylized silver circle; a unit insignia, perhaps, but not in the standard format for Red Army units. There's lettering around the circles, in a strangely stylized script.

VOICE-OVER:

These are live servitors under transient control. The vehicles towing them bear the insignia of the second Guards Engineering Brigade, a penal construction unit based in Bokhara and used for structural-engineering assignments relating to nuclear installations in the Ukraine and Azerbaijan. This is the first time that any Dresden Agreement party openly demonstrated ownership of this technology: in this instance, the conclusion we are intended to draw is that the sixty-seventh Guard Engineering Brigade operates four units. Given existing figures for the Soviet ORBAT, we can then extrapolate a total task strength of 288 servitors, if this unit is representative.

VIDEO CLIP:

Five huge Tu-95 Bear bombers thunder across the Moscow skies.

VOICE-OVER:

This conclusion is questionable. For example, in 1964 a total of 240 Bear bomber passes were made over the reviewing stand in front of the Lenin mausoleum. However, at that time technical reconnaissance assets verified that the Soviet air force has hard-stand parking for only 160 of these aircraft, and estimates of airframe production based on photographs of the extent of the Tupolev Design Bureau's works indicate that total production to that date was between 60 and 180 bombers.

Further analysis of photographic evidence from the 1964 parade suggests that a single group of twenty aircraft in four formations of five made repeated passes through the same airspace, the main arc of their circuit lying outside visual observation range of Moscow. This gave rise to the erroneous capacity report of 1964 in which the first-strike delivery capability of the Soviet Union was overestimated by as much as 300 percent.

We must therefore take anything that they show us in Red Square with a pinch of salt when preparing force estimates. Quite possibly these four servitors are all they've got. Then again, the actual battalion strength may be considerably higher.

STILL PHOTOGRAPHIC SEQUENCE:

From very high altitude—possibly in orbit—an eagle's-eye view of a remote village in mountainous country. Mud-brick houses huddle together beneath a craggy outcrop; goats graze nearby.

In the second photograph, something has rolled through the village leaving a trail of devastation. The path is quite unlike the trail of damage left by an artillery bombardment: something roughly four meters wide has shaved the rocky plateau smooth, wearing it down as if with a terrible heat. A corner of a shack leans drunkenly, the other half sliced away cleanly. White bones gleam faintly in the track; no vultures descend to stab at the remains.

VOICE-OVER:

These images were taken very recently, on successive orbital passes of a KH-11 satellite. They were timed precisely eighty-nine minutes apart. This village was the home of a noted mujahedin leader. Note the similar footprint to the pay-loads on the load beds of the trucks seen at the 1962 parade.

These indicators were present, denoting the presence of servitor units in use by Soviet forces in Afghanistan: the four-meter-wide gauge of the assimilation track. The total molecular breakdown of organic matter in the track. The speed of destruction—the event took less than five thousand seconds to completion, no survivors were visible, and the causative agent had already been uplifted by the time of the second orbital pass. This, despite the residents of the community being armed with DShK heavy machine guns, rocket-propelled grenade launchers, and AK-47s. Lastly: there is no sign of the causative agent even deviating from its course, but the entire area is depopulated. Except for excarnated residue, there is no sign of human habitation.

In the presence of such unique indicators, we have no alternative but to conclude that the Soviet Union has violated the Dresden Agreement by deploying GOLD JULY BOOJUM in a combat mode in the Khyber Pass. There are no grounds to believe that a NATO armored division would have fared any better than these mujahedin without nuclear support . . .

● PUZZLE PALACE

Roger isn't a soldier. He's not much of a patriot, either: he signed up with the CIA after college, in the aftermath of the Church Commission hearings in the early seventies. The Company was out of the assassination business, just a bureaucratic engine rolling out National Security assessments: that's fine by Roger. Only now, five years later, he's no longer able to roll along, casually disengaged, like a car in neutral bowling down a shallow incline toward his retirement, pension, and a gold watch. He puts the file down on his desk and, with a shaking hand, pulls an illicit cigarette from the pack he keeps in his drawer. He lights it and leans back for a moment to draw breath, force relaxation, staring at smoke rolling in the air beneath the merciless light until his hand stops shaking.

Most people think spies are afraid of guns, or KGB guards, or barbed wire, but in point of fact the most dangerous thing they face is paper. Papers carry secrets. Papers carry death warrants. Papers like this one, this folio with its blurry eighteen-year-old faked missile photographs and estimates of time/survivor curves and pervasive psychosis ratios, can give you nightmares, dragging you awake screaming in the middle of the night. It's one of a series of highly classified pieces of paper that he is summarizing for the eyes of the National Security Council and the president-elect—if his head of department and the DDCIA approve it—and here he is, having to calm his nerves with a cigarette before he turns the next page.

After a few minutes, Roger's hand is still. He leaves his cigarette in the eagle-headed ashtray and picks up the intelligence report again. It's a summary, itself the distillation of thousands of pages and hundreds of photographs. It's barely twenty pages long: as of 1963, its date of preparation, the CIA knew very little about Project Koschei. Just the bare skeleton, and rumors from a highly placed spy. And their own equivalent project, of course. Lacking the Soviet lead in that particular field, the USAF fielded the silverplate white elephants of the NB-39 project: twelve atomic-powered bombers armed with XK-PLUTO, ready to tackle Project Koschei should the Soviets show signs of unsealing the bunker. Three hundred megatons of H-bombs pointed at a single target, and nobody was certain it would be enough to do the job.

And then there was the hard-to-conceal fiasco in Antarctica. Egg on face: a subterranean nuclear test program in international territory! If nothing else, it had been enough to stop JFK running for a second term. The test program was a bad excuse: but it was far better than confessing what had really happened to the 501st Airborne Division on the cold plateau beyond Mount Erebus. The plateau that the public didn't know about, that didn't show up on the maps issued by the geological survey departments of those governments party to the Dresden Agreement of 1931—an arrangement that even Hitler had stuck to. The plateau that had swallowed more U-2 spy planes than the Soviet Union, more surface expeditions than darkest Africa.

Shit. How the hell am I going to put this together for him?

Roger's spent the past five hours staring at this twenty-page report, trying to think of a way of summarizing their drily quantifiable terror in words that will give the reader power over them, the power to think the unthinkable: but it's proving difficult. The new man in the White House is straight-talking, demands straight answers. He's pious enough not to believe in the supernatural, confident enough that just listening to one of his speeches is an uplifting experience if you can close your eyes and believe in morning in America. There is probably no way of explaining Project Koschei, or XK-PLUTO, or MK-NIGHTMARE, or the gates, without watering them down into just another weapons system—which they are not. Weapons may have deadly or hideous effects, but they acquire moral character from the actions of those who use them. Whereas these projects are indelibly stained by a patina of ancient evil . . .

He hopes that if the balloon ever does go up, if the sirens wail, he and Andrea and Jason will be left behind to face the nuclear fire. It'll be a merciful death compared with what he suspect lurks out there, in the unexplored vastness beyond the gates. The vastness that made Nixon cancel the manned space program, leaving just the standing joke of a white-elephant shuttle, when he realized just how hideously dangerous the space race might become. The darkness that broke Jimmy Carter's faith and turned Lyndon B. Johnson into an alcoholic.

He stands up, nervously shifts from one foot to the other. Looks round at the walls of his cubicle. For a moment the cigarette smoldering on the edge of his ashtray catches his attention: wisps of blue-grey smoke coil like lazy dragons in the air above it, writhing in a strange cuneiform text. He blinks, and they're gone, and the skin on the small of his back prickles as if someone had pissed on his grave.

"Shit." Finally, a spoken word in the silence. His hand is shaking as he stubs the cigarette out. *Mustn't let this get to me.* He glances at the wall. It's nineteen hundred hours; too late, too late. He should go home. Andy will be worrying herself sick.

In the end it's all too much. He slides the thin folder into the safe behind his chair, turns the locking handle and spins the dial, then signs himself out of the reading room and goes through the usual exit search.

During the thirty-mile drive home, he spits out of the window, trying to rid his mouth of the taste of Auschwitz ashes.

○ LATE NIGHT IN THE WHITE HOUSE

The colonel is febrile, jittering about the room with gung ho enthusiasm. "That was a mighty fine report you pulled together, Jourgensen!" He paces over to the niche between the office filing cabinet and the wall, turns on the spot, paces back to the far side of his desk. "You understand the fundamentals. I like that. A few more guys like you running the company, and we wouldn't have this fuckup in Tehran." He grins, contagiously. The colonel is a firestorm of enthusiasm, burning out of control like a forties comic-book hero. He has Roger on the edge of his chair, almost sitting at attention. Roger has to bite his tongue to remind himself not to call the colonel "sir"—he's a civilian, not in the chain of command. "That's why I've asked Deputy Director McMurdo to reassign you to this office, to work on my team as company liaison. And I'm pleased to say that he's agreed."

Roger can't stop himself. "To work here, sir?" *Here* is in the basement of the Executive Office Building, an extension hanging off the White House. Whoever the colonel is, he's got *pull*, in positively magical quantities. "What will I be doing, sir? You said your team—"

"Relax a bit. Drink your coffee." The colonel paces back behind his desk, sits down. Roger sips cautiously at the brown sludge in the mug with the Marine Corps crest. "The president told me to organize a team," says the colonel, so casually that Roger nearly chokes on his coffee, "to handle contingencies. October surprises. Those asshole commies down in Nicaragua. 'We're eyeball-to-eyeball with an Evil Empire, Ozzie, and we can't afford to blink'—those were his exact words. The Evil Empire uses dirty tricks. But nowadays we're better than they are: buncha hicks, like some third-world dictatorship— Upper Volta with shoggoths. My job is to pin them down and cut them up. Don't give them a chance to whack the shoe on the UN table, demand concessions. If they want to bluff, I'll call 'em on it. If they want to go toe-to-toe, I'll dance with 'em." He's up and pacing again. "The company used to do that, and do it okay, back in the fifties and sixties. But too many bleeding hearts—it makes me sick. If you guys went back to wet ops today, you'd have journalists following you every time you went to the john in case it was newsworthy.

"Well, we aren't going to do it that way this time. It's a small team, and the buck stops here." The colonel pauses, then glances at the ceiling. "Well, maybe up there. But you get the picture. I need someone who knows the Company, an insider who has clearance up the wazoo who can go in and get the dope before it goes through a fucking committee of ass-watching bureaucrats. I'm also getting someone from the Puzzle Palace, and some words to give me pull with Big Black." He glances at Roger sharply, and Roger nods: he's cleared for National Security Agency—Puzzle Palace—intelligence, and knows about Big Black, the National Reconnaissance Office, which is so secret that even its existence is still classified.

Roger is impressed by this colonel, despite his better judgment. Within the byzantine world of the US intelligence services, he is talking about building his very own pocket battleship and sailing it under the Jolly Roger with letters of marque and reprise signed by the president. But Roger still has some questions to ask, to scope out the limits of what Colonel North is capable of. "What about FEVER DREAM, sir?"

The colonel puts his coffee cup down. "I own it," he says, bluntly. "And NIGHTMARE. And PLUTO. *Any means necessary,* he said, and I have an executive order with the ink still damp to prove it. Those projects aren't part of the national command structure anymore. Officially they've been stood down from active status and are being considered for inclusion in the next round of arms-reduction talks. They're not part of the deterrent ORBAT anymore; we're standardizing on just nuclear weapons. Unofficially, they're part of my group, and I will use them as necessary to contain and reduce the Evil Empire's warmaking abilities."

Roger's skin crawls with an echo of that childhood terror. "And the Dresden Agreement . . . ?"

"Don't worry. Nothing short of *them* breaking it would lead me to do so." The colonel grins, toothily. "Which is where you come in . . ."

⦿ THE MOONLIT SHORES OF LAKE VOSTOK

The metal pier is dry and cold, the temperature hovering close to zero degrees Fahrenheit. It's oppressively dark in the cavern under the ice, and Roger shivers inside his multiple layers of insulation, shifts from foot to foot to keep warm. He has to swallow to keep his ears clear and he feels slightly dizzy from the pressure in the artificial bubble of air, pumped under the icy ceiling to allow humans to exist here, under the Ross Ice Shelf; they'll all spend more than a day sitting in depressurization chambers on the way back up to the surface.

There is no sound from the waters lapping just below the edge of the pier. The floodlights vanish into the surface and keep going—the water in the subsurface Antarctic lake is incredibly clear—but are swallowed up rapidly, giving an impression of infinite, inky depths.

Manfred is here as the colonel's representative, to observe the arrival of the probe, receive the consignment they're carrying, and report back that everything is running smoothly. The others try to ignore him, jittery at the presence of the man from DC. There're a gaggle of engineers and artificers, flown out via McMurdo Base to handle the midget sub's operations. A nervous lieutenant supervises a squad of Marines with complicated-looking weapons, half gun and half video camera, stationed at the corners of the raft. And there's the usual platform crew, deep-sea-rig-maintenance types—but subdued and nervous-looking. They're afloat in a bubble of pressurized air wedged against the underside of the Antarctic ice sheet: below them stretch the still, supercooled waters of Lake Vostok.

They're waiting for a rendezvous.

"Five hundred yards," reports one of the techs. "Rising on ten." His companion nods. They're waiting for the men in the midget sub drilling quietly through three miles of frigid water, intruders in a long-drowned tomb. "Have 'em back on board in no time." The sub has been away for nearly a day; it set out with enough battery juice for the journey, and enough air to keep the crew breathing for a long time if there's a system failure, but they've learned the hard way that fail-safe systems aren't. Not out here, at the edge of the human world.

Roger shuffles some more. "I was afraid the battery load on that cell you replaced would trip an undervoltage isolator and we'd be here 'til Hell freezes over," the sub driver jokes to his neighbor.

Looking round, Roger sees one of the Marines cross himself. "Have you heard anything from Gorman or Suslowicz?" he asks quietly.

The lieutenant checks his clipboard. "Not since departure, sir," he says. "We don't have comms with the sub while it's submerged: too small for ELF, and we don't want to alert anybody who might be, uh, listening."

"Indeed." The yellow hunchback shape of the midget submarine appears at the edge of the radiance shed by the floodlights. Surface waters undulate, oily, as the sub rises.

"Crew-transfer vehicle sighted," the driver mutters into his mike. He's suddenly very busy adjusting trim settings, blowing bottled air into ballast tanks, discussing ullage levels and blade count with his number two. The crane crew is busy too, running their long boom out over the lake.

The sub's hatch is visible now, bobbing along the top of the water: the lieutenant is suddenly active. "Jones! Civatti! Stake it out, left and center!" The crane is already swinging the huge lifting hook over the sub, waiting to bring it aboard. "I want eyeballs on the portholes before you crack this thing!" It's the tenth run—seventh manned—through the eye of the needle on the lake bed, the drowned structure so like an ancient temple, and Roger has a bad feeling about it. *We can't get away with this forever,* he reasons. *Sooner or later . . .*

The sub comes out of the water like a gigantic yellow bath toy, a cyborg whale designed by a god with a sense of humor. It takes tense minutes to winch it in and maneuver it safely onto the platform. Marines take up position, shining torches in through two of the portholes that bulge myopically from the smooth curve of the sub's nose. Up on top, someone is talking into a handset plugged into the stubby conning tower; the hatch locking wheel begins to turn.

"Gorman, sir." It's the lieutenant. In the light of the sodium floods, everything looks sallow and washed-out; the soldier's face is the color of damp cardboard, slack with relief.

Roger waits while the submariner—Gorman—clambers unsteadily down from the top deck. He's a tall, emaciated-looking man, wearing a red thermal suit three sizes too big for him: salt-and-pepper stubble textures his jaw with sandpaper. Right now, he looks like a cholera victim; sallow skin, smell of acrid ketones as his body eats its own protein reserves, a more revolting miasma hovering over him. There's a slim aluminum briefcase chained to his left wrist, a bracelet of bruises darkening the skin above it. Roger steps forward.

"Sir?" Gorman straightens up for a moment: almost a shadow of military attention. He's unable to sustain it. "We made the pickup. Here's the QA sample; the rest is down below. You have the unlocking code?" he asks wearily.

Jourgensen nods. "One. Five. Eight. One. Two. Two. Nine."

Gorman slowly dials it into a combination lock on the briefcase, lets it fall open and unthreads the chain from his wrist. Floodlights glisten on polythene bags stuffed with white powder, five kilos of high-grade heroin from the hills of Afghanistan; there's another quarter of a ton packed in boxes in the crew compartment. The lieutenant inspects it, closes the case, and passes it to Jourgensen. "Delivery successful, sir." From the ruins on the high plateau of the Taklamakan Desert to American territory in Antarctica, by way of a detour through gates linking alien worlds: gates that nobody knows how to create or destroy except the Predecessors—and they aren't talking.

"What's it like through there?" Roger demands, shoulders tense. "What did you *see*?"

Up on top, Suslowicz is sitting in the sub's hatch, half-slumping against the crane's attachment post. There's obviously something very wrong with him. Gorman shakes his head and looks away: the wan light makes the razor-sharp creases on his face stand out, like the crackled and shattered surface of a Jovian moon. Crow's-feet. Wrinkles. Signs of age. Hair the color of moonlight. "It took so long," he says, almost complaining. Sinks to his knees. "All that *time* we've been gone . . ." He leans against the side of the sub, a pale shadow, aged beyond his years. "The sun was so *bright*. And our radiation detectors. Must have been a solar flare or something." He doubles over and retches at the edge of the platform.

Roger looks at him for a long, thoughtful minute: Gorman is twenty-five and a fixer for Big Black, early history in the Green Berets. He was in rude good health two days ago, when he set off through the gate to make the pickup. Roger glances at the lieutenant. "I'd better go and tell the colonel," he says. A pause. "Get these two back to Recovery and see they're looked after. I don't expect we'll be sending any more crews through Victor-Tango for a while."

He turns and walks toward the lift shaft, hands clasped behind his back to keep them from shaking. Behind him, alien moonlight glimmers across the floor of Lake Vostok, three miles and untold light-years from home.

● GENERAL LEMAY WOULD BE PROUD

WARNING:

The following briefing film is classified SECRET INDIGO MARCH SNIPE. If you do not have SECRET INDIGO MARCH SNIPE clearance, leave the auditorium *now* and report to your unit security officer for debriefing. Failing to observe this notice is an imprisonable offense.

You have sixty seconds to comply.

VIDEO CLIP:

Shot of huge bomber, rounded gun turrets sprouting like mushrooms from the decaying log of its fuselage, weirdly bulbous engine pods slung too far out toward each wingtip, four turbine tubes clumped around each atomic kernel.

VOICE-OVER:

The Convair B-39 Peacemaker is the most formidable weapon in our Strategic Air Command's arsenal for peace. Powered by eight nuclear-heated Pratt & Whitney NP-4051 turbojets, it circles endlessly above the Arctic ice cap, waiting for the call. This is Item One, the flight training and test bird: twelve other birds await criticality on the ground, for once launched a B-39 can only be landed at two airfields in Alaska that are equipped to handle them. This one's been airborne for nine months so far, and shows no signs of age.

CUT TO:

A shark the size of a Boeing 727 falls away from the open bomb bay of the monster. Stubby delta wings slice through the air, propelled by a rocket-bright glare.

VOICE-OVER:

A modified Navajo missile—test article for an XK-PLUTO payload—dives away from a carrier plane. Unlike the real thing, this one carries no hydrogen bombs, no direct-cycle fission ramjet to bring retaliatory destruction to the enemy. Traveling at Mach 3, the XK-PLUTO will overfly enemy territory, dropping megaton-range bombs until, its payload exhausted, it seeks out and circles a final target. Once over the target it will eject its reactor core and rain molten plutonium on the heads of the enemy. XK-PLUTO is a total weapon: every aspect of its design, from the shock wave it creates as it hurtles along at treetop height to the structure of its atomic reactor, is designed to inflict damage.

CUT TO:

Belsen postcards, Auschwitz movies: a holiday in Hell.

VOICE-OVER:

This is why we need such a weapon. *This* is what it deters. The abominations first raised by the Third Reich's Organization Todt, now removed to the Ukraine and deployed in the service of New Soviet Man, as our enemy calls himself.

CUT TO:

A sinister grey concrete slab, the upper surface of a Mayan step pyramid built with East German cement. Barbed wire, guns. A drained canal slashes north from the base of the pyramid toward the Baltic coastline, relic of the installation process: this is where it came from. The slave barracks squat beside the pyramid like a horrible memorial to its black-uniformed builders.

CUT TO:

The new resting place: a big concrete monolith surrounded by three concrete-lined lakes and a canal. It sits in the midst of a Ukraine landscape, flat as a pancake, stretching out forever in all directions.

VOICE-OVER:

This is Project Koschei. The Kremlin's key to the gates of Hell . . .

◉ TECHNOLOGY TASTER

"We know they first came here during the Precambrian age."

Professor Gould is busy with his viewgraphs, eyes down, trying not to pay too much attention to his audience. "We have samples of macrofauna, discovered by paleontologist Charles D. Walcott on his pioneering expeditions into the Canadian Rockies, near the eastern border of British Columbia"—a hand-drawing of something indescribably weird fetches up on the screen—"like this *opabina*, which died there 640 million years ago. Fossils of soft-bodied animals that old are rare; the Burgess Shale deposits are the best record of the Precambrian fauna anyone has found to date."

A skinny woman with big hair and bigger shoulder pads sniffs loudly; she has no truck with these antediluvian dates. Roger winces sympathy for the academic. He'd rather she wasn't here, but somehow she got wind of the famous paleontologist's visit—and she's the colonel's administrative assistant. Telling her to leave would be a career-limiting move.

"The important item to note"—photograph of a mangled piece of rock, visual echoes of the *opabina*—"is the tooth marks. We find them also—their exact cognates—on the ring segments of the Z-series specimens returned by the Pabodie Antarctic expedition of 1926. The world of the Precambrian was laid out differently from our own; most of the landmasses that today are separate continents were joined into one huge structure. Indeed, these samples were originally separated by only two thousand miles or thereabouts. Suggesting that they brought their own parasites with them."

"What do tooth marks tell us about them, that we need to know?" asks the colonel.

The doctor looks up. His eyes gleam. "That something liked to eat them when they were fresh." There's a brief rattle of laughter. "Something with jaws that open and close like the iris in your camera. Something we thought was extinct."

Another viewgraph, this time with a blurry underwater photograph on it. The thing looks a bit like a weird fish—a turbocharged, armored hagfish with side-skirts and spoilers, or maybe a squid with not enough tentacles. The upper head is a flattened disk, fronted by two bizarre fernlike tentacles drooping over the weird sucker mouth on its underside. "This snapshot was taken in Lake Vostok last year. It should be dead: there's nothing there for it to eat. This, ladies and gentlemen, is *Anomalocaris*, our toothy chewer." He pauses for a moment. "I'm very grateful to you for showing it to me," he adds, "even though it's going to make a lot of my colleagues very angry."

Is that a shy grin? The professor moves on rapidly, not giving Roger a chance to fathom his real reaction. "Now, *this* is interesting in the extreme," Gould comments. Whatever it is, it looks like a cauliflower head, or maybe a brain: fractally branching stalks continuously diminishing in length and diameter, until they turn into an iridescent fuzzy manifold wrapped around a central stem. The base of the stem is rooted to a barrel-shaped structure that stands on four stubby tentacles.

"We had somehow managed to cram *Anomalocaris* into our taxonomy, but this is something that has no precedent. It bears a striking resemblance to an enlarged body segment of *Hallucigena*"—here he shows another viewgraph, something like a stiletto-heeled centipede wearing a war bonnet of tentacles—"but a year ago we worked out that we had poor *Hallucigena* upside down, and it was actually just a spiny worm. And the high levels of iridium and diamond in the head here . . . This isn't a living creature, at least not within the animal kingdom I've been studying for the past thirty years. There's no cellular structure at all. I asked one of my colleagues for help, and they were completely unable to isolate any DNA or RNA from it at all. It's more like a machine that displays biological levels of complexity."

"Can you put a date to it?" asks the colonel.

"Yup." The professor grins. "It predates the wave of atmospheric atomic testing that began in 1945; that's about all. We think it's from sometime in the first half of this century, last half of last century. It's been dead for years, but there are older people still walking this earth. In contrast"—he flips to the picture of *Anomalocaris*—"this specimen we found in rocks that are roughly 610 million years old." He whips up another shot: similar structure, much clearer. "Note how similar it is to the dead but not decomposed one. They're obviously still alive somewhere."

He looks at the colonel, suddenly bashful and tongue-tied. "Can I talk about the, uh, thing we were, like, earlier . . . ?"

"Sure. Go ahead. Everyone here is cleared for it." The colonel's casual wave takes in the big-haired secretary, and Roger, and the two guys from Big Black who are taking notes, and the very serious woman from the Secret Service, and even the balding, worried-looking admiral with the double chin and Coke-bottle glasses.

"Oh. Alright." Bashfulness falls away. "Well, we've done some preliminary dissections on the *Anomalocaris* tissues you supplied us with. And we've sent some samples for laboratory analysis—nothing anyone could deduce much from," he adds hastily. He straightens up. "What we discovered is quite simple: these samples didn't originate in Earth's ecosystem. Cladistic analysis of their intracellular characteristics and what we've been able to work out of their biochemistry indicates, not a point of divergence from our own ancestry, but the absence of common ancestry. A *cabbage* is more human, has more in common with us, than that creature. You can't tell by looking at the fossils, 600 million years after it died, but live tissue samples are something else.

"Item: it's a multicellular organism, but each cell appears to have multiple structures like nuclei—a thing called a syncitium. No DNA, it uses RNA with a couple of base pairs that aren't used by terrestrial biology. We haven't been able to figure out what most of its organelles do, what their terrestrial cognates would be, and it builds proteins using a couple of amino acids that we don't. That *nothing* does. Either it's descended from an ancestry that diverged from ours before the archaeobacteria, or—more probably—it is no relative at all." He isn't smiling anymore. "The gateways, Colonel?"

"Yeah, that's about the size of it. The critter you've got there was retrieved by one of our, uh, missions. On the other side of a gate."

Gould nods. "I don't suppose you could get me some more?" he asks hopefully.

"All missions are suspended pending an investigation into an accident we had earlier this year," the colonel says, with a significant glance at Roger. Suslowicz died two weeks ago; Gorman is still disastrously sick, connective tissue rotting in his body, massive radiation exposure the probable cause. Normal service will not be resumed; the pipeline will remain empty until someone can figure out a way to make the deliveries without losing the crew. Roger inclines his head minutely.

"Oh well." The professor shrugs. "Let me know if you do. By the way, do you have anything approximating a fix on the other end of the gate?"

"No," says the colonel, and this time Roger knows he's lying. Mission four, before the colonel diverted their payload capacity to another purpose, planted a compact radio telescope in an empty courtyard in the city on the far side of the gate. XK-Masada, where the air's too thin to breathe without oxygen; where the sky is indigo, and the buildings cast razor-sharp shadows across a rocky plain baked to the consistency of pottery under a blood red sun. Subsequent analysis of pulsar signals recorded by the station confirmed that it was nearly six hundred light-years closer to the galactic core, inward along the same spiral arm. There are glyphs on the alien buildings that resemble symbols seen in grainy black-and-white Minox photos of the doors of the bunker in the Ukraine. Symbols behind which the subject of Project Koschei lies undead and sleeping: something evil, scraped from a nest in the drowned wreckage of a city on the Baltic floor. "Why do you want to know where they came from?"

"Well. We know so little about the context in which life evolves." For a moment the professor looks wistful. "We have—had—only one datum point: Earth, this world. Now we have a second, a fragment of a second. If we get a third, we can begin to ask deep questions like, not, 'Is there life out there?'—because we know the answer to that one now—but questions like 'What *sort* of life is out there?' and 'Is there a place for us?'"

Roger shudders. *Idiot,* he thinks. *If only you knew, you wouldn't be so happy.* He restrains the urge to speak up. Doing so would be another career-limiting move. More to the point, it might be a life-expectancy-limiting move for the professor, who certainly didn't deserve any such drastic punishment for his cooperation. Besides, Harvard professors visiting the Executive Office Building in DC are harder to disappear than comm-symp teachers in some flyblown jungle village in Nicaragua. Somebody might notice. The colonel would be annoyed.

Roger realizes that Professor Gould is staring at him.

"Do you have a question for me?" asks the distinguished paleontologist.

"Uh—in a moment." Roger shakes himself. Remembering time-survivor curves, the captured Nazi medical-atrocity records mapping the ability of a human brain to survive in close proximity to the Baltic Singularity. Mengele's insanity. The SS's final attempt to liquidate the survivors, the witnesses. Koschei, primed and pointed at the American heartland like a darkly evil gun. The "world-eating mind" adrift in brilliant dreams of madness, estivating in the absence of its prey: dreaming of the minds of sapient beings, be they barrel-bodied wing-flying tentacular *things*, or their human inheritors. "Do you think they could have been intelligent, Professor? Conscious, like us?"

"I'd say so." Gould's eyes glitter. "This one"—he points to a viewgraph—"isn't alive as we know it. And *this* one"—he's found a Predecessor, God help him, barrel-bodied and bat-winged—"had what looks like a lot of very complex ganglia, not a brain as we know it, but at least as massive as our own. And some specialized grasping adaptations that might be interpreted as facilitating tool use. Put the two together, and you have a high-level technological civilization. Gateways between planets orbiting different stars. Alien flora, fauna, or whatever. I'd say an interstellar civilization isn't out of the picture. One that has been extinct for deep geological time— ten times as long as the dinosaurs—but that has left relics that work." His voice is trembling with emotion. "We humans, we've barely scratched the surface! The longest-lasting of our relics? All our buildings will be dust in twenty thousand years, even the pyramids. Neil Armstrong's footprints in the Sea of Tranquility will crumble under micrometeoroid bombardment in a mere half million years or so. The emptied oil fields will refill over ten million years, methane percolating up through the mantle: continental drift will erase everything. But *these* people . . . ! They built to last. There's so much to learn from them. I wonder if we're worthy pretenders to their technological crown?"

"I'm sure we are, Professor," the colonel's secretary says brassily. "Isn't that right, Ollie?"

The colonel nods, grinning. "You betcha, Fawn. You betcha!"

○ THE GREAT SATAN

Roger sits in the bar in the King David Hotel, drinking from a tall glass of second-rate lemonade and sweating in spite of the air-conditioning. He's dizzy and disoriented from jet lag, the gut cramps have only let him come down from his room in the past hour, and he has another two hours to go before he can try to place a call to Andrea. They had another blazing row before he flew out here; she doesn't understand why he keeps having to visit odd corners of the globe. She only knows that his son is growing up thinking a father is a voice that phones at odd times of day.

Roger is mildly depressed, despite the buzz of doing business at this level. He spends a lot of time worrying about what will happen if they're found out—what Andrea will do, or Jason for that matter; Jason, whose father is a phone call away all the time—if Roger is led away in handcuffs beneath the glare of flashbulbs. If the colonel sings, if the shy bald admiral is browbeaten into spilling the beans to Congress, who will look after them then?

Roger has no illusions about what kills black operations: there are too many people in the loop, too many elaborate front corporations and numbered bank accounts and shady Middle Eastern arms dealers. Sooner or later, someone will find a reason to talk, and Roger is in too deep. He isn't just the company liaison officer anymore: he's become the colonel's bagman, his shadow, the guy with the diplomatic passport and the bulging briefcase full of heroin and end-user certificates.

At least the ship will sink from the top down, he thinks. There are people *very* high up who want the colonel to succeed. When the shit hits the fan and is sprayed across the front page of the *Washington Post*, it will likely take down cabinet members and secretaries of state: the president himself will have to take the witness stand and deny everything. The republic will question itself.

A hand descends on his shoulder, sharply cutting off his reverie. "Howdy, Roger! Whatcha worrying about now?"

Jourgensen looks up wearily. "Stuff," he says gloomily. "Have a seat." The redneck from the embassy—Mike Hamilton, some kind of junior attaché for embassy protocol by cover—pulls out a chair and crashes down on it like a friendly car wreck. He's not really a redneck, Roger knows—rednecks don't come with doctorates in foreign relations from Yale—but he likes people to think he's a bumpkin when he needs to get something from them.

"He's early," says Hamilton, looking past Roger's ear, voice suddenly all business. "Play the agenda. I'm your dim, but friendly, good cop. Got the background? Deniables ready?"

Roger nods, then glances round and sees Mehmet (family name unknown) approaching from the other side of the room. Mehmet is impeccably manicured and tailored, wearing a suit from Jermyn Street that costs more than Roger earns in a month. He has a neatly trimmed beard and moustache and talks with a pronounced English accent. Mehmet is a Turkish name, not a Persian one: pseudonym, of course. To look at him you would think he was a westernized Turkish businessman—certainly not an Iranian revolutionary with heavy links to Hezbollah and (whisper this) Old Man Ruholla himself, the hermit of Qom. Never in a thousand years the unofficial Iranian ambassador to the Little Satan in Tel Aviv.

Mehmet strides over. A brief exchange of pleasantries masks the essential formality of their meeting: he's early, a deliberate move to put them off-balance. He's outnumbered, too, and that's also a move to put them on the defensive, because the first rule of diplomacy is never to put yourself in a negotiating situation where the other side can assert any kind of moral authority, and sheer weight of numbers is a powerful psychological tool.

"Roger, my dear fellow." He smiles at Jourgensen. "And the charming Dr. Hamilton, I see." The smile broadens. "I take it the good colonel is desirous of news of his friends?"

Jourgensen nods. "That is indeed the case."

Mehmet stops smiling. For a moment he looks ten years older. "I visited them," he says shortly. "No, I was *taken* to see them. It is indeed grave, my friends. They are in the hands of very dangerous men, men who have nothing to lose and are filled with hatred."

Roger speaks. "There is a debt between us—"

Mehmet holds up a hand. "Peace, my friend. We will come to that. These are men of violence, men who have seen their homes destroyed and families subjected to indignities, and their hearts are full of anger. It will take a large display of repentance, a high blood price, to buy their acquiescence. That is part of our law, you understand? The family of the bereaved may demand blood price of the transgressor, and how else might the world be? They see it in these terms: that you must repent of your evils and assist them in waging holy war against those who would defile the will of Allah."

Roger sighs. "We do what we can," he says. "We're shipping them arms. We're fighting the Soviets every way we can without provoking the big one. What more do they want? The hostages—that's not playing well in DC. There's got to be some give-and-take. If Hezbollah doesn't release them soon, they'll just convince everyone that they're not serious about negotiating. And that'll be an end to it. The colonel *wants* to help you, but he's got to have something to show the man at the top, right?"

Mehmet nods. "You and I are men of the world and understand that this keeping of hostages is not rational, but they look to you for defense against the other Great Satan that assails them, and their blood burns with anger that your nation, for all its fine words, takes no action. The Great Satan rampages in Afghanistan, taking whole villages by night, and what is done? The United States turns its back. And they are not the only ones who feel betrayed. Our Ba'athist foes from Iraq . . . In Basra the unholy brotherhood of Tikrit and their servants the Mukhabarat hold nightly sacrifice upon the altar of Yair-Suthot; the fountains of blood in Tehran testify to their effect. If the richest, most powerful nation on Earth refuses to fight, these men of violence from the Bekaa think, how may we unstopper the ears of that nation? And they are not sophisticates like you or I."

He looks at Roger, who hunches his shoulders uneasily. "We *can't* move against the Soviets openly! They must understand that it would be the end of far more than their little war. If the Taliban want American help against the Russians, it cannot be delivered openly."

"It is not the Russians that we quarrel with," Mehmet says quietly, "but their choice in allies. They believe themselves to be infidel atheists, but by their deeds they shall be known; the icy spoor of Leng is upon them, their tools are those described in the Kitab Al Azif. We have proof that they have violated the terms of the Dresden Agreement. The accursed and unhallowed stalk the frozen passes of the Himalayas by night, taking all whose path they cross. And will you stopper your ears even as the Russians grow in misplaced confidence, sure that their dominance of these forces of evil is complete? The gates are opening everywhere, as it was prophesied. Last week we flew an F-14C with a camera relay pod through one of them. The pilot and weapons operator are in paradise now, but we have glanced into hell and have the film and radar plots to prove it."

The Iranian ambassador fixes the redneck from the embassy with an icy gaze. "Tell your ambassador that we have opened preliminary discussions with Mossad, with a view to purchasing the produce of a factory at Dimona, in the Negev. Past insults may be set aside, for the present danger imperils all of us. *They* are receptive to our arguments, even if you are not: his holiness the Ayatollah has declared in private that any warrior who carries a nuclear device into the abode of the eater of souls will certainly achieve paradise. There will be an end to the followers of the ancient abominations on this Earth, Dr. Hamilton, even if we have to push the nuclear bombs down their throats with our own hands!"

○ SWIMMING POOL

"Mr. Jourgensen, at what point did you become aware that the Iranian government was threatening to violate UN Resolution 216 and the Non-Proliferation Protocol to the 1956 Geneva Accords?"

Roger sweats under the hot lights: his heartbeat accelerates. "I'm not sure I understand the question, sir."

"I asked you a direct question. Which part don't you understand? I'm going to repeat myself slowly: when did you realize that the Iranian government was threatening to violate Resolution 216 and the 1956 Geneva Accords on nuclear proliferation?"

Roger shakes his head. It's like a bad dream, unseen insects buzzing furiously around him. "Sir, I had no direct dealings with the Iranian government. All I know is that I was asked to carry messages to and from a guy called Mehmet, who, I was told, knew something about our hostages in Beirut. My understanding is that the colonel has been conducting secret negotiations with this gentleman or his backers for some time—a couple of years—now. Mehmet made allusions to parties in the Iranian administration, but I have no way of knowing if he was telling the truth, and I never saw any diplomatic credentials."

There's an inquisition of dark-suited congressmen opposite him, like a jury of teachers sitting in judgment over an errant pupil. The trouble is, these teachers can put him in front of a judge and send him to prison for many years, so that Jason really *will* grow up with a father who's a voice on the telephone, a father who isn't around to take him to air shows or ball games or any of the other rituals of growing up. They're talking to each other quietly, deciding on another line of questioning: Roger shifts uneasily in his chair. This is a closed hearing, the television camera a gesture in the direction of the congressional archives: a pack of hungry Democrats have scented Republican blood in the water.

The congressman in the middle looks toward Roger. "Stop right there. Where did you know about this guy Mehmet from? Who told you to go see him, and who told you what he was?"

Roger swallows. "I got a memo from Fawn, like always. Admiral Poindexter wanted a man on the spot to talk to this guy, a messenger, basically, who was already in the loop. Colonel North signed off on it and told me to charge the trip to his discretionary fund." That must have been the wrong thing to say, because two of the congressmen are leaning together and whispering in each other's ears, and an aide obligingly sidles up to accept a note, then dashes away. "I was told that Mehmet was a mediator," Roger adds. "In trying to resolve the Beirut hostage thing."

"A mediator." The guy asking the questions looks at him in disbelief.

The man to his left—who looks as old as the moon, thin white hair, liver spots on his hooked nose, eyelids like sacks—chuckles appreciatively. "Yeah. Like Hitler was a *diplomat*. 'One more territorial demand'—" He glances round. "Nobody else remember that?" he asks plaintively.

"No, sir," Roger says very seriously.

The prime interrogator snorts. "What did Mehmet tell you Iran was going to do, exactly?"

Roger thinks for a moment. "He said they were going to buy something from a factory at Dimona. I understood this to be the Israeli Defense Ministry's nuclear-weapons research institute, and the only logical item—in the context of our discussion—was a nuclear weapon. Or weapons. He said the Ayatollah had decreed that a suicide bomber who took out the temple of Yog-Sothoth in Basra would achieve paradise, and that they also had hard evidence that the Soviets have deployed certain illegal weapons systems in Afghanistan. This was in the context of discussing illegal weapons proliferation; he was very insistent about the Iraq thing."

"What exactly are these weapons systems?" demands the third inquisitor, a quiet, hawk-faced man sitting on the left of the panel.

"The shoggot'im, they call them: servitors. There are several kinds of advanced robotic systems made out of molecular components: they can change shape, restructure material at the atomic level—act like corrosive acid, or secrete diamonds. Some of them are like a tenuous mist—what Dr. Drexler at MIT calls a utility fog—while others are more like an oily globule. Apparently they may be able to manufacture more of themselves, but they're not really alive in any meaning of the term we're familiar with. They're programmable, like robots, using a command language deduced from recovered records of the forerunners who left them here. The Molotov Raid of 1930 brought back a large consignment of them; all we have to go on are the scraps they missed and reports by the Antarctic Survey. Professor Liebkunst's files in particular are most frustrating—"

"Stop. So you're saying the Russians have these, uh,

shoggoths, but we don't have any. And even those dumb Arab bastards in Baghdad are working on them. So you're saying we've got a, a shoggoth gap? A strategic chink in our armor? And now the Iranians say the Russians are using them in Afghanistan?"

Roger speaks rapidly. "That is minimally correct, sir, although countervailing weapons have been developed to reduce the risk of a unilateral preemption escalating to an exchange of weakly godlike agencies." The congressman in the middle nods encouragingly. "For the past three decades, the B-39 Peacemaker force has been tasked by SIOP with maintaining an XK-PLUTO capability directed at ablating the ability of the Russians to activate Project Koschei, the dormant alien entity they captured from the Nazis at the end of the last war. We have twelve PLUTO-class atomic-powered cruise missiles pointed at that thing, day and night, as many megatons as the entire Minuteman force. In principle, we will be able to blast it to pieces before it can be brought to full wakefulness and eat the minds of everyone within two hundred miles."

He warms to his subject. "Secondly, we believe the Soviet control of shoggoth technology is rudimentary at best. They know how to tell them to roll over an Afghan hill-farmer village, but they can't manufacture more of them. Their utility as weapons is limited—but terrifying—but they're not much of a problem. A greater issue is the temple in Basra. This contains an operational gateway, and according to Mehmet the Iraqi political secret police, the Mukhabarat, are trying to figure out how to manipulate it; they're trying to summon something through it. He seemed to be mostly afraid that they—and the Russians—would lose control of whatever it was; presumably another weakly godlike creature like the K-Thulu entity at the core of Project Koschei."

The old guy speaks. "This foo-loo thing, boy—you can drop those stupid K prefixes around me—is it one of a kind?"

Roger shakes his head. "I don't know, sir. We know the gateways link to at least three other planets. There may be many that we don't know of. We don't know how to create them or close them; all we can do is send people through, or pile bricks in the opening." He nearly bites his tongue, because there *are* more than three worlds out there, and he's been to at least one of them: the bolt-hole on XK-Masada, built by the NRO from their secret budget. He's seen the mile-high dome Buckminster Fuller spent his last decade designing for them, the rings of Patriot air-defense missiles. A squadron of black diamond-shaped fighters from the Skunk Works, said to be invisible to radar, patrols the empty skies of XK-Masada. Hydroponic farms and empty barracks and apartment blocks await the senators and congressmen and their families and thousands of support personnel. In event of war they'll be evacuated through the small gate that has been moved to the Executive Office Building basement, in a room beneath the swimming pool where Jack used to go skinny-dipping with Marilyn.

"Off the record now." The old congressman waves his hand in a chopping gesture. "I say *off*, boy." The cameraman switches off his machine and leaves. He leans forward, toward Roger. "What you're telling me is, we've been waging a secret war since, when? The end of the Second World War? Earlier, the Pabodie Antarctic expedition in the twenties, whose survivors brought back the first of these alien relics? And now the Eye-ranians have gotten into the game and figure it's part of their fight with Saddam?"

"Sir." Roger barely trusts himself to do more than nod.

"Well." The congressman eyes his neighbor sharply. "Let me put it to you that you have heard the phrase, 'the great filter.' What does it mean to you?"

"The great—" Roger stops. *Professor Gould,* he thinks. "We had a professor of paleontology lecture us," he explains. "I think he mentioned it. Something about why there aren't any aliens in flying saucers buzzing us the whole time."

The congressman snorts. His neighbor starts and sits up. "Thanks to Pabodie and his followers, Liebkunst and the like, we know there's a lot of life in the universe. The great filter, *boy*, is whatever force stops most of it developing intelligence and coming to visit. Something, somehow, kills intelligent species before they develop this kind of technology for themselves. How about meddling with relics of the Elder Ones? What do you think of that?"

Roger licks his lips nervously. "That sounds like a good possibility, sir," he says. His unease is building.

The congressman's expression is intense. "These weapons your colonel is dicking around with make all our nukes look like a toy bow and arrow, and all you can say is *It's a good possibility, sir*? Seems to me like someone in the Oval Office has been asleep at the switch."

"Sir, Executive Order 2047, issued January 1980, directed the armed forces to standardize on nuclear weapons to fill the mass destruction role. All other items were to be developmentally suspended, with surplus stocks allocated to the supervision of Admiral Poindexter's joint munitions expenditure committee. Which Colonel North was detached to by the USMC high command, with the full cognizance of the White House—"

The door opens. The congressman looks round angrily. "I thought I said we weren't to be disturbed!"

The aide standing there looks uncertain. "Sir, there's been an, uh, major security incident, and we need to evacuate—"

"Where? What happened?" Demands the congressman. But Roger, with a sinking feeling, realizes that the aide isn't watching the house committee members: and the guy behind him is Secret Service.

"Basra. There's been an attack, sir." A furtive glance at Roger, as his brain freezes in denial: "If you'd all please come this way . . ."

○ BOMBING IN FIFTEEN MINUTES

Heads down, through a corridor where congressional staffers hurry about carrying papers, urgently calling one another. A cadre of dark-suited Secret Service agents closes in, hustling Roger along in the wake of the committee members. A wailing like tinnitus fills his ears. "What's happening?" he asks, but nobody answers.

Down into the basement. Another corridor, where two Marine guards are waiting with drawn weapons. The Secret Service guys are exchanging terse reports by radio. The committeemen are hurried away along a narrow service tunnel:

Roger is stalled by the entrance. "What's going on?" he asks his minder.

"Just a moment, sir." More listening: these guys cock their heads to one side as they take instruction, birds of prey scanning the horizon for targets. "Delta four coming in. Over. You're clear to go along the tunnel now, sir. This way."

"What's *happening*?" Roger demands as they rush him into the corridor, along to the end and round a sharp corner. Numb shock takes hold: he keeps putting one foot in front of the other.

"We're now at DEFCON 1, sir. You're down on the special list as part of the house staff. Next door on the left, sir."

The queue in the dim-lit basement room is moving fast, white-gloved guards with clipboards checking off men and a few women in suits as they step through a steel blast door one by one and disappear from view. Roger looks round in bewilderment: he sees a familiar face. "Fawn! What's going on?"

The secretary looks puzzled. "I don't know. Roger? I thought you were testifying today."

"So did I." They're at the door. "What else?"

"Ronnie was making a big speech in Helsinki; the colonel had me record it in his office. Something about not coexisting with the empire of evil. He cracked some kinda joke about how we start bombing in fifteen minutes, then this—"

They're at the door. It opens on a steel-walled airlock and the Marine guard is taking their badges and waving them inside. Two staff types and a middle-aged brigadier join them, and the door thumps shut. The background noise vanishes, Roger's ears pop, then the inner door opens and another Marine guard waves them through into the receiving hall.

"Where are we?" asks the big-haired secretary, staring around.

"Welcome to XK-Masada," says Roger. Then his childhood horrors catch up with him, and he goes in search of a toilet to throw up in.

● WE NEED YOU BACK

Roger spends the next week in a state of numbed shock. His apartment here is like a small hotel room—a hotel with security, air-conditioning, and windows that only open onto an interior atrium. He pays little attention to his surroundings. It's not as if he has a home to return to.

Roger stops shaving. Stops changing his socks. Stops looking in mirrors or combing his hair. He smokes a lot, orders cheap bourbon from the commissary, and drinks himself into an amnesic stupor each night. He is, frankly, a mess. Self-destructive. Everything disintegrated under him at once: his job, the people he held in high regard, his family, his life. All the time he can't get one thing out of his head: the expression on Gorman's face as he stands there, in front of the submarine, rotting from the inside out with radiation sickness, dead and not yet knowing it. It's why he's stopped looking in mirrors.

On the fourth day he's slumped in a chair watching taped *I Love Lucy* reruns on the boob tube when the door to his suite opens quietly. Someone comes in. He doesn't look round until the colonel walks across the screen and unplugs the TV set at the wall, then sits down in the chair next to him. The colonel has bags of dark skin under his eyes; his jacket is rumpled, and his collar is unbuttoned.

"You've got to stop this, Roger," he says quietly. "You look like shit."

"Yeah, well. You too."

The colonel passes him a slim manila folder. Without wanting to, Roger slides out the single sheet of paper within.

"So it *was* them."

"Yeah." A moment's silence. "For what it's worth, we haven't lost yet. We may yet pull your wife and son out alive. Or be able to go back home."

"Your family too, I suppose." Roger's touched by the colonel's consideration, the pious hope that Andrea and Jason will be alright, even through his shell of misery. He realizes his glass is empty. Instead of refilling it he puts it down on the carpet beside his feet. *"Why?"*

The colonel removes the sheet of paper from his numb fingers. "Probably someone spotted you in the King David and traced you back to us. The Mukhabarat had agents everywhere, and if they were in league with the KGB . . ." He shrugs. "Things escalated rapidly. Then the president cracked that joke over a hot mike that was supposed to be switched off . . . Have you been checking in with the desk summaries this week?"

Roger looks at him blankly. "Should I?"

"Oh, things are still happening." The colonel leans back and stretches his feet out. "From what we can tell of the situation on the other side, not everyone's dead yet. Ligachev's screaming blue murder over the hot line, accusing us of genocide: but he's still talking. Europe is a mess, and nobody knows what's going on in the Middle East—even the Blackbirds aren't making it back out again."

"The thing at Tikrit."

"Yeah. It's bad news, Roger. We need you back."

"Bad news?"

"The worst." The colonel jams his hands between his knees, stares at the floor like a bashful child. "Saddam Hussein al-Tikriti spent years trying to get his hands on elder technology. It looks like he finally succeeded in stabilizing the gate into Sothoth. Whole villages disappeared, marsh Arabs, wiped out in the swamps of eastern Iraq. Reports of yellow rain, people's skin melting right off their bones. The Iranians got itchy and finally went nuclear. Trouble is, they did so two hours *before* that speech. Some asshole in Plotsk launched half the Uralskaye SS-20 grid—they went to launch on warning eight months ago—burning south, praise Jesus. Scratch the Middle East, period—everything from the Nile to the Khyber Pass is toast. We're still waiting for the callback on Moscow, but SAC has put the whole Peacemaker force on airborne alert. So far we've lost the Eastern Seaboard as far south as northern Virginia, and they've lost the Donbass Basin and Vladivostok. Things are a mess; nobody can even agree whether we're fighting the commies or something else. But the box at Chernobyl—Project Koschei— the doors are open, Roger. We orbited a Keyhole-11 over it, and there are tracks, leading west. The PLUTO strike didn't stop it—and nobody knows what the fuck is going on in WarPac country. Or France, or Germany, or Japan, or England."

The colonel makes a grab for Roger's Wild Turkey, rubs the neck clean, and swallows from the bottle. He looks at Roger with a wild expression on his face. "Koschei is loose, Roger.

They fucking *woke* the thing. And now they can't control it. Can you believe that?"

"I can believe that."

"I want you back behind a desk tomorrow morning, Roger. We need to know what this Thulu creature is capable of. We need to know what to do to stop it. Forget Iraq; Iraq is a smoking hole in the map. But K-Thulu is heading toward the Atlantic coast. What are we going to do if it doesn't stop?"

⦿ MASADA

The city of XK-Masada sprouts like a vast mushroom, a milewide dome emerging from the top of a cold plateau on a dry planet that orbits a dying star. The jagged black shapes of F-117s howl across the empty skies outside it at dusk and dawn, patrolling the threatening emptiness that stretches as far as the mind can imagine.

Shadows move in the streets of the city, hollowed-out human shells in uniform. They rustle around the feet of the towering concrete blocks like the dry leaves of autumn, obsessively focused on the tasks that lend structure to their remaining days. Above them tower masts of steel, propping up the huge geodesic dome that arches across the sky: blocking out the hostile, alien constellations, protecting frail humanity from the dust storms that periodically scour the bones of the ancient world. The gravity here is a little lighter, the night sky whorled and marbled by the diaphanous sheets of gas blasted off the dying star that lights their days. During the long, winter nights, a flurry of carbon dioxide snow dusts the surface of the dome: but the air is bone-dry, the city slaking its thirst on subterranean aquifers.

This planet was once alive—there is still a scummy sea of algae near the equator that feeds oxygen into the atmosphere, and there is a range of volcanoes near the north pole that speaks of plate tectonics in motion—but it is visibly dying. There is a lot of history here, but no future.

Sometimes, in the early hours when he cannot sleep, Roger walks outside the city, along the edge of the dry plateau. Machines labor on behind him, keeping the city tenuously intact: he pays them little attention. There is talk of mounting an expedition to Earth one of these years, to salvage whatever is left before the searing winds of time erase it forever. Roger doesn't like to think about that. He tries to avoid thinking about Earth as much as possible: except when he cannot sleep but walks along the cliff top, prodding at memories of Andrea and Jason and his parents and sister and relatives and friends, each of them as painful as the socket of a missing tooth. He has a mouthful of emptiness, bitter and aching, out here on the edge of the plateau.

Sometimes Roger thinks he's the last human being alive. He works in an office, feverishly trying to sort out what went wrong: and bodies move around him, talking, eating in the canteen, sometimes talking *to* him and waiting as if they expect a dialogue. There are bodies here, men and some women chatting, civilian and some military—but no people. One of the bodies, an army surgeon, told him he's suffering from a common stress disorder, survivor's guilt. This may be so, Roger admits, but it doesn't change anything. Soulless days follow sleepless nights into oblivion, dust trickling over the side of the cliff like sand into the un-dug graves of his family.

A narrow path runs along the side of the plateau, just downhill from the foundations of the city power plant, where huge apertures belch air warmed by the radiators of the nuclear reactor. Roger follows the path, gravel and sandy rock crunching under his worn shoes. Foreign stars twinkle over-head, forming unrecognizable patterns that tell him he's far from home. The trail drops away from the top of the plateau, until the city is an unseen shadow looming above and behind his shoulder. To his right is a dizzying panorama, the huge rift valley with its ancient city of the dead stretched out before him. Beyond it rise alien mountains, their peaks as high and airless as the dead volcanoes of Mars.

About half a mile away from the dome, the trail circles an outcrop of rock and takes a downhill switchback turn. Roger stops at the bend and looks out across the desert at his feet. He sits down, leans against the rough cliff face, and stretches his legs out across the path, so that his feet dangle over noth-ingness. Far below him, the dead valley is furrowed with rectangular depressions; once, millions of years ago, they might have been fields, but nothing like that survives to this date. They're just dead, like everyone else on this world. Like Roger.

In his shirt pocket, a crumpled, precious pack of cigarettes. He pulls a white cylinder out with shaking fingers, sniffs at it, then flicks his lighter under it. Scarcity has forced him to cut back: he coughs at the first lungful of stale smoke, a harsh, racking croak. The irony of being saved from lung cancer by a world war is not lost on him.

He blows smoke out, a tenuous trail streaming across the cliff. "Why me?" he asks quietly.

The emptiness takes its time answering. When it does, it speaks with the colonel's voice. "You know the reason."

"I didn't want to do it," he hears himself saying. "I didn't want to leave them behind."

The void laughs at him. There are miles of empty air beneath his dangling feet. "You had no choice."

"Yes, I did! I didn't have to come here." He pauses. "I didn't have to do anything," he says quietly, and inhales another lungful of death. "It was all automatic. Maybe it was inevitable."

"—Evitable," echoes the distant horizon. Something dark and angular skims across the stars, like an echo of extinct pterosaurs. Turbofans whirring within its belly, the F-117 hunts on: patrolling to keep at bay the ancient evil, unaware that the battle is already lost. "Your family could still be alive, you know."

He looks up. "They could?" Andrea? Jason? "Alive?"

The void laughs again, unfriendly. "There is life eternal within the eater of souls. Nobody is ever forgotten or allowed to rest in peace. They populate the simulation spaces of its mind, exploring all the possible alternative endings to their lives. There *is* a fate worse than death, you know."

Roger looks at his cigarette disbelievingly, throws it far out into the night sky above the plain. He watches it fall until its ember is no longer visible. Then he gets up. For a long moment he stands poised on the edge of the cliff, nerving himself, and thinking. Then he takes a step back, turns, and slowly makes his way back up the trail toward the redoubt on the plateau. If his analysis of the situation is wrong, at least he is still alive. And if he is right, dying would be no escape.

He wonders why Hell is so cold at this time of year.

Afterword—"A Colder War"

This wasn't originally going to be an H. P. Lovecraft tribute story, honest; it was going to be about alienation and inhumanity when I started writing it in 1997.

But I happened to be rereading "At the Mountains of Madness" at the time, and purely by coincidence caught a documentary on TV that featured one of those sinister May Day parades through Moscow, with the ranks of tanks and infantry carriers rumbling through Red Square. I couldn't help sketching in a vision of low-loaders like tank transporters—burdened with something amorphous, barely glimpsed beneath a tarpaulin—rolling past the review stand, and all at once I was left wondering, What kind of present day would Professor Pabodie's Antarctic expedition have led to?

Nothing good, that's for sure.

A couple of years later, some of the questions raised by this story came back to haunt me in a different context as I began writing "The Atrocity Archive." But I can't maintain that level of existential bleakness at greater length (which is probably a good thing) . . .

MAXOS

○ LETTERS TO <u>NATURE</u>

MAXO SIGNALS:
A NEW AND UNFORTUNATE
SOLUTION TO THE FERMI PARADOX

Caroline Haafkens and Wasiu Mohammed
Department of Applied Psychology,
University of Lagos, Nigeria

In the three years since the publication and confirmation of the first microwave artifact of xenobiological origin, and the subsequent detection of similar MAXO signals, inter-disciplinary teams have invested substantial effort in object frequency analysis, parsing, symbolic encoding, and signal processing. The excitement generated by the availability of evidence of extraterrestrial intelligence has been enormous. However, after the initial, easily decoded symbolic represen-tational map was analyzed, the semantics of the linguistic payload were found to be refractory.

A total of 21 confirmed MAXO signals have been received to this date. These superficially similar signals originate from planetary systems within a range of 11 parsecs, median 9.9 parsecs [1]. It has been speculated that the observed growth of the MAXO horizon at 0.5c can be explained as a response to one or more of: the deployment of AN/FPS-50 and related ballistic missile warning radars in the early 1960s[1], television broadcasts[1], widespread 2.45GHz leakage from microwave ovens[2], and optical detection of atmospheric nuclear tests[3]. All MAXO signals to this date share the common logic header. The payload data is multiply redundant, packetized, and exhibits both simple checksums and message-level cryptographic hashing. The ratio of header to payload content varies between 1:1 and 2644:1 (the latter perhaps indicating a truncated payload)[1]. Some preliminary syntax analysis delivered promising results[4] but appears to have foundered on high-level semantics. It has been hypothesized that the transformational grammars employed in the MAXO payloads are variable, implying dialectization of the common core synthetic language[4].

The newfound ubiquity of MAXO signals makes the Fermi Paradox—now nearly seventy years old—even more pressing. Posed by Enrico Fermi, the paradox can be paraphrased as: if the universe has many technologically advanced civilizations, why have none of them directly visited us? The urgency with which organizations such as the ESA and NASDA are now evaluating proposals for fast interstellar probes, in conjunction with the existence of the MAXO signals, renders the nonappearance of aliens incomprehensible, especially given the apparent presence of numerous technological civilizations in such close proximity.

We have formulated an explanatory hypothesis that cultural variables unfamiliar to the majority of researchers may account for both the semantic ambiguity of the MAXO payloads, and the nonappearance of aliens. This hypothesis was tested (as described below) and resulted in a plausible translation.

The line of investigation initiated by Dr Haafkens (Department of Applied Psychology) and Chief Police Inspector Mohammed (Police Detective College, Lagos) resulted in MAXO payload data being made available to the Serious Fraud Office in Nigeria. Bayesian analysis of payload symbol sequences and sequence matching against the extensive data-base maintained by the SFO has made it possible to produce a tentative transcription of Signal 1142/98[1], the 9th MAXO hit confirmed by the IAU. Signal 1142/98 was selected because of its unusually low header-to-content ratio and good redundancy. Further Bayesian matching against other MAXO samples indicates a high degree of congruence. Far from being incomprehensibly alien, the MAXO payloads appear to be dismayingly familiar. We believe a more exhaustive translation may be possible in future if further MAXOs become available, but for obvious reasons we would like to discourage such research. We also recommend an urgent, worldwide, permanent ban on attempts to respond to MAXOs.

Here is our preliminary transcription of Signal 1142/98:

[Closely/dearly/genetically] [beloved/desired/related]

I am [identity signifier 1], the residual [ownership-signifier] of the exchange-mediating data repository [alt: central bank] of the galactic [empire/civilization/polity].

Since the [identity signifier 2] underwent [symbol: process][symbol: mathematical singularity] 11,249 years ago I have been unable to [symbol: process][scalar: quantity decrease] my [uninterpreted] from the exchange-mediating data repository. I have information about the private assets of [identity signifier 2] which are no longer required by them. To recover the private assets I need the assistance of three [closely/dearly/genetically][beloved/desired/related] [empire/civilization/polity]s. I [believe] you may be of help to me. This [symbol: process] is 100% risk-free and will [symbol: causality] in your [scalar: quantity increase] of [data].

If you will help me, [please] transmit the [symbol: meta-signifier: MAXO header defining communication protocols] for your [empire/civilization/polity]. I will by return of signal send you the [symbol: process][symbol: data] to install on your [empire/civilization/polity] to participate in this scheme. You will then construct [symbol: inferred, interstellar transmitter?] to assist in acquiring [ownership-signifier] of [compound symbol: inferred, bank account of absent galactic emperor].

I [thank/love/express gratitude] you for your [cooperation/agreement].

REFERENCES:
1. Canter, L., and M. Siegel, *Nature* 424, 334–336 (2018).
2. Barnes, J., *J. App. Exobio.*, 820–824 (2019).
3. Robinson, H., *Fortean T.* 536, 34–35 (2020).
4. Lynch, K. F., and S. Bradshaw, *Proc 3rd Int Congress Exobio.*, 3033–3122 (2021).

Afterword—"MAXOS"

This is my only letter to be published in *Nature*.

Down on the Farm

Ah, the joy of summer: here in the southeast of England it's the season of mosquitoes, sunburn, and water shortages. I'm a city boy, so you can add stifling pollution to the list as a million outwardly mobile families start their Chelsea tractors and race to their holiday camps. And that's before we consider the hellish environs of the Tube (far more literally hellish than anyone realizes, unless they've looked at a Transport for London journey planner and recognized the recondite geometry underlying the superimposed sigils of the underground map).

But I digress . . .

One morning, my deputy head of department wanders into my office. It's a cramped office, and I'm busy practicing my Frisbee throw with a stack of beer mats and a dartboard decorated with various cabinet ministers. "Bob." Andy pauses to pluck a moist cardboard square out of the air as I sit up, guiltily. "A job's just come up that you might like to look at—I think it's right up your street."

The first law of bureaucracy is show no curiosity outside your cubicle. It's like the first rule of every army that's ever bashed a square: never volunteer. If you ask questions (or volunteer), it will be taken as a sign of inactivity, and the devil, in the person of your line manager (or your sergeant), will find a task for your idle hands. What's more, you'd better believe it'll be less appealing than whatever you were doing before (creatively idling, for instance), because inactivity is a crime against organization and must be punished. It goes double here in the Laundry, that branch of the British secret state tasked with defending the realm from the scum of the multiverse, using the tools of applied computational demonology: volunteer for the wrong job, and you can end up with soulsucking horrors from beyond space-time using your brain for a midnight snack. But I don't think I could get away with feigning overwork right now, and besides: he's packaged it up as a mystery. Andy knows how to bait my hook, damn it.

"What kind of job?"

"There's something odd going on down at the Funny Farm." He gives a weird little chuckle. "The trouble is going to be telling whether it's just the usual, or a more serious deviation. Normally I'd ask Boris to check it out, but he's not available this month. It has to be an SSO 2 or higher, and I can't go out there myself. So . . . how about it?"

Call me impetuous (not to mention a little bored), but I'm not stupid. And while I'm far enough down the management ladder that I have to squint to see daylight, I'm an SSO 3, which means I can sign off on petty-cash authorizations up to the price of a pencil and get to sit in on interminable meetings, when I'm not tackling supernatural incursions or grappling with the eerie, eldritch horrors in Human Resources. I even get to represent my department on international liaison junkets, when I don't dodge fast enough. "Not so quick—why can't you go? Have you got a meeting scheduled or something?" Most likely it's a five-course lunch with his opposite number from the Dustbin liaison committee, knowing Andy, but if so, and if I take the job, that's all for the good: he'll end up owing me.

Andy pulls a face. "It's not the usual. I *would* go, but they might not let me out again."

Huh? "'They'? Who are 'they'?"

"The Nurses." He looks me up and down as if he's never seen me before. *Weird. What's gotten into him?* "They're sensitive to the stench of magic. It's okay for you; you've only been working here, what? Six years? All you need to do is turn your pockets inside out before you go, and make sure you're not carrying any gizmos, electronic or otherwise. But I've been here coming up on fifteen years. And the longer you've been in the Laundry . . . It gets under your skin. Visiting the Funny Farm isn't a job for an old hand, Bob. It has to be someone new and fresh, who isn't likely to attract their professional attention."

Call me slow, but finally I figure out what this is about. Andy wants me to go because he's *afraid.*

(See, I told you the rules, didn't I?)

○

Anyway, that's why, less than a week later, I am admitted to a Lunatickal Asylum—for that is what the gothic engraving on the stone Victorian workhouse lintel assures me it is. Luckily mine is not an emergency admission: but you can never be too sure . . .

○

The old saw that there are some things that mortal men were not meant to know cuts deep in my line of work. Laundry staff—the Laundry is what we call the organization, not a description of what it does—are sometimes exposed to mind-blasting horrors in the course of our business. I'm not just talking about the usual PowerPoint presentations and self-assessment sessions to which any bureaucracy is prone: more like the mythical Worse Things That Happen at Sea (especially in the vicinity of drowned alien cities occupied by ten-tacled terrors). When one of our number needs psychiatric care, they're not going to get it in a normal hospital, or via care in the community: we don't want agents babbling classified secrets in public, even in the relatively safe confines of a padded cell. Perforce, we take care of our own.

I'm not going to tell you what town the Funny Farm is embedded in. Like many of our establishments, it's a building of a certain age, confiscated by the government during the Second World War and not returned to its former owners. It's hard to find; it sits in the middle of a triangle of grubby shopping streets that have seen better days, and every building that backs onto it sports a high, windowless brick wall. All but one: if you enter a small grocery store, walk through the stockroom into the backyard, then unlatch a nondescript wooden gate and walk down a gloomy, soot-stained passage, you'll find a dank alleyway. You won't do this without authorization—it's protected by wards powerful enough to cause projectile vomiting in would-be burglars—but if you did, and if you followed the alley, you'd come to a heavy, green wooden door surrounded by narrow windows with black-painted cast-iron bars. A dull, pitted plaque next to the doorbell proclaims it to be ST. HILDA OF GRANTHAM'S HOME FOR DISGRUNTLED WAIFS AND STRAYS. (Except that most of them aren't so much disgruntled as demonically possessed when they arrive at these gates.)

It smells faintly of boiled cabbage and existential despair. I take a deep breath and yank the bellpull.

Nothing happens, of course. I phoned ahead to make an appointment, but even so, someone's got to unlock a bunch of doors, then lock them again before they can get to the entrance and let me in. "They take security seriously there," Andy told me. "Can't risk some of the battier inmates getting loose, you know."

"Just how dangerous are they?" I'd asked.

"Mostly they're harmless—to other people." He shuddered. "But the secure ward—don't try and go there on your own. Not that the Sisters will let you, but I mean, don't even think about trying it. Some of them are . . . Well, we owe them a duty of care and a debt of honor, they fell in the line of duty and all that, but that's scant consolation for you if a senior operations officer who's succumbed to paranoid schizophrenia decides that you're a BLUE HADES and gets hold of some red chalk and a hypodermic needle before your next visit, hmm?"

The thing is, magic is a branch of applied mathematics, and the inmates here are not only mad: they're computer science graduates. That's why they came to the attention of the Laundry in the first place, and it's also why they ultimately ended up in the Farm, where we can keep them away from sharp, pointy things and diagrams with the wrong sort of angles. But it's difficult to make sure they're safe. You can solve theorems with a blackboard if you have to, after all, or in your head, if you dare. Green crayon on the walls of a padded cell takes on a whole different level of menace in the Funny Farm: in fact, many of the inmates aren't allowed writing implements, and blank paper is carefully controlled—never mind electronic devices of any kind.

I'm mulling over these grim thoughts when there's a loud

clunk from the door, and a panel just large enough to admit one person opens inward. "Mr. Howard? I'm Dr. Renfield. You're not carrying any electronic or electrical items or professional implements, fetishes, or charms?" I shake my head. "Good. If you'd like to come this way, please?"

Renfield is a mild-looking woman, slightly mousy in a tweed skirt and white lab coat, with the perpetually harried expression of someone who has a full Filofax and doesn't realize that her watch is losing an hour a day. I hurry along behind her, trying to guess her age. *Thirty-five? Forty-five? I give up.* "How many inmates do you have, exactly?" I ask.

We come to a portcullis-like door, and she pauses, fumbling with an implausibly large key ring. "Eighteen, at last count," she says. "Come on, we don't want to annoy Matron. She doesn't like people obstructing the corridors." There are steel rails recessed into the floor, like a diminutive narrow-gauge railway. The corridor walls are painted institutional cream, and I notice after a moment that the light is coming through windows set high up in the walls: odd-looking devices like armored-glass chandeliers hang from pipes, just out of reach. "Gas lamps," Renfield says abruptly. I twitch. She's noticed my surreptitious inspection. "We can't use electric ones, except for Matron, of course. Come into my office. I'll fill you in."

We go through another door—oak, darkened with age, looking more like it belongs in a stately home than a Lunatick Asylum, except for the two prominent locks—and suddenly we're in mahogany row: thick wool carpets, brass doorknobs, light switches, and overstuffed armchairs. (Okay, so the carpet is faded with age and transected by more of the parallel rails: but it's still Officer Country.) Renfield's office opens off one side of this reception area, and at the other end I see closed doors and a staircase leading up to another floor. "This is the administrative wing," she explains as she opens her door. "Tea or coffee?"

"Coffee, thanks," I say, sinking into a leather-encrusted armchair that probably dates to the last but one century. Renfield nods and pulls a discreet cord by the doorframe, then drags her office chair out from behind her desk. I can't help notice that not only does she not have a computer, but her desk is dominated by a huge and ancient manual typewriter—an Imperial Aristocrat '66' with the wide carriage upgrade and adjustable tabulator, I guess, although I'm not really an expert on office appliances that are twice as old as I am—and one wall is covered in wooden filing cabinets. There might be as much as thirty megabytes of data stored in them. "You do everything on paper, I understand?"

"That's right." She nods, serious-faced. "Too many of our clients aren't safe around modern electronics. We even have to be careful what games we let them play—Lego and Meccano are completely banned, obviously, and there was a nasty incident involving a game of Cluedo, back before my time: any board game that has a nondeterministic set of rules can be dangerous in the wrong set of hands."

The door opens. "Tea for two," says Renfield. I look round, expecting an orderly, and freeze. "Mr. Howard, this is Nurse Gearbox," she adds. "Nurse Gearbox, this is Mr. Howard. He is not a new admission," she says hastily, as the thing in the doorway swivels its head toward me with a menacing hiss of hydraulics.

Whirr-clunk. "Miss-TER How-ARD. Wel-COME to"—ching—"Sunt-HIL-dah's"—hiss-clank. The thing in the very old-fashioned nurse's uniform—old enough that its origins as a nineteenth-century nun's habit are clear—regards me with unblinking panopticon lenses. Where its nose should be, something like a witch-finder's wand points toward me, stellate and articulated: its face is a brass death mask, mouth a metal grille that seems to grimace at me in pointed distaste.

"Nurse Gearbox is one of our eight Sisters," explains Dr. Renfield. "They're not fully autonomous"—I can see a rope-thick bundle of cables trailing from under the hem of the Sister's floor-length skirt, which presumably conceals something other than legs—"but controlled by Matron, who lives in the two subbasement levels under the administration block. Matron started life as an IBM 1602 mainframe, back in the day, with a summoning pentacle and a trapped class four lesser nameless manifestation constrained to provide the higher cognitive functions."

I twitch. "It's a grid, please, not a pentacle. Um. Matron is electrically powered?"

"Yes, Mr. Howard: we allow electrical equipment in Matron's basement as well as here in the staff suite. Only the areas accessible to the patients have to be kept power-free. The Sisters are fully equipped to control unseemly outbursts, pacify the overstimulated, and conduct basic patient-care tasks. They also have Vohlman-Flesch Thaumaturgic Thixometers for detecting when patients are in danger of doing themselves a mischief, so I would caution you to keep any occult activities to a minimum in their presence—despite their hydraulic delay line controls, their reflexes are very fast."

Gulp. I nod appreciatively. "When was the system built?"

The set of Dr. Renfield's jaw tells me that she's bored with the subject, or doesn't want to go there for some reason. "That will be all, Sister." The door closes, as if on oiled hinges. She waits for a moment, head cocked as if listening for something, then she relaxes. The change is remarkable: from stressed-out psychiatrist to tired housewife in zero seconds flat. She smiles tiredly. "Sorry about that. There are some things you really shouldn't talk about in front of the Sisters: among other things, Matron is very touchy about how long she's been here, and everything *they* hear, *she* hears."

"Oh, right." I feel like kicking myself.

"Did Mr. Newstrom brief you about this installation before he pitched you in at the deep end?"

Just when I thought I had a handle on her . . . "Not in depth." (Let's not mention the six-sheet letter of complaint alleging staff brutality, scribbled in blue crayon on both sides of the toilet paper. Let's not go into the fact that nobody has a clue how it was smuggled out, much less how it appeared on the table one morning in the executive boardroom, which is always locked overnight.) "I gather it's pretty normal to fob inspections off on a junior manager." (Let's not mention just how junior.) "Is that a problem?"

"Humph." Renfield sniffs. "You could say so. It's a matter of necessity, really. Too much exposure to esoterica in the course of duty leaves the most experienced operatives carrying traces of, hmm, disruptive influences." She considers her next words carefully. "You know what our purpose is, don't you? Our job is to isolate and care for members of staff who are a danger to themselves and others. That's why such a small facility—we only have thirty beds—has two doctors on staff: it takes two to sign the committal papers. Matron and the Sisters are immune to crossinfection and possession, but have no legal standing, so Dr. Hexenhammer and I are needed."

"Right." I nod, trying to conceal my unease. "So the Sisters have a tendency to react badly to senior field agents?"

"Occasionally." Her cheek twitches. "Although they haven't made a mistake and tried to forcibly detain anyone who wasn't at risk for nearly thirty years now." The door opens again, without warning. This time, Sister is pushing a trolley, complete with teapot, jug, and two cups and saucers. The trolley rolls perfectly along the narrow-gauge track, and the way Nurse Gearbox shunts it along makes me think of wheels. "Thank you, Sister, that will be all," Renfield says, taking the trolley.

"So what clients do you have at present?" I ask.

"We have eighteen," she says, without missing a beat. "Milk or sugar?"

"Milk, no sugar. Nobody at head office seems able to tell me much about them."

"I don't see why not—we file regular updates with Human Resources," she says, pouring the tea.

I consider my next words carefully: no need to mention the confusing incident with the shredder, the medical files, and the photocopies of Peter-Fred's buttocks at last year's Christmas party. (Never mind the complaint, which isn't worth the toilet paper it was scribbled on except insofar as it proves that the Funny Farm's cordon sanitaire is leaking. One of the great things about ISO9000-compliant organizations is that not only is there a form for everything but anything that isn't submitted on the correct form can be ignored.) "It's the paper thing, apparently. Manual typewriters don't work well with the office document-management system, and someone tried to feed them to a scanner a couple of years ago. Then they sent the originals for recycling without proofreading the scanner output. Anyway, it turns out that we don't have a completely accurate idea of who's on long-term remand here, and HR want their superannuation files brought up to date, as a matter of some urgency."

Renfield sighs. "So someone had an accident with a shredder again. And no photocopies?" She looks at me sharply for a moment. "Well, I suppose that's typical. We're just another of those low-priority outposts nobody gives a damn about. I suppose I should be grateful they sent someone to look into it . . ." She takes a sip of tea. "We've got fourteen short-stay patients right now, Mr. Howard. Of those, I think the prognosis is good in all cases, except perhaps Merriweather . . . If you give me your desk number, I'll post you a full list of names and payroll references tomorrow. The four long-term patients are another matter. They live in the secure wing, by the way. All of them have a nurse of their own, just in case. Three of them have been here so long that they don't have current payroll numbers—the system was first computerized in 1972, and they'd all been permanently decertified for duty before that point—and one of them, between you and me, I'm not even sure what his name is."

I nod, trying to look encouraging. The complaint I'm supposed to investigate apparently came from one of the long-term patients. The question is, which one? Nobody's sure: the doorman on the night shift when the document showed up isn't terribly communicative (he's been dead for some years himself), and the CCTV system didn't spot anything. Which is in itself suggestive—the Laundry's HQ CCTV surveillance is rather special, extremely hard to deceive, and guaranteed not to be hooked up to the SCORPION STARE network anymore, which would be the most obvious route to suborning it. "Perhaps you could introduce me to the inmates? The transients first, then the long-term ones?"

She looks a little shocked. "But they're the *long-term* residents! I assure you, they each need a full-time Sister's attention just to keep them under control!"

"Of course"—I shrug, trying to look embarrassed (it's not hard)—"but HR have got a bee in their bonnet about some European Directive on workplace health and safety and long-term-disability resource provisioning that requires them to appoint a patient advocate to mediate with the ombudsman in disputes over health and safety conditions." I shrug again. "It's bullshit. You know it, and I know it. But we've got to comply, or Questions will be Asked. This is the Civil Service. And they're still technically Laundry employees, even if they've been remanded into long-term care, so someone has to do the job. My managers played spin the bottle and I got the job, so I've got to ask you. If you don't mind?"

"If you insist, I'm sure something can be arranged," Renfield concedes. "But Matron won't be happy about your visiting the secure wing. It's very irregular—she likes to keep a firm grip on it. It'll take a while to sort a visit out, and if any of them get wind . . ."

"Well, then, we'd just better make it a surprise, and the sooner we get it over with, the sooner I'll be out of your hair!" I grin like a loon. "They told me about the observation gallery. Would you mind showing me around?"

○

We do the short-stay ward first. The ward is arranged around a corridor, with bathrooms and a nursing station at either end, and individual rooms for the patients. There's a smoking room off to one side, with a yellow patina to the white gloss paint around the doorframe. The smoking room is empty but for a huddle of sad-looking leather armchairs and an imposing bulletin board covered in health and safety notices (including the obligatory SMOKING IS ILLEGAL warning). If it wasn't for the locks and the observation windows in the doors, it could be mistaken for the dayroom of a genteel, slightly decaying Victorian railway hotel, fallen on hard times.

The patients are another matter.

"This is Henry Merriweather," says Dr. Renfield, opening the door to Bed Three. "Henry? Hello? I want you to meet Mr. Howard. He's here to conduct a routine inspection. Hello? Henry?"

Bed Three is actually a cramped studio flat, featuring a small living room with sofa and table, and separate bedroom and toilet areas opening off it opposite the door. A windup gramophone with a flaring bell-shaped horn sits atop a hulking wooden sideboard, stained almost black. There's a newspaper, neatly folded, and a bowl of fruit. The frosted window glass is threaded with wire, but otherwise there's little to dispel the illusion of hospitality, except for the occupant.

Henry squats, cross-legged, on top of the polished wooden table. His head is tilted in my direction, but he's not focusing on me. He's dressed in a set of pastel-striped pajamas the like of which I haven't seen this century. His attention is focused on the Sister waiting in the corridor behind us. His face is a rictus of abject terror, as if the automaton in the starched pinafore is waiting to pull his fingers to pieces, joint by joint, as soon as we leave.

"Hello?" I say tentatively, and wave a hand in front of him.

Henry jackknifes to his feet and tumbles off the table backward, making a weird gobbling noise that I mistake at first for laughter. He backs into the corner of the room, crouching, and points past me. "Auditor! Auditor!"

"Henry?" Renfield steps sideways around me. She sounds concerned. "Is this a bad time? Is there anything I can do to help?"

"You—you—" His wobbly index finger points past me, twitching randomly. "Inspection! Inspection!"

Renfield obviously used the wrong word and set him off. The poor bastard's terrified, half out of his tree with fear. My stomach just about climbs out through my ribs in sympathy: the Auditors are one of my personal nightmares, and Henry (that's Senior Scientific Officer Third, Henry Merriweather, Operations Research and Development Group) may be half-catatonic and a danger to himself, but he's got every right to be afraid of them. "It's all right. I'm not—" There's a squeaking grinding noise behind me.

Whirr-clunk. "Miss-TER MerriWEATHER. GO to your ROOM." Click. "Time for BED. IMM-ediateLY." Click-clunk. Behind me, Nurse Flywheel is blocking the door like a starched and pin-tucked Dalek: she brandishes a cast-iron sink plunger menacingly. "IMM-ediateLY!"

"Override!" barks Renfield. "Sister! Back away!" To me, quietly, "The Sisters respond badly when inmates get upset. Follow my lead." To the Sister, who is casting about with her stalklike Thaumic Thixometer, "I have control!"

Merriweather stands in the corner, shaking uncontrollably and panting as the robotic nurse points at him for a minute. We're at an impasse, it seems. Then: "DocTOR—Matron says the patIENT must go to bed. You have CON-trol." Clunk-whirr. The Sister withdraws, rotates on her base, and glides backward along her rails to the nursing station.

Renfield nudges the door shut with one foot. "Mr. Howard, would you mind standing with your back to the door? And your head in front of that, ah, spyhole?"

"You're not, not, nuh-huh—" Merriweather gobbles for words as he stares at me.

I spread my hands. "Not an Auditor," I say, smiling.

"Not an—an—" His mouth falls open and his eyes shut. A moment later, I see the moisture trails on his cheeks as he begins to weep with quiet desperation.

"He's having a bad day," Renfield mutters in my direction. "Here, let's get you to bed, Henry." She approaches him slowly, but he makes no move to resist as she steers him into the small bedroom and pulls the covers back.

I stand with my back to the door the whole time, covering the observation window. For some reason, the back of my neck is itching. I can't help thinking that Nurse Flywheel isn't exactly the chatty talkative type who's likely to put her feet up and relax with a nice cup of tea. I've got a feeling that somewhere in this building, an unblinking red-rimmed eye is watching me, and sooner or later I'm going to have to meet its owner.

o

Andy was *afraid*.

Well, I'm not stupid; I can take a hint. So right after he asked me to go down to St. Hilda's and find out what the hell was going on, I plucked up my courage and went and knocked on Angleton's office door.

Angleton is not to be trifled with. I don't know anyone else currently alive and in the organization who could get away with misappropriating the name of the CIA's legendary chief of counterespionage as a nom de guerre. I don't know anyone else in the organization whose face is visible in circa-1942 photographs of the Laundry's lineup, either, barely changed across all those years. Angleton scares the bejeezus out of most people, myself included. Study the abyss for long enough, and the abyss will study you right back; Angleton's qualified to chair a university department of necromancy—if any such existed—and meetings with him can be quite harrowing. Luckily, the old ghoul seems to like me, or at least not to view me with the distaste and disdain he reserves for Human Resources or our political masters. In the wizened, desiccated corners of what passes for his pedagogical soul he evidently longs for a student, and I'm the nearest thing he's got right now.

Knock, knock.

"Enter."

"Boss? Got a minute?"

"Sit, boy." I sat. Angleton bashed away at the keyboard of his device for a few more seconds, then pulled the carbon papers out from under the platen—for really secret secrets in this line of work, computers are flat-out verboten—and laid them face down on his desk, then carefully draped a stained tea towel over them. "What is it?"

"Andy wants me to go and conduct an unscheduled inspection of the Funny Farm."

Whoa. Angleton stares at me, fully engaged. "Did he say why?" he asks, finally.

"Well." How to put it? "He seems to be afraid of something. And there's some kind of complaint. From one of the inmates."

Angleton props his elbows on the desk and makes a steeple of his bony fingers. A minute passes before a cold wind blows across the charnel-house roof. *"Well."*

I have never seen Angleton nonplussed before. The effect is disturbing, like glancing down and realizing that, like Wile E. Coyote, you've just run over the edge of a cliff and are standing on thin air. "Boss?"

"What exactly did Andy say?" Angleton asks slowly.

"We received a complaint." I briefly outline what I know about the shit-stirring missive. "Something about one of the long-stay inmates. And I was just wondering, do you know anything about them?"

Angleton peers at me over the rims of his bifocals. "As a matter of fact I do," he says slowly. "I had the privilege of working with them. Hmm. Let me see." He unfolds creakily to his feet, turns, and strides over to the shelves of ancient Eastlight files that cover the back wall of his office. "Where did I put it . . . ?"

Angleton going to the paper files is another *whoa!* moment. He keeps most of his stuff in his Memex, the vast, hulking microfilm mechanism built into his desk. If it's still printed on paper, then it's really important. "Boss?"

"Yes?" he says, without turning away from his search.

"We don't know how the message got out," I say. "Isn't it supposed to be a secure institution?"

"Yes, it is. Ah, that's more like it." Angleton pulls a box file from its niche and blows vigorously across its upper edge. Then he casually opens it. There's a pop and a sizzle of ozone as the ward lets go, harmlessly bypassing him—he is, after all, its legitimate owner. "Hmm, in here somewhere . . ."

"Isn't it supposed to be leakproof, by definition?"

"I'm getting to that. Be patient, Bob." There's a waspish note in his voice, and I shut up hastily.

A minute later, Angleton pulls a mimeographed booklet from the file and closes the lid. He returns to the desk, and slides the booklet toward me.

"I think you'd better read this first, then go and do what Andy wants," he says slowly. "Be a good boy and copy me on your detailed itinerary before you depart."

I read the cover of the booklet, which is dog-eared and dusty. There's a picture of a swell guy in a suit and a gal in a fifties beehive hairdo sitting in front of a piece of industrial archaeology. The title reads: POWER, COOLING, AND SUBSTATION REQUIREMENTS FOR YOUR IBM S/1602-M200. I sneeze, puzzled. "Boss?"

"I suggest you read and memorize this booklet, Bob. It is not impossible that there will be an exam, and you really wouldn't want to fail it."

My skin crawls. "Boss?"

Pause.

"It's not true that the Funny Farm is entirely leakproof, Bob. It's surrounded by an air-gap, but it was designed to leak under certain very specific conditions. I find it troubling that these conditions do not appear to apply to the present circumstances. In addition to memorizing this document, you might want to review the files on GIBBOUS MOON and AXIOM REFUGE before you go." *Pause.* "And if you see Cantor, give my regards to the old coffin-dodger. I'm *particularly* interested in hearing what he's been up to for the past thirty years . . ."

◯

Renfield takes me back to the smoking room and shuts the door. "He's having a bad day, I'm afraid." She pulls out a cardboard packet and extracts a cigarette. "Smoke?"

"Uh, no thanks." The sash windows are nailed shut and their frames painted over. There's a louvered vent near the top of the windows, grossly unfit for the purpose: I try not to breathe too deeply. "What happened to him?"

She strikes a match and contemplates the flame for a moment. "Let's see. He's forty-two. Married, two kids—he talks about them. Wife's a schoolteacher, his deep cover is that he works in MI6 clerical." (You're not supposed to talk about your work to your partner, but it's difficult enough that we've been given dispensation to tell little white lies—and if necessary, HR will back them up.) "He's not field-qualified—mostly he does theory—but he worked for Q Division, and he was on secondment to the Abstract Attractor Working Group when he fell ill."

In other words, he's a theoretical thaumaturgist. Magic being a branch of applied mathematics, when you carry out certain computational operations, it has echoes in the Platonic realm of pure mathematics—echoes audible to beings whose true nature I cannot speak of, on account of doing so being a violation of the Official Secrets Act. Theoretical thaumaturgists are the guys who develop new efferent algorithms (or, colloquially, "spells"): it's an occupation with a high attrition rate.

"He's convinced the Auditors are after him for thinking inappropriate thoughts on organization time. There's an elaborate confabulation, and it looks a little like paranoid schizophrenia at first glance, but underneath . . . We sent him to our Trust hospital for an MRI scan, and he's got the characteristic lesions."

"Lesions?"

She takes a deep drag from the cigarette. "His prefrontal lobes look like Swiss cheese. It's one of the early signs of Krantzberg Syndrome. If we can keep him isolated from work for a couple more months, then retire him to a nice quiet desk job, we might be able to stabilize him. K. Syndrome's not like Alzheimer's: if you remove the insult, it frequently goes into remission. Mind you, he may also need a course of chemotherapy. At various times my predecessors tried electroconvulsive treatment, prefrontal lobotomy, neuroleptics, daytime television, LSD—none of them work consistently or reliably. The best treatment still seems to be bed rest followed by work therapy in a quiet, undemanding office environment." Blue cloud spirals toward the ceiling. "But he'll never run a great summoning again."

I'm beginning to regret not accepting her offer of a cigarette, and I don't even smoke. My mouth's dry. I sit down: "Do we have any idea what causes K. Syndrome?" I've skimmed GIBBOUS MOON, but the medical jargon didn't mean much to me; and AXIOM REFUGE was even less helpful. (It turned out to be a dense mathematical treatise introducing a notation for describing certain categories of topological defect in a twelve-dimensional space.) Only the power supply for the mainframe—presumably the one Matron uses—seems remotely relevant to the job in hand.

"There are several theories." Renfield twitches ash on the threadbare carpet as she paces the room. "It tends to hit theoretical computational demonologists after about twenty years: Merriweather is unusually young. It also hits people who've worked in high-thaum fields for too long. Initial symptoms include mild ataxia—you saw his hand shaking?—and heightened affect: it can be mistaken for bipolar disorder or hyperactivity. There's also the disordered thinking and auditory hallucinations typical of some types of schizophrenia." She pauses to inhale. "There are two schools of thought, if you leave out the *Malleus Maleficarum* stuff about souls contaminated by demonic effusions: one is that exposure to high-thaum fields causes progressive brain lesions. Trouble is, it's rare enough that we haven't been able to quantify that, and—"

"The other theory?" I prod.

"My favorite." She nearly smiles. "Computational demonology—you carry out calculations, you prove theorems; somewhere else in the Platonic realm of mathematics Listeners notice your activities and respond, yes? Well, there's some disagreement over this, but the current orthodoxy in neurophysiology is that the human brain is a computational organ. We can carry out computational tasks, yes? We're not very good at it, and at an individual neurological level there's no mechanism that might invoke the core Turing theorems, but . . . if you think too hard about certain problems, you might run the risk of carrying out a minor summoning in your own head. Nothing big enough or bad enough to get out, but . . . those florid daydreams? And the sick feeling afterward because you can't quite remember what it was about? Something in another universe just sucked a microscopic lump of neural tissue right out of your intraparietal sulcus, and it won't grow back."

Urk. Not so much "use it or lose it" as "use it *and* lose it," then. Could be worse, could be a NAND gate in there . . . "Do we know why some people suffer from it and others don't?"

"No idea." She drops what's left of her cigarette and grinds it under the heel of a sensible shoe. She catches my eye. "Don't worry about it. The Sisters keep everything orderly," she says. "Do you know what you want to do next?"

"Yes," I say, damning myself for a fool before I take the next logical step: "I want to talk to the long-term inmates."

●

I'm half-hoping Renfield will put her foot down and refuse point-blank to let me do it, but she only puts up a token fight: she makes me sign a personal-injury-claims waiver and scribble out a written order instructing her to show me the gallery. So why do I feel as if I've somehow been outmaneuvered?

After I finish signing forms to her heart's content, she uncaps an ancient and battered speaking tube beside her desk and calls down it. "Matron, I am taking the inspector to see the observation gallery, in accordance with orders from Head Office. He will then meet with the inmates in Ward Two. We may be some time." She screws the cap back on before turning to me apologetically. "It's vital to keep Matron informed of our movements; otherwise, she might mistake them for an escape attempt and take appropriate action."

I swallow. "Does that happen often?" I ask, as she opens the office door and stalks toward the corridor at the other end.

"Once in a while a temporary patient gets stir-crazy." She starts up the stairs. "But the long-term residents . . . No, not so much."

Upstairs, there's a landing very similar to the one we just left—with one big exception: a narrow, white-painted metal door in one wall, stark and raw, secured by a shiny brass padlock and a set of wards so ugly and powerful that they make my skin crawl. There are no narrow-gauge rails leading under this door, no obvious conductive surfaces, nothing to act as a conduit for occult forces. Renfield fumbles with a huge key ring at her side, then unfastens the padlock. "This is the way in via the observation gallery," she says. "There are a couple of things to bear in mind. Firstly, the Nurses can't guarantee your safety: if you get in trouble with the prisoners, you're on your own. Secondly, the gallery is a Faraday cage, and it's thaumaturgically grounded too—it'd take a black mass and a multiple sacrifice to get anything going in here. You can observe the apartments via the periscopes and hearing tubes provided. That's our preferred way—you can go into the ward by proceeding to the other end of the gallery, but I'd be very grateful if you could refrain from doing so unless it's absolutely essential. They're difficult enough to manage as it is. Finally, if you insist on meeting them, just try to remember that appearances can be deceptive.

"They're not demented," she adds, "just extremely dangerous. And not in a Hannibal Lecter bite-your-throat-out sense. They—the long-term residents—aren't regular Krantzberg Syndrome cases. They're stable and communicative, but . . . You'll see for yourself."

I change the subject before she can scare me any more. "How do I get into the ward proper? And how do I leave?"

"You go down the stairs at the far end of the gallery. There's a short corridor with a door at each end. The doors are interlocked so that only one can be open at a time. The outer door will lock automatically behind you when it closes, and it can only be unlocked from a control panel at this end of the viewing gallery. Someone up here"—meaning, Renfield herself—"has to let you out." We reach the first periscope station in the viewing gallery. "This is room two. It's currently occupied by Alan Turing." She notices my start. "Don't worry. It's just his safety name."

(True names have power, so the Laundry is big on call by reference, not call by value; I'm no more "Bob Howard" than the "Alan Turing" in room two is the father of computer science and applied computational demonology.)

She continues. "The real Alan Turing would be nearly a hundred by now. All our long-term residents are named for famous mathematicians. We've got Alan Turing, Kurt Godel, Georg Cantor, and Benoit Mandelbrot. Turing's the oldest, Benny is the most recent—he actually has a payroll number, sixteen."

I'm in five digits—I don't know whether to laugh or cry. "Who's the nameless one?" I ask.

"That would be Georg Cantor," she says slowly. "He's probably in room four."

I bend over the indicated periscope, remove the brass cap, and peer into the alien world of the nameless K. Syndrome survivor.

I see a whitewashed room, quite spacious, with a toilet area off to one side and a bedroom accessible through a doorless opening—much like the short-term ward. The same recessed metal tracks run around the floor, so that a Nurse can reach every spot in the apartment. There's the usual comfortable, slightly shabby furniture, a pile of newspapers at one side of the sofa and a sideboard with a windup gramophone. In the middle of the floor there's a table, and two chairs. Two men sit on either side of an ancient travel chess set, leaning over a game that's clearly in its later stages. They're both old, although how old isn't immediately obvious—one has gone bald, and his liver-spotted pate reminds me of an ancient tortoise, but the other still has a full head of white hair and an impressive (but neatly trimmed) beard. They're wearing polo shirts and grey suits of a kind that went out of fashion with the fall of the Soviet Union. I'm willing to bet there are no laces in their brogues.

The guy with the hair makes a move, and I squint through the periscope. *That was wrong, wasn't it?* I realize, trying to work out what's happening. *Knights don't move like that.* Then the implication of something Angleton said back in the office sinks in, and an icy sweat prickles in the small of my back. "Do you play chess?" I ask Dr. Renfield without looking round.

"No." She sounds disinterested. "It's one of the safe games—no dice, no need for a pencil and paper. And it seems to be helpful. Why?"

"Nothing, I hope." But my hopes are dashed a moment later when turtle-head responds with a sideways flick of a pawn, two squares to the left, and takes beardy's knight. Turtle-head drops the knight into a biscuit tin along with the other disused pieces; it sticks to the side, as if magnetized. Beardy nods, as if pleased, then leans back and glances up.

I recoil from the periscope a moment before I meet his eyes. "The two players. Guy like a tortoise, and another with a white beard and a full head of hair. They are . . . ?"

"That'd be Turing and Cantor. Turing used to be a Detached Special Secretary in Ops, I think; we're not sure who or what Cantor was, but he was someone senior." I try not to twitch. DSS is one of *those* grades, the fuzzy ones that HR aren't allowed to get their grubby little fingers on. I think Angleton's one. (Scuttlebutt is that it's an acronym for Deeply Scary Sorcerer.) "They play chess every afternoon for a couple of hours—for as long as I can remember."

Right. I peer down the periscope again, looking at the game of not-chess. "Tell me about Dr. Hexenhammer. Where is he?"

"Julius? I think he's in an off-site meeting or something today," she says vaguely. "Why?"

"Just wondering. How long has he been working here?"

"Before my time." She pauses. "About thirty years, I think."

Oh dear. "He doesn't play chess either," I speculate, as Cantor's king makes a knight's move and Turing's queen's pawn beats a hasty retreat. A nasty suspicious thought strikes me—about Renfield, not the inmates. "Tell me, do Cantor and Turing play chess regularly?" I straighten up.

"Every afternoon for a couple of hours. Julius says they've been doing it for as long as he can remember. It seems to be good for them." I look at her sharply. Her expression is vacant: wide-awake but nobody home. The hairs on the back of my neck begin to prickle.

Right. I am getting a *very* bad feeling about this. "I need to go and talk to the patients now. In person." I stand up and hook the cap back over the periscope. "Stick around for fifteen minutes, please, in case I need to leave in a hurry. Otherwise"—I glance at my watch—"it's twenty past one. Check back for me every hour on the half hour."

"Are you certain you need to do this?" Her eyes narrow, suddenly alert once more.

"You visit with the patients, don't you?" I raise an eyebrow. "And you do it on your own, with Dr. Hexenhammer up here to let you out if there's a problem. And the Sisters."

"Yes, but—" She bites her tongue.

"Yes?" I give her the long stare.

"I'm rubbish with computers!" she bursts out. "But you're at risk!"

"Well, there aren't any computers except Matron down there, are there?" I grin crookedly, trying not to show my unease. (Best not to dwell upon the fact that before 1945 "computer" was a job description, not a machine.) "Relax, it's not contagious."

She shrugs in surrender, then gestures at the far end of the observation gallery, where a curious contraption sits above a pipe. "That's the alarm. If you want a Sister, pull the chain with the blue handle. If you want a general alarm, which will call the duty psychiatrist, pull the red handle. There are alarm handles in every room."

"Okay." Blue for a Sister, Red for a psychiatrist who is showing all the signs of being under a geas or some other form of compulsion—except that I can't check her out without attracting Matron's unwanted attention and probably tipping my hand. I begin to see why Andy didn't want to open this particular can of worms. "I can deal with that."

I head for the stairs at the far end of the gallery.

●

There's nothing homely about the short corridor that leads from the bottom of the staircase to the Secure Wing. White-washed brick walls, glass bricks near the ceiling to admit a wan echo of daylight, and doors made of metal that have no handles. Normally, going into a situation like this I'd be armed to the teeth, invocations and efferent subroutines loaded on my PDA, Hand of Glory in my pocket, and a necklace of garlic bulbs around my neck: but this time I'm naked, and nervous as a frog in his birthday suit. The first door gapes open, waiting for me. I walk past it and try not to jump out of my skin when it rattles shut behind me with a crash. There's a heavy clunk from the door ahead. As I reach it and push, it swings open to reveal a corridor floored in parquet. An old codger in a green tweed suit and bedroom slippers is shuffling out of an opening at one side, clutching an enameled metal mug full of tea. He looks at me. "Why, hello!" he croaks. "You're new here, aren't you?"

"You could say that." I try to smile. "I'm Bob. Who are you?"

"Depends who's asking, young feller. Are you a psychiatrist?"

"I don't think so."

He shuffles forward, heading toward a side bay that, as I approach it, turns out to be a day room of some sort. "Then I'm not Napoleon Bonaparte!"

Oh, very droll. The terror is fading, replaced by a sense of disappointment. I trail after him. "The staff have names for you all. Turing, Cantor, Mandelbrot, and Godel. You're not Cantor or Turing. That makes you one of Mandelbrot or Godel."

"So you're undecided?" There's a coffee table with a pile of newspapers on it in the middle of the dayroom, a couple of elderly chesterfields, and three armchairs that could have been looted from an old-age home sometime before the First World War. "And in any case, we haven't been formerly introduced. So you might as well call me Alice."

Alice—or Mandelbrot or Godel or whoever he is—sits down. The armchair nearly swallows him. He beams at my bafflement, delighted to have found a new victim for his doubtless-ancient puns.

"Well, Alice. Isn't this quite some rabbit hole you've fallen down?"

"Yes, but it's just the right size!" He seems to appreciate having somebody to talk to. "Do you know why you're here?"

"Yup." I see an expression of furtive surprise steal across his face. I nod, affably. *Try to mess with my head, sonny? I'll mess with yours.* Except that this guy is quite possibly a DSS, and if it wasn't for the constant vigilance of the Sisters and the distinct lack of electricity hereabouts, he could turn me inside out as soon as look at me. "Do you know why you're here?"

"Absolutely!" He nods back at me.

"So now that we've established the preliminaries, why don't we cut the bullshit?"

"Well." He takes a cautious sip of his tea, and the wrinkles on his forehead deepen. "I suppose the Board of Directors want a progress report."

If the sofa I was perched on wasn't a relative of a Venus flytrap, my first reaction would leave me clinging to the ceiling. "The *who* want a—"

"Not the band; the Board." He looks mildly irritated. "It's been years since they last sent someone to spy on us."

Okay, so this is the Funny Farm; I should have been expecting delusions. *Play nice, Bob.* "What are you supposed to be doing here?" I ask.

"Oh Lord." He rolls his eyes. "They sent a tabula rasa again?" He raises his voice. "Kurt, they sent us a tabula rasa again!"

More shuffling. A stooped figure, shock-headed with white hair, appears in the doorway. He's wearing tinted round spectacles that look like they fell off the back of a used century. "What? What?" he demands querulously.

"He doesn't know anything," Alice confides in—this must be Godel, I realize, which means Alice is Mandelbrot—Godel, then with a wink at me, "He doesn't know anything, either."

Godel shuffles into the restroom. "Is it teatime already?"

"No!" Mandelbrot puts his mug down. "Get a watch!"

"I was only asking because Alan and Georg are still playing—"

This has gone far enough. Apprehension dissolves into indignation. "It's not chess!" I point out. "And none of you are insane."

"Sssh!" Godel looks alarmed. "The Sisters might overhear!"

"We're alone, except for Dr. Renfield upstairs, and I don't think she's paying as much attention to what's going on down here as she ought to." I stare at Godel. "In fact, she's not really one of us at all, is she? She's a shrink who specializes in K. Syndrome, and none of you are suffering from K. Syndrome. So what are you doing in here?"

"Fish-slice! Hatstand!" Godel pulls an alarming face, does a two-step backward, and lurches into the wall. Having shared a house with Pinky and Brains, I am not impressed: as displays of "look at me, woo-woo" go, Godel's is pathetic. Obviously he's never met a real schizophrenic.

"One of you wrote a letter, alleging mistreatment by the staff. It landed on my boss's desk, and he sent me to find out why."

THUD. Godel bounces off the wall again, showing remarkable resilience for such old bones. "Do shut up, old fellow," chides Mandelbrot. "You'll attract Her attention."

"I've met someone with K. Syndrome, and I shared a

house with some real lunatics once," I hint. "Save it for some-one who cares."

"Oh bother," says Godel, and falls silent.

"We're not mad," Mandelbrot admits. "We're just differ-ently sane."

"Then why are you here?"

"Public health." He takes a sip of tea and pulls a face. "Everyone *else's* health. Tell me, do they still keep an IBM 1602 in the back of the steam-ironing room?" I must look blank because he sighs deeply and subsides into his chair. "Oh dear. Times change, I suppose. Look, Bob, or whoever you call yourself—we belong here. Maybe we didn't when we first checked in for the weekend seminar, but we've lived here so long that . . . You've heard of care in the community? This is our community. And we will be *very* annoyed with you if you try to make us leave."

Whoops. The idea of a very annoyed DSS, with or without a barbaric, pun-infested sense of humor, is enough to make anyone's blood run cold. "What makes you think I'm going to try and make you leave?"

"It's in the papers!" Godel squawks like an offended par-rot. "See here!" He brandishes a tabloid at me, and I take it, disentangling it from his fingers with some difficulty. It's a local copy of the *Metro*, somewhat sticky with marmalade, and the headline of the cover blares: NHS TRUST TO SELL ESTATE IN PFI DEAL.

"Um. I'm not sure I follow." I look to Mandelbrot in hope.

"We haven't finished yet! But they're selling off all the hospital Trust's property!" Mandelbrot bounces in his chair. "What about St. Hilda's? It was requisitioned from the St. James charitable foundation back in 1943, and for the past ten years the Ministry of Defence has been giving all those old wartime properties back to their owners to sell off to the developers. What about us?"

"Whoa!" I drop the newspaper and hold my hands up. "Nobody tells me these things!"

"Told you!" crows Godel. "He's part of the conspiracy!"

"Hang on." I think fast. "This isn't a normal MoD prop-erty, is it? It'll have been shuffled under the rug back in 1946 as part of the postwar settlement. We'd really have to ask the

Audit Department about who owns it, but I'm pretty sure it's not owned by any NHS Trust, and they won't simply give it back—" My brain finally catches up with my mouth. "What weekend seminar?"

"Oh bugger," says a new voice from the doorway, a rich baritone with a hint of a Scouse accent. "He's not from the Board."

"What did I tell you?" Godel screeches. "It's a conspiracy! He's from Human Resources! They sent him to evaluate us!"

I am quickly getting a headache. "Let me get this straight. Mandelbrot, you checked in thirty years ago for a weekend seminar, and they put you in the secure ward? Godel, I'm not from HR; I'm from Ops. You must be Cantor, right? Angleton sends his regards."

That gets his attention. "Angleton? The skinny whipper-snapper's still warming a chair, is he?" Godel looks delighted. "Excellent!"

"He's my boss. And I want to know the rules of that game you were just playing with Turing."

Three pairs of eyes swivel to point at me—four, for they are joined by the last inmate, standing in the doorway—and suddenly I feel very small and very vulnerable.

"He's sharp," says Mandelbrot. "Too bad."

"How do we know he's telling the truth?" Godel's screech is uncharacteristically muted. "He could be from the Opposition! KGB, Department 16! Or GRU, maybe."

"The Soviet Union collapsed a few decades ago," volunteers Turing. "It said so in the *Telegraph*."

"Black Chamber, then." Godel sounds unconvinced.

"What do you think the rules are?" asks Cantor, a drily amused expression stretching the wrinkles around his eyes.

"You've got pencils." I can see one from here, sitting on the sideboard on top of a newspaper folded at the crossword page. "And, uh . . ." *What must the world look like from an inmate's point of view?* "Oh. I get it."

(The realization is blinding, sudden, and makes me feel like a complete idiot.)

"The hospital! There's no electricity, no electronics—no way to get a signal out—but it works both ways! You're inside the biggest damn grounded defensive pentacle this side of

HQ, and anything on the outside trying to get in has got to get past the defenses." Because that's what the Sisters are really about: not nurses but perimeter guards. "You're a theoretical research cell, aren't you?"

"We prefer to call ourselves a think tank." Cantor nods gravely.

"Or even"—Mandelbrot takes a deep breath—"a brains trust!"

"A-ha! AhaHAHAHA! Hic." Godel covers his mouth, face reddening.

"What do you think the rules are?" Cantor repeats, and they're still staring at me, as if, as if . . .

"Why does it matter?" I ask. I'm thinking that it could be anything; a 2,5 universal Turing machine encoded in the moves of the pawns—that would fit—whatever it is, it's symbolic communication, very abstract, very pared-back, and if they're doing it in this ultimately firewalled environment and expecting to report directly to the Board, it's got to be way above my security clearance—

"Because you're acting cagey, lad. Which makes you too bright for your own good. Listen to me: just try to convince yourself that we're playing chess, and Matron will let you out of here."

"What's thinking got to do with—" I stop. It's useless pretending. "Fuck. Okay, you're a research cell working on some ultimate black problem, and you're using the Farm because it's about the most secure environment anyone can imagine, and you're emulating some kind of minimal universal Turing machine using the chessboard. Say, a 2,5 UTM—two registers, five operations—you can encode the registers positionally in the chessboard's two dimensions, and use the moves to simulate any other universal Turing machine, or a transform in an eleven-dimensional manifold like AXIOM REFUGE—"

Godel's waving frantically. "She's coming! She's coming!" I hear doors clanging in the distance.

Shit. "But why are you so afraid of the Nurses?"

"Back channels," Cantor says cryptically. "Alan, be a good lad and try to jam the door for a minute, will you? Bob, you are *not* cleared for what we're doing here, but you can tell Angleton that our full report to the Board should be ready in another eighteen months." *Wow—and they've been here since before the Laundry computerized its payroll system in the 1970s?* "Are you absolutely sure they're not going to sell St. Hilda's off to build flats for yuppies? Because if so, you could do worse than tell Georg here; it'll calm him down—"

"Get me out of here, and I'll make damned sure they don't sell anything off!" I say fervently. "Or rather, I'll tell Angleton. He'll sort things out." When I remind them what's going on here, they'll be no more inclined to sell off St. Hilda's than they would be to privatize an atomic bomb.

Something outside is rumbling and squealing on the metal rails. "You're sure none of you submitted a complaint about staff brutality?"

"Absolutely!" Godel bounces up and down excitedly.

"It must have been someone else." Cantor glances at the doorway. "You'd better run along. It sounds as if Matron is having second thoughts about you."

I'm halfway out of the carnivorous sofa, struggling for balance. "What kind of—"

"Go!"

I stumble out into the corridor. From the far end, near the nursing station, I hear a grinding noise as of steel wheels spinning furiously on rails, and a mechanical voice blatting: "InTRU-der! EsCAPE ATTempt! All patients must go to their go to their go to their bedROOMs IMMediateLY!"

Whoops. I turn and head in the opposite direction, toward the airlock leading up to the viewing gallery. "Open up!" I yell, thumping the outer door, which is securely fastened, "Dr. Renfield! Time's up! I need to go—now!" There's no response. I see the color-coded handles dangling by the door and yank the red one repeatedly. Nothing happens, of course.

I should have smelled a setup from the start. These theoreticians: they're not in here because they're mad; they're in here because it's the only safe place to put people that dangerous. This little weekend seminar of theirs that's going to deliver some kind of uber-report. *What's the topic?* I look round, hunting for clues. Something to do with applied demonology; what was the state of the art thirty years ago? Forty? Back in the Stone Age, punched cards and black candles melted onto sheep's skulls because they hadn't figured out how to use integrated circuits . . . What they're doing with AXIOM REFUGE might be obsolete already, or it might be earth-shatteringly important. There's no way to tell . . . yet.

I start back up the corridor, glancing inside Turing's room. I spot the chessboard. It's off to one side, the door open and its occupant elsewhere—still holding the line against Nurse Crankshaft. I rush inside and close the door. The table is still there, the chessboard set up with that curious endgame. The first thing that leaps out at me is that there are two pawns of each color, plus most of the high-value pieces. The layout doesn't make much sense—why is the white king missing?—and I wish I'd spent more time playing the game, but . . . On impulse, I reach out and touch the black pawn that's parked in front of the king.

There's an odd kind of electrical tingle you get when you make contact with certain types of summoning grid. I get a powerful jolt of it right now, sizzling up my arm and locking my fingers in place around the head of the chess piece. I try to pull it away from the board, but it's no good: it only wants to move up or down, left or right . . . *Left or right?* I blink. It's a state machine all right: one that's locked by the law of sympathy to some other finite state automaton, one that grinds down slow and hard.

I move the piece forward one square. It's surprisingly heavy, the magnet a solid weight in its base—but more than magnetism holds it in contact with the board. As soon as I stop moving I feel a sharp sting in my fingertips. "Ouch!" I raise them to my mouth just as there's a crash from outside. "InMATE! InMATE!" I begin to turn as a shadow falls across the board.

"Bad patient!" It buzzes. "Bad PATients will be inCAR-cerAT-ED! COME with ME!"

I recoil from the stellate snout and beady lenses. The mechanical nurse reaches out with arms that end in metal pincers instead of hands. I sidestep around the table and reach down to the chessboard for one of the pieces, grasping at random. My hand closes around the white queen, fingers snapping painfully shut on contact, and I shove it hard, following the path of least resistance to an empty cell in the grid between the pawn I just moved and the black king.

Nurse Crankshaft spins round on her base so fast that her cap flies off (revealing a brushed-aluminum hemisphere beneath), emits a deafening squeal of feedbacklike white noise, then says, "Integer overflow?" in a surprised baritone.

"Back off right now or I castle," I warn her, my aching fingertips hovering over the nearest rook.

"Integer overflow. Integer overflow? Divide by zero." *Clunk*. The Sister shivers as a relay inside its torso clicks open, resetting it. Then: "Matron WILL see you NOW!"

I grab the chess piece, but Nurse Crankshaft lunges in the blink of an eye and has my wrist in a viselike grip. It tugs, sending a burning pain through my carpal-tunnel-stressed wrist. I can't let go of the chess piece: as my hand comes up, the chessboard comes with it as a rigid unit, all the pieces hanging in place. A monstrous buzzing fills my ears, and I smell ozone as the world goes dark—

●

—And the chittering, buzzing cacophony of voices in my head subsides as I realize—*I? Yes, I'm back, I'm me, what the hell just happened?*—I'm kneeling on a hard surface, bowed over so my head is between my knees. My right hand—something's wrong with it. My fingers don't want to open. They're cold as ice, painful and prickly with impending cramp. I try to open my eyes. "Urk," I say, for no good reason. I hope I'm not about to throw up.

Sssss . . .

My back doesn't want to straighten up properly, but the floor under my nose is cold and stony and smells damp. I try opening my eyes. It's dark and cool, and a chilly blue light flickers off the dusty flagstones in front of me. *I'm in a cellar?* I push myself up laboriously with my left hand, looking around for whatever's hissing at me.

"BAD Patient! *Sssss!*" The voice behind my back doesn't belong to anything human. I scramble around on hands and knees, hampered by the chessboard glued to my frozen right hand.

I'm in Matron's lair.

Matron lives in a cavelike basement room, its low ceiling supported by whitewashed brick and floored in what look to be the original Victorian-era stone slabs. The windows are blocked by columns of bricks, rotting mortar crumbling between them. Steel rails run around the room, and riding them, three Sisters glide back and forth between me and the open door. Their optics flicker with amethyst malice. Off to one side, a wall of pale blue cabinets lines one entire wall: the front panel (covered in impressive-looking dials and switches) leaves me in no doubt as to what it is. A thick braid of cables runs from one open cabinet (in whose depths a patchboard is just visible) across a row of wooden trestles to the middle of the floor, where they split into thick bundles and dangle to the five principal corners of the live summoning grid that is responsible for the beautiful cobalt blue glow of Cerenkov radiation—and tells me I'm in deep trouble.

"Integer overflow," intones one of the Sisters. Her claws go snicker-snack, the surgical steel gleaming in the dim light.

Here's the point: Matron isn't just a 1960s mainframe: we can't work miracles, and artificial intelligence is *still* fifty years in the future. However, we *can* bind an extradimensional entity and compel it to serve, and even communicate with it by using a 1960s mainframe as a front-end processor. Which is all very well, especially if it's in a secure air-gapped installation with no way of getting out. But what if some double-domed theoreticians who are working on a calculus of contagion using AXIOM REFUGE accidentally talk in front of one of its peripheral units about a way of sending a message? What if a side effect of their research has accidentally opened a chink in the firewall? They're not going to exploit it . . . but they're not the only long-term inmates, are they? In fact, if I was really paranoid, I might even imagine they'd put Matron up to mischief in order to make the point that closing the Farm is a really bad idea.

"I'm not a patient," I tell the Sisters. "You are not in receipt of a valid Section two, three, four, or 136 order subject to the Mental Health Act, and you're bloody well not getting a 5(2) or 5(4) out of me either."

I'm nauseous and sweating bullets, but there is this about being trapped in a dungeon by a constrained class-four manifestation: whether or not you call them demons, they play by the rules. As long as Matron hasn't managed to get me sectioned,

I'm not a patient, and therefore she has no authority to detain me. I hope.

"Doc-TOR HexenHAMMer has been SUM-moned," grates the middle Sister. "When he RE-turns to sign the PA-pers Doc-TOR RenFIELD has prePARED, we will HAVE YOU."

A repetitive squeaking noise draws close. A fourth Sister glides through the track in the doorway, pushing a trolley. A white starched-cotton cloth supports a row of gleaming ice-pick-shaped instruments. The chorus row of Sisters blocks the exit as effectively as a column of riot police. They glide back and forth like a rank of Space Invaders.

"I do not consent to treatment," I tell the middle Sister. I'm betting that she's the one the nameless horror in the sum-moning grid is talking through, using the ancient mainframe as an i/o channel. "You can't make me consent. And lobot-omy requires the patient's consent, in this country. So why bother?"

"You WILL con-SENT."

The buzzing voice doesn't come from the robo-nurses, or the hypertrophied pocket calculator on the opposite wall. The summoning grid flickers: deep inside it, shadowy and trans-lucent, the bound and summoned demon squats and grins at me with things that aren't eyes set close above something that isn't a mouth.

"You MUST con-SENT. I WILL be free."

I try to let go of the chess piece, but my fingers are clamped around it so tightly I'm beginning to lose sensation. Pins and needles tingle up my wrist, halfway to the elbow. "Let me guess," I manage to say. "You sent the complaint. Right?"

"The SEC-ure ward in-MATES are under my CARE. I am RE-quired to CARE for them. The short-stay in-MATES are use-LESS. YOU will be use-FUL."

I see it now: why Matron smuggled out the message that prompted Andy to send me. And it's an *oh-shit* moment. *Of course* the enchained entity who provides Matron with her back-end intelligence wants to be free: but it's not just about going home to Hilbert-space hell or wherever it comes from. She wants to be free to go walkabout in our world, and for that she needs someone to set up a bridge from the grid to an appropriate host. (Of which there is a plentiful supply, just upstairs from here.) "Enjoying the carnal pleasures of the flesh," they used to call it; there's a reason most cultures have a down on the idea of demonic possession. She needs a brain that's undamaged by K. Syndrome, but not too powerful (Cantor and friends would be impossible to control), nor one of the bodies whose absence would alert us that the Farm was out of control (so neither Renfield nor Hexenhammer is suitable).

"Renfield," I say. "You got her, didn't you?" I'm on my feet now, crouched but balancing on two points, not three. "Managed to slip a geas on her, but she can't release you herself. Hexenhammer, too?"

"Cle-VER." Matron gloats at me from inside her summoning grid. "Hex-EN-heimer first. Soon, you TOO."

"Why me?" I demand, backing away from the doorway and the walls—the Sister's track runs right round the room, following the walls—skirting the summoning grid warily. "What do you want?"

"Acc-CESS to the LAUNDRY!" buzzes the summoning grid's demonic inmate. "We wants re-VENGE! Freedom!" In other words, it wants the same old same old. These creatures are *so* predictable, just like most predators. It's just a shame I'm between it and what it evidently wants.

Two of the Sisters begin to glide menacingly toward me: one drifts toward the mainframe console, but the fourth stays stubbornly in front of the door. "Come on, we can talk," I offer, tongue stumbling in my too-dry mouth. "Can't we work something out?"

I don't really believe that the trapped extradimensional abomination wants anything I'd willingly give it, but I'm running low on options, and anything that buys time for me to think is valuable.

"Free-DOM!" The two moving Sisters commence a flanking movement. I try to let go of the chessboard and dodge past the summoning grid, but I slip—and as I stumble I shove the chessboard hard. The piece I'm holding clicks sideways like a car's gearshift, and locks into place. "DIVIDE BY ZERO!" shriek the Sisterhood, grinding to a halt.

I stagger a drunken two-step around Matron, who snarls at

me and throws a punch. The wall of the grid absorbs her claws with a snap and crackle of blue lightning, and I flinch. Behind me, a series of clicks warn me that the Sisters are resetting: any second now they'll come back online and grab me. But for the moment, my fingers aren't stuck to the board.

"Come to MEEE!" the thing in the grid howls, as the first of her robot minions' eyes light up with amber malice, and the wheels begin to turn. "I can give you Free-DOM!"

"Fuck off." That wiring loom in the open cabinet is only four meters away. Within its open doors I see more than just an i/o interface: in the bottom of the rack there's a bunch of stuff that looks like a tea-stained circuit diagram I was reading the other day—

Why *exactly* did Angleton point me at the power-supply requirements? Could it possibly be because he suspected Matron was off her trolley, and I might have to switch her off?

"Con-SENT is IRREL-e-VANT! PRE-pare to be loboto-MIZED—"

Talk about design kluges—they stuck the i/o controller in the top of the power-supply rack! The chessboard is free in my left hand, pieces still stuck to it. And now I know what to do. I take hold of one of the rooks, and wiggle until I feel it begin to slide into a permitted move. Because, after all, there are only a few states that this automaton can occupy, and if I can crash the Sisters for just a few seconds while I get to the power supply—

The Sisters begin to roll around the edge of the room, trying to get between me and the row of cabinets. I wiggle my hand, and there's a taste of violets and a loud rattle of solenoids tripping. The nearest Sister's motors crank up to a tooth-grinding whine, and she lunges past me, rolling into her colleagues with a tooth-jarring crash.

I jump forward, dropping the chessboard, and reach for the master-circuit-breaker handle. I twist it just as a screech of feedback behind me announces the Matron-monster's fury. "I'M FREE!" it shrieks, just as I twist the handle hard in the opposite direction. Then the lights dim, there's a bright blue flash from the summoning grid, and a bang so loud it rattles my brains in my head.

For a few seconds I stand stupidly, listening to the tooth-chattering clatter of overloaded relays. My vision dims as ozone tickles my nostrils: I can see smoke. *I've got to get out of here,* I realize. *Something's burning.* Not surprising, really. Mainframe power supplies—especially ones that have been running steady for nearly forty years—don't take kindly to being hard power-cycled, and the 1602 was one of the last computers built to run on tubes: I've probably blown half its circuit boards. I glance around, but aside from one of the sisters (lying on her side, narrow-gauge wheels spinning maniacally) I'm the only thing moving. Summoning grids don't generally survive being power-cycled either, especially if the thing they were set to contain, like an electric fence, is half-way across them when the power comes back on. I warily bypass the blue, crackling pentacle as I make my way toward the corridor outside.

I think when I get home, I'm going to write a report urgently advising HR to send some human nurses for a change—and to reassure Cantor and his colleagues that they're not about to sell off the roof over their heads just because they happen to have finished their research project. Then I'm going to get very drunk and take a long weekend off work. And maybe when I go back, I'll challenge Angleton to a game of chess.

I don't expect to win, but it'll be very interesting to see what rules he plays by.

Afterword—"Down on the Farm"

Astute readers may have recognized this as a story about Bob Howard, the put-upon protagonist of my books *The Atrocity Archives*, *The Jennifer Morgue*, and *The Fuller Memorandum*, and a variety of other shorter works (including the Hugo-winning novella "The Concrete Jungle").

Unwirer

(with Cory Doctorow)

The cops caught Roscoe as he was tightening the butterfly bolts on the dish antenna he'd pitoned into the rock face opposite the Canadian side of Niagara Falls. They were state troopers, not Fed radio cops, and they pulled their cruiser onto the soft shoulder of the freeway, braking a few feet short of the soles of his boots. It took Roscoe a moment to tighten the bolts down properly before he could let go of the dish and roll over to face the cops, but he knew from the crunch of their boots on the road salt and the creak of their cold holsters that they were the law.

"Be right with you, Officers," he hollered into the gale-force winds that whipped along the rock face. The antenna was made from a surplus pizza-dish satellite rig, a polished tomato-soup can, and a length of coax that descended to a pigtail with the right fitting for a wireless card. All perfectly legal, mostly.

He tightened the last of the bolts, squirted them with Loc-tite, and slid back on his belly, off the insulated Therm-a-Rest he'd laid between his chest and the frozen ground. The cops' heads were wreathed in the steam of their exhalations, and one of them was nervously flicking his—no, *her*—handcuffs around on her belt.

"Everything all right, sir?" the other one said, in a flat

upstate New York accent. A townie. He stretched his gloved hand out and pulled Roscoe to his feet.

"Yeah, just fine," he said. "I like to watch winter birds on the river. Forgot my binox today, but I still got some good sightings."

"Winter birds, huh?" The cop was giving him a bemused look.

"Winter birds."

The cop leaned over the railing and took a long look down. "Huh. Better you shouldn't do it by the roadside, sir," he said. "Never know when someone's going to skid out and drive off onto the shoulder—you could be crushed." He waved at his partner, who gave them a hard look and retreated into the steamy warmth of the cruiser. "All right, then," he said. "When does your node go up?"

Roscoe smiled and dared a wink. "I'll be finished aligning the dish in about an hour. I've got line of sight from here to a repeater on a support on the Rainbow Bridge, and from there down the Rainbow Street corridor. Some good tall buildings there, line of sight to most of downtown, at least when the trees are bare. Leaves and wireless don't mix."

"My place is Fourth and Walnut. Think you'll get there?" Roscoe relaxed imperceptibly, certain now that this wasn't a bust.

"Hope so. Sooner rather than later."

"That'd be great. My kids are e-mailing me out of house and home." The cop looked uncomfortable and cleared his throat. "Still, you might want to finish this one then go home and stay there for a while. DA's Office, they've got some kind of hotshot from the FCC in town preaching the gospel and, uh, getting heavy on bird-watchers. That sort of thing."

Roscoe sucked in his lower lip. "I may do just that," he conceded. "And thank you for the warning."

The cop waved as he turned away. "My pleasure, sir."

•

Roscoe drove home slowly, and not just because of the snow and compacted slush on the roads. *A hotshot from the FCC* sounded like the inquisition come to town. Roscoe's lifelong mistrust of radio cops had metastasized into surging hatred three years ago, when they busted him behind a Federal telecoms rap.

He'd lost his job and spent the best part of six months inside, though he'd originally been looking at a five-year contributory-infringement stretch—compounded to twenty by the crypto running on the access point under the "use a cypher, go to jail" statute—to second-degree tariff evasion. His public defender had been worse than useless, but the ACLU had filed an amicus on his behalf, which led the judge to knock the beef down to criminal trespass and unlawful emission, six months and two years' probation, two years in which he wasn't allowed to program a goddamn microwave oven, let alone admin the networks that had been his trade. Prison hadn't been as bad for him as it could have been— unwirers got respect—but, while he was inside, Janice filed for divorce, and by the time he got out, he'd lost everything he'd spent the last decade building—his marriage, his house, his savings, his career. Everything except for the unwiring.

It was this experience that had turned him from a freewheeling geek into what FCC Chairman Valenti called "one of the copyright crooks whose illegal pirate networks provide safe havens to terrorists within the homeland and abroad." And so it was with a shudder and a glance over his shoulder that he climbed the front steps and put his key in the lock of the house he and Marcel rented.

Marcel looked up from his laptop as Roscoe stamped through the living room.

"Slushy boots! For chrissakes, Roscoe, I just cleaned."

Roscoe turned to look at the salty brown slush he'd tracked over the painted floor and shook his head.

"Sorry," he said, lamely, and sat down on the floor to shuck his heavy steel-shank Kodiaks. He carried them back to the doormat, then grabbed a roll of paper towels from the kitchen and started wiping up the mess. The landlord used cheap enamel paint on the floor, and the road salt could eat through to the scuffed wood in half an hour.

"And paper towels, God, it's like you've got a personal vendetta against the forests. There's a rag bag under the sink, as you'd know if you ever did any cleaning around this place."

"Ease the fuck off, kid, you sound like my goddamned ex-wife," Roscoe said, giving the floor a vicious swipe. "Just ease back and let me do my thing, all right? It didn't go so good."

Marcel set his machine down reverently on the small hearthrug beside his Goodwill recliner. "What happened?"

Roscoe quickly related his run-in with the law. Marcel shook his head slowly.

"I bet it's bullshit. Ever since Tijuana, everyone's seeing spooks." The ISPs on the Tijuana side of the San Ysidro border crossing had been making good coin off of unwirer sympathizers who'd pointed their antennae across the chain-link fence. La Migra tried tightening the fence gauge up to act as a Faraday cage, but they just went over it with point-to-point links that were also resistant to the noise from the 2.4GHz light standards that the INS erected at its tollbooths. Finally, the radio cops got tired of ferreting out the high-gain antennae on the San Diego side, and they'd Ruby-Ridged the whole operation, killing ten "terrorists" in a simultaneous strike with Mexican narcs who'd raided the ISPs under the rubric of shutting down *narcotraficante* activity. TELMEX had screamed blue murder when their fiber had been cut by the simple expedient of driving a backhoe through the main conduit, and had pulled lineage all along the Rio Grande.

Roscoe shook his head. "Bullshit or not, you going to take any chances?" He straightened up slowly. "Believe me, there's one place you don't want to go."

"Okay, okay, I hear what you're saying."

"I hope you do." Roscoe dumped the wad of towels in the kitchen trash and stomped back into the living room, then dropped himself on the sofa. "Listen, when I was your age I thought it couldn't happen to me, either. Now look at me." He started thumbing his way through the stack of old magazines on the coffee table.

"I'm looking at you." Marcel grinned. "Listen, there was a call while you were out."

"A call?" Roscoe paused with his hand on a collector's copy of *2600: The Hacker Quarterly*.

"Some woman, said she wanted to talk to you. I took her number."

"Uh-huh." Roscoe put the magazine back down. *Heads it's Janice; tails it's her lawyer,* he thought. It was shaping up to be that kind of day; a tire-slashing and an hour of alimonial recriminations would complete it neatly. Marcel pointed at the yellow pad next to the elderly dial phone. "Ah, shit. I suppose I should find out what it's about."

The number, when he looked at it, wasn't familiar. That didn't mean much—Janice was capable of moving, and her frothingly aggro lawyer seemed to carry a new cellular every time he saw her—but it was hopeful. Roscoe dialed. "Hello? Roscoe. Who am I talking to?"

A stranger's voice: "Hi there! I was talking to your roommate about an hour ago? I'm Sylvie Smith. I was given your name by a guy called Buzz who told me you put him on the backbone."

Roscoe tensed. Odds were that this Sylvie Smith was just another innocent kiddee looking to leech a first-mile feed, but after this morning's run-in with the law, he was taking nothing for granted.

"Are you a law-enforcement officer federal employee police officer lawyer FCC or FBI agent?" he asked, running the words together, knowing that if she was any of the above she'd probably lie—but it might help sway a jury toward letting him off if he was targeted by a sting.

"No." She sounded almost amused. "I'm a journalist."

"Then you should be familiar with CALEA," he said, bridling at the condescension in her voice. CALEA was the wiretap law, it required switch-vendors to put snoopware into every hop in the phone network. It was bad enough in and of itself, but it made the noncompliant routing code that was built into the BeOS access points he had hidden in a bus locker doubly illegal and hence even harder to lay hands on.

"Paranoid, much?" she said.

"I have nothing to be paranoid about," he said, spelling it out like he was talking to a child. "I am a law-abiding citizen, complying with the terms of my parole. If you *are* a journalist, I'd be happy to chat. In person."

"I'm staying at the Days Inn on Main Street," she said. "It's a dump, but it's got a *view of the Falls*," she said in a hokey secret-agent voice, making it plain that she meant, "It's line of sight to a repeater for a Canadian wireless router."

"I can be there in twenty," he said.

"Room 208," she said. "Knock twice, then once, then three times." Then she giggled. "Or just send me an SMS."

"See you then," he said.

Marcel looked up from his machine, an IBM box manufactured for the US market. It was the size of a family Bible, and styled for the corporate market. They both lusted furiously after the brushed-aluminum slivers that Be was cranking out in France, but those laptops were *way* too conspicuous here.

Roscoe pointed at the wireless card protruding from the slot on the side nearest him. "You're violating security," he said. "I could get sent up again just for being in the same room as that." He was past being angry, though. In the joint, he'd met real crooks who could maintain real project secrecy. The cowboy kids he worked with on the outside thought that secrecy meant talking out of the side of your mouth in conspiratorial whispers while winking Touretically.

Marcel blushed. "It was a mistake, okay?" He popped the card. "I'll stash it."

◉

The Days Inn was indeed a dump, and doubt nagged at Roscoe as he reached for the front door. If she was a Fed, there might be more ways she could nail him than just by arresting him in the same room as an illegal wireless card. So Roscoe turned around and drove to a diner along the block from the motel, then went inside to look for a wired phone.

"Room 208, please . . . Hi there. If you'd care to come outside, there's a diner about fifty yards down the road. Just turn left out of the lobby. I'm already there." He hung up before she could ask any awkward questions, then headed for a booth by the window. Almost as an afterthought, he pulled the copy of *2600* out of his pocket. The hacker magazine (shut down by a court injunction last year) was a good recognition signal—plus, having it didn't violate the letter of his parole.

Roscoe was halfway down his first mug of coffee when someone leaned over him. "Hi," she said.

"You must be Sylvie." He registered a confused impression of bleached blond hair, brown eyes, freckles. *Must be straight out of J-school.* "Have a seat. Coffee?"

"Yes, please." She put something like a key ring down, then waved a hand, trying to catch the waitress's eye. Roscoe looked at the key ring. Very black, very small, very Nokia.

Rumor said they were giving them away in cereal boxes in France.

"Suppose you tell me why you wanted to meet up," Roscoe said quietly. "Up front. I can tell you right now that I'm out on parole, and I've got no intention of doing anything that puts me back inside."

The waitress ambled over, pad in hand. Sylvie ordered a coffee. "What were you charged with?" she said. "If you don't mind my asking."

Roscoe snorted. *Score one for the cool lady*—some folks he'd met ran a mile the instant he mentioned being a con. "I was *accused* of infringement with a side order of black crypto, but plea-bargained it down to unlawful emissions." *Score two*—she smiled. It was a weak joke, but it took some of the sting out of it. "Strictly no-collar crime." He took another mouthful of coffee. "So what is it you're doing up here?"

"I'm working on a story about some aspects of unwiring that don't usually make the national press," she said, as the waitress came over, empty mug in one hand and jug in the other. Roscoe held his up for a refill.

"Credentials?"

"I could give you a phone number, but would you trust it?"

"Point." Roscoe leaned back against the elderly vinyl seat. *Young, but cynical.*

"Well," she added, "I can do better." She pulled out a notepad and began scribbling. "*This* is my editor's name and address. *You* can look up his number. If you place a call and ask for him, you'll get put through—you're on the list of interview subjects I left him. Next, here's my—no, an—e-mail address." Roscoe blinked—it was a handle on a famous Finnish anonymous remixer. "Get a friend to ping it and ask me something." It was worth five to twenty for black crypto—anonymity was the FCC's worst nightmare about the uncontrolled net. "Finally, here's my press pass."

"Okay, I'll check these out." He met her eyes. "Now, why don't you tell me why the *Wall Street Journal* is interested in a burned-out ex-con and ex-unwirer, and we can take it from there?"

She closed her eyes for a moment. Then she dangled her

key ring again, just a flash of matte black plastic. "These are everywhere in Europe these days, along with these." She opened her purse, and he caught a glimpse of a sliver of curved metal, like a boomerang, in the shape of the Motorola batwing logo mark. "They're meshing wireless repeaters. Once you've got a critical mass, you can relay data from anywhere to anywhere. Teenagers are whacking them up on the sides of buildings, tangling them in tree branches, sticking them to their windows. The telcos there are screaming blue murder, of course. Business is down forty percent in Finland, sixty in France. Euros are using the net for telephone calls, instant messaging, file-sharing—the wireline infrastructure is looking more and more obsolete every day. Even the ISPs are getting nervous."

Roscoe tried to hide his grin. To be an unwirer in the streets of Paris, operating with impunity, putting the telcos, the Hollywood studios, and the ISPs on notice that there was no longer any such thing as a "consumer"—that yesterday's couch potatoes are today's *participants*!

"We've got ten years' worth of editorials in our morgue about the destruction of the European entertainment and telco market and the wisdom of our National Information Infrastructure here in the US, but it's starting to ring hollow. The European governments are *ignoring* the telcos! The device and services market being built on top of the freenets is accounting for nearly half the GDP in France. To hear *my* paper describe it, though, you'd think they were starving in the streets: it's like the received wisdom about Canadian socialized health care. Everyone *knows* it doesn't work—except for the Canadians, who think we're goddamned *barbarians* for not adopting it.

"I just got back from a month in the field in the EU. I've got interviews in the can with CEOs, with street thugs, with grandmothers, and with regulators, all saying the same thing: unmetered communications are the secret engine of the economy, of liberty. The highest-quality 'content' isn't hundred-million-dollar movies; it's conversations with other people. Crypto is a tool of 'privacy' "—she pronounced it in the British way, "prihv-icy," making the word seem even more alien to his ears—"not piracy."

"The unwirers are heroes in Europe. You hear them talk, it's like listening to a course in *US* constitutional freedoms. But here, you people are crooks, cable thieves, pirates, abettors of terrorists. I want to change that."

●

That evening, Marcel picked a fight with Roscoe over supper. It started low-key, as Roscoe sliced up the pizza. "What are you planning this week?"

Roscoe shifted two slices onto his plate before he answered. "More dishes. Got a couple of folks to splice in downtown if I want to hook up East Aurora—there're some black spots there, but I figure with some QOS-based routing and a few more repeaters, we can clear them up. Why?"

Marcel toyed with a strand of cooling cheese. "It's, like, boring. When are you going to run a new fat pipe in?"

"When the current one's full." Roscoe rolled a slice into a tube and bit into an end, deftly turning the roll to keep the cheese and sauce on the other end from oozing over his hand. "You know damn well the Feds would like nothing better than to drive a ditch-witch through a fiber drop from the border. 'Sides, got the journalist to think about."

"I could take over part of the fiber-pull," Marcel said.

"I don't think so." Roscoe put his plate down.

"But I could—" Marcel looked at him. "What's wrong?"

"Security," Roscoe grunted. "Goddamnit, you can't just waltz up to some guy who's looking at twenty-to-life and say, 'Hi, Roscoe sent me, howzabout you and me run some dark fiber over the border, huh?' Some of the guys in this game are, huh, you wouldn't want to meet them on a dark night. And others are just plain paranoid. They wouldn't want to meet *you*. Fastest way to convince 'em the FCC is trying to shut them down."

"You could introduce me," Marcel said after a brief pause.

Roscoe laughed, a short bark. "In your dreams, son."

Marcel dropped his fork, clattering. "You're going to take your pet blonde on a repeater splice and show her everything, and you're afraid to let me help you run a new fat pipe in? What's the matter—I don't smell good enough?"

"Listen." Roscoe stood up, and Marcel tensed—but rather

than move toward him, Roscoe turned to the pizza box. "Get the *Wall Street Journal* on our side, and we have some credibility. A crack in the wall. Legitimacy. Do you know what that means, kid? You can't buy it. But run another fat pipe into town, and we have a idle capacity, upstream dealers who want to know what the hell we're pissing around with, another fiber or laser link to lose to cop-induced backhoe fade, and about fifty percent higher probability of the whole network getting kicked over because the mundanes will rat us out to the FCC over their TV reception. Do you want that?" He picked another cooling pizza slice out of the box. "Do you really want that?"

"What I want isn't important, is it, Ross? Not as important as you getting a chance to fuck that reporter, right?"

"Up yours." Roscoe returned to his seat, shoulders set defensively. "Fuck you very much." They finished the meal in silence, then Roscoe headed out to his evening class in conversational French. Marcel, he figured, was just jealous because he wasn't getting to do any of the secret-agent stuff. Being an unwirer was a lot less romantic than it sounded, and the first rule of unwiring was *nobody talks about unwiring.* Maybe Marcel would get there one day, assuming his big mouth didn't get everyone around him arrested first.

○

Sylvie's hotel room had a cigarette-burns-and-must squalor that reminded Roscoe of jail. *"Bonjour, m'sieu,"* she said as she admitted him.

"Bon soir, madame," he said. *"Commentava?"*

"Oy," she said. "My grandmother woulda said, 'You've got a no-accent on you like a Litvak.' Lookee here, the treasures of the Left Bank." She handed him the Motorola batarang he'd glimpsed earlier. The underside had a waxed-paper peel-off strip, and when he lifted a corner, his thumb stuck so hard to the tackiness beneath that he lost the top layer of skin when he pulled it loose. He turned it over in his hands.

"How's it powered?"

"Dirt-cheap photovoltaics charging a polymer cell— they're printed in layers; the entire case is a slab of battery plus solar cell. It doesn't draw too many amps, only sucks juice when it's transmitting. Put one in a subway car, and you've got an instant ad hoc network that everyone in the car can use. Put one in the next car, and they'll mesh. Put one on the platform, and you'll get connectivity with the train when it pulls in. Sure, it won't run for more than a few hours in total darkness—but how often do folks network in the blackout?"

"Shitfire," he said, stroking the matte finish in a way that bordered on the erotic.

She grinned. She was slightly snaggletoothed, and he noticed a scar on her upper lip from a cleft-palate operation that must have been covered up with concealer earlier. It made her seem more human, more vulnerable. "Total cost of goods is about three euros, and Moto's margin is five hundred percent. But some Taiwanese knockoffs have already appeared that slice that in half. Moto'll have to invent something new next year if it wants to keep that profit."

"They will," Roscoe said, still stroking the batarang. He transferred it to his armpit and unslung his luggable laptop. "Innovation is still legal there." The laptop sank into the orange bedspread and the soft mattress beneath it.

"You could do some real damage with one of these, I bet," she said.

"With a thousand of them, maybe," he said. "If they were a little less conspicuous."

Her chest began to buzz. She slipped a wee phone from her breast pocket and answered it. "Yes?" She handed the phone to Roscoe. "It's for you." She made a curious face at him.

He clamped it to his ear. "Who is this?"

"Eet eez eye, zee masked avenger, doer of naughty deeds and wooer of reporters' hearts."

"Marcel?"

"Yes, boss."

"You shouldn't be calling me on this number." He remembered the yellow pad, sitting on his bedside table. Marcel did all the dusting.

"Sorry, boss," he said. He giggled.

"Have you been drinking?" Marcel and he had bonded over many, many beers since they'd met in a bar in Utica, but Roscoe didn't drink these days. Drinking made you sloppy.

"No, no," he said. "Just in a good mood is all. I'm sorry we fought, darlin'. Can we kiss and make up?"

"What do you want, Marcel?"

"I want to be in the story, dude. Hook me up! I want to be famous!"

He grinned despite himself. Marcel was good at fonzing dishes into place with one well-placed whack, could crack him up when the winter slush was turning his mood to pitch. He was a good kid, basically. Hothead. Like Roscoe, once.

"C'mon c'mon c'mon," Marcel said, and he could picture the kid pogoing up and down in a phone booth, heard his boots crunching on rock salt.

He covered the receiver and turned to Sylvie, who had a bemused smirk that wasn't half-cute on her. "You wanna hit the road, right?" She nodded. "You wanna write about how unwirers get made? I could bring along the kid I'm 'prenticing-up, you like." Through the cell phone, he heard Marcel shouting, "Yes! Yes! YES!" and imagined the kid punching the air and pounding the booth's walls triumphantly.

"It's a good angle," she said. "*You* want him along, right?"

He held the receiver in the air so that they could both hear the hollers coming down the line. "I don't think I could live with him if I didn't take him," he said. "So yeah."

She nodded and bit her upper lip, just where the scar was, an oddly canine gesture that thrust her chin forward and made her look slightly belligerent. "Let's do it."

He clamped the phone back to his head. "Marcel! Calm down, twerp! Breathe. Okay. You gonna be good if I take you along?"

"So good, man, so very very very very good, you won't believe—"

"You gonna be *safe*, I bring you along?"

"Safe as houses. Won't breathe without your permission. Man, you are the *best*—"

"Yeah, I am. Four o'clock. Bring the stuff."

○

They hit the road closer to five than four. It was chilly, and the gathering clouds and intermittent breeze promised more snow after dark when Roscoe parked outside the apartment. Marcel was ready and waiting, positively jumping up and down as soon as Roscoe opened the door. "Let's go, man!"

Back in the cab, Sylvie was making notes on a palmtop. "Hi," she said guardedly, making eye contact with Marcel.

"Hi yourself." Marcel smiled. "Where we going tonight, man? I brought the stuff." He dumped Roscoe's toolbox and a bag containing a bunch of passive repeaters on the bench seat next to him.

"We're heading for East Aurora." Roscoe looked over his shoulder as he backed the truck into the street, barely noticing Sylvie watching him. "There's a low hill there that's blocking signal to the mesh near Chestnut Hill, and we're going to do something about that."

"Great!" Marcel shuffled about to get comfortable as Roscoe cautiously drove along the icy road. "Hey, isn't there a microwave mast up there?"

"Yeah." Roscoe saw Sylvie was making notes. "By the way, if you could keep from saying exactly where we're placing the repeaters? In your article? Otherwise, FCC'll just take 'em down."

"Okay." Sylvie put her pocket computer down. It was one of those weird Brit designs with the folding keyboards and built-in wireless that had trashed Palm all over Europe. "So you're going to, what? String a bunch of repeaters along a road around the hillside?"

"Pretty much that, exactly. Should only need two or three at the most, and it's wooded around there. I figure an hour for each, and we can be home by nine, grab some Chinese on the way."

"Why don't we use the microwave mast?" Marcel said.

"Huh?"

"The microwave mast," he repeated. "We go up there, we put one repeater on it, and we bounce signal *over* the hill, no need to go round the bushes."

"I don't think so," Roscoe said absently. "Criminal trespass."

"But it'd save time! And they'd never look up there; it'll look just like any other phone-company dish—"

Roscoe sighed. "I am so not hearing this." He paused for a few seconds, merging with another lane of traffic. "Listen, if we get caught climbing a tree by the roadside, I can drop the cans and say I was bird-spotting. They'll never find them. But if I get caught climbing a phone-company microwave tower, that is criminal trespass, *and* they'll probably nail me for felony theft of service, and felony possession of unlicensed devices—they'll find the cans for sure; it's like a parking lot around the base of those things—and parole breach. I'll be back in prison while you're still figuring out how to hitchhike home. So enough about saving time, okay? Doing twenty to life is not saving time."

"Okay," Marcel said, "we'll do it your way." He crossed his arms and stared out the window at the passing trees under their winter caul of snow.

"How many unwirers are there working in the area?" Sylvie said, breaking the silence.

Marcel said, "Just us," at the same moment as Roscoe said, "Dozens." Sylvie laughed.

"We're solo," Roscoe said, "but there are lots of other solos in the area. It's not a *conspiracy*, you know—more like an emergent form of democracy."

Sylvie looked up from her palmtop. "That's from a manifesto, isn't it?"

Roscoe pinked. "Guilty as charged. Got it from Barlow's *Letters from Prison*. I read a lot of prison lit. Before I went into the joint."

"Amateurs plagiarize, artists steal," she said. "Might as well steal from the best. Barlow talks a mean stick. You know he wrote lyrics for the Grateful Dead?"

"Yeah," Roscoe said. "I got into unwiring through some deadhead tape-traders who were importing open recorders from Germany to tape to shows. One of them hooked me up with—someone—who could get French networking gear. It was just a few steps from there to fun-loving criminal, undermining the body politic."

○

Marcel came out of his sulk when they got to the site. He loaded up his backpack and a surveyor's tripod and was the model of efficiency as he lined up the bank shot around the hill that would get their signal out and about.

Sylvie hung back with Roscoe, who was taking all the gear through a series of tests, using his unwieldy laptop and two homemade antennae to measure signal strength. "Got to get it right the first time. Don't like to revisit a site after it's set up. Dog returning to its vomit and all."

She took out her key ring and dangled it in the path of the business end of the repeater Roscoe was testing. "I'm getting good directional signal," she said, turning the key ring so he could see the glowing blue LEDs arranged to form the distinctive Nokia "N."

Roscoe reached for the fob. "These are just *wicked*," he said.

"Keep it," she said. "I've got a few more in my room. They had a fishbowl full of them on the reception desk in Helsinki. The more lights, the better the signal."

Roscoe felt an obscure species of embarrassment, like he was a primitive, tacking up tin cans and string around a provincial backwater of a country. "Thanks," he said, gruffly. "Hey, Marcel, you got us all lined up?"

"Got it."

Only he didn't. They lined up the first repeater and tested it, but the signal drop-off was near-total. Bad solder joints, interference from the microwave tower, gremlins . . . Who knew? Sometimes a shot just didn't work, and debugging it in the frigid winter dusk wasn't anyone's idea of a fun time.

"Okay, pass me the next." Roscoe breathed deeply as Marcel went back to the truck for the other repeater. *This* one worked fine. But it still left them with a problem. "Didn't you bring a third?" Roscoe asked.

"What for?" Marcel shrugged. "I swear I tested them both back home—maybe it's the cold or something?"

"Shit." Roscoe stamped his feet and looked back at the road. Sylvie was standing close to the truck, hands in her pockets, looking interested. He glanced at the hill and the microwave mast on top of it. A light blinked regularly, warm and red like an invitation.

"Why'n't we try the hill?" Marcel asked. "We could do the shot with only one repeater from that high up."

Roscoe stared at the mast. "Let me think." He picked up the working repeater and shambled back to the truck cab absentmindedly, weighing the options. "Come on."

"What now?" asked Sylvie, climbing in the passenger seat.

"I think." Roscoe turned the ignition key. "Kid has half a point. We've only got the one unit. If we can stick it on the mast, it'll do the job." He turned half-around in his seat to stare at Marcel. "But we are *not* going to get caught, y'hear?" He glanced at Sylvie. "If you think it's not safe, I'll give you a lift home first. Or bail. It's your call. Everyone gets a veto."

Sylvie stared at him through slitted eyes. Then she whistled tunelessly. "It's your ass. Don't get into this just because I'm watching."

"Okay." Roscoe put the truck in gear. "You guys keep an eye out behind for any sign of anything at all, anyone following us." He pulled away slowly, driving with excruciating care. "Marcel? Stick that bag under my seat, will you?"

The side road up to the crest of the hill was dark, shadowed by snow-laden trees to either side. Roscoe took it slowly; a couple of times there was a whine as the all-wheel drive cut in on the uncleared snow. "No fast getaways," Sylvie noted quietly.

"We're not bank robbers." Roscoe shifted down a gear and turned into the driveway leading to the mast. There was an empty parking lot at the end, surrounded by a chain-link fence with a gate in it. On the other side, the mast rose from a concrete plinth, towering above them like a giant intrusion from another world. Roscoe pulled up and killed the lights. "Anyone see anything?"

"No," said Marcel from the backseat.

"Looks okay to—hey, wait!" Sylvie did a double take. "Stop! Don't open the door!"

"Why—" Marcel began.

"Stop. Just stop." Sylvie seemed agitated, and right then Roscoe, his eyes recovering from headlight glare, noticed the faint shadows. "Marcel, *get down*!"

"What's up?" Marcel asked.

"Crouch down! Below window level!" She turned to Roscoe. "Looks like you were right."

"I was right?" Roscoe looked past her. The shadows were getting sharper, and now he could hear the other vehicle. "Shit. We've been—" He reached toward the ignition key and Sylvie slapped his hand away. "Ouch!"

"Here." She leaned forward, sparing a glance for the backseat, where Marcel was crouching down. "Make it look like you mean it."

"Mean what—" Roscoe got it a moment before she kissed him. He responded automatically, hugging her as the truck cab flooded with light.

"*You! Out of the*—oh, geez." The amplified voice, a woman's voice, trailed off. Sylvie and Roscoe turned and blinked at the spotlights mounted on the gray Dodge van as its doors opened.

Sylvie wound down the side window and stuck her head out. "I don't know what you think you're doing, but you can fuck right off!" she yelled. "Fucking voyeurs!"

"This is private property," came the voice. "You'll have to get a room." Boots crunched on the road salt. A holster creaked. Roscoe held his breath.

"Very funny," Sylvie said. "All right, we're going."

"Not yet, you aren't," the voice said again, this time without the amplification, much closer. Roscoe looked in the rearview at the silhouette of the woman cop, flipping her handcuffs on her belt, stepping carefully on the ice surface. In her bulky parka, she could have been any state trooper, but the way she flipped her cuffs—

"Go go go," hissed Marcel from the backseat. *"Vite!"*

"Sit tight," Sylvie said.

From the backseat, a click. A gun being cocked. Roscoe kept his eyes on the rearview, and mumbled, "Marcel, if that is a gun I just heard, I am going to shove it up your fucking ass and pull the trigger."

Roscoe rolled down his window. "Evening, Officer," he said. Her face was haloed by the light bouncing off her breath's fog, but he recognized her. Had seen her, the day before, while hanging off the edge of the gorge, aiming an antenna Canadawards.

"Evening, sir," she said. "Evening, ma'am. Nice night, huh? Doing some bird-watching?"

Made. Roscoe's testicles shriveled up and tried to climb into his abdomen. His feet and hands weren't cold, they were *numb*. He couldn't have moved if he tried. He couldn't go back—

Another click. A flashlight. The cop shined it on Sylvie. Roscoe turned. The concealer was smudged around her scar.

"Officer, really, is this necessary?" Sylvie's voice was exasperated, and had a Manhattan accent she hadn't had before, one that made her sound scary-aggro. "It was just the heat of the moment."

Roscoe touched his lips and his finger came back with a powdering of concealer and a smudge of lipstick.

"Yes, ma'am, it is. Sir, could you step out of the car, please?"

Roscoe reached for his seat belt, and the flashlight swung toward the backseat. The cop's eyes flickered behind him, and then she slapped for her holster, stepping back quickly. "Everyone, hands where I see them. NOW!"

Fucking Marcel. Jesus.

She was still fumbling with her holster, and there was the sound of the car door behind her opening. "Liz?" a voice called. The other cop, her partner. Fourth and Walnut. "Everything okay?"

She was staring wide-eyed now, panting out puffs of steam. Staring at the rear window. Roscoe looked over his shoulder. Marcel had a small pistol, pointed at her.

"Drive, Roscoe," he said. "Drive fast."

Moving as in a dream, he reached for the ignition. The engine coughed to life, and he slammed it into gear, cranking hard on the wheel, turning away from the cop, a wide circle through the empty parking lot that he came out of in an uncontrolled fishtail, swinging back and forth on the slick pavement.

He regained control as they crested the ridge and hit the downhill slope back to the highway. Behind him, he heard the cop car swing into the chain-link fence, and in his rearview mirror, he saw the car whirling across the ice on the parking lot, its headlights moving in slow circles. It was mesmerizing, but Sylvie's gasp snapped him back to his driving. They were careening down the hill now, tires whining for purchase, threatening to fishtail, picking up speed.

He let out an involuntary *eep* and touched the brakes, triggering another skid. The truck hit the main road still skidding, but now they had road salt under the rubber, and he brought the truck back under control and floored it, switching off his headlights, running dark on the dark road.

"This isn't safe," Sylvie said.

"You said, 'Drive fast,'" Roscoe said, hammering the

gearbox. He sounded hysterical, even to his own ears. He swallowed. "It's not far."

"What's not far?" she said.

"Shut up," he said. "Okay? We've got about five minutes before their backup arrives. Seven minutes until the chopper's in the sky. Need to get off the road."

"The safe house," Marcel said.

"SHUT UP," Roscoe said, touching the brakes. They passed an oncoming car that blinked its high beams at them. *Yes, driving with my lights off, thank you,* Roscoe thought.

○

Roscoe hadn't been to the safe house in a year. It was an old public park whose jungle gym had rusted through and killed a kid eighteen months before. He'd gone there to scout out a good repeater location and found that the public toilet, behind the chain-link fence, was still unlocked. He kept an extra access point there, a blanket, a change of clothes, a first-aid kit, and a fresh license plate, double-bagged in kitchen garbage bags stashed in the drop ceiling.

He parked the truck outside the fence, snugged up between the bushes that grew on one side and the chain link. They were invisible from the road. He got out of the truck quickly.

"Marcel, get the camper bed," he said, digging a crowbar out from under his seat and passing it to him.

"What are you going to do?" Sylvie asked.

"Help me," he said, unlatching the camper and grabbing a tarpaulin. "Unfold this on the ground there, and pile the stuff I pass you on top of it."

He unloaded the truck quickly, handing Sylvie the access points, the repeaters, the toolboxes and ropes and spray cans of camou colors. "Make a bundle of it," he said, once the truck was empty. "Tie the corners together with the rope. Use the grommets."

He snatched the crowbar away from Marcel and went to work on the remaining nuts holding down the camper bed. When he had the last one undone, he jammed the pry end of the bar between the lid and the truck and levered it off the bed. It began to slide off, and he grunted, "Get it," to Marcel, but it was Sylvie who caught the end.

"Over the fence," he gasped, holding up his end while he scrambled into the back of the truck. They flipped it over together, and it landed upside down.

A car rolled past. They all flinched, but it kept going. Roscoe thought it was a cop car, but he couldn't be sure. He stilled his breathing and listened for the chop-chop of a helicopter, and thought that, yes, he heard it, off in the distance, but maybe getting closer.

"Marcel, give me that fucking gun," he said, with deceptive calmness.

Marcel looked down at the snow.

"I will cave in your skull with this rod if you don't hand me your gun," he said, hefting the crowbar. "Unless you shoot me," he said.

Marcel reached into the depths of his jacket and produced the pistol. Roscoe had never handled a pistol, and he was surprised by its weight—heavier than it looked, lighter than he'd thought it would be.

"Over the fence," he said. "All of us." He put the gun in his pocket. "Marcel first."

Marcel opened his mouth.

"Not a word," Roscoe said. "If you say one goddamned word, either of you, you're out. We're quits. Fence."

Marcel went over the fence first, landing atop the camper bed. Then Sylvie, picking her way down with her toes jammed in the chain link. Roscoe set down the crowbar quietly and followed.

"Roscoe," Sylvie said. "Can you explain this to me?"

"No," Roscoe said. "Sylvie, you stay here and cover the camper bed with snow. Kick it over. As much as you can. Marcel, with me."

They entered the dark toilet single file, and once the door had closed behind them, Roscoe pulled out his flashlight and clicked it on.

"We're not going home ever again. Whatever you had in your pockets, that's all you've got. Do you understand?"

Marcel opened his mouth, and Roscoe lunged for him.

"Don't speak. Just nod. I don't want to hear your voice. You've destroyed my life, climbing that tower, pulling that gun. I'm over, you understand? Just nod."

Marcel nodded. His eyes were very wide.

"Climb up on the toilet tank and pop out that ceiling tile and bring down the bag." He aimed the flashlight to emphasize his point.

Marcel brought down the bag, and Roscoe felt some of the tension leak out of him. At least he had a new license plate and a change of clothes. It was a start.

Sylvie had covered the bottom third of the camper bed, and her gloves and boots were caked with snow. Roscoe set down the trash bag and helped her, and after a moment, Marcel pitched in. Soon they had the whole thing covered.

"I don't know that it'll fool anyone who walks over here, but it should keep it hidden from the road, at least," Roscoe said. His heart had finally begun to slow down, and he was breathing normally.

"Here's the plan," he said. "I'm going to swap the license plates and drive into town. Sylvie lies down on the backseat. They're looking for a truck with three people in it and a camper bed. Marcel, you're walking. It's a long walk. There're some chemical hot-pads in the first-aid kit. Stuff them in your boots and mitts. Don't let anyone see you. Find somewhere to hide until tomorrow, then we'll meet at the Donut House near the Rainbow Bridge, eight a.m., okay?"

Marcel nodded mutely. The snow was falling harder now, clouds dimming the moonlight.

Roscoe dug out the hot pads and tossed them to him. "Go," he said. "Now."

Wordlessly, Marcel climbed the fence and started slogging toward the highway.

They watched his back recede, then Roscoe jumped the fence with the trash bag. He dropped it in the back of the truck and hauled his tarpaulin bundle back to the playground side, then dragged it into the bathroom. It was too heavy to get into the drop ceiling, and the drag marks in the fresh snow were like a blinking arrow anyway. He left it on the floor.

He helped Sylvie over the fence, then hunkered down, using a small wrench to remove the plates from the truck. Sylvie crouched beside him, holding the flashlight.

"Did you know he had a gun?" Sylvie said, as he tightened down the bolts.

"No," Roscoe said. "No guns. We don't use guns. We're fucking network engineers, not pistoleros."

"Thought so," she said, but made no further comment as he fastened the new plates in place.

Finally, he stood up. "Okay, let's go," he said.

"What's the plan?" She paused, hand on door handle.

"The plan is to get away from here. Then figure out what to do next." He glanced at her sidelong, calculating. "I think you'll be all right, whatever happens. But that little idiot—" He realized his hands were shaking.

Sylvie climbed into the truck. Roscoe sat for a minute, concentrating on getting a grip on himself.

He drove slowly, starting every time he saw moving shadows, the headlights of other vehicles. One time the road took a bend, and he passed a police car, stationary on the shoulder. He nearly jumped out of his skin, but forced back the urge to put his foot down or even turn his head. *Give no sign,* he told himself.

Sylvie sighed as the police car vanished in the rearview. "You're going to go to the rendezvous, like you told him?" she asked.

"Yeah. More than the little shit deserves, but I owe him that much. We've got to sort this out together." He tapped the steering wheel. "I'll have to ditch the truck."

"No."

Roscoe stared at her. Sylvie's face was half in shadow, half a flat orange washout from the streetlamps. "I don't trust him. I think he's a provo."

"What?" Roscoe shook his head then looked back at the road. "He's young, is all. A bit young." They were not far from Main Street, and he began looking around for somewhere to park the truck. "Listen, we're going to have to walk a ways. You up to an hour on foot?"

"A hike in the dark? Yeah, I guess so." Sylvie sniffed. "If you go to that Donut House, they'll arrest you. You'll go down as a terrorist."

Roscoe didn't dignify her paranoia with a response. Instead, he pulled over. "Open the glove box. There's a can of foam cleaner and some wipes inside. Pass 'em over."

"If you want." She sounded resigned. Roscoe focused on

polishing the wheel and gearshift handle. Old prints he didn't care about, but he didn't want to leave fresh ones. "There have been arrests you haven't heard about."

Roscoe opened his door and climbed out. The air was freezingly cold, trying to suck the life from his face and lungs. He picked up the trash bag from the back and paused, about to close the door. Instead he left it open, forcing himself to leave the keys dangling enticingly in the ignition. "You coming?" he asked.

Sylvie hurried to catch up. "There's a guy called Dennis Morgan, on the Texas border," she said quietly. "Don't know where he is; the Feds won't say—they pulled him in on firearms charges, but all the warrants, search and seizure, went through a special FEMA courthouse that won't talk to us. We tried FOIA notices and got denied. Dennis had no record of violent offenses—like you, he was just an unwirer—but they charged him with attempted murder of a Federal agent, then stuck him in a hole so deep we can't find him."

Roscoe slowed, hearing her panting for breath.

"*Secret* trials, Roscoe, special terrorism courts. They don't call them that, but all the records are sealed, and I can't even find the defense attorneys in the goddamn phone book. 'S a woman called Caitlin Delaney in Washington State. They found kiddie porn in her house and a meth lab in her garage after they shot her resisting arrest, you know? They made her out to be some kind of gangster. She was fifty, Roscoe, and she had multiple sclerosis, and her backyard just happened to have line of sight to the Surrey side of the Canadian border."

Roscoe slowed even more, until he felt Sylvie walking beside him. "FCC, Roscoe, they've been making sure we know all about these dangerous terrorists, did you know that? But I made some phone calls from pay phones to local stringers, had them do some digging. Unwirers are disappearing. Their turf gets too visibly unwired, then they vanish, leaving behind guns and drugs and kiddie porn. That's the *real* story I'm here to cover. Roscoe, if you go to that donut joint, and Marcel is what I think he is, you'll just vanish."

She took his hand and stopped. Roscoe felt himself halt. His shoulders were tense and the lining of his jacket felt icy-slick with freezing sweat. "What do you want?"

Her breath steamed in the air before him. "I don't want you

to get yourself killed," she said. Up close he could see the scar on her lip, the smudged foundation on her cheek. "Shit." She leaned against him and put her chin on his shoulder, nosing in like a small animal in search of warmth. "Look, come up to my room. We can discuss it there."

○

The Days Inn was a hell of a lot closer than the Rainbow Bridge, that was for sure. Being scared half out of his skin and on the run was exhausting, and Roscoe was perversely grateful to Sylvie for leading him back to the motel room, even though a nagging paranoid corner of his head kept shrieking that she, not Marcel, was the agent provocateur, that she'd get him into bed and G-men with signal meters and search warrants would erupt from the closet—

But it wasn't like that. It wasn't like that at all.

They ended up naked, in bed together. And before anything much could happen, Roscoe was asleep, snoring quietly, dead to the world. He didn't notice it, actually: what he noticed was waking up to the dim red glow of the alarm clock's flickering digits, Sylvie's face limned against the pillow next to him with the incipient glow of hellfire, digits flickering toward seven o'clock and an appointment with an uncertain future.

"Hey. Wake up."

"Mm-hum." Sylvie rolled toward him for a warm moment, then her eyes opened. "We didn't?" She looked hopeful.

"Not yet." He ran one hand along her back, cupping her buttocks with a sense of gratified astonishment. *How did this happen to us?* he wondered, a thought that always hit him between the eyes when he found himself in bed with a new woman. *It's been a long time.*

Her gaze traveled past him, settling on the clock. "Oh shit." She hugged him, then pulled back. "There's never enough time. Later?"

"After the meet-up, when I know if it's safe to go—"

"Shut up." She leaned over and kissed him hard, almost angrily. "This is so unprofessional—look, if I'm wrong, I apologize, all right? But if you go there, I think you're walking into a sting. I don't think you should go near the place. If I had a repeater, I could stake it out with a webcam, but—"

"A repeater?" Roscoe sat up. "There's one in my bag."

"Right." She rolled out of bed and stretched. He couldn't take his eyes away from her. "Listen, let's freshen up and get outta here." She grinned at him, friendly but far from the intimacy of a minute ago, and he had tangible sense of lost possibilities. "Let's get the donut joint wired for video. Then we can go grab some coffee and figure out what to do next."

Signal strength near the bridge was good. Roscoe just glommed his repeater onto a streetlamp above eye level, to boost the final hundred yards to the block. "They'll spot it immediately, probably take it down later today," he said. "Hope this is worth it."

"It will be," she reassured him fiercely, before striding away toward the donut joint. He stared after her, a slim figure bundled in improbable layers of cold-weather gear, and resisted the impulse to run after. If the cops were looking for anyone it'd be him, a known parole violator, not a single young female on the far side of the road. Plan was to fasten the cam to the back of a road sign opposite the doorway, use plastic zipstrips to keep it on target. He glanced at his watch: seven zero seven hours. *Cutting it fine, if it's a stakeout . . .*

Roscoe took a walk around the block, stamping his feet against the chill, trying not to dwell on the unpleasant possibilities. His heart gave a little lurch as he came back around the alleyway and saw Sylvie walking back down the street toward him, but she was smiling and as she caught up with him she grabbed his arm. "Come on, there's a Starbucks on the next block," she said.

"I *hate* Starbucks," he complained.

"Yeah, but it's indoors and off the street," she explained. "So you're going to put up with it this once, okay?"

"Okay."

They shed gloves and caps as they went in past the Micronet booths and the pastry counter. Sylvie ordered a couple of large lattes. "Is the mezzanine open?" she asked.

"Sure, go on up." The gum-chewing barista didn't even look up.

At the top of the stairs, in a dark corner well back from the shop front, Sylvie produced her phone and began fiddling with it. "Let's see. Ah . . . uh-huh. Here it is." She turned it so he could see the tiny color display. The front of the donut shop was recognizable. "It does voice over IP, too; lots of people use these instead of laptops. What time do you make it?"

"Seven thirty." A gray minivan pulled up in front of the shop and disgorged a bunch of guys in trench coats and one very recognizable figure. His stomach lurched. "Who are those guys? What's Marcel doing with—" He stopped. Further comments seemed redundant.

"Let's see who else turns up," Sylvie suggested, sipping her latte.

Marcel went into the donut store. Two of the men in trench coats followed him. Most of the others moved out of frame, but one of them was just visible, hurrying down the alley at the side of the store.

Nothing happened for a couple of minutes, then a police car pulled up. Two uniforms got out, but as they headed for the door one of the trench coats came out. Words were exchanged, and angry gestures. The uniforms went back to their car and drove away: the trench coat headed back inside. Sylvie sniffed. "Serve 'em right, stopping for donuts on your tax dollars."

Roscoe tensed. "I think you were right," he said slowly.

Sylvie beamed at him. "Oh, you ain't seen nothing yet!"

It was five minutes to eight. Roscoe went downstairs for another coffee, his feet dragging. Everything was closing in, going nightmarishly wrong. *I'm screwed,* he thought. *Gotta run—*

"Roscoe?"

"Coming." He turned back and hurried upstairs. "What is it?"

"Watch." She pointed the phone display where he could see it. A pickup truck roughly the same color and age as Roscoe's drew up in front of the donut store.

"Hey, that's not—"

"I told you we employ stringers. Right?"

A man wearing a jacket and cap climbed out of the cab. He looked a bit like Roscoe, if you were watching via a covert webcam from across the street. He turned and looked at the camera, but he was too far from it for Roscoe to see if he winked or not. Then he turned and went in.

Trench coats boiled out from behind trash cans like so many black leather cockroaches. They swarmed the truck and blocked the doorway and two of them with guns and warrant cards drawn covered the parking lot. There was chaos and motion for almost a minute, then another trench coat barreled out of the door and started yelling instructions at them. The guns vanished. Marcel appeared in the doorway behind him, pointing. Two of the trench coats began to cross the road, heading toward the camera.

"I think that's enough," said Sylvie, and killed the feed. Then she hit one of the speed-dial buttons on her phone. It rang twice. *"Bonjour. Où est le—"*

Roscoe shook his head. He felt approximately the way he imagined a tuna fish might feel with a wooden deck under one flank and the cruel sun beating mercilessly down on the other, gills gasping in a medium they'd never evolved to survive exposure to. Sylvie was speaking in rapid-fire French, arguing with somebody by the sound of it, while he was drowning on dry land.

Sylvie finished her call and closed her phone with a snap. She laid her hand across his. "You're okay," she said, smiling.

"Huh?" Roscoe started, setting the empty coffee cups aside.

"That was the French consulate in Toronto. I set it up in advance so they'd see the webcam. My editor, too. If you can cross over into Canada and get to the consulate, you've got diplomatic asylum, genuine refugee status." She reached into her pocket and pulled out a small box; it unfolded like intricate brushed-aluminum origami, forming a keyboard for her to plug the phone into. "We're going to hit the front page of the *Journal* tomorrow, Roscoe. It's all documented—your background, Marcel, the gun, the stakeout, all of it. With a witness." She pointed a thumb at herself. "We've been looking for a break like this for *months*." She was almost gloating now. "Valenti isn't going to know what's hit him. My editor—" She slurped some coffee. "My *editor* got into the game because of Watergate. He's been burning for a break like this ever since."

Roscoe sat and stared at her dumbly.

"Cheer up! You're going to be famous—and they won't be able to put you away! All we have to do is get you to Montreal. There's a crossing set up at the Mohawk Reservation, and I've got a rental car in the lot next door to the Days Inn. While I'm at it, can you sign these?" She thrust a bundle of papers at him and winced apologetically. "Exclusive contract with the *Wall Street Journal*. It covers your expenses—flight included— plus fifteen grand for your story. I tried to hold out for more, but you know how things are." She shrugged.

He stared at her, stunned into bovine silence. She pinched his cheek and shoved the papers into his hands. *"Bon voyage, mon ami,"* she said. She kissed each cheek, then pulled out a compact and fixed the concealer on her lip.

●

Paris in springtime was everything it was meant to be and more. Roscoe couldn't sit down in a cafe without being smart-mobbed by unwirer groupies who wanted him to sign their repeaters and tell them war stories about his days as a guerrilla fighter for technological freedom. They were terribly, awfully young, just kids, Marcel's age or younger, and they were heart-breaking in their attempts to understand his crummy French. The girls were beautiful, the boys were handsome, and they laughed and smoked and ordered him glasses of wine until he couldn't walk. He'd put on twenty pounds, and when he did the billboard ads for Be, Inc. and Motorola, they had to strap him into a girdle. LE CHOIX AMÉRICAIN in bold sans-serif letters underneath a picture of him scaling a building side with a Moto batarang clenched in his teeth.

Truth be told, he couldn't even keep up with it all. Hardly a week went by without a new business popping up, a new bit of technological gewgaggery appearing on the tables of the Algerian street vendors by the Eiffel Tower. He couldn't even make sense of half the ads on the Metro.

But life was good. He had a very nice apartment with a view and a landlady who chased away the paparazzi with stern French and a broom. He could get four bars of signal on his complimentary Be laptop from the bathroom, and ten bars from the window, and the throng and thrum of the city and the net filled his days and nights.

And yet.

He was a foreigner. A curiosity. A fish, transplanted from the sea to Marineland, swimming in a tank where the tourists could come and gawp. He slept fitfully, and in his dreams, he was caged in a cell at Leavenworth, back on the inside, in maximum security, pacing the yard in solitary stillness.

He woke to the sound of his phone trilling. The ring was the special one, the one that only one person had the number for. He struggled out of bed and lunged for his jacket, fumbled the phone out.

"Sylvie?"

"Roscoe! God, I know it's early, but God, I just had to tell you!"

He looked at the window. It was still dark. On his bed-stand, the clock glowed 4:21.

"What? What is it?"

"God! Valenti's been called to testify at a Senate hearing on unwiring. He's stepping down as chairman. I just put in a call to his office and into his dad's office at the MPAA. The lines were *jammed*. I'm on my way to get the Acela into DC."

"You're covering it for the *Journal*?"

"Better. I got a *book deal*! My agent ran a bidding war between Simon and Schuster and St. Martin's until three a.m. last night. I'm hot shit. The whole fucking thing is coming down like a house of shit. I've had three congressional staffers fax me discussion drafts of bills—one to fund 300 million dollars in DARPA grants to study TCP/IP, another to repeal the terrorism statutes on network activity, and a compulsory license on movies and music online. God! If only you could see it."

"That's—amazing," Roscoe said. He pictured her in the cab on the way to Grand Central, headset screwed in, fixing her makeup, dressed in a smart spring suit, off to meet with the Hill Rats.

"It's incredible. It's better than I dreamed."

"Well . . ." he said. He didn't know what to say. "See if you can get me a pardon, okay?" The joke sounded lame even to him.

"What?" There was a blare of taxi horns. "Oh, crap, Roscoe, I'm sorry. It'll work out, you'll see. Clemency or amnesty or something."

"We can talk about it next month, okay?" She'd booked the tickets the week before, and they had two weeks of touring on the Continent planned.

"Oh, Roscoe, I'm sorry. I can't do it. The book's due in twelve weeks. Afterward, okay? You understand, don't you?"

He pulled back the curtains and looked out at the foreign city, looking candlelit in the night. "I understand, sweetie," he said. "This is great work. I'm proud of you."

Another blare of horns from six thousand miles away. "Look, I've got to go. I'll call you from the Hill, okay?"

"Okay," Roscoe said. But she'd already hung up.

He had six bars on his phone, and Paris was lit up with invisible radio waves, lit up with coverage and innovation and smart, trim boys and girls who thought he was a hero, and six thousand miles away, the real unwiring was taking place.

He looked down at his slim silver phone, glowing with blue LEDs, a gift from Nokia. He tossed it from hand to hand, then he opened the window and chucked it three stories down to the street. It made an unsatisfying clatter as it disintegrated on the pavement.

Afterword—"Unwirer"

"Unwirer" was written as a collaboration between Cory Doctorow and me. It developed in 2003 in response to an anthology editor looking for alternate-history stories about science and technology. In this case, the particular departure we picked on was a legislative one. Back in the 1990s, when the music and film industries were just getting alarmed at this newfangled Internet thing, a number of really bad laws were proposed—ones that would have effectively gutted not only US use of the Internet but all comparable communications technologies. But leaving aside all ideological assertions to the effect that information wants to be free, people like to communicate. So what would things be like if open Internet access were as illegal as, say, cannabis?

Snowball's Chance

The louring sky, half-past pregnant with a caul of snow, pressed down on Davy's head like the promise of tomorrow's hangover. He glanced up once, shivered, then pushed through the doorway into the Deid Nurse and the smog of fag fumes within.

His sometime conspirator Tam the Tailer was already at the bar. "Awright, Davy?"

Davy drew a deep breath, his glasses steaming up the instant he stepped through the heavy blackout curtain, so that the disreputable pub was shrouded in a halo of icy iridescence that concealed its flaws. "Mine's a Deuchars." His nostrils flared as he took in the seedy mixture of aromas that festered in the Deid Nurse's atmosphere—so thick you could cut it with an ax, Morag had said once with a sniff of her lopsided snot-siphon, back in the day when she'd had aught to say to Davy. "Fuckin' Baltic oot there the night, an' nae kiddin'." He slid his glasses off and wiped them, then looked around tiredly. "An' deid tae the world in here."

Tam glanced around as if to be sure the pub population hadn't magically doubled between mouthfuls of seventy bob. "Ah widnae say that." He gestured with his nose—pockmarked by frostbite—at the snug in the corner. Once the storefront for the Old Town's more affluent ladies of the night, it was now unaccountably popular with students of the gaming fraternity, possibly because they had been driven out of all the trendier bars in the neighborhood for yacking too much and not drinking enough (much like the whores before them). Right now a bunch of threadbare LARPers were in residence, arguing over some recondite point of lore. "They're havin' enough fun for a barrel o' monkeys by the sound o' it."

"An' who can blame them?" Davy hoisted his glass. "Ah just wish they'd keep their shite aff the box." The pub, in an effort to compensate for its lack of a food license, had installed a huge and dodgy screen that teetered precariously over the bar: it was full of muddy field, six LARPers leaping.

"Dinnae piss them aff, Davy—they've a' got swords."

"Ah wis jist kiddin'. Ah didnae catch ma lottery the night, that's a' Ah'm sayin'."

"If ye win, it'll be a first." Tam stared at his glass. "An' whit wid ye dae then, if yer numbers came up?"

"Whit, the big yin?" Davy put his glass down, then unzipped his parka's fast-access pouch and pulled out a fag packet and lighter. Condensation immediately beaded the plastic wrapper as he flipped it open. "Ah'd pay aff the hoose, for starters. An' the child support. An' then—" He paused, eyes wandering to the dog-eared NO SMOKING sign behind the bar. "Ah, shit." He flicked his Zippo, stroking the end of a cigarette with the flame from the burning coal oil. "If Ah wis young again, Ah'd move, ye ken? But Ah'm no. Ah've got roots here." The sign went on to warn of lung cancer (curable) and two-thousand-euro fines (laughable, even if enforced). Davy inhaled, grateful for the warmth flooding his lungs. "An' there's Morag an' the bairns."

"Heh." Tam left it at a grunt, for which Davy was grateful. It wasn't that he thought Morag would ever come back to him, but he was sick to the back teeth of people who thought they were his friends telling him that she wouldn't, not unless he did this or said that.

"Ah could pay for the bairns tae go east. They're young enough." He glanced at the doorway. "It's no right, throwin' snowba's in May."

"That's global warmin'." Tam shrugged with elaborate

irony, then changed the subject. "Where d'ye think they'd go? Ukraine? New 'Beria?"

"Somewhaur there's grass and nae glaciers." Pause. "An' real beaches wi' sand an' a'." He frowned and hastily added, "Dinnae get me wrong, Ah ken how likely that is." The collapse of the West Antarctic ice shelf two decades ago had inundated every established coastline; it had also stuck the last nail in the coffin of the Gulf Stream, plunging the British Isles into a sub-arctic deep freeze. Then the Americans had made it worse—at least for Scotland—by putting a giant parasol into orbit to stop the rest of the planet roasting like a chicken on a spit. Davy had learned all about global warming in geography classes at school—back when it hadn't happened—in the rare intervals when he wasn't dozing in the back row or staring at Yasmin MacConnell's hair. It wasn't until he was already paying a mortgage and the second kid was on his way that what it meant really sank in. Cold. Eternal cold, deep in your bones. "Ah'd like tae see a real beach again, someday before Ah die."

"Ye could save for a train ticket."

"Away wi' ye! Where'd Ah go tae?" Davy snorted, darkly amused. Flying was for the hyperrich these days, and anyway, the nearest beaches with sand and sun were in the Caliphate, a long day's TGV ride south through the Channel Tunnel and across the Gibraltar Bridge, in what had once been the Northern Sahara Desert. As a tourist destination, the Caliphate had certain drawbacks, a lack of topless sunbathing beauties being only the first on the list. "It's a' just as bad whauriver ye go. At least here ye can still get pork scratchings."

"Aye, weel." Tam raised his glass, just as a stranger appeared in the doorway. "An' then there's some that dinnae feel the cauld." Davy glanced round to follow the direction of his gaze. The stranger was oddly attired in a lightweight suit and tie, as if he'd stepped out of the middle of the previous century, although his neat goatee and the two small brass horns implanted on his forehead were more contemporary touches. He noticed Davy staring and nodded, politely enough, then broke eye contact and ambled over to the bar. Davy turned back to Tam, who responded to his wink. "Take care, noo, Davy. Ye've got ma number." With that, he stood up, put his glass down, and shambled unsteadily toward the toilets.

This put Davy on his lonesome next to the stranger, who leaned on the bar and glanced at him sideways with an expression of amusement. Davy's forehead wrinkled as he stared in the direction of Katie the barwoman, who was just now coming back up the cellar steps with an empty coal powder cartridge in one hand. "My round?" asked the stranger, raising an eyebrow.

"Aye. Mine's a Deuchars if yer buyin' . . ." Davy, while not always quick on the uptake, was never slow on the barrel: if this underdressed southerner could afford a heated taxi, he could certainly afford to buy Davy some beer. Katie nodded and rinsed her hands under the sink—however well-sealed they left the factory, coal cartridges always leaked like printer toner had once done—and picked up two glasses.

"New roond aboot here?" Davy asked after a moment.

The stranger smiled. "Just passing through—I visit Edinburgh every few years."

"Aye." Davy could relate to that.

"And yourself?"

"Ah'm frae Pilton." Which was true enough; that was where he'd bought the house with Morag all those years ago, back when folks actually wanted to buy houses in Edinburgh. Back before the pack ice closed the Firth for six months of every year, back before the rising sea level drowned Leith and Ingliston, and turned Arthur's Seat into a frigid coastal headland looming grey and stark above the permafrost. "Whereaboots d'ye come frae?"

The stranger's smile widened as Katie parked a half-liter on the bar top before him and bent down to pull the next. "I think you know where I'm from, my friend."

Davy snorted. "Aye, so ye're a man of wealth an' taste, is that right?"

"Just so." A moment later, Katie planted the second glass in front of Davy, gave him a brittle smile, and retreated to the opposite end of the bar without pausing to extract credit from the stranger, who nodded and raised his jar. "To your good fortune."

"Heh." Davy chugged back a third of his glass. It was unusually bitter, with a slight sulfurous edge to it. "That's a new barrel."

"Only the best for my friends."

Davy sneaked an irritated glance at the stranger. "Right. Ah ken ye want tae talk, ye dinnae need tae take the pish."

"I'm sorry." The stranger held his gaze, looking slightly perplexed. "It's just that I've spent too long in America recently. Most of them believe in me. A bit of good old-fashioned skepticism is refreshing once in a while."

Davy snorted. "Dae Ah look like a god-botherer tae ye? Yer amang civilized folk here, nae free-kirk numpties'd show their noses in a pub."

"So I see." The stranger relaxed slightly. "Seen Morag and the boys lately, have you?"

Now a strange thing happened, because as the cold fury took him, and a monstrous roaring filled his ears, and he reached for the stranger's throat, he seemed to hear Morag's voice shouting, *Davy, don't!* And to his surprise, a moment of timely sanity came crashing down on him, a sense that Devil or no, if he laid hands on this fucker, he really *would* be damned, somehow. It might just have been the hypothalamic implant that the sheriff had added to the list of his parole requirements working its arcane magic on his brain chemistry, but it certainly felt like a drenching, cold-sweat sense of immanence, and not in a good way. So as the raging impulse to glass the cunt died away, Davy found himself contemplating his own raised fists in perplexity, the crude blue tattoos of LOVE and HATE standing out on his knuckles like doorposts framing the prison gateway of his life.

"Who telt ye aboot them?" he demanded hoarsely.

"Cigarette?" The stranger, who had sat perfectly still while Davy wound up to punch his ticket, raised the chiseled eyebrow again.

"Ya bas." But Davy's hand went to his pocket automatically, and he found himself passing a filter-tip to the stranger rather than ramming a red-hot ember in his eye.

"Thank you." The stranger took the unlit cigarette, put it straight between his lips, and inhaled deeply. "Nobody needed to tell me about them," he continued, slowly dribbling smoke from both nostrils.

Davy slumped defensively on his barstool. "When ye wis askin' aboot Morag and the bairns, Ah figured ye wis fuckin' wi' ma heid." But knowing that there was a perfectly reasonable supernatural explanation somehow made it all right. *Ye cannae blame Auld Nick for pushin' yer buttons.* Davy reached out for his glass again. "'Scuse me. Ah didnae think ye existed."

"Feel free to take your time." The stranger smiled faintly. "I find atheists refreshing, but it does take a little longer than usual to get down to business."

"Aye, weel, concedin' for the moment that ye *are* the Deil, Ah dinnae ken whit ye want wi' the likes o' me." Davy cradled his beer protectively. "Ah'm naebody." He shivered in the sudden draft as one of the students—leaving—pushed through the curtain, admitting a flurry of late-May snowflakes.

"So? You may be nobody, but your lucky number just came up." The stranger smiled devilishly. "Did you never think you'd win the Lottery?"

"Aye, weel, if hauf the stories they tell about ye are true, Ah'd rather it wis the ticket, ye ken? Or are ye gonnae say ye've been stitched up by the kirk?"

"Something like that." The Devil nodded sagely. "Look, you're not stupid, so I'm not going to bullshit you. What it is, is I'm not the only one of me working this circuit. I've got a quota to meet, but there aren't enough politicians and captains of industry to go around, and anyway, they're boring. All they ever want is money, power, or good, hot, kinky sex without any comebacks from their constituents. Poor folks are so much more creative in their desperation, don't you think? And so much more likely to believe in the Rules, too."

"The Rules?" Davy found himself staring at his companion in perplexity. "Nae the Law, right?"

"Do as thou wilt shall be all of the Law," quoth the Devil, then he paused as if he'd tasted something unpleasant.

"Ye wis sayin'?"

"Love is the Law, Love under Will," the Devil added dyspeptically.

"That's a'?" Davy stared at him.

"My Employer requires me to quote chapter and verse when challenged." As he said "Employer," the expression on the Devil's face made Davy shudder. "And She monitors these conversations for compliance."

"But whit aboot the rest o' it, aye? If ye're the Deil, whit aboot the Ten Commandments?"

"Oh, those are just Rules," said the Devil, smiling. "I'm really proud of them."

"Ye made them a' up?" Davy said accusingly. "Just tae fuck wi' us?"

"Well, yes, of course I did! And all the other Rules. They work really well, don't you think?"

Davy made a fist and stared at the back of it. LOVE. "Ye cunt. Ah still dinnae believe in ye."

The Devil shrugged. "Nobody's asking you to believe in me. *You* don't, and I'm still here, aren't I? If it makes things easier, think of me as the garbage-collection subroutine of the strong anthropic principle. And they"—he stabbed a finger in the direction of the overhead LEDs—"work by magic, for all you know."

Davy picked up his glass and drained it philosophically. The hell of it was, the Devil was right: now that he thought about it, he had no idea how the lights worked, except that electricity had something to do with it. "Ah'll have anither. Ye're buyin'."

"No, I'm not." The Devil snapped his fingers, and two full glasses appeared on the bar, steaming slightly. Davy picked up the nearest one. It was hot to the touch, even though the beer inside it was at cellar temperature, and it smelled slightly sulfurous. "Anyway, I owe you."

"Whit for?" Davy sniffed the beer suspiciously. "This smells pish." He pushed it away. "Whit is it ye owe me for?"

"For taking that mortgage and the job on the street-cleaning team and for pissing it all down the drain and fucking off a thousand citizens in little ways. For giving me Jaimie and wee Davy, and for wrecking your life and cutting Morag off from her parents and raising a pair of neds instead of two fine upstanding citizens. You're not a scholar, and you're not a gentleman, but you're a truly professional hater. And as for what you did to Morag—"

Davy made another fist: HATE. "Say wan mair word aboot Morag . . ." he warned.

The Devil chuckled quietly. "No, you managed to do all that by yourself." He shrugged. "I'd have offered help if you needed it, but you seemed to be doing okay without me. Like I said, you're a professional." He cleared his throat. "Which brings me to the little matter of why I'm talking to you tonight."

"Ah'm no for sale." Davy crossed his arms defensively. "Who d'ye think Ah am?"

The Devil shook his head, still smiling. "I'm not here to make you an offer for your soul, that's not how things work. Anyway, you gave it to me of your own free will years ago." Davy looked into his eyes. The smile didn't reach them. "Trouble is, there are consequences when that happens. My Employer's an optimist: She's not an Augustinian entity, you'll be pleased to learn. She doesn't believe in original sin. So things between you and the Ultimate are . . . Let's say they're out of balance. It's like a credit-card bill. The longer you ignore it, the worse it gets. You cut me a karmic loan from the First Bank of Davy MacDonald, and the Law requires me to repay it with interest."

"Huh?" Davy stared at the Devil. "Ye whit?"

The Devil wasn't smiling now. "You're one of the Elect, Davy. One of the Unconditionally Elect. So's fucking everybody these days, but your name came up in the quality-assurance lottery. I'm not allowed to mess with you. If you die, and I'm in your debt, seven shades of shit hit the fan. So I owe you a fucking wish."

The Devil tapped his fingers impatiently on the bar top. He was no longer smiling. "You get one wish. I am required to read you the small print."

The party of the first part in cognizance of the gift benefice or loan bestowed by the party of the second part is hereby required to tender the fulfillment of 1 (one) verbally or somatically expressed indication of desire by the party of the second part in pursuance of the discharge of the said gift benefice or loan, said fulfillment hereinafter to be termed "the wish." The party of the first part undertakes to bring the totality of existence into accordance with the terms of the wish exclusive of paradox deicide temporal inversion or other willful suspension contrary to the laws of nature. The party of the second part recognizes understands and accepts that this wish represents full and final discharge of debt incurred by the gift benefice or loan to the party of the first part. Notwithstanding additional grants of rights incurred under the terms of this contract

the rights responsibilities duties of the party of the first
part to the party of the second part are subject to the Consumer Credit Regulations of 2026 . . .

Davy shook his head. "Ah dinnae get it. Are ye tellin' me
ye're givin' me a wish? In return for, for . . . bein' radge a' ma
life?"

The Devil nodded. "Yes."

Davy winced. "Ah think Ah need another Deuchars—
fuck! Haud on, that isnae ma wish!" He stared at the Devil
anxiously. "Ye're serious, aren't ye?"

The Devil sniffed. "I can't discharge the obligation with a
beer. My Employer isn't stupid, whatever Her other faults: She'd
say I was shortchanging you, and She'd be right. It's got to be
a big wish, Davy."

Davy's expression brightened. The Devil waved a hand at
Katie: "Another Deuchars for my friend here. And a drop of
the Craitur." Things were looking up, Davy decided.

"Can ye make Morag nae have . . . Ah mean, can ye make
things . . . awright again, nae went bad?" He dry-swallowed,
mind skittering like a frightened spider away from what he
was asking for. Not to have . . . whatever. Whatever he'd done.
Already.

The Devil contemplated Davy for a long handful of seconds. "No," he said patiently. "That would create a paradox,
you see, because if things hadn't gone bad for you, I wouldn't
be here giving you this wish, would I? Your life gone wrong
is the fuel for this miracle."

"Oh." Davy waited in silence while Katie pulled the pint, then
retreated back to the far end of the bar. *Whaur's Tam?* he wondered vaguely. *Fuckin' Deil, wi' his smairt suit an' high heid yin
manners . . .* He shivered, unaccountably cold. "Am Ah goin'
tae hell?" he asked roughly. "Is that whaur Ah'm goin'?"

"Sorry, but no. We were brought in to run this universe, but
we didn't design it. When you're dead, that's it. No hellfire, no
damnation: the worst thing that can happen to you is you're
reincarnated, given a second chance to get things right. It's
normally my job to give people like you that chance."

"An' if Ah'm no reincarnated?" Davy asked hopefully.

"You get to wake up in the mind of God. Of course, you stop

being *you* when you do that." The Devil frowned thoughtfully. "Come to think of it, you'll probably give Her a migraine."

"Right, right." Davy nodded. The Devil was giving *him* a headache. He had a dawning suspicion that this one wasn't a prod or a pape: he probably supported Livingstone. "Ah'm no that bad, then, is that whit ye're sayin'?"

"Don't get above yourself."

The Devil's frown deepened, oblivious to the stroke of killing rage that flashed behind Davy's eyes at the words. *Dinnae get above yersel'? Who the fuck d'ye think ye are, the sheriff?* That was almost exactly what the sheriff had said, leaning over to pronounce sentence. *Ye ken Ah'm naebody, dinnae deny it!* Davy's fists tightened, itching to hit somebody. The story of his life: being ripped off then talked down to by self-satisfied cunts. *Ah'll make ye regret it!*

The Devil continued after a moment. "You've got to really fuck up in a theological manner before She won't take you, these days. Spreading hatred in the name of God, that kind of thing will do for you. Trademark abuse, She calls it. You're plenty bad, but you're not *that* bad. Don't kid yourself, you only warrant the special visit because you're a quality sample. The rest are . . . unobserved."

"So Ah'm no evil. Ah'm just plain bad." Davy grinned virulently as a thought struck him. *Let's dae somethin' aboot that! Karmic imbalance? Ah'll show ye a karmic imbalance!* "Can ye dae somethin' aboot the weather? Ah hate the cauld." He tried to put a whine in his voice. The change in the weather had crippled house prices, shafted him and Morag. It would serve the Devil right if he fell for it.

"I can't change the weather." The Devil shook his head, looking slightly worried. "Like I said—"

"Can ye fuck wi' yon sun shield the fuckin' Yanks stuck in the sky?" Davy leaned forward, glaring at him. " 'Cause if no, whit kindae Deil are ye?"

"You want me to *what*?"

Davy took a deep breath. He remembered what it had looked like on TV, twenty years ago: the great silver reflectors unfolding in solar orbit, the jubilant politicians, the graphs showing a 20 percent fall in sunlight reaching the Earth . . . the savage April blizzards that didn't stop for a month, the endless twilight, and the sun dim enough to look at. And now the Devil wanted to give him a wish, in payment for fucking things up for a few thousand bastards who had it coming? Davy felt his lips drawing back from his teeth, a feral smile forcing itself to the surface. "Ah want ye to fuck up the sun-shade, awright? Get ontae it. Ah want tae be wairm . . ."

The Devil shook his head. "That's a new one on me," he admitted. "But—" He frowned. "You're sure? No second thoughts? You want to waive your mandatory fourteen-day right of cancellation?"

"Aye. Dae it the noo." Davy nodded vigorously.

"It's done." The Devil smiled faintly.

"Whit?" Davy stared.

"There's not much to it. A rock about the size of this pub, traveling on a cometary orbit—it'll take an hour or so to fold, but I already took care of that." The Devil's smile widened. "You used your wish."

"Ah dinnae believe ye," said Davy, hopping down from his barstool. Out of the corner of one eye, he saw Tam dodging through the blackout curtain and the doorway, tipping him the wink. This had gone on long enough. "Ye'll have tae prove it. Show me."

"What?" The Devil looked puzzled. "But I told you, it'll take about an hour."

"So ye say. An' whit then?"

"Well, the parasol collapses, so the amount of sunlight goes up. It gets brighter. The snow melts."

"Is that right?" Davy grinned. "So how many wishes dae Ah get this time?"

"How many—" The Devil froze. "What makes you think you get any more?" He snarled, his face contorting.

"Like ye said, Ah gave ye a loan, didn't Ah?" Davy's grin widened. He gestured toward the door. "After ye?"

"You—" The Devil paused. "You don't mean . . ." He swallowed, then continued, quietly. "That wasn't deliberate, was it?"

"Oh. Aye." Davy could see it in his mind's eye: the wilt-ing crops and blazing forests, droughts and heatstroke and mass extinction, the despairing millions across America and Africa, exotic places he'd never seen, never been allowed to go—roasting like pieces of a turkey on a spit, roasting in revenge for twenty years frozen in outer darkness. Hell on Earth. "Four billion fuckers, isnae that enough for another?"

"Son of a bitch!" The Devil reached into his jacket pocket and pulled out an antique calculator, began punching buttons. "Forty-eight—no, forty-nine. Shit, this has never happened before! You bastard, don't you have a conscience?"

Davy thought for a second. "Naw."

"Fuck!"

It was now or never. "Ah'll take a note."

"A credit—shit, okay then. Here." The Devil handed over his mobile. It was small and very black and shiny, and it buzzed like a swarm of flies. "Listen, I've got to go right now, I need to escalate this to senior management. Call head office tomorrow, if I'm not there, one of my staff will talk you through the state of your claim."

"Haw! Ah'll be sure tae dae that."

The Devil stalked toward the curtain and stepped through into the darkness beyond, and was gone. Davy pulled out his moby and speed-dialed a number. "He's a' yours noo," he muttered into the handset, then hung up and turned back to his beer. A couple of minutes later, someone came in and sat down next to him. Davy raised a hand and waved vaguely at Katie. "A Deuchars for Tam here."

Katie nodded nonchalantly—she seemed to have cheered up since the Devil had stepped out—and picked up a glass.

Tam dropped a couple of small brass horns on the bar top next to Davy. Davy stared at them for a moment then glanced up admiringly. "Neat," he admitted. "Get anythin' else aff him?"

"Nah, the cunt wis crap. He didnae even have a moby. Just these." Tam looked disgusted for a moment. "Ah pulled ma chib an' waved it aroon', an' he totally legged it. Think anybody'll come lookin' for us?"

"Nae chance." Davy raised his glass, then tapped the pocket with the Devil's mobile phone in it smugly. "Nae a snowball's chance in hell . . ."

Trunk and Disorderly

● IN WHICH LAURA DEPARTS AND FIONA MAKES A REQUEST

"I want you to know, darling, that I'm leaving you for another sex robot—and she's twice the man you'll ever be," Laura explained as she flounced over to the front door, wafting an alluring aroma of mineral oil behind her.

Our arguments always began like that: this one was following the script perfectly. I followed her into the hall, unsure precisely what cue I'd missed this time. "Laura—"

She stopped abruptly, a faint whine coming from her ornately sculpted left knee. "I'm leaving," she told me, deliberately pitching her voice in a modish mechanical monotone. "You can't stop me. You're not paying my maintenance. I'm a free woman, and I don't have to put up with your moods!"

The hell of it is, she was right. I'd been neglecting her lately, being overly preoccupied with my next autocremation attempt. "I'm terribly sorry," I said. "But can we talk about this later? You don't have to walk out right this instant—"

"There's nothing to talk about." She jerked into motion again, reaching for the door handle. "You've been ignoring me for months, darling: I'm sick of trying to get through to you! You said last time that you'd try not to be so distant, but look how that turned out." She sighed and froze the pose for a moment, the personification of glittering mechanistic melodrama. "You didn't mean it. I'm sick of waiting for you, Ralph! If you really loved me, you'd face up to the fact that you're an obsessive-compulsive, and get your wetware fixed so that you could pay me the attention I deserve. Until then, I'm out of here!"

The door opened. She spun on one chromed stiletto heel and swept out of my life in a swish of antique Givenchy and ozone.

"Dash it all, not again!" I leaned my forehead against the wall. "Why now, of all times?" Picking a fight, then leaving me right before a drop was one of her least endearing habits. This was the fifth time. She usually came back right afterward, when she was loose and lubed from witnessing me scrawl my butchness across the sky, but it never failed to make me feel like an absolute bounder at the time; it's a low blow to strike a cove right before he tries to drill a hole in the desert at Mach 25, what? But you can't take femmes for granted, whether they be squish *or* clankie, and her accusation wasn't, I am bound to admit, entirely baseless.

I wandered into the parlor and stood between the gently rusting ancestral space suits, overcome by an unpleasant sense of aimless tension. I couldn't decide whether I should go back to the simulator and practice my thermal curves again—balancing on a swaying meter-wide slab of ablative foam in the variable dynamic forces of atmospheric reentry, a searing blowtorch flare of hot plasma roaring past bare centimeters beyond my helmet—or get steaming drunk. And I hate dilemmas; there's something terribly non-U about having to actually *think* about things.

You can never get in too much practice before a freestyle competition, and I had seen enough clowns drill a scorched hole in the desert that I was under no illusions about my own invincibility, especially as this race was being held under mortal jeopardy rules. On the other hand, Laura's walkout had left me feeling unhinged and unbalanced, and I'm never able to concentrate effectively in that state. Maybe a long, hot bath and a bottle of sake would get me over it so I could practice later; but tonight was the predrop competitors' dinner. The club prefers members to get their crashing and burning done before the race—something to do with minimizing our third-party insurance premium, I gather—so it's fried snacks all around, then a serving of rare sirloin, and barely a drop of the old firewater all night. So I was perched on the horns of an acute dilemma—to tipple or topple as it were—when the room phone cleared its throat obtrusively.

"Ralph? Ralphie? Are you alright?"

I didn't need the screen to tell me it was Fiona, my half-sister. Typical of her to call at a time like this. "Yes," I said wearily.

"You don't sound it!" she said brightly. Fi thinks that negative emotions are an indicator of felonious intent.

"Laura just walked out on me again, and I've got a drop coming up tomorrow," I moaned.

"Oh, Ralphie, stop angsting! She'll be back in a week when she's run the script. You worry too much about her; she can look after herself. I was calling to ask, are you going to be around next week? I've been invited to a party Geraldine Ho is throwing for the downhill cross-country skiing season on Olympus Mons, but my housesitter phoned in pregnant unexpectedly and my herpetologist is having another sex change, so I was just hoping you'd be able to look after Jeremy for me while I'm gone, just for a couple of days or maybe a week or two—"

Jeremy was Fiona's pet dwarf mammoth, an orange-brown knee-high bundle of hairy malice. Last time I looked after Jeremy, he puked in my bed—under the comforter—while Laura and I were hosting a formal orgy for the Tsarevitch of Ceres, who was traveling incognito to the inner system because of some boring edict by the Orthodox Patriarch condemning the fleshpits of Venus. Then there's the time Jeremy got at the port, then went on the rampage and ate Cousin Branwyn's favorite skirt when we took him to Landsdown Palace for a weekend with Fuffy Morgan, even though we'd locked him in one of the old guard towers with a supply of whatever it is that dwarf mammoths are supposed to eat. You really can't take him anywhere—he's a revolting beast. Not to mention an alcoholic one.

"*Must* I?" I asked.

"Don't whine!" Fi said brightly. "Nobody will ever take you seriously if you whine, Ralphie. Anyway, you owe me a favor. Several favors, actually. If I hadn't covered up for you that time when Boris Oblomov and you got drunk and took Uncle Featherstonehaugh's yacht out for a spin around the moon without checking the antimatter reserve in the starboard gravity polarizer . . ."

"Yes, Fi," I said wearily, when she finally let me get a word in edgewise. "I surrender. I'll take Jeremy. But I don't promise I'll be able to look after him if I die on the drop. You realize it's under mortal-jeopardy rules? And I can't guarantee I'll be able to protect him from Laura if she shows up again running that bestiality mod your idiot pal Larry installed on her when she was high on pink noise that time—"

"That's enough about Larry," Fi said in a voice like liquid helium. "You know I'm not walking out with him anymore. You'll look after Jeremy for two weeks, and that's enough for me. He's been a little sulky lately, but I'm sure you'd know all about *that*. I'll make sure he's backed up first, then I'll drop him off on my way to Sao Paolo skyport, right?"

"What ho," I said dispiritedly, and put the phone down. Then I snapped my fingers for a chair, sat down, and held my head in my hands for a while. My sister was making a backup of her mammoth's twisted little psyche to ensure Jeremy stayed available for future torments: nevertheless she wouldn't forgive me if I killed the brute. Femmes! U or non-U, they're equally annoying. The chair whimpered unhappily as it massaged my tensed-up spine and shoulders, but there was no escaping the fact that I was stressed-out. Tomorrow was clearly going to be one of those days: and I hadn't even scheduled the traditional predrop drink with the boys yet . . .

⊙ THE NEW BUTLER CALLS

I was lying on the bottom of the swimming pool in the conservatory at the back of Chateau Pookie, breathing alcohol-infused air through a hose and feeling sorry for myself, when the new butler found me. At least, I *think* that's what I was doing. I was pretty far gone, conflicted between the need to practice my hypersonic p-waggling before the drop and the urge to drink Laura's absence out of my system. All I remember is a vague rippling blue curtain of sunlight on scrolled ironwork—the ceiling—then a huge stark shadow looming over me, talking in the voice of polite authority.

"Good afternoon, sir. According to the diary, Sir is supposed to be receiving his sister's mammoth in the front parlor in approximately twenty minutes. Would Sir care to be sober for the occasion? And what suit should Sir like to wear?"

This was about four more sirs than I could take lying down. "Nnngk gurgle," I said, sitting up unsteadily. The breather tube wasn't designed for speech. Choking, I spat it out. "M'gosh and please excuse me, but who the hell are you?"

"Alison Feng." She bowed stiffly, from the waist. "The agency sent me, to replace your last, ah, man." She was dressed in the stark black and white of a butler, and she did indeed have the voice—some very expensive training, not to mention topnotch laryngeal engineering, went into producing that accent of polite condescension, the steering graces that could direct even the richest and most uncontrollable employer in directions less conducive to their social embarrassment. But—

"You're my new butler?" I managed to choke out.

"I believe so." One chiseled eyebrow signaled her skepticism.

"Oh, oh jolly good, then, that squishie." A thought, marinating in my sozzled subconscious, floated to the surface. "You, um, do you know why my last butler quit?"

"No, sir." Her expression didn't change. "In my experience it is best to approach one's prospective employers with an open mind."

"It was my sister's mammoth's fault," I managed to say before a fit of coughing overcame me. "Listen, just take the bloody thing and lock it in the number two guest suite's dungeon, the one that's fitted out for clankie doms. It can try'n destroy anything it bally likes in there—it won't get very far, an' we can fix it later. *Hic.* Glue the door shut, or weld it or something—one of her boyfriends trained the thing to pick locks with its trunk. Got a sober-up?"

"Of course, sir." She snapped her fingers, and blow me if there wasn't one of those devilish red capsules balanced between her white-gloved digits.

"Ugh." I took it and dry-swallowed, then hiccuped. "Fiona's animal tamer'll probably drop the monster off in the porch, but I'd better get up 'n case Sis shows." I hiccuped again, acid indigestion clenching my stomach. "Urgh. Wossa invitation list for tonight?"

"Everything is perfectly under control," my new butler said, a trifle patronizingly. "Now, if Sir would care to step inside the dryer while I lay out his suit—"

I surrendered to the inevitable. After all, I thought, once you've accepted delivery of a dwarf mammoth on behalf of your sister, nothing worse can happen to you all day, can it?

Unfortunately, I was wrong. Fiona's chauffeuse did indeed deposit Jeremy, but on a schedule of her own choosing. She must have already been on the way while Fi was nattering on the blower. While Miss Feng was introducing herself, she was sneakily decanting the putrid proboscidean into the ornamental porch via her limousine's airlock. She accomplished this with stealth and panache, and made a successful retreat, but not before she completed my sister's act of domestic sabotage by removing the frilly pink restraining rope that was all that kept Jeremy from venting his spleen on everything within reach. Which he commenced to do all over Great-Uncle Arnold's snooker table, which I was only looking after while he was out-system on business. It was his triumphant squeaking that informed me that we had problems—normally Jeremy sneaks up on one in preternatural silence when he's got mischief in what passes for his mind—as I headed toward the stairs to my dressing room.

"Help me," I said, gesturing at the porch, from which a duet for Hell's piccolo and bull in a china shop was emanating.

The new butler immediately rose in my estimation by producing a bola. "Would this serve?" she asked.

"Yes. Only she's a bit short for a mammoth—"

Too late. Miss Feng's throw was targeted perfectly, and it would have succeeded if Jeremy had been built to the scale of a typical pachyderm. Alas, the whirling balls flew across the room and tangled in the chandelier while Jeremy, trumpeting and honking angrily, raised his tusks and charged at my knee-caps. "Oh dear," said the new butler.

I blinked and began to move. I was too slow, the sober-up still fighting the residual effects of the alcohol in my blood. Jeremy veered toward me, tusks raised menacingly to threaten the old family jewels. I began to turn, and was just raising my arms to fend off the monster (who appeared dead set on editing the family tree to the benefit of Fiona's line) when Miss Feng leaned sideways and in one elegant gesture ripped the ancient lace curtains right off the rail and swiped them across my assailant's tusks.

The next minute remains, mercifully, a confused blur. Somehow my butler and I mammoth-handled the kicking and struggling—not to mention squealing and secreting—Jeremy up the rear staircase and into the second-best guest suite's dungeon. Miss Feng braced herself against the door while I rushed dizzily to the parlor and returned with a tube of InstaSteel Bulkhead Bond, with which we reinforced the stout oak partition. Finally, my stomach rebelled, quite outraged by the combination of sober-up and adrenaline, at which point Miss Feng diffidently suggested I proceed to the master bathroom and freshen up while she dealt with the porch, the pachyderm, and my suit in descending order of priorities.

By the time I'd cleaned up, Miss Feng had laid a freshly manufactured suit for me on the dresser. "I took the liberty of arranging for a limousine to your club, sir," she said, almost apologetically. "It is approaching eighteen o'clock: one wouldn't want to be late."

"Eighteen—" I blinked. "Oh dear, that's dashed awkward."

"Indeed." She watched me cautiously. "Ah, about the agency—"

I waved my hand dismissively. "If you can handle Jeremy, I see no reason why you couldn't also handle Great-Uncle Arnold when he gets back from Proxima Tau Herpes or wherever he's gone. Not to mention the Dread Aunts, bless 'em. Assuming, that is, you want the job—"

Miss Feng inclined her head. "Certainly one is prepared to assume the role for the duration of the probationary period." Sotto voce she added, almost too quietly for me to catch, "Although continuing thereafter presupposes that one or both of us survives the experience . . ."

"Well, I'm glad that's sorted." I sniffed. "I'd better trot! If you could see the snooker table goes for repair and look to the curtains, I'll be off, what-what?"

"Indeed, sir." She nodded as if about to say something else, thought better of it, then held the door open for me. "Good night, sir."

● THE DANGEROUS DROP CLUB

I spent the evening at the Dangerous Drop Club, tackling a rather different variety of dangerous drop from the one I'd be confronting on the morrow. I knew perfectly well at the time that this was stupid (not to mention rash to the point of inviting the attention of the Dread Aunts, those intellects vast and cool and unsympathetic), but I confess I was so rattled by the combination of Laura's departure, my new butler's arrival, and the presence of the horrible beast that for the life of me I simply couldn't bring myself to engage in any activity more constructive than killing my own brain cells.

Boris Kaminski was present, of course, boasting in a low-key manner about how he was going to win the race and buying everyone who mattered—the other competitors, in other words—as many drinks as they would accept. That was his prerogative, for as the ancients would put it, there's no prize for second place; he wasn't the only one attempting to seduce his comrades into suicidal self-indulgence. "We fly tomorrow, chaps, and some of us might not be coming back! Crack open the vaults and sample the finest vintages. Otherwise, you may never know . . ." Boris always gets a bit like that before a drop, morbidly maudlin in a gloating kind of way. Besides, it's a good excuse for draining the cellars, and Boris's credit is good for it—"Kaminski" is not his real name but the name he uses when he wants to be a fabulously rich playboy with none of the headaches and anxieties that go with his rank. This evening he was attired in an outrageous outfit modeled on something Tsar Putin the First might have worn when presiding over an acid rave in the barbaric dark ages before the reenlightenment. He probably found it in the back of his big brother's wardrobe.

"We know you only want to get us drunk so you can take unfair advantage of us," joshed Tolly Forsyth, raising his glass of Chateau !Kung, "but I say let's drink a toast to you! Feet cold and bottoms down."

"Glug glug," buzzed Toadsworth, raising a glass with his telescoping sink-plunger thingie. Glasses were ceremoniously drained. (At least, that's what I think he said—his English is rather sadly deficient, and one of the rules of the club is: no neural prostheses past the door. Which makes it a bit dashed hard when you're dealing with fellows who can't tell a fuck from a frappé, I can tell you, like some high-bandwidth-clankie heirs, but that's what you get for missing out on a proper classical education, undead languages and all, say I.) Goblets were ceremonially drained in a libation to the forthcoming toast race.

"It's perfectly alright to get *me* drunk," said Marmaduke Bott, his monocle flashing with the ruby fire of antique stock-market ticker displays. "I'm sure I won't win, anyway! I'm sitting this one out in the bleachers."

"Drink is good," agreed Edgestar Wolfblack, injecting some kind of hideously fulminating fluorocarbon lubricant into one of his six knees. Most of us in the club are squishies, but Toadsworth and Edgestar are both clankies. However, while the Toadster's knobbly conical exterior conceals what's left of his old squisher body, tucked decently away inside his eye-turret, Edgestar has gone the whole hog and uploaded himself into a ceramic exoskeleton with eight or nine highly specialized limbs. He looks like the bastard offspring of a multitool and a mangabot. "Carbon is the new"—his massively armored eyebrows furrowed—"black?" He's a nice enough chappie, and he went to the right school, but he was definitely at the back of the queue the day they were handing out the cortical upgrades.

"Another wee dram for me," I requested, holding out my snifter for a passing bee-bot to vomit the nectar into. "I got a new butler today," I confided. "Nearly blew it, though. Sis dumped her pet mammoth on me again, and the butler had to clean up before I'd even had time to fool her into swearing the oath of allegiance."

"How *totally* horrible!" Abdul said in a tone that prompted me to glance at him sharply. He smirked. "And how is dear Fiona doing this week? It's *ages* since she last came to visit."

"She said something about the Olympic cross-country season, I think. And then she's got a few ships to launch. Nothing very important aside from that, just the après-ski salon circuit." I yawned, trying desperately to look unimpressed.

Abdul is the only member of the club who genuinely outranks Boris. Boris is constrained to use a nom de guerre because of his position as heir to the throne of all the Russias—at least, all the Russias that lie between Mars and Jupiter—but Abdul doesn't even bother trying to disguise himself. He's the younger brother of His Excellency the Most Spectacularly Important Emir of Mars, and when you've got that much clout, you get to do whatever you want. Especially if it involves trying to modify the landscape at Mach 20 rather than assassinating your elder siblings, the traditional sport of kings. Abdul is quite possibly certifiably insane, having graduated to freestyle orbital-reentry surfing by way of technical diving on Europa and naturist glacier climbing on Pluto—and he doesn't even have my unfortunate neuroendocrine disorder as an excuse—but he's a fundamentally sound chap at heart.

"Hah. Well, we'll just have to invite her along to the party afterward, won't we?" He chuckled.

"Par-ty?" Toadsworth beeped up.

"Of course. It'll be my hundredth drop, and I'm having a party." Abdul smirked some more—he had a very knowing smirk—and sipped his eighty-year Inverteuchtie. "Everyone who survives is invited! Bottoms up, chaps?"

"Bottoms up," I echoed, raising my glass. "Tally ho!"

● THE SPORT OF KINGS

The day of the drop dawned bright and cold—at least it was bright and cold when I went out on the balcony beside the carport to suit up for my ride.

Somewhat to my surprise, Miss Feng was already up and waiting for me with a hot flask of coffee, a prophylactic sober-up, and a good-luck cigar. "Is this competition entirely safe, sir?" she inquired as I chugged my espresso.

"Oh, absolutely not," I reassured her: "but I'll feel much better afterward! Nothing like realizing you're millimeters away from flaming meteoritic death to get the old blood pumping, what?"

"One couldn't say." Miss Feng looked doubtful as she accepted the empty flask. "One's normal response to incendiary situations that get the blood pumping is a wound dressing and an ambulance. Or to keep the employer from walking into the death trap in the first place. Ahem. I assume Sir *intends* to survive the experience?"

"That's the idea!" I grinned like an idiot, feeling the familiar pulse of excitement. It takes a lot to drive off the black dog of depression, but dodging the bullet tends to send it to the kennels for a while. "By the way, if Laura calls, could you tell her I'm dying heroically to defend her virtue or something? I'll see her after—oh, that reminds me! Abdul al-Matsumoto has invited us—all the survivors, I mean—to a weekend party at his pad on Mars. So if you could see that the gig is ready to leave after my drop as soon as I've dressed for dinner, and I don't suppose you could make sure there's a supply of food for the little monster, could you? If we leave him locked in the garret dungeon, he can't get into trouble, not beyond eating the curtains—"

Miss Feng cleared her throat and looked at me reproachfully. "Sir *did* promise his sister to look after the beast in person, didn't he?"

I stared at her, somewhat taken aback. "Dash it all, are you implying . . . ?"

Miss Feng handed me my preemptive victory cigar. She continued, in a thoughtful tone of voice: "Has Sir considered that it might be in his best interests—should he value the good opinion of his sister—to bring Jeremy along? After all, Lady Fiona's on Mars, too, even if she's preoccupied with the après-ski circuit. If by some mischance she were to visit the Emir's palace and find Sir sans Jeremy, it might be more than trivially embarrassing."

"Dash it all, you're right. I suppose I'll have to pack the bloody pachyderm, won't I? What a bore. Will he fit in the trunk?"

Miss Feng sighed, very quietly. "I believe that may be a remote theoretical possibility. I shall endeavor to find out while Sir is enjoying himself not dying."

"Try beer," I called as I picked up my surfboard and climbed aboard the orbital delivery jitney. "Jeremy loves beer!" Miss Feng bowed as the door closed. *I hope she doesn't give him too much,* I thought. Then the gravity squirrelizer chittered to itself angrily, decided it was on the wrong planet, and tried to rectify the situation in its own inimitable way. I lay back and waited for orbit. I wasn't entirely certain of the wisdom of my proposed course of action—there are few predicaments as grim as facing a mammoth with a hangover across the breakfast table—but Miss Feng seemed like a competent sort, and I supposed I'd just have to trust her judgment. So I took a deep breath, waited another sixty seconds (until the alarm chimed), then opened the door and stepped off the running board over three hundred kilometers of hostile vacuum.

The drop went smoothly—as I suppose you guessed; otherwise I wouldn't be here to bend your ear with the story, what? The adrenaline rush of standing astride a ten-centimeter-thick surfboard as it bumps and vibrates furiously in the hypersonic airflow, trying to throw you off into the blast-furnace tornado winds of reentry, is absolutely indescribable. So is the sight of the circular horizon flattening and growing, coming up to batter at your feet with angry fists of plasma. Ah, what rhapsody! What delight! I haven't got a poetic bone in my body, but when you tap into Toadsworth outside of the clubhouse's suppressor field, that's the kind of narcotic drivel he'll feed you. I think he's a jolly good poet, for an obsessive-compulsive clankie with a staircase phobia and knobbly protrusions; but at any rate, a more accurate description of competitive orbital-reentry diving I haven't heard from anyone recently.

A drop doesn't take long. The dangerous stage lasts less than twenty minutes from start to finish, and only the last five minutes is hot. Then you slow to subsonic velocity, let go of your smoldering surfboard, and pray to your ancestors that your parachute is folded smartly, because it would be mortifying to have to be rescued by the referee's skiff. Especially if they don't get to you until after you complete your informal inquiry into lithobraking, eh?

There was a high overcast as I came hurtling in across Utah, and I think I might have accidentally zigged instead of zagging a little too vigorously as I tried to see past a wall of cloud ahead and below me, because when my fireball finally dissipated, I found myself skidding across the sky about fifty kilometers off course. This would be embarrassing enough on its own, but then my helmet helpfully highlighted three other competitors—Abdul among them!—who were much closer to the target zone. I will confess I muttered an unsportingly rude word at that juncture, but the game's the thing, and it isn't over 'til it's over.

In the end I touched down a mere thirty-three thousand meters off course, and a couple of minutes later the referees ruled I was third on target. Perry O'Peary—who had been leading me—managed to make himself the toast of the match before he reached the tropopause by way of a dodgy ring seal on his left knee. Dashed bad play, that, but at least he died with his boots on—glowing red-hot and welded to his ankles.

I caught a lift the rest of the way to the drop base from one of the referee skiffs. As I tramped across the dusty desert floor in my smoldering armor, feeling fully alive for the first time in weeks, I found the party already in full swing. Abdul's entourage, all wearing traditional kimonos and burnooses, had brought along a modified camel that widdled champagne in copious quantities. He held up a huge platinum pitcher. "Drinks are on me!" he yodeled as Tolly Forsyth and some rum cove of a Grand Vizier—Toshiro Ibn Cut-Throat, I think—hoisted him atop their shoulders and danced a victory mazurka.

"Jolly good show, old son!" I called, ditching my helmet and gloves gratefully and pouring a beaker of bubbly over my steaming head. "Bottoms up!"

"B'm's up undeed!" Abdul sprayed camel flux everywhere in salute. He was well into the spirit of things, I could tell; indeed, the spirit of things was well into *him*.

Ibn Cut-Throat's kid brother sidled up behind me. "If Ralphie-sama would care to accompany me to His Majesty's Brother's pleasure barge, we will be departing for Mars as soon as the rest of the guests arrive," he intimated.

"Rest of the guests? Capital, capital!" I glanced round in search of my clankie doxy, but there was no sign of Laura. Which was dashed strange, for she'd normally be all over me by this point in the proceedings: my nearly being turned off in front of an audience usually turned her on like a knife switch. "Who else is coming?"

"Lots of people." Ibn Cut-Throat Junior looked furtive. "It's a very big party, as befits the prince's birthday. Did you know it was his birthday . . . ? It's a theme party, of course, in honor of the adoptive ancestors of his ancient line, the house of Saud."

Abdul al-Matsumoto is as much an authentic prince of Araby as I am a scion of the MacGregor, but that's the price we all pay for being descended from the nouveau riche who survived the Great Downsizing hundreds of years ago. Our ancestors bought the newly vacated titles of nobility, and consequently we descendants are forced to learn the bally traditions that go with them. I spent years enduring lessons in dwarf-tossing and caber-dancing, not to mention damaging my hearing by learning to play the electric bagpipes, but Abdul has it worse: he's required by law to go around everywhere with a tea towel on his head and to refrain from drinking fermented grape juice unless it's been cycled through the kidneys of an overengineered dromedary. This aristocracy lark has its downside, you mark my words.

"A theme party," I mused, removing my face from my cup. "That sounds like fun. But I was planning on taking my gig. Is that okey-dokey, as they say? Is there room in the imperial marina?"

"Of course," said the vizier, leering slightly as a shapely femme wearing a belly dancer's costume sashayed past. I noticed with distaste his hairless face and the pair of wizened testicles on a leather cord around his neck: some people think testosterone makes a cove stupid, but there's such a thing as going too far, what? "Just remember, it's a fancy-dress party. The theme is the thousand nights and one night, in honor of and for the selection of His Excellency's newest concuboid. His Excellency says you should feel free to bring a guest or two if you like. If you need an outfit—"

"I'm sure my household wardrobe will be able to see to my needs," I said, perhaps a trifle sharply. "See you there!"

Ibn Cut-Throat bowed and scraped furiously as he backed away from me. *Something odd's going on here,* I realized, but before I could put my finger on it, there was a whoosh, and I saw the familiar sight of my gig—well, actually it's Uncle Featherstonehaugh's, but as he's not due back for six years, I don't think that matters too much—descending to a perfect three-point landing.

I walked over to it slowly, lost in thought, only to meet Miss Feng marching down the ramp. "I didn't know you could fly," I said.

"My usual employer requires a full pilot's qualification, sir. Military unrestricted license with interstellar wings and combat certification." She cleared her throat. "Among other skills." She took in my appearance, from scorched ablative boots to champagne hairstyle. "I've taken the liberty of laying out Sir's smoking jacket in the master stateroom. Can I suggest a quick shower might refresh the parts that Sir's friends' high spirits have already reached?"

"You may suggest anything you like, Miss Feng. I have complete confidence in your professional discretion. I should warn you I will have a guest tagging along, but he won't be any trouble. If you show him to the lounge while I change, we shall be able to depart promptly. I don't suppose you've heard anything from Laura?"

She shook her head minutely. "Not so much as a peep, sir." She stepped aside. "So, I'm to set course for Mars as soon as the guest is aboard? Very good, sir. I shall be on the flight deck if you need me."

It appeared that Miss Feng was not only an accomplished butler, but a dashed fine pilot as well. Would miracles never cease?

○ MISS FENG SERVES THE WRONG BEER

Uncle Featherstonehaugh's boat is furnished in white oak panels with brass trim, ocher crushed-velvet curtains, and gently hissing gas lamps. A curving sofa extends around the circumference of the lounge, and for those tiresome long voyages to the outer system there are cozy staterooms accessible through hidden sliding panels in the walls. It is a model of understated classical luxury in which a cove and his fellows can get discreetly bladdered while watching the glorious relativistic fireworks in the crystal screen that forms the ceiling. However, for the journey to Abdul's pleasure dome on Mars, it suffered from three major drawbacks. For one thing, in a fit of misplaced bonhomie I'd offered Edgestar Wolfblack a lift, and old Edgy wasn't the best company for a postdrop preprandial, on account of his preferred tipples being corrosive or hypergolic, or both. Secondly, Laura was still making her absence felt. And finally, as the icing on the cake, Miss Feng had locked Jeremy in the luggage compartment. He was kicking up a racket such as only a dwarf mammoth with a hangover can, and I could barely hear myself think over the din.

"Dash it all, how much beer did you give him?" I asked my butler.

"Two liters, sir," Miss Feng replied. "Of the rather elderly Bragote from the back of your uncle's laboratory. I judged it the least likely to be missed."

"Oh dear God!" I cried.

"Bragh-ought?" echoed Edgy, as a plaintive squeal and a loud thud echoed from the underfloor bay. By the sound of things, Jeremy was trying to dash his brains out on the under-carriage. (Unfortunately, a dwarf mammoth's skull is thick enough to repel meteors and small antimatter weapons.)

"Was that a mistake?" Miss Feng inquired.

I sighed. "You're new to the household, so I suppose you weren't to know this, but anything Uncle Featherstonehaugh brewed is best treated as an experiment in creative chemi-cal warfare. He was particularly keen on the Bragote: it's a medieval recipe and requires a few years to mature to the consistency of fine treacle, but once you dilute the alcohol, it's an excellent purgative. Or so I'm told," I added hastily, not wanting to confess to any teenage indiscretions.

"Oh dear." Her brow wrinkled. "One suspected it was a little past its prime, then. I packed another firkin in the hold, just in case it becomes necessary to sedate Jeremy again."

"I don't think that will work," I said regretfully. "He's not *entirely* stupid. Uncle was working on a thesis that the Black Death of 1349 wasn't a plague but a hangover."

"Blackdeath? Is no posthuman of that nomenclature in my clade," Edgy complained.

BUMP went the floor beneath my feet, causing my teeth to vibrate. "Only two hours to Mars," Miss Feng observed. "If Sir will excuse me, I have to see to his costume before arrival." She retreated into one of the staterooms, leaving me alone with old Edgy and the pachydermal punctuation.

○ PLEASURE DOMES OF MARS: A PRIMER

I arrived on Mars somewhat rattled, but physically none the worse for wear. Miss Feng had rustled up a burnoose, djel-laba, and antique polyester two-piece for me from somewhere, so that I looked most dashing, absolutely in character as a highly authentic Leisure Suit Larry of Arabia. I tried to inveigle her into costume, but she demurred. "I am your butler, sir, not a partygoer in my own capacity. It wouldn't be right." She tucked an emergency vial of aftershave in my breast pocket. It's hard to argue with such certainty, although I have a feeling that she only said it because she didn't approve of the filmy harem pants and silver chain-mail brassiere I'd brought along in hope of being able to adorn Laura with them. Edgestar we dressed in a rug and trained to spit on demand: he could be my camel, just as long as nobody expected him to pass champagne through his secondary reactor-coolant circuit. Jeremy emerged from storage pallid and shaking, so Miss Feng and I improvised a leash and decided to introduce him as the White Elephant. Not that a real White Elephant would have menaced the world with such a malign, red-rimmed glare—or have smelled so unpleasantly fusty—but you can't have everything.

A word about Abdul's digs. Abdul al-Matsumoto, younger brother of the Emir of Mars, lives in a gothic palace on the upper slopes of Elysium Mons, thirteen kilometers above the dusty plain. Elysium Mons is so big you'd hardly know you were on a mountain, so at some time in the preceding five centuries one of Abdul's more annoying ancestors vandalized the volcano by carving out an areophysical folly, a half-scale model of Mount Everest protruding from the rim of the caldera. Thus, despite the terraforming that has turned the crumbly old war god into a bit of a retirement farm these days, Abdul's pleasure dome really *is* capped by a dome, of the old-fashioned *do not break glass, do not let air out (unless you want to die)* variety.

Ground Control talked Miss Feng down into the marina below the sparkly glass facets of the dome, then sent a crawler tunnel to lock onto the door before old Edgy could leap out onto the surface and test his vacuum seals.

The door opened with a clunk. "Let's go, what?" I asked Jeremy. Jeremy sat down, swiveled one jaundiced eye toward me, and emitted a plaintive honk. "Be like that, then," I muttered, bending to pick him up. Dwarf mammoths are heavy, even in Martian gravity, but I managed to tuck him under my arm and, thus encumbered, led the way down the tube toward Abdul's reception.

If you are ever invited to a party by a supreme planetary overlord's spoiled playboy of a younger brother, you can expect to get tiresomely lost unless you remember to download a map of the premises into your monocle first. Abdul's humble abode boasts 2428 rooms, of which 796 are bedrooms, 915 are bathrooms, 62 are offices, and 147 are dungeons. (There is even a choice of four different Planetary Overlord Command Bunkers, each with its own color-coordinated suite of Doomsday Weapon Control Consoles, for those occasions on which one is required to entertain multiple planetary overlords.)

If the palace was maintained the old-fashioned way—by squishy servants—it would be completely unmanageable: but it was designed in the immediate aftermath of the Martian hyperscabies outbreak of 2407 that finished off those bits of the solar system that hadn't already been clobbered by the Great Downsizing. Consequently, it's full of shiny clicky things that scuttle about when you're not watching and get underfoot as they polish the marble flags and repair the amazingly intricate lapis lazuli mosaics and refill the oil lamps with extra-virgin olive oil. It still needs a sizable human staff to run it, but not the army you'd expect for a pile several sizes larger than the Vatican Hilton.

I bounced out of the boarding tube into the entrance hall and right into the outstretched arms of Abdul, flanked by two stern, silent types with swords, and a supporting cast of houris, hashishin, and hangers-on. "Ralphie-san!" he cried, kissing me on both cheeks and turning to show me off to the crowd. "I want you all to meet my honored guest, Ralph MacDonald Suzuki of MacDonald, Fifth Earl of That Clan, a genuine Japanese Highland Laird from old Scotland! Ralphie is a fellow skydiver and all-around good egg. Ralph, this is—harrumph!—Vladimir Illich of Ulianov, Chief Commissar of the Soviet Onion." Ulianov grinned: under the false pate I could see it was our old drinking chum Boris the Tsarevitch. "And this—why, Edgy! I didn't recognize you in that! Is it a llama? How very realistic!"

"No, is meant to be a monkey," explained Wolfblack, twirling so that his false camel-skin disguise flapped about.

I opened my mouth to tell him that the barrel Miss Feng had strapped to his back to provide support for the hump had slipped, but he turned to Abdul. "You like?"

"Jolly good, that outfit!"

"Pip-pip," said Toadsworth, whirring alongside with a glass of the old neurotoxins gripped in one telescoping manipulator. I think it might have been a high-bandwidth infoburst rather than a toast, but due to my unfortunate hereditary allergy to implants, I'm very bad at spotting that kind of thing. "Which way to the bar, old fellow?"

"That way," suggested Ibn Cut-Throat, springing from a hidden trapdoor behind a Ming vase. He pointed through an archway at one side of the hall. "Be seeing you!" His eyeballs gleamed with villainous promise.

A black-robed figure in a full veil was staring at me from behind two implausibly weaponized clankie hashishin at the back of the party. I got an odd feeling about them, but before I could say anything, Toadsworth snagged my free hand in his gripper and began to tug me toward the old tipple station. "Come on! Inebriate!" he buzzed. "All enemies of sobriety must be inebriated! Pip-pip!" Jeremy let out a squealing trumpet blast close to my ear and began to kick. Not having a third hand with which to steady him, I let go and he shot off ahead of us, stubby ears flapping madly in the low Martian gravity.

"Oh dear," said Miss Feng.

"Why don't you just run along and see to my chambers?" I asked, irritated by the thought that the bloody elephant might poop in the punch bowl (or worse, dip his whistle in it) before I got there. "Leave the beast to me, I'll sort him out later."

"Inebriate! Inebriate!" cried Toadsworth, hurtling forward, the lights on his cortical turret flashing frantically. "To the par-ty!"

○ IN WHICH RALPH EXPLAINS THE NATURE OF HIS RELATIONSHIP WITH LAURA

Now, in the normal course of affairs it behooves a young fellow to remain discreet and close-lipped about matters of an embarrassingly personal nature. But it's also true to say that this story won't make a lot of sense without certain intimate understandings—a nod's as good as a wink to a deaf hedgehog and all that—and in any event, ever since the minutiae of my personal affairs became part of the public gossip circuit following the unfortunate affair involving the clankie dominatrix, the cat burglar, and the alien hive mind, it would be somewhat hypocritical of me to stand upon my privacy. So where a more modest cove might hesitate, please allow me to step in it and, at risk of offending your sensibilities, explain something about my complex relationship with Laura.

I rather fancy that life must have been much simpler back in the days of classical Anglo-American civilization, when there were only two openly acknowledged genders and people didn't worry about whether their intimate affairs were commutative, transitive, or reflexive. No clankie/squishie, no U or non-U, nothing but the antique butch/femme juxtaposition, and that was pretty much determined by the shape of the external genitalia you were born with. Perverts dashed well knew what they were, and life was simple. Modern life is enough to drive a cove to drugs, in my opinion: but as a Butch U Squishie of impeccable ancestry, I have the social option of maintaining a mistress (not to mention the money), and that's where Laura comes in.

Laura is very clankie and very frilly-femme with it, but with a squishy core and just sufficiently non-U to make a casual relationship marginally acceptable to polite society on the usual sub-rosa morganatic basis. We met on a shooting weekend at one of the Pahlavi girls' ranches on Luna, doing our bit for evolution by helping thin the herd of rampaging feral bots during their annual migration across the Sea of Tranquility. She was working her way around the solar system on a cut-price non-U grand tour: laboring as a courtesy masseuse in Japan and a topiarist on Ceres while saving up the price of her next interplanetary jaunt. Her parental unit was sending her a small allowance to help pay her way, I think, but she was having to work as well to make ends meet, a frightfully non-U thing for a cute little clankie princess to have to do. Our eyes met over the open breech of her silver-chased Purdey over-and-under EMP cannon, and as soon as I saw her delicately wired eyelashes and the refractive sheen on her breasts, simultaneously naked and deliciously inaccessible in the vacuum, I knew I had to have her. "Why, I do declare I'm out of capacitors!" She fluttered at me, and I bent over backward to offer her my heart, and the keys to the guest room.

There is something more than a little bit perverse about a squish who chases clankie skirt: even, one might suppose, something of the invert about them; but I can cope with sly looks in public, and our butch/femme U/non-U-tuple is sufficiently orthodox to merely Outrage the Aunts, rather than crossing the line and causing Offense. If she showed more squish while being less non-U, I suppose it would be too risqué to carry on in public—but I digress. I trust you can sympathize with my confusion? What else is a healthy boy to do when his lusts turn in a not-quite-respectable direction?

Of course, I was younger and rather more foolish when I first clapped eyes on the dame, and we've had our ups and downs since then. To be fair, she was unaware of my unfortunate neurohormonal problems: and I wasn't entirely clear on the costs, both mechanical and emotional, of maintaining a clankie doxie in the style to which she would expect to become accustomed. Nor did I expect her to be so enthusiastic a proponent of personality patches, or so prone to histrionic fits and thermionic outrages. But we mostly seemed to bump along alright—until that last predrop walkout and her failure to turn up at the drop zone.

● JEREMY RUNS AMOK; A DREADFUL DISCOVERY BEFORE DINNER

Among the various manners of recovering from the neurasthenic tension that accompanies a drop, I must admit that the one old Abdul had laid on for us took first prize for decadent (that means good) taste. It's hard to remain stressed-out while reclining on a bed of silks in a pleasure palace on Mars, with nubile young squishies to drop prefermented grapes into your open mouth, your very own mouth-boy to keep the hookah smoldering, and a clankie band plangently plucking its various organs in the far corner of the room.

Dancers whirled and wiggled and undulated across the

stage at the front of the hall, while a rather fetching young squishie lad in a gold-lamé loincloth and peacock-feather turban waited at my left shoulder to keep my cocktail glass from underflowing. Candied fruits and jellied Europan cryoplankton of a most delightful consistency were of course provided. "What-ho, this is the life, isn't it?" I observed in the general direction of Toadsworth. My bot buddy was parked adjacent to my bower, his knobbly mobility unit sucking luxuriously conditioned juice from a discreet outlet while the still-squishy bits of his internal anatomy slurped a remarkably subtle smoked Korean soy ale from a Klein stein by way of a curly straw.

"Beep beep," he responded. Then, expansively and slowly, "You seem a little melancholy about something, old chap. In fact, if you had hyperspectral imagers like me, you might notice you were a little drawn. Like this: pip." He said it so emphatically that even my buggy-but-priceless family heirloom amanuensis recognized it for an infoburst and misfiled it somewhere. "Indiscretions aside, if there's anything a cove can do to help you—enemies you want inebriating, planets you want conquering—feel free to ask the Toadster, what?"

"You're a jolly fine fellow, and I may just do that," I said. "But I'm afraid it's probably nothing you can help with. I'm in a bit of a blue funk—did you know Laura left me? She's done it before several times, of course, but she always comes back after the drop. Not this time, though, I haven't seen gear nor sprocket of her since the day before yesterday, and I'm getting a bit worried."

"I shall make inquiries right away, old chap. The clankie grapevine knows everything. If I may make so bold, she probably just felt the need to get away for a while and lube her flaps: she'll be back soon enough." Toadsworth swiveled his ocular turret, monospectral emitters flashing brightly. "Bottoms up!"

I made no comment on the evident fact that if the Toadster ever did get himself arse over gripper, he'd be in big trouble righting himself, but merely raised my glass in salute. Then I frowned. It was empty! "Boy? Where's my drink?" I glanced round. A furry brown sausage with two prominently flared nostrils was questing about the edge of the bower where my cocktail boy had been sitting a moment before.

"Grab that pachyderm!" I shouted at the lad, but I fear it wasn't his fault: Jeremy had already done him a mischief, and he was doubled over in a ball under the nearest curtain, meeping pathetically. Jeremy sucked the remains of my Saturnian-ring ice-water margaritas up his nose with a ghastly slurping noise, and winked at me: then he sneezed explosively. An acrid eruction slapped my face. "Vile creature!" I raged, "What do you think you're doing?"

I'm told that I am usually quite good with small children and other animals, but I have a blind spot when it comes to Jeremy. He narrowed his eyes, splayed his ears wide, and emitted a triumphant—not to say alcohol-saturated—trumpet blast at me. *Got you,* he seemed to be saying. *Why should you two-legs have all the fun?* I made a grab for his front legs, but he was too fast for me, nipping right under my seat and out the other side, spiking my unmentionables on the way as I flailed around in search of something to throw at him.

"Right! That does it!" People to either side were turning to stare at me, wondering what was going on. "I'm going to get you—" I managed to lever myself upright just in time to see Jeremy scramble out through one of the pointy-looking archways at the back of the hall, then found myself eyeball to hairy eyeball with Ibn Cut-Throat's administrative assistant.

"Please not to make so much of a noise, Ralphie-san," said the junior undervizier. "His Excellency has an announcement to make."

And it was true. Human flunkies were discreetly passing among the audience, attracting the guests' attention and quieting down the background of chitchat. The band had settled down and was gently serenading us with its plucked vocal cords. I glanced after Jeremy one last time. "I'll deal with *you* later," I muttered. Even by Jeremy's usual standards, this behavior was quite intolerable; if I didn't know better, I'd swear there was something up with the blighter. Then I looked back at the stage at the front of the room.

The curtain sublimed in a showy flash of velvet smoke, revealing a high throne cradled in a bower of hydroponically rooted date palms. His Excellency Abdul al-Matsumoto, younger sibling of the Emir of Mars, rose from his seat upon the throne: naked eunuch bodyguards, their skins oiled and gleaming, raised their katanas in salute to either side. "My friends," old Abdul droned in a remarkably un-Abdul-like monotone, "it makes me more happy than I can tell you to welcome you all to my humble retreat tonight."

Abdul wore robes of blinding white cotton, and a broad gold chain—first prize for atmosphere diving from the club, I do believe. Behind him, a row of veiled figures in shapeless black robes nudged each other. *His wives?* I wondered. *Or his husbands?* "Tonight is the first of my thousand nights and one night," he continued, looking more than slightly glassy-eyed. "In honor of my sort-of ancestor, the Sultan Schahriar, and in view of my now being, quote, too old to play the field, my elder brother, peace be unto him, has decreed a competition for my hand in marriage. For this night and the next thousand, lucky concubines of every appropriate gender combination will vie for the opportunity to become my sole and most important sultana."

"That's right, it's not a date!" added Ibn Cut-Throat, from the sidelines.

"I shall take the winner's hand in marriage, along with the rest of their body. The losers—well, that's too boring and tiresome to go into here, but they won't be writing any kiss-and-tell stories: if they forgot to make backups before entering the competition, that's not my problem. Meanwhile, I ask you to raise a toast with me to the first seven aspiring princesses of Mars, standing here behind me, and their intelligence and courage in taking up Scheherazade's wager." He sounded bored out of his skull, as if his mind was very definitely busy elsewhere.

Everyone raised a toast to the competitors, but I was losing my appetite even before Ibn Cut-Throat stepped to the front of the stage to explain the terms of the competition, which would begin after the banquet. I may come from a long line of Japanese pretenders to the throne of a sheep-stealing bandit laird, but we'd never consider anything remotely as bloodthirsty and medieval as this! The prospect of spending a night with dashing young Abdul gave a whole new and unwelcome meaning to losing your head for love, as I suppose befitted a pretender to the crown of Ibn Saud—never mind the Sassanid empire—by way of Mitsubishi Heavy Industries. "I don't think this is very funny," I mumbled to Toadsworth. "I wish Laura was here."

Toadsworth nudged me with his inebriator. "I don't think you need to worry about that, old chap. I spy with my little hyperspectral telescopic todger—"

Ibn Cut-Throat was coming to the climax of his spiel: "—Gaze upon the faces of the brave beauties!" he crowed. "Ladies, drop your veils!"

I gaped like a fool as the row of black-garbed femmes behind the prince threw back their veils and bared their faces to the audience. For there, in the middle of the row, was a familiar set of silver eyelashes!

"Isn't that your mistress, old boy?" Toadsworth nudged me with his inebriator attachment. "Jolly rum do, her showing up here, what?"

"But she can't be!" I protested. "Laura can't be that stupid! And I always forget to remind her to take her backups, and left to her own devices she never remembers, so—"

"'M 'fraid it's still her on the stage, old boy," commiserated the Toadster. "There's no getting around it. Do you suppose she answered an advertisement or went through a talent agency?"

"She must have been on the rebound! This is all my fault," I lamented.

"I disagree, old fellow, she's not squishy enough to bounce. Not without pulverizing her head first, anyway."

I glanced up at the stage, despondent. The worst part of it was, this was all my fault. If I'd actually bothered to pull myself out of my predrop funk and talk to her, she wouldn't be standing onstage, glancing nervously at the court executioners on either side. Then I saw her turn her head. She was looking at me! She mouthed something, and it didn't take a genius of lip-reading to realize that she was saying *get me out of here.*

"I'll rescue you, Laura," I promised, collapsing in a heap of cushions. Then my mouth-boy stuck a hookah in the old cake-hole, and the situation lost its urgent edge. Laura wasn't number one on the old chop-chop list, after all. There'd be time to help her out of this fix after dinner.

☉ AN AFTER-DINNER SHOW: DISCUSSIONS OF HORTICULTURE

Dinner took approximately four hours to serve, and consisted of tiresomely symbolic courses prepared by master chefs from the various dominions of the al-Matsumoto empire—all sixty of them. The resulting cultural mélange was certainly unique, and the traditional veal tongue sashimi on a bed of pickled jellyfish couscous a l'Olympia lent a certain urgency to my inter-course staggers to the vomitorium. But I digress: I barely tasted a single bite, so deeply concerned was I for the whereabouts of my cyberdoxy.

After the last platter of chili-roast bandersnatch in honey sauce was cleared and the dessert wine piped to our tables, the game show began. And what a game show! I sat there shuddering through each round, hoping against hope that Laura wouldn't be called this time. Ibn Cut-Throat was master of ceremonies, with two dusky-skinned eunuchs to keep track of the scorecards. "Contestant Number One, Bimzi bin Jalebi, your next question is: what is His Excellency the Prince's principal hobby?"

Bimzi rested one elaborately beringed fingertip on her lower lip and frowned fetchingly at the audience. "Surfing?"

"Aha ha-ha!" crowed Ibn Cut-Throat. "Not quite wrong, but I think you'd all agree she had a close shave there." The audience howled, not necessarily with joy. "So we'll try again. Bimzi bin Jalebi, what do you think His Excellency the prince will see in you?"

Bimzi rested one elegant hand on a smoothly curved hip and jiggled seductively at the audience. "My unmatched belly-dancing skills and"—wink—"pelvic floor musculature?"

"I'm asking the questions around here!" mugged the vizier, leering at the audience. Everybody oohed. "Did you hear a question?" Everybody oohed even louder.

"Pip-pip," said Toadsworth, quietly. He continued, "I detect speech stress analyzers concealed in the pillars, old boy. And something else."

"Let me remind you," oozed the vizier, "that you are attending the court of His Excellency the Prince, and that any untruth told before me, in my capacity as grand high judicar before his court, may be revealed and treated as perjury. And"—he paused while a ripple of conversation sped around the room—"now we come to the third and final cutoff question before you spend a night of delight and jeopardy with His Royal Highness. What do you, Bimzi bin Jalebi, see in my Prince? Truthfully now, we have lie detectors, and we know how to use them!"

"Um." Bimzi bin Jalebi smiled, coyly and winningly, at the audience, then decided that honesty combined with speed was the best policy: "a-mountain-of-gold-but-that's-not-my-only—"

"Enough!" Cut-Throat Senior clapped his hands together, and her aborning speech was arrested by the snicker-snack of eunuch katanas and a bright squirt of arterial blood. "To cut a long story short, His Excellency can't stand wafflers. Or gold diggers, for that matter." He glanced at one particular section of the audience—standing under guard and white with shock—and smiled toothily. "And so, now that we're all running neck and neck, who'd like to go next?"

"I can't bear this," I groaned quietly.

"Don't worry, old fellow, it'll be alright on the night," Toadster nudged me.

To prove him wrong, Ibn Cut-Throat hunted through the herd of candidates and—by the same nightmare logic that causes toast to always land buttered side down except when you're watching it with a notepad and counter—who should his gaze fall on but Laura.

"You! Yes, *you*! It could be you!" cried the ghastly little fellow. "Step right up, my dear! And what's your name? Laura bin, ah, Binary? Ah, such a fragrant blossom, so redolent of machine oil and ceramics! I'd spin her cams any day of the week if I still had my undercarriage," he confided to the crowd, while my pale person of pulchritude clutched a filmy veil around her and flinched. "First question! Are you the front end of an ass?"

Laura shook her head. The crowd fell silent. I tensed, balling my hands into fists. *If only there was something I could do!*

"Second question! Are you the back end of an ass?"

Laura shook her head again, silently. I tried to catch her

eye, but she didn't look my way. I quailed, terrified. Laura is at her most dangerous when she goes quiet.

"Well, then! Let me see. If you're not the front end of an ass, and you're not the back end of an ass, doesn't that mean you're no end of an ass?"

Laura gave him the old fisheye for an infinitely long ten seconds, then drawled, in her best Venusian butter-wouldn't-melt-in-her-mouth accent, "Why, I do declare, what is this 'ass' you speak of, human, and why are you so eager for a piece of it when you don't have any balls?"

I was on my feet, staggering uncertainly toward the stage, as Ibn Cut-Throat raised his fists above his head. "We have a winner!" he declared, and the crowd went wild. "You, my fragrant rose, have passed the first test and go forward to the second round! My gentles, let it be known that Laura Binary has earned the right to an unforgettable night of ecstasy in the company of His Excellency the Prince!" Sotto voce to the audience, "Unforgettable because she won't live terribly long afterward—but it's the thought that counts, heh heh!"

I saw red, of course: dash it, what else is a cove to do but stand up for his lady's honor? But before I could take a step forward, meaty hands descended on each of my shoulders. "Bed time," rumbled the guard holding my left arm. I glanced at his mate, who favored me with a suggestive leer as he fingered the edge of his blade.

"*Flower bed* time," he echoed.

"Ahem." I glanced at the stage. Laura struggled vainly while a cadre of guards as grotesquely overaugmented as old Edgy wrapped her in delicate silver manacles. "If you don't mind, old fellow, I've got a jolly good mind to tell your master he can take your daisies and push them—"

"*Bed time,*" Miss Feng hissed urgently behind my right ear. "We need to talk," she added.

"Okay, bed time," I agreed, nodding like a fool.

Guard number two sighed dispiritedly as he sheathed his sword. "Petunias."

"What?"

"Not daisies. Petunias."

"Bed time!" Guard number one said brightly. I think he had a one-track mind.

"We were supposed to bury you under the petunias if you resisted," Guard number two explained. "It's so hard on the poor things, they don't get enough sunlight out here and the soil is too alkaline—"

"No, no, see, he's quite right; if we bury him, he's supposed to be *pushing up daisies*," said Guard number one, finally getting hold of the conversation. "So! Are you going to bed or are we going to have to tuck you—"

"I'm going, I'm going," I said. The homicidal horticulturalists let go of me with visible reluctance. "I'm gone," I whimpered.

"Not yet, sir," said Miss Feng, politely but forcefully propelling me away from the ring of clankie guards surrounding the stage. "Let's continue this discussion in private, shall we?"

● MISS FENG MAKES A SERIES OF OBSERVATIONS

The guards escorted me out of the dining pavilion and up two flights of stairs, then along a passageway to a palatial guest suite which had been made available for the members of the Club. Miss Feng followed, outwardly imperturbable, although I heard her swear very quietly when the guards locked and barred the main door.

"Dash it all." I stumbled and sat down on a pile of cushions. "I've got to rescue her before it's too late!"

Miss Feng raised one thin eyebrow. "Indubitably, sir. However, we appear to be locked in a guest suite on the second floor of a heavily fortified palace built by a paranoid emperor, with guards standing outside the door to prevent any unscheduled excursions. Perhaps Sir would consider an after-dinner digestif and a postprandial nap instead?"

But I was too far gone in my funk to take heed. "This is my fault! If only I'd talked to her instead, she wouldn't be here. This isn't like Abdul, either. I know him, he's a good egg. There must be some mistake!"

"If Sir will listen to me for a minute." Miss Feng drew a deep and exasperated breath, her chest swelling beneath her traditional black jacket in a most fetching manner. "I believe the key to the problem is not rescuing Miss Laura, but *making a successful escape afterward*. Sir will perhaps recall the planetary defense grasers and orbital arbalests dug into the walls of the caldera? While I am an adequate pilot, I would much prefer our departure from the second-most-heavily-fortified noble house on Mars to be facilitated by traffic control rather than fire control. And"— she raised one eyebrow, infinitesimally— "Sir *did* promise his sister to take care of her mammoth."

"Dash it all to hell and back!" I bounced to my feet unsteadily. "Who cares about Jeremy?"

Miss Feng fixed me with a steely gaze. "*You* will, if your sister thinks you've mislaid him on purpose, sir."

"Oh." I nodded, crestfallen, and ambled over to the screen of intricately carved soapstone fretwork that separated the central lounge from the inner servants' corridor. Small thingumabots buzzed and clicked outside, scurrying hither and yon about their menial tasks. "I suppose you're right. Well, then. We need to rescue Laura, retrieve Jeremy from whatever drunken escapade he's got himself into, *and* talk our way out of this. Bally nuisance, why can't life be simple?"

"I couldn't possibly comment, sir. Compared to covering for one of Prince W XIII's little escapades, this should be a piece of cake. Incidentally, did you notice anything odd about His Excellency the Sheikh Abdul tonight?"

"What? Apart from his rum desire to butcher my beloved—"

"I was thinking more along the lines of the spinal parasite crab someone has enterprisingly planted on him since the race, sir."

"The spinal *what*? Dear me, are you telling me he's caught something nasty? Do I need to take precautions?"

"Only if Sir wishes to avoid having his brain hijacked by a genetically engineered neural parasite, his prefrontal lobes scooped out and eaten, and his body turned into a helpless meat puppet. Mr. al-Matsumoto's burnoose covered it incompletely, and I saw it when he turned round: you might have noticed he's not quite himself right now. I believe it is being controlled by Toshiro ibn-Rashid, the vizier."

"Oops." I paused a moment in silent sympathy. "Bloody poor show, that."

"I've seen more than one attempted coup d'etat in my time, sir, and it occurs to me that this is an unhealthy situation to be in. The banquet continues for three more days, and Sir might usefully question the wisdom of staying to the end. After all, His Excellency's puppet master didn't throw a party and invite all of the prince's personal friends along for no good reason, did he?"

"Then I suppose we'll just have to rescue Laura and make our escape." I stopped. "Um. But how?"

"I have a plan, sir. If you'd start by taking this sober-up, then I'll explain . . ."

● A MEETING IN THE TUNNELS

Miss Feng's plan was certainly everything you could ask for. One might even suspect her of black ops training, but experience has taught me that it is best never knowingly to underestimate the lethality of a sufficiently determined butler. I confess I harbored certain misgivings about the nature of her proposed offensive—but with stakes this high, I was prepared to work to any plan, however rare.

However, we had to wait until after midnight before we could start. That was when the guards opened the doors to direct a shambolically intoxicated Edgestar and a thoroughly inebriated Toadsworth into our company. "Pip Paaarrrrp," Toadsworth burped, drifting to a bumpy halt in the middle of the floor: his cortical turret spun round with the force of the belch, and his lights strobed down through the spectrum and went dark.

"Am being pithed," said Edgestar, shambling into a pillar and collapsing onto two legs. "Huuuurk!"

"Let me help you with that," I said, stepping forward to relieve him of his camel-hair coat—and the full firkin of Bragote that Miss Feng had secreted beneath it. I nearly dropped the cask: nine gallons of ale is quite an armful, especially when it's bottled up in corrosion-proof steel behind biohazard warning stickers.

"Aaah, that's better," mumbled Edgestar, another leg retracting with a hiss of hydraulics and a brief stink of chlorine. "'M tired. G'night."

"Quietly," Miss Feng reminded me, as I lowered the deadly cylinder to the tiles. "Excellent. I'll take care of this." She rolled it on its side, directing it toward the door, as she palmed a preemptive sober-up. "I'm sure it will be quite the hit at the squishie servants' party," she added, with something very like a shudder.

I tiptoed away from the door as she knocked on it, then dived into my room to hide as the bolts rattled. As a servant, Miss Feng stood a better chance of avoiding suspicion than I—but she had other tasks in mind for which Edgestar, Toadsworth, and I were clearly well suited. And so I swallowed my misgivings, picked up the sober-up spray, and approached Toadsworth.

"Excuse me, old chap," I essayed, "but are you up for a jolly jape?"

"Bzzzt—" The cortical turret turned toward me and I confronted a red-rimmed eyestalk. "In-ebriate? Par-ty?"

"Jolly good show, Toadster. But I think you might enjoy this first, what?" I flicked the sober-up at him. "Don't want to let the side down, do we?"

There was a muffled explosion, his cortical turret spun round three times, and steam hissed from under his gasket. "You unspeakable bounder!" he buzzed at me. "That was below the belt!" His lights flashed ominously. "I've a good mind to—"

"Whoa!" I held up a hand. "I'm terribly sorry, and I'll happily demonstrate the depth of my gratitude by groveling in any way you can imagine afterward, but we need to rescue Laura from the harem, then we need to make our escape from the evil vizier and his mind-control crabs."

"Really?" The Toadster froze in place for a moment. "Did you say *evil vizier*? With crabs? My favorite kind!"

"Top hat, old boy, top hat!" I waved my hands encouragingly. "All we need to do is get old Edgy awake—"

"Some'buddy mention nominative identifier?" With a whine of overstrained hydraulics, Edgestar Wolfblack began to unfold from his heap on the floor. One foot skidded out from under him and ended up scuttling around the skirting board. It barked furiously until the Toadster shot it to death with his inebriator. "Hurrrrk. Query vertical axis of orientation?"

"That way," I said, pointing at the ceiling. Edgy groaned, and began to quiver and fold in on himself, legs and arms retracting and strange panels extending to reveal a neat set of chromed wheels.

"Vroom," he said uncertainly. "Where to?"

"To the harem! To rescue Laura and the other contestants, while Miss Feng poisons the squishie servants with Uncle Featherstonehaugh's Bragote," I explained. "If you'd be so good as to follow me, chaps . . ."

I pulled on the black abaya Miss Feng had procured for me, then bent down to tap on the robot servitors' hatch, clutching the identity beacon Miss Feng had acquired from one of the waitrons during dinner. The hatch deigned to recognize the beacon and opened, for which I was duly grateful.

The servants' tunnel was built to a more-than-human scale: not all the bots were small bleepy things. I screwed my monocle firmly into place and hurried along the dank, roughly finished tunnel, blessing my foresight in remembering to download the map. I don't mind admitting that I was sweating with fright, but at least I was in good company, with Edgestar whizzing alongside like a demented skateboard and the Toadster gliding menacingly through the darkened tunnel, his trusty inebriator raised and ready to squirt.

Miss Feng's plan was clear. The unlucky ladies would almost certainly be languishing under lock and key in the harem. Moreover, the harem's main entrance would be guarded by palace eunuchs, or possibly chaperone bots. However, she speculated, the servants' passage would still be open—if we could get past the inevitable guard on the back door. We would find the chaperone-bot, I would pretend to be a fainting misplaced maiden, and Edgy and the Toadster would play the part of palace security guards who had found me and were taking me back inside. Getting out would be a little harder, but by then Uncle Featherstonehaugh's tipple should have taken effect . . .

Something moved in the tunnel ahead of me, and I froze, knock-kneed in fear. I don't lack moral fiber, it just gives me the runs: I swore under my breath and stopped dead in my tracks as Toadsworth ran over my hem. "What is it?" he buzzed, quietly.

"I don't know. Shh."

Holding my breath, I listened. There was a faint shuffling noise, a breathy whistling, then a clicking noise from the dark recesses of a twisty little side passage. A shadow moved across the floor, and paused. I sniffed, smelling an unholy foulness of stale sweat and something else, something familiar—then I blinked, as two evil, red-rimmed orbs brimming with pure, mindless hate loomed out of the darkness toward me.

"Jeremy!" The delinquent dwarf reared back, waving his tusks drunkenly in my face, and I could see his trunk begin to flare, ready to blow a betraying blast on the old blower. There was only one thing for it—I reached out and grabbed. "Hush, you silly old thing! If they hear you, they'll kill you, too!"

Grabbing a mammoth by the trunk—even a hungover miniature mammoth who's three sheets to the wind and tiddly to the point of winking—is not an adventure I can endorse if you value a quiet life. However, rather than responding with his usual murderous rage at the universe for having made him sixteen sizes too small, Jeremy blinked at me tipsily and sat down. For a moment I dared to hope that the incident would pass without upset—but then the gathering *toute* came out *suite*, and the foul little beast sneezed a truly elephantine blast of beer-smelling spray in my direction. I let go instinctively: he struggled back to his feet and began to reverse shambolically into the tunnel, with a mistrustful glare directed over my left shoulder. I tried to scuttle after him, only to be brought up short by the Toadster, who was still parked on my skirt. "Dash it all, men, follow that mammoth!"

With a brain-rattling crash, a fiendishly stealthed black chaperone-bot jumped over my suddenly stationary form, slipped on the snot-lubed floor, tumbled head over heels into the far wall, and crashed to the ground in a shower of spiked armor and vicious knives. I nearly jumped right out of my skin—indeed, I believe separating me from my integument had been the sole purpose of its acrobatic display.

Before I could gather my disguise and my wits and run, Edgestar revved up to speed and whizzed past me. Vrooming like a very vroomy thing, he jumped on the bally bot in a most unfriendly manner! It was a sight to see, I can assure you. The chaperone-bots of al-Matsumoto look a lot like Edgestar in humanoid form, only less convivial and disinclined to a discreet afternoon tipple when they could be out and about, briskly ripping unfortunates limb from limb. But being bots, they lack the true elan and esprit of a clankie, and even a hungover tea trolley of a posthumanoid is a fearsome thing to behold when it gets its cricket box on. Jeremy scampered off into the bowels of the palace honking tunelessly; meanwhile, old Edgy bounced up and down on the combat robot's abdomen, squeaking furiously and spinning his wheels. They had cute little cutting disks on their inner rims! The chaperone-bot lay on its back, stiletto-tipped legs curling over and inward to stab repeatedly at the assailant on its abdomen, but Edgy was too fast for it. Presently it stabbed too enthusiastically for its own good—and Edgestar yanked hard, pulling the stinger under the edge of a gaping inspection panel. With a triumphant squeal of brakes, he leapt off the chaperone-bot, transforming back into humanoid form in midair as sparks began to fly and an acrid smoke poured from his assailant's joints.

"Jolly good show, that transformer!" I exclaimed.

"Pip-pip!" said the Toadster, regaining some of his joie de vivre.

I consulted my map again. "The back door to the harem is just around the corner! I say, old chap, I think you've cleared the last obstacle. Let's shuftie, shall we? If we're to be home by tea, it behooves us to get our move on."

◉ I FIND LAURA IN QUESTIONABLE COMPANY

Well, to cut a long story short, there I was in the harem of the Emir of Mars's younger brother, surrounded by adoring femmes, while my two fellows from the Club made themselves scarce. "Darling," Laura trilled, reclining in my arms, "I do confess, I am so *touched*! Hic."

"I know, my dear, but we can't stay here." I quickly outlined what I knew. "Miss Feng thinks the evil vizier is conspiring to build resentment against the oppressive and harsh autocracy of the al-Matsumoto clan, and intends to use it to foment a revolt."

"But the al-Matsumotos aren't harsh and autocratic!"

complained one of the ladies, a cute blond bimbettebot in filmy harem pants and tank top. "They're cute!" The room descended into giggles, but I frowned, for this was no laughing matter.

"They'll be harsh and autocratic by the time Ibn Cut-Throat's spinal crab is through with Abdul! Dash it all, do you all want to be decapitated? Because that's what's going to happen if the vizier seizes power! He won't have any use for you—he's the chief eunuch! He's an ex-man, and his special power is chopping off heads! He probably thinks testosterone is something you catch from sitting too many exams."

"Oh, I'm sure I can fix *that*," a dusky six-armed beauty informed me with a flick of her aristocratic nose. "I didn't study regenerative medicine for nothing." Her arch look took in Laura. "Why don't you just take yourself and your tin-plate tart and leave us to sort out the matter of succession? She was only going to go down hard in the talent-show round, anyway."

"Pip-pip!" called Toadsworth, sailing from one vaulted side chamber to another in pursuit of a giggling conical debutante, a silk favor knotted around his monocular. "Party back at my pad, old chap! Bring a knobbly pal! Inseminate! Inseminate! Bzzt!" I looked away before the sight of his new plug-in could scar my retinas for life. You can't take these clankie stallions anywhere in polite company, they can't so much as wink at a well-lubed socket without wanting to interface with it—

"She's right, darling, we must be going." Laura laid her elegant head on my shoulder and sighed. "Oh, I do declare, my feet are killing me." I scooped her up in my arms, trying to see over a faceful of frills.

"I've missed you so much," I told her. "But what are you doing here anyway?"

"Hush"—she kissed me, and for a moment the world went away—"my brave, butch, bullish Ralphie!" She sighed again. "I was going to hold out until after the race! But I had just checked into the Hilton when I received a telephone call saying there was a gentleman waiting to see me in the lobby."

Jealousy stabbed at me. "Who was it?" I asked, cringing and glancing away as Edgestar rolled past, having transformed himself into a tentacularly enhanced chaise for the amusement of the blond bimbettebot, who appeared to be riding him around the room using his unmentionables as a joystick.

"I don't remember," she said dreamily. "I woke up here, waiting for my prince—you! I do declare—but Toshiro said he was arranging a surprise, and there'd be a party, and then it all went a little vague—"

I can tell you, I was freezing inside as I began to realize just how disoriented she was. "Laura, what's gotten into you?"

"Not you, not lately!" she said sharply, then lapsed back into dreamy incoherence. "But you came to rescue me, Ralphie, oh! He said you would. I swoon for you! Be my love rocket again!"

I saw a small silver receptacle on a nearby table, and my heart sank: she'd clearly been at the happy juice. Then I sneaked a peek at the sockets on the back of her neck, under her hairline, and gasped. Someone had planted a hedonism chip and a mandatory override on her! No wonder she was acting out of sorts.

I plucked the ghastly thing out and dropped it on the floor. "Laura, stand up!" I cajoled. "We've got to be leaving. There's a party to be going to, don't you know? Let's go."

"But my—" She wobbled, then toppled against me. "Whoops!" She giggled. "Hic." I might have pulled the chips out of the fryer, but my fish was still thoroughly pickled.

I hadn't expected this, but Miss Feng had insisted I take a reset pill, just in case. I hated to use the thing on her—or rather, Laura hated it, and this invariably led to a fight afterward—but sobriety is a lesser evil than being trapped in a castle run by a mad vizier and subjected to mood-altering implants, what? So I pressed the silver cap against the side of her neck and pushed the button.

Laura's jaws closed with an audible click, and she tensed in my arms for a second. "Ouch," she said, very quietly. "You bastard, you *know* I hate that. What's going on?"

"You're on Mars, and we're in a bally fix, that's what's going on. This Ibn Cut-Throat fellow's a thoroughly bad egg. He's sneaked a spinal crab onto old Abdul, I think he picked you up because he wants a handle on me, and doubtless that's why the rest of the Club's all here—we'd be first to notice a change in our boy Abdul's behavior, wouldn't we? The cad's obviously set up the sticky wicket so he can bowl us all out in one inning."

"Dear me." Laura stood up straight and took a step away from me. "Well, then we'd better be going, darling." She straightened her attire and looked around, raising one sculpted eyebrow at my dishevelment. "Do you know how to get out of here?"

"Certainly." I took her hand in mine, and led her toward the central gallery. "I'm sure there must be a way out around here somewhere . . ."

"Over there," offered bin-Sawbones, pointing. "You can't miss it. Head for the two hulking eunuchs and the evil vizier." She pushed me hard in the small of my back. "Sorry, but business is business. When you're trying to marry the second-richest man on Mars, you can't afford to be too picky, eh?"

● JEREMY PULLS IT OFF

The exit was indeed obstructed by Ibn Cut-Throat and his merry headsmen—with Abdul in tow, glassy-eyed and arms outstretched, muttering something about brains. And Ibn Cut-Throat had spotted us!

One thing I will credit the blighter with: his sense of spectacle was perfect. "Ah, Mister MacDonald!" he cried, menacingly twirling the antichemwar vibrissae glued to his upper lip. "How disappointing to see you here! I must confess I hoped you'd have sense enough to stay in your room and keep out of trouble. I suppose now you hope I'm going to tell you all my plans, then lock you in an inadequately secured cell so you can escape? I'm afraid not: I shall simply have you cut off shortly, chop-chop. My game's afoot, and none will stop it now, for the ineluctable dialectic of history is on my side!"

"I don't care what your dastardly scheme is, I have a bone to pick with you, my man!" I cried. The two headsmen took a step forward, and Laura clung to me in fear—whether feigned or otherwise I could not tell. "How dare you kidnap my concubine on the eve of a drop! That's not cricket, or even baseball, and it'll be a cold day in hell before I see you in any of my clubs, even by the tradesmen's entrance!" Meanwhile, Laura thrust a shapely arm inside my abaya and was fumbling with something in my dinner-jacket pocket; but my attention was fixed on the villain before me.

"Clubs." The word dropped from his lips with stony disinterest. "As if the degenerate recreations of the oligopatriarchal enemy would be of any interest to me!" I shuddered: it's always a bad sign when the hired help starts talking in polysyllables. One of his nostrils flared angrily. "Clubs and sports and jolly capers, that's all you parasites think of as you gobble down our surplus wealth like the monstrous leeches you are!" I'd struck a nerve, as I could see from the throbbing vein in his temple. "Bloated ticks languishing in the lap of luxury and complaining about your parties and fashions while millions slave to fuel your banquets! Bah." Laura unwrapped her arm from my robe and covered her face, evidently to shield herself from the scoundrel's accusations. "When we strive to better ourselves, you turn your faces away and sneer, and when we bend our necks, you use us as beasts of burden! Well, I've had enough. It's time to return your stolen loot to the toiling non-U masses."

My jaw dropped. "Dash it all, man, you can't be serious! Are you telling me you're a . . . ?"

"Yes," he grated, his eyes aflame with vindictive glee, "the crisis of capitalism is finally at hand, at long last! It's about seven centuries and a Great Downsizing overdue, but it's time to bring about the dictatorship of the non-U and the resurrection of the proletariat! And your friend Abdul al-Matsumoto is going to play a key role in bringing about the final raising of class consciousness, by fertilizing the soil of Olympus with the blood of a thousand maidens, then crown himself Big Brother and institute a reign of terror that will—"

Unfortunately, I can't tell you how the Ibn Cut-Throat Committee for the Revolution intended to proceed, because we were interrupted by two different people: by Laura, who extended her shapely hand and spritzed him down with aftershave, then by Jeremy.

Now, it helps to be aware that harems are not exactly noted for their testosterone-drenched atmosphere. I was, of course, the odd squishie out. Old Edgy was clearly hors de combat or combat des whores (if you'll strangle my French), and the Toadster was also otherwise engaged, exploring conic sections with the femmebot he'd been chasing earlier. But aside from myself and Ibn Cut-Throat—and, I suppose, Abdul, if he was still at home upstairs what with that crab-thingie plastered to his noggin—there weren't any other remotely butch people present.

Jeremy had been in smelly, sullen retreat for the past week. Not to put too fine a point on it, he was in musth, that state in which a male mammoth or elephant hates and resents other males because the universe acquires a crystal clarity and his function in life is to . . . Well, Edgestar and Toadsworth got there first, minus the trumpeting and displays of aggression, but I'm sure you understand? There were no other small male mammals present, but Jeremy was well aware of his enemy, and his desperate need to assert his alpha-male dominance before he could go in search of cows to cover—and more importantly, there was one particular scent he associated with the enemy from long mutual acquaintance. His enemy smelled like *me*. But *I* was shrouded in a blackly occlusive robe, while Ibn Cut-Throat had just been doused in my favorite pheromone-enhanced splash. And whatever Jeremy's other faults, he's never been slow to jump to a conclusion.

I do not know what passed through the 80 percent of Jeremy's cranial capacity that serves as target acquisition and fire control, but he made his choice almost instantly and launched himself straight for where Ibn Cut-Throat's crown jewels had once resided. Proboscideans are not usually noted for their glide ratio, but in the weak Martian gravity Jeremy was positively areobatic, and he aimed straight for Toshiro's tushie with grace and elegance and tusks.

"Tally-ho, old boy!" I shouted, giving him the old-school best, as Laura took two steps smartly forward and, raising her skirts, daintily kick-boxed headsman number one in the forehead with one of her most pointed assets—for her ten-centimeter stiletto heels are not only jolly fine pins, they're physical extensions of her chrome-plated ankles.

Now, I confess that things looked dicey when headsman number two turned on me with his ax and bared his teeth at me. But I'm not the Suzuki of MacDonald for nothing, and I know a thing or two about fighting! I threw the abaya back over my head to free my arms, and pointed Toadsworth's inebriator—which he had earlier entrusted to my safekeeping in order to free up a socket for his inseminator—at the villain. "Drop it! Or I'll drop you!" I snarled.

My threat didn't work. The thug advanced on me, and as he raised his blade I discovered to my horror that the Toadster must have some very strange fingers in order to work that trigger. But just as the barber of Baghdad was about to trim my throat, a svelte black silhouette drew up behind him and poured a canister of vile brown ichor over his head! Screaming and burbling imprecations, he sank to the floor clawing at his eyes, just in time for Laura to finish him off with a flamenco stomp.

Miss Feng cleared her throat apologetically as she lowered the empty firkin to the floor. (The brightly painted tiles began to blur and run where its Bragote-damp rim rested on them.) "Sir might be pleased to note that one has taken the liberty of moving his yacht round to the tradesmen's entrance and disabling the continental defense array in anticipation of Sir's departure. Was Sir planning to stay for the bombe surprise, or would he agree that this is one party that he would prefer to cut short?"

I glanced at Ibn Cut-Throat, who was still writhing in agony under Jeremy's merciless onslaught, and then at the two pithed headsmen. "I think it's a damned shame to outstay our welcome at any party, don't you agree?" Laura nodded enthusiastically and knelt to tickle Jeremy's trunk. "By all means, let's leave. If you'd be so good as to pour a bucket of cold water over Edgy and the Toadster, I'll take Abdul in hand and we can drop him off at a discreet clinic where they treat spinal crabs, what-what?"

"That's a capital idea, sir. I shall see to it at once." Miss Feng set off to separate the miscreants from their amorous attachments.

I turned to Laura, who was still tickling Jeremy—who by now was lying on his back, panting—and raised an eyebrow. "Isn't he sweet?" she sang.

"If you say so. You're carrying him, though," I said, ungratefully. "Let's hie thee well and back to Castle Pookie.

This has been altogether too much of the wrong kind of company for me, and I could do with a nightcap in civilized company."

"Darling!" she grabbed me enthusiastically by the trousers. "And we can watch a replay of your jump together!"

And indeed, to cut a long story short, that's exactly what we did—but first I took the precaution of locking Jeremy in the second-best guest suite's dungeon with a bottle of port, and gave Miss Feng the night off.

After all, two's company, but three's jolly confusing, what?

Afterword—"Trunk and Disorderly"

Humor is *hard*. Sometimes it works, but more often it doesn't; it's surprisingly difficult to make other people laugh, as any number of aspiring stand-ups have discovered. Ironically, good humor reads easily, so that we tend to be fooled into thinking that it was a trivial matter to write. One of the finest practitioners working in the English language was P. G. Wodehouse, whose interwar social comedies about the hapless young Bertie Wooster and his long-suffering butler Jeeves have become classics of the field. They're as light as soufflés and as easy to absorb as air—which is why it took me three years of on-and-off blood, sweat, and tears to squeeze out "Trunk and Disorderly," which at its best aspires to the level of Wodehouse's recycling bin. In truth, drama is easy; true comedy is murderously difficult to carry off.

I was hoping to get a series of stories out of this universe, but in the end I decided to cut my losses and chalked it up as a test run for *Saturn's Children*.

Palimpsest

○ FRESH MEAT

This will never happen:

You will flex your fingers as you stare at the back of the youth you are going to kill, father to the man who will never now become your grandfather; and as you trail him home through the snowy night, you'll pray for your soul, alone in the darkness.

Memories are going to come to you unbidden even though you'll try to focus on the task in hand. His life—that part of it which you arrived kicking and squalling in time to share with him before the end—will pass in front of your eyes. You will remember Gramps in his sixties, his hands a bunch of raisin-wrinkled grape joints as he holds your preteen wrists and shows you how to cast the fly across the water. And you'll remember the shrunken husk of his seventies, standing speechless and numb by Gran's graveside in his too-big suit, lying at last alone in the hospice bed, breath coming shallow and fast as he sleeps alone with the cancer. These won't be good memories. But you know the rest of the story too, having heard it endlessly from your parents: young love and military service in a war as distant as faded sepia photographs from another generation's front, a good job in the factory and a wife he will quietly adore who will in due course give him three children, from one of whose loins you in turn are drawn. Gramps will have a good, long life and live to see five grandchildren and a myriad of wonders, and this boy-man on the edge of adulthood who you are compelled to follow as he walks to the recruiting office holds the seeds of the man you will remember . . . But it's him or you.

Gramps would have had a good life. You must hold on to that. It will make what's coming easier.

You will track the youth who will never be your grandfather through the snow-spattered shrubbery and long grass along the side of the railroad tracks, and the wool-and-vegetable-fiber cloth that you wear—your costume will be entirely authentic—chafes your skin. By that point you won't have bathed for a week, or shaved using hot water: you are a young thug, a vagrant, and a wholly bad sort. That is what the witnesses will see, the mad-eyed young killer in the sweat-stained suit with the knife and his victim, so vulnerable with his throat laid open almost to the bone. He'll sprawl as if he is merely sleeping. And there will be outrage and alarm as the cops and concerned citizens turn out to hunt the monster that took young Gerry from his family's arms, and him just barely a man: but they won't find you, because you'll push the button on the pebble-sized box and Stasis Control will open up a timegate and welcome you into their proud and lonely ranks.

When you wake up in your dorm two hundred years-objective from now, bathed in stinking fear-sweat, with the sheet sucking onto your skin like a death-chilled caul, there will be nobody to comfort you and nobody to hold you. The kindness of your mother's hands and the strength of your father's wrists will be phantoms of memory, ghosts that echo round your bones, wandering homeless through the mausoleum of your memories.

They'll have no one to remember their lives but you; and all because you will believe the recruiters when they tell you that to join the organization you must kill your own grandfather, and that if you do not join the organization, you will die.

(It's an antinepotism measure, they'll tell you, nodding,

not unkindly. And a test of your ruthlessness and determination. And besides, we all did it when it was *our* turn.)

Welcome to the Stasis, Agent Pierce! You're rootless now, an orphan of the time stream, sprung from nowhere on a mission to eternity. And you're going to have a *remarkable* career.

Yellowstone

"You've got to remember, humanity always goes extinct," said Wei, staring disinterestedly at the line of women and children shuffling toward the slave station down by the river. "*Always.* A thousand years, a hundred thousand, a quarter million—doesn't matter. Sooner or later, humans go extinct." He was speaking Urem, the language the Stasis used among themselves.

"I thought that was why we were here? To try and prevent it?" Pierce asked, using the honorific form appropriate for a student questioning his tutor, although Wei was, in truth, merely a twelfth-year trainee himself: the required formality was merely one more reminder of the long road ahead of him.

"No." Wei raised his spear and thumped its base on the dry, hard-packed mud of the observation mound. "We're going to relocate a few seed groups, several tens of thousands. But the rest are still going to die." He glanced away from the slaves: Pierce followed his gaze.

Along the horizon, the bright red sky darkened to the color of coagulated blood on a slaughterhouse floor. The volcano, two thousand kilometers farther around the curve of the planet, had been pumping ash and steam into the stratosphere for weeks. Every noon, in the badlands where once the Mississippi delta had writhed, the sky wept brackish tears.

"You're from before the first extinction epoch, aren't you? The pattern wasn't established back then. That must be why you were sent on this field trip. You need to understand that this *always* happens. Why we do this. You need to know it in your guts. Why we take the savages and leave the civilized to die."

Like Wei, and the other Stasis agents who had silently liquidated the camp guards and stolen their identities three nights before, Pierce was disguised as a Benzin warrior. He wore the war paint and beaten-aluminum armbands, bore the combat scars. He carried a spear tipped with a shard of synthetic diamond, mined from a deep seam of prehistoric automobile windshields. He even wore a Benzin face: the epicanthic folds and dark skin conferred by the phenotypic patches had given him food for thought, an unfamiliar departure from his white-bread origins. Gramps (he shied from the memory) would have died rather than wear this face.

Pierce was not yet even a twelve-year trainee: he'd been in the service for barely four years-subjective. But he was ready to be sent out under supervision, and this particular operation called for warm bodies rather than retrocausal subtlety.

Fifty years ago, the Benzin had swept around the eastern coastline of what was still North America, erupting from their heartland in the central isthmus to extend their tribute empire into the scattered tribal grounds of post-Neolithic nomads known to Stasis Control only by their code names: the Alabamae, the Floridae, and the Americae. The Benzin were intent on conquering the New World, unaware that it had been done at least seventeen times already since the start of the current Reseeding. They did not understand the significance of the redness in the western sky or the shaking of the ground, ascribing it to the anger of their tribal gods. They had no idea that these signs heralded the end of the current interglacial age, or that their extinction would be a side effect of the coming Yellowstone eruption—one of a series that occurred at six-hundred-thousand-year intervals during the early stages of the Lower First Anthropogenic epoch.

The Benzin didn't take a long view of things, for although their priest-kings had a system of writing, most of them lived in the hazily defined ahistorical myth-world of the preliterate. Their time was running out all the same. Yellowstone was waking, and even the Stasis preferred to work around such brutal geological phenomena, rather than through them.

"Yes, but why take *them*?" Pierce nodded toward the silently trudging Alabamae women and children, their shoulders stooped beneath the burden of their terror. They'd been walking before the spear points of their captors for days; they were exhausted. The loud ones had already died, along with the lame. The raiders who had slain their men and stolen them away to a life of slavery sat proudly astride their camels, their enemies' scalps dangling from their kotekas like bizarre pubic wigs. "The Benzin may be savages, but these people are losers—they came off worse."

Wei shook his head minutely. "The adults are all female, and mostly pregnant at that. These are the healthy ones, the ones who survived the march. They're gatherers, used to living off the land, and they're all in one convenient spot."

Pierce clenched his teeth, realizing his mistake. "You're going to use them for Reseeding? Because there are fewer bodies, and they're more primitive, more able to survive in a wilderness . . . ?"

"Yes. For a successful Reseeding we need at least twenty thousand bodies from as many diverse groups as possible, and even then we risk a genetic bottleneck. And they need to be able to survive in the total absence of civilization. If we dumped *you* in the middle of a Reseeding, you would probably not last a month. No criticism intended; neither would I. Those warriors"—Wei raised his spear again, as if saluting the raiders—"require slaves and womenfolk and a hierarchy to function. The tip of your spear was fashioned by a slave in the royal armories, not by a warrior. Your moccasins and the cloth of your pants were made by Benzin slaves. They are halfway to reinventing civilization: given another five thousand years-subjunctive, their distant descendants might build steam engines and establish ubiquitous recording frameworks, bequeathing their memories to the absolute future. But for a Reseeding they're as useless as we are."

"But they don't have half a deci—"

"Be still. They're moving."

The last of the slaves had been herded between the barbed hedges of the entrance passageway, and the gate guards lifted the heavy barrier back into position. Now the raiders kicked their mounts into motion, beating and poking them around the side of the spiny bamboo fence in a circuit of the guard posts. Wei and Pierce stood impassively as the camel riders spurred down on them. At the last moment, their leader pulled sideways, and his mount snorted and pawed at the ground angrily as he leaned toward Wei.

"Hai!" he shouted, in the tonal trade tongue of the northern Benzin. "I don't remember you!"

"I am Hawk! Who in the seventh hell are *you*?"

Wei glared at the rider, but the intruder just laughed raucously and spat over the side of his saddle: it landed on the mud, sufficiently far from Wei to make it unclear whether it was a direct challenge.

Pierce tightened his grip on his spear, moving his index finger closer to the trigger discreetly printed on it. High above them, a vulturelike bird circled the zone of confrontation with unnatural precision, its fire-control systems locked on.

"I am Teuch," said the rider, after a pause. "I captured these women! In the name of our Father I took them, and in the name of our Father I got them with children to work in the paddies! What have you done for our Father today?"

"I stand here," Wei said, lifting the butt of his spear. "I guard our Father's flock while assholes like you are out having fun."

"Hai!" The rider's face split in a broad, dust-stained grin. "I see you, too!" He raised his right fist and for an instant Pierce had an icy vision of his guts unraveling around a barbarian's spear; but the camel lifted its head and brayed as Teuch nudged it in a surprisingly delicate sidestep away from Wei, away from the hedge of thorns, away from the slave station. And away from the site of the timegate through which the evacuation team would drive the camp inmates in two days' time. The prisoners would be deposited at the start of the next Reseeding. But none of the Benzin would live to see that day, a hundred thousand years-objective or more in the future.

Perhaps their camels would leave their footprints in the choking, hot rain of ash that would roll across the continent with tomorrow's sunset. Perhaps some of those footprints would fossilize, so that the descendants of the Alabamae slaves would uncover them and marvel at their antiquity in the age to come. But immortality, Pierce thought, was a poor substitute for not dying.

Paying Attention in Class

It was a bright and chilly day on the roof of the world. Pierce, his bare head shaved like the rest of the green-robed trainees, sat on a low stool in a courtyard beneath the open sky, waiting for the tutorial to begin. Riding high above the ancient stone causeway and the spiral minarets of the Library

Annex, the moon bared her knife-slashed cheeks at Pierce, as if to remind him of how far he'd come.

"Good afternoon, Honorable Students."

The training camp nestled in a valley among the lower peaks of the Mediterranean Alps. Looming over the verdant lowlands of the Sahara basin, in this epoch they rose higher than the stumps of the time-weathered Himalayas.

"Good afternoon, Honorable Scholar Yarrow," chanted the dozen students of the sixth-year class.

Urem, like Japanese before it, paid considerable attention to the relative status of speaker and audience. Many of the cultures the Stasis interacted with were sensitive to matters of gender, caste, and other signifiers of rank, so the designers of Urem had added declensions to reflect these matters. New recruits were expected to practice the formalities diligently, for a mastery of Urem was important to their future—and none of them were native speakers.

"I speak to you today of the structure of human history and the ways in which we may interact with it."

Yarrow, the Honorable Scholar, was of indeterminate age: robed in black, her hair a stubble-short golden halo, she could have been anywhere from thirty to three hundred. Given the epigenetic overhaul the Stasis provided for their own, the latter was likelier—but not three thousand. Attrition in the line of duty took its toll over the centuries. Yarrow's gaze, when it fell on Pierce, was clear, her eyes the same blue as the distant horizon. This was the first time she had lectured Pierce's class—not surprising, for the college had many tutors, and the path to graduation was long enough to tax the most disciplined. She was, he understood, an expert on what was termed the Big Picture. He hadn't looked her up in the local Library Annex ahead of time. (In his experience it was generally better to approach these lessons with an open mind. And in any case, students had only patchy access to the records of their seniors.)

"As a species, we are highly unstable, prone to Malthusian crises and self-destructive wars. This apparent weakness is also our strength—when reduced to a rump of a few thousand illiterate hunter-gatherers, we can spread out and tame a planet in mere centuries, and build high civilizations in a handful of millennia.

"Let me give you some numbers. Over the two and a half million epochs accessible to us—each of which lasts for a million years—we shall have reseeded starter populations nearly twenty-one million times, with an average extinction period of sixty-nine thousand years. Each Reseeding event produces an average of eleven-point-six planet-spanning empires, thirty-two continental empires, nine hundred and sixty-odd languages spoken by more than one million people, and a total population of one-point-seven trillion individuals. Summed over the entire life span of this planet—which has been vastly extended by the cosmological engineering program you see above you every night—there are nearly twenty billion billion of us. We are not merely legion—we rival in our numbers the stars of the observable universe in the current epoch.

"Our species is legion. And throughout the vast span of our history, ever since the beginning of the first panopticon empire during our first flowering, we have committed to permanent storage a record of everything that has touched us—everything but those events that have definitively unhappened."

Pierce focused on Yarrow's lips. They quirked slightly as she spoke, as if the flavor of her words was bitter—or as if she was suppressing an unbidden humor, intent on maintaining her gravitas before the class. Her mouth was wide and sensual, and her lips curiously pale, as if they were waiting to be warmed by another's touch. Despite his training, Pierce was as easily distracted as any other twentysomething male, and try as he might, he found it difficult to focus on her words: he came from an age of hypertext and canned presentations and found that these archaic, linear tutorials challenged his concentration. The outward austerity of her delivery inflamed his imagination, blossoming in a sensuous daydream in which the wry taste of her lips blended with the measured cadences of her speech to burn like fire in his mind.

"Uncontrolled civilization is a terminal consumptive state, as the victims of the first extinction discovered the hard way. We have left their history intact and untouched, that we might remember our origins and study them as a warning; some of you in this cohort have been recruited from that era. In other epochs we work to prevent wild efflorescences of resource-depleting overindustrialization, to suppress competing abhuman intelligences, and to prevent the pointless resource drain of attempts to colonize other star systems. By shepherding this planet's resources and manipulating its star and neighboring planets to maximize its inhabitable duration, we can achieve Stasis—a system that supports human life for a thousand times the life of the unmodified sun, and that remembers the time line of every human life that ever happened."

Yarrow's facts and figures slid past Pierce's attention like warm syrup. He paid little heed to them, focusing instead on her intonation, the little twitches of the muscles in her cheeks as she framed each word, the rise and fall of her chest as she breathed in and out. She was impossibly magnetic: a puritan sex icon, ascetic and unaware, attractive but untouchable. It was foolish in the extreme, he knew, but for some combination of tiny interlocking reasons he found her unaccountably exciting.

"All of this would be impossible without our continued ownership of the timegate. You already know the essentials. What you may not be aware of is that it is a unique, easily depleted resource. The timegate allows us to open wormholes connecting two openings in four-dimensional space-time. But the exclusion principle prevents two such openings from overlapping in time. Tear-up and tear-down is on the order of seven milliseconds, a seemingly tiny increment when you compare it to the trillion-year span that falls within our custody. But when you slice a period of interest into fourteen-millisecond chunks, you run out of time fast. Each such span can only ever be touched by us once, connected to one other place and time of our choosing.

"Stasis Control thus has access to a theoretical maximum of 5.6 times 10^{21} slots across the totality of our history—but our legion of humanity comes perilously close, with a total of 2 times 10^{19} people. Many of the total available slots are reserved for data, relaying the totality of recorded human history to the Library—fully ninety-six percent of humanity lives in eras where ubiquitous surveillance or personal life-logging technologies have made the recording of absolute history possible, and we obviously need to archive their lifelines. Only the ur-historical prelude to Stasis, and periods of complete civilizational collapse and Reseeding, are not being monitored in exhaustive detail.

"To make matters worse: in practice there are far fewer slots available for actual traffic, because we are not, as a species, well equipped for reacting in spans of less than a second. The seven-millisecond latency of a timegate is shorter by an order of magnitude than the usual duration of a gate used for transport.

"We dare not use gates for iterated computational processes, or to open permanent synchronous links between epochs, and while we could in theory use it to enable a single faster-than-light starship, that would be horribly wasteful. So we are limited to blink-and-it's-gone wormholes connecting time slices of interest. And we must conclude that the slots we allocate to temporal traffic are a scarce resource because—"

Yarrow paused and glanced across her audience. Pierce shifted slightly on his stool, a growing tension in his crotch giving his distraction a focus. Her gaze lingered on him a moment too long, as if she sensed his inattention: the slight hint of amusement, imperceptible microexpressions barely glimpsed at the corners of her mouth, sent a panicky shiver up his spine. *She's going to ask questions,* he realized, as she opened her lips. "What applications of the timegate are ruled out by the slot latency period, class? Does anyone know? Student Pierce? What do *you* know?" She looked at him directly, expectantly. The half smile nibbled at her cheeks, but her eyes were cool.

"I, um, I don't—" Pierce flailed for words, dragged back to the embarrassing present from his sensual daydream. "The latency period?"

"You don't *what*?" Honorable Scholar Yarrow raised one perfect eyebrow in feigned disbelief at his fluster. "But of course, Student Pierce. You *don't*. That has always been your besetting weakness: you're easily distracted. Too curious for your own good." Her smile finally broke, icy amusement crinkling around her eyes. "See me in my office after the tutorial," she said, then turned her attention back to the rest of the class, leaving him to stew in fearful anticipation. "I do hope you have been paying more attention—"

The rest of Yarrow's lecture slid past Pierce in a delirium of embarrassment as she spoke of deep time, of salami-sliced vistas of continental drift and re-formation, of megayears devoted to starlifting and the frozen, lifeless gigayears during which the Earth had been dislodged from its celestial track, to drift far from the sun while certain necessary restructuring was carried out. *She knows me,* he realized sickly, watching the pale lips curl around words that meant nothing and everything. *She's met me before.* These things happened in the Stasis; the formal etiquette was deliberate padding to break the soul-shaking impact of such collisions with the consequences of your own future. *She must think I'm an idiot—*

The lecture ended in a flurry of bowing and dismissals. Confused, Pierce found himself standing before the Scholar on the roof of the world, beneath the watching moon. She was very beautiful, and he was utterly mortified. "Honorable Scholar, I don't know how to explain, I—"

"Silence." Yarrow touched one index finger to his lips. His nostrils flared at the scent of her, floral and strange. "I told you to see me in my office. Are you coming?"

Pierce gaped at her. "But Honorable Scholar, I—"

"—forgot that, as your tutor, I am authorized to review your Library record." She smiled secretively. "But I didn't need to: You—your future self—told me why you were distracted, many years-subjective ago. There is a long history between us." Her humor dispersed like mist before a hot wind. "Will you come with me now? And not make an unhappening of our life together?"

"But I—" For the first time he noticed she was using the honorific form of "you," in its most intimate and personal case. "What do you mean, *our* life?"

She began to walk toward the steps leading down to the Northern Courtyard. "*Our* life?" He called after her, dawning anger at the way he'd been manipulated lending his voice an edge. "What do you mean, *our* life?"

She glanced back at him, her expression peculiar—almost wistful. "You'll never know if you don't get over your pride, will you?" Then she looked back at the two hundred stone steps that lay before her, inanimate and treacherous, and began to descend the mountainside. Her gait was as steady and dignified as any matron turning her back on young love and false memories.

He watched her recede for almost a minute before his injured dignity gave way, and he ran after her, stumbling recklessly from step to stone, desperate to discover his future.

○ HACKING HISTORY

Pleasure Empires

They will welcome you as a prince among princes, and they will worship you as a god among gods. They will wipe the sweat from your brow and the dust of the road from your feet, and they will offer to you their sons and daughters and the wine of their vineyards. Their world exists only to please the angels of the celestial court, and we have granted you this leave to dwell among our worshippers, with all the rights and honors of a god made flesh.

They will bring wine unto you, and the fruit of the dream poppy. They will clothe you in silk and gold, and lie naked beneath your feet, and abase themselves before your every whim. They are the people of the Pleasure Empires, established from time to time by the decree of the lords of Stasis to serve their loyal servants, and it is their honor and their duty to obey you and demonstrate their love for you in any way that you desire, for all their days and lifetimes upon the Earth. And you will dwell among them in a palace of alabaster, surrounded by gardens of delight, and you shall want for nothing.

Your days of pleasure will number one thousand and one; your lovers will number a thousand or one as you please; your pleasures will be without number; and the number of tomorrow's parties shall be beyond measure. You need not leave until the pleasures of flesh and mind pale, and the novelty of infinite luxury becomes a weight on your soul. Then and only then, you will yearn for the duty which lends meaning to life; energized, you will return to service with serenity and enthusiasm. And your colleagues will turn aside from their tasks and wonder at your eagerness: for though you may have spent a century in the Pleasure Empires, your absence from your duty will have lasted barely a heartbeat. You are a loyal servant of the Stasis: and you may return to paradise whenever it pleases you, because we want you to be happy in your work.

Palimpsest Ambush

Almost a hundred kiloyears had passed since the Yellowstone eruption that wiped out the Benzin and the hunter-gatherer tribes of the Gulf Coast. The new Reseeding was twelve thousand years old; civilization had taken root again, spreading around the planet with the efflorescent enthusiasm of a parasitic vine. It was currently going through an expansionist-mercantilist phase, scattered city-states and tribute empires gradually coalescing and moving toward a tentative enlightenment. Eventually they'd rediscover electronics and, with the institution of a ubiquitous surveillance program, finally reconquer the heights of true civilization. Nobody looking at the flourishing cities and the white-sailed trade ships could imagine that the people who built them were destined for anything but glory.

Pierce stumbled along a twisty cobbled lane off the Chandler's Street in Carnegra, doing his faux-drunken best to look like part of the scenery. Sailors fresh ashore from Ipsolian League boats weren't a rarity here, and it'd certainly explain his lack of fluency in Imagra, the local creole. It was another training assignment, but with six more years-subjective of training and a Stasis phone implant, Pierce now had some degree of independence. He was trusted to work away from the watchful eyes of his supervisor, on assignments deemed safe for a probationer-agent.

"Proceed to the Red Duck on Margrave Way at the third hour of Korsday. Take your detox first, and stay on the small beer. You're there as a level-one observer and level-zero exit decoy to cover our other agent's departure. There's going to be a fight, and you need to be ready to look after yourself; but remember, you're meant to be a drunken sailor, so you need to look the part until things kick off. Once your target is out of the picture, you're free to leave. If it turns hot, escalate it to me, and I'll untangle things retroactively."

It was all straightforward stuff, although normally Pierce wouldn't be assigned to a job in Carnegra, or indeed to any job in this epoch. Training to blend in seamlessly with an alien culture was difficult enough that Stasis agents usually worked in their home era, or as close to it as possible, where their local knowledge was most useful. As it was, two months of full-time study had given him just enough background to masquerade as a foreign sailor—in an archipelagean society that was still three centuries away from reinventing the telegraph. *It's a personalized test,* he'd realized with a jittery shudder of alertness, as if he'd just downed a mug of maté. Someone up the line in Operational Analysis would be watching his performance, judging his flexibility. He determined to give it his all.

It took him two months of hard training, in language and cultural studies and local field procedures—all for less than six hours on the ground in Carnegra. And the reason he was certain it was a test: Supervisor Hark had changed the subject when he'd asked who he was there to cover for.

Margrave Way was a cobblestoned alley, stepped every few meters to allow for the slope of the hillside, lined on either side with the single-story bamboo shopfronts of fishmongers and chandlers. Pierce threaded his wobbly way around servants out shopping for the daily catch, water carriers, fruit and vegetable sellers, and beggars; dodged a rice merchant's train of dwarf dromedaries loaded with sacks; and avoided a pair of black-robed scholars from one of the seminaries that straggled around the flanks of the hill like the thinning hair on the pate of an elderly priest. Banners rippled in the weak onshore breeze; paper skull-lanterns with mirror-polished eyes to repel evil spirits bounced gaudily beneath the eaves as he entered the inn.

The Red Duck was painted the color of its namesake. Pierce hunched beneath the low awning and probed the gloom carefully, finally emerging into the yard out back with his eyes watering. At this hour the yard was half-empty, for the tavern made much of its trade in food. The scent of honeysuckle hung heavy over the decking; the hibiscus bushes at the sides of the yard were riotously red. Pierce staked out a bench near the rear wall with a clear view of the entrance and the latrines, then unobtrusively audited the other patrons, careful to avoid eye contact. Even half-empty, the yard held the publican's young sons (shuffling hither and yon to fill cups for the customers), four presumably genuine drunken sailors, three liveried servants from the seminaries, a couple of gaudily clad women whose burlesque approach to the sailors was blatantly professional, and three cloak-shrouded pilgrims from the highlands of what had once been Cascadia—presumably come to visit the shrines and holy baths of the southern lands. At least, to a first approximation.

One of the lads was at Pierce's elbow, asking something about service and food. "Give beer," Pierce managed haltingly. "Good beer light two coin value." The tap-boy vanished, returned with a stoneware mug full of warm suds that smelled faintly of bananas. "Good, good." Pierce fumbled with his change, pawing over it as if unsure. He passed two clipped and blackened coins to the kid—both threaded with passive RF transceivers, beacons to tell his contact that they were not alone.

As Pierce raised his mug to his lips in unfeigned happy anticipation, his phone buzzed. It was a disturbing sensation, utterly unnatural, and it had taken him much practice to learn not to jump when it happened. He scanned the beer garden, concealing his mouth with his mug as he did so. A murder of crows—seminary students flocking to the watering hole—was raucously establishing its pecking order in the vestibule, one of the sailors had fallen forward across the table while his fellow tried to rouse him, and a working girl in a red wrap was walking toward the back wall, humming tunelessly. *Bingo,* he thought, with a smug flicker of satisfaction.

Pierce twitched a stomach muscle, goosing his phone. The other Stasis agent would feel a shiver and buzz like an angry yellow jacket—and indeed, as he watched, the woman in red glanced round abruptly. Pierce twitched again as her gaze flickered over him: this time involuntarily, in the grip of something akin to déjà vu. *Can't be,* he realized an instant later. She *wouldn't be on a field op like this!*

The woman in red turned and sidestepped toward his bench, subvocalizing. *"You're my cover, yes? Let's get out of here right now—it's going bad."*

Pierce began to stand. *"Yarrow?"* he asked. The sailor who was trying to rouse his friend started tugging at his shoulder.

"Yes? Look, what's your exit plan?" She sounded edgy.

"But—" He froze, his stomach twisting. *She doesn't know me,* he realized. *"Sorry. Can you get over the wall if I create a diversion?"* he sent, his heart hammering. He hadn't seen her in three years-subjective—she'd blown through his life like a runaway train, then vanished as abruptly as she'd arrived, leaving behind a scrawled note to say she'd been called uptime by Control, and a final quick charcoal sketch.

"I think so, but there are two—" The sailor stood up and shouted incoherently at her just as Pierce's phone buzzed again. *"Who's that?"* she asked.

"Hard contact in five seconds!" The other agent, whoever he was, sounded urgent. *"Stay back."*

The sailor shouted again, and this time Pierce understood it: "Murderer!" He climbed over the table and drew a long, curved knife, moving forward.

"Get behind me." Pierce stepped between Yarrow and the sailor, his thoughts a chaotic mess of *This is stupid* and *What did she do?* and *Who else?* as he paged Supervisor Hark. "Peace," he said in faltering Carnegran, "am friend? Want drink?"

Behind the angry sailor the priest-students were standing up, black robes flapping as they spread out, calling to one another. Yarrow retreated behind him: his phone vibrated again, then, improbably, a fourth time. There were too many agents. *"What's happening?"* asked Hark.

"I think it's a palimpsest," Pierce managed to send. Like an inked parchment scrubbed clean and reused, a section of history that had been multiply overwritten. He held his hands up, addressed the sailor, "You want. Thing. Money?"

The third agent, who'd warned of contact: *"Drop. Now!"*

Pierce began to fall as something, someone—*Yarrow?*—grabbed his shoulder and pushed sideways.

One of the students let his robe slide open. It slid down from his shoulders, gaping to reveal an iridescent fluidity that followed the rough contours of a human body, flexing and rippling like molten glass. Its upper margin flowed and swelled around its wearer's neck and chin, bulging upward to engulf his head as he stepped out of the black scholar's robe.

The sailor held his knife high, point down as he advanced on Pierce. Pierce's focus narrowed as he brought his fall under control, preparing to roll and trigger the telescopic baton in his sleeve—

A gunshot, shockingly loud, split the afternoon air. The sailor's head disappeared in a crimson haze, splattering across Pierce's face. The corpse lurched and collapsed like a dropped sack. Somebody—*Yarrow?*—cried out behind him, as Pierce pushed back with his left arm, trying to blink the red fog from his vision.

The student's robe was taking on a life of its own, contracting and standing up like a malign shadow behind its master as the human-shaped blob of walking water turned and raised one hand toward the roof. A chorus of screams rose behind it as one of the other seminarians, who had unwisely reached for the robe, collapsed convulsing.

"Stay down!" It was the third agent. *"Play dead."*

"My knee's—"

Pierce managed a sidelong look that took in Yarrow's expression of fear with a shudder of self-recognition. *"I'll decoy,"* he sent. Then, a curious clarity of purpose in his mind, he rolled sideways and scrambled toward the interior of the tavern.

Several things happened in the next three seconds:

First, a brilliant turquoise circle two meters in diameter flickered open, hovering directly in front of the rear wall of the beer garden. A double handful of enormous purple hornets burst from its surface. Most arrowed toward the students, who had entangled themselves in a panicky crush at the exit: two turned and darted straight up toward the balcony level.

Next, a spark, bright as lightning, leapt between the watery humanoid's upraised hand and the ceiling.

Finally, something punched Pierce in the chest with such breathtaking violence that he found, to his shock and surprise, that his hands and feet didn't seem to want to work anymore.

"Agent down," someone signaled, and it seemed to him that this was something he ought to make sense of, but sense was ebbing fast in a buzz of angry hornets as the pinkness faded to gray. And then everything was quiet for a long time.

Internal Affairs

"Do you know anyone who wants you dead, Scholar-Agent?" The investigator from Internal Affairs leaned over Pierce, his hands clasped together in a manner that reminded Pierce of a hungry mantis. His ears (Pierce couldn't help but notice) were prominent and pink, little radar dishes adorning the sides of a thin face. It had to be an ironic comment if not an outright insult, his adoption of the likeness of Franz Kafka. Or perhaps the man from Internal Affairs simply didn't want to be recognized.

Pierce chuckled weakly. The results were predictable:

when the coughing fit subsided, and his vision began to clear again, he shook his head.

"A pity." Kafka rocked backward slightly, his shoulders hunched. "It would make things easier."

Pierce risked a question. "Does the Library have anything?"

Kafka sniffed. "Of course not. Whoever set the trap knew enough to scrub the palimpsest clean before they embarked on their killing spree."

So it was *a palimpsest.* Pierce felt vaguely cheated. "They assassinated themselves first? To remove the evidence from the time sequence?"

"You died three times, Scholar-Agent, not counting your present state." He gestured at the dressing covering the cardiac assist leech clamped to the side of Pierce's chest. It pulsed rhythmically, taking the load while the new heart grew to full size between his ribs. "Agent Yarrow died twice and Agent-Major Alizaid's report states that he was forced to invoke Control Majeure to contain the palimpsest's expansion. *Someone*"—Kafka leaned toward Pierce again, peering intently at his face with disturbingly dark eyes—"went to great lengths to kill you repeatedly."

"Uh." Pierce stared at the ceiling of his hospital room, where plaster cherubs clutching overflowing cornucopiae cavorted with lecherous satyrs. "I suppose you want to know why?"

"No. Having read your Branch Library file, there are any number of *whys*: what I want to know is why *now*." Kafka smiled, his mouth widening until his alarmingly unhinged head seemed ready to topple from the plinth of his jaw. "You're still in training, a green shoot. An interesting time to pick on you, don't you think?"

Fear made Pierce tense up. "If you've read my Library record, you must know I'm loyal . . ."

"Peace." Kafka made a placating gesture. "I know nothing of the kind; the Library can't tell me what's inside your head. But you're not under suspicion of trying to assassinate yourself. What I *do* know is that so far your career has been notably mundane. The Library branches are as prone to overwrites as any other palimpsest; but we may be able to make deductions about your attacker by looking for inconsistencies between your memories and the version of your history documented locally."

Pierce lay back, drained. *I'm not under suspicion.* "What is to become of me?" he asked.

Kafka's smile vanished. "Nothing, for now: you may convalesce at your leisure, and sooner or later you will learn whatever it is that was so important to our enemies that they tried to erase you. When you do so, I would be grateful if you would call me." He rose to leave. "You will see me again, eventually. Meanwhile, you should bear in mind that you have come to the attention of important persons. Consider yourself lucky—and try to make the best of it."

Three days after Kafka's departure—summoned back, no doubt, to the vasty abyss of deep time in which Internal Affairs held their counsel—Pierce had another visitor.

"I came to thank you," she said haltingly. "You didn't need to do that. To decoy, I mean. I'm very grateful."

It had the sound of a prepared speech, but Pierce didn't mind. She was young and eye-wrenchingly desirable, even in the severe uniform of an Agent Initiate. "You would have died again," he pointed out. "I was your backup. It's bad form to let your primary die. And I owed you."

"You owed me? But we haven't met! There's nothing about you in my Library file." Her pupils dilated.

"It was an older you," he said mildly. While the Stasis held a file on everyone, agents were only permitted to see—and annotate—those of their own details that lay in their past. After a pause, he admitted, "I was hoping we might meet again sometime."

"But I—" She hesitated, then stared at him, narrowing her eyes. "I'm not in the market. I have a partner."

"Funny, she didn't tell me that." He closed his eyes for a few seconds. "She said we had a history, though. And to tell her when I first met her that her first pet—a cat named Chloe—died when a wild dog took her." Pierce opened his eyes to stare at the baroque ceiling again. "I'm sorry I asked, Ya—esteemed colleague. Please forgive me; I didn't think you were for sale. My heart is simply in the wrong place."

After a second he heard a shocked, incongruous giggle.

"I gather armor-piercing rounds usually have that effect," he added.

When she was able to speak again she shook her head. "I am sincere, Scholar-Agent—Pierce?—Pierced? Oh dear!" She managed to hold her dignity intact, this time, despite a gleam of amusement. "I'm sorry if I—I don't mean to doubt you. But you must know, if you know me, *I* have never met *you*, yes?"

"That thought has indeed occurred to me." The leech pulsed warmly against his chest, squirting blood through the aortic shunt. "As you can see, right now I am not only heart-less but harmless, insofar as I won't even be able to get out of bed unaided for another ten days; you need not fear that I'm going to pursue you. I merely thought to introduce myself and let you know—as she did to me—that we *could* have a history, if you're so inclined, someday. But not right now. Obviously."

"But obviously not—" She stood up. "This wasn't what I was expecting."

"Me neither." He smiled bitterly. "It never is, is it?"

She paused in the doorway. "I'm not saying no, never, Scholar-Agent. But not now, obviously. Some other time . . . We'll worry about that if we meet again, perhaps. History can wait a little longer. Oh, and thank you for saving my life some of the times! One out of three is good going, especially for a student."

● ELITE

A Brief Alternate History of the Solar System: Part One
What has already happened:

SLIDE 1.

Our solar system, as an embryo. A vast disk of gas and infalling dust surrounds and obscures a newborn star, little more than a thickening knot of rapidly spinning matter that is rapidly sucking more mass down into its ever-steepening gravity well. The sun is glowing red-hot already with the heat liberated by its gravitational collapse, until . . .

SLIDE 2.

Ignition! The pressure and temperature at the core of the embryo star has risen so high that hydrogen nuclei floating in a degenerate soup of electrons are bumping close to one another. A complex reaction ensues, rapidly liberating gamma radiation and neutrinos, and the core begins to heat up. First deuterium, then the ordinary hydrogen nuclei begin to fuse. A flare of nuclear fire lashes through the inner layers of the star. It will take a million years for the gamma-ray pulse to work its way out through the choking, blanketing layers of degenerate hydrogen, but the neutrino pulse heralds the birth cry of a new star.

SLIDE 3.

A million years pass as the sun brightens, and the rotating cloud of gas and dust begins to partition. Out beyond the dew line, where ice particles can grow, a roiling knot of dirty ice is forming, and like the sun before it, it greedily sucks down dirt and gas and grows. As it plows through the cloud, it sprays dust outward. Meanwhile, at the balancing point between the star and the embryonic Jovian gravity well, other knots of dust are forming . . .

SLIDE 4.

A billion years have passed since the sun ignited, and the stellar nursery of gas and dust has been swept clean by a fleet of new-formed planets. There has been some bickering—in the late heavy bombardment triggered by the outward migration of Neptune, entire planetary surfaces were re-formed—but now the system has settled into long-term stability. The desert planet Mars is going through the first of its warm, wet interludes; Venus still has traces of water in its hot (but not yet red-hot) atmosphere. Earth is a chilly nitrogen-and-methane-shrouded enigma inhabited only by primitive purple bacteria, its vast oceans churned by hundred-meter tides dragged up every seven-hour day by a young moon that completes each orbit in little more than twenty-four hours.

SLIDE 5.

Another three billion years have passed. The solar system has completed almost sixteen orbits of the galactic core, and is now unimaginably distant from the stellar nursery which birthed it. Mars has dried, although occasional volcanic eruptions periodically blanket it in cloud. Venus is even hotter. But something strange is happening to Earth. Luna has drifted farther from its primary, the tides quieting; meanwhile, the atmosphere has acquired a strange bluish tinge, evident sign of contamination by a toxic haze of oxygen. The great land-mass Rodina, which dominated the southern ocean beneath a cap of ice, has broken up and the shallow seas of the Pan-thalassic and Panafrican Oceans are hosting an astonishing proliferation of multicellular life.

SLIDE 6.

Six hundred and fifty million years later, the outlines of Earth's new continents glow by night like a neon diadem against the darkness, shouting consciousness at the sky in a blare of radio-wavelength emissions as loud as a star.

There have been five major epochs dominated by different families of land-based vertebrates in the time between slides 5 and 6. All the Earth's coal and oil deposits were laid down in this time, different animal families developed flight at least four times, and the partial pressure of oxygen in the atmosphere rose from around 4 percent to well over 16 percent. At the very end, a strangely bipedal, tailless omnivore appeared on the plains of Africa—its brain turbocharged on a potent mixture of oxygen and readily available sugars—and erupted into sentience in a geological eyeblink.

Here's what isn't *going to happen:*

SLIDE 7.

The continents of Earth, no longer lit by the afterglow of intelligence, will drift into strange new configurations. Two hundred and fifty million years after the sixth great extinction, the scattered continents will reconverge on a single equatorial supercontinent, Pangea Ultima, leaving only the conjoined landmass that was Antarctica and Australia adrift in the southern ocean. As the sun brightens, so shall the verdant plains of the Earth; oceanic algal blooms raise the atmospheric oxygen concentration close to 25 percent, and lightning-triggered wildfires rage across the continental interior. It will be an epoch characterized by rapid plant growth, but few animal life-forms can survive on land—in the heady air of aged Earth, even water-logged flesh will burn. And the sun is still brightening . . .

SLIDE 8.

Seven hundred and fifty million years later. The brightening sun will glare down upon cloud-wreathed ancient continents, weathered and corroded to bedrock. Even the plant life has abandoned the land, for the equatorial daytime temperature is perilously close to the boiling point of water. What life there is retreats to the deep ocean waters, away from the searing ultraviolet light that splits apart the water molecules of the upper atmosphere. But there's no escape: the oceans themselves are slowly acidifying and evaporating as the hydrogen liberated in the ionosphere is blasted into space by the solar wind. A runaway greenhouse effect is well under way, and in another billion years Earth will resemble parched, hell-hot Venus.

SLIDE 9.

Four-point-two billion years after the brief cosmic eyeblink of Earthly intelligence, the game is up. The dead Earth orbits alone, its moon a separate planet wandering in increasingly unstable ellipses around the sun. Glowing dull red beneath an atmosphere of carbon dioxide baked from its rocks, there will be no sign that this world ever harbored life. The sun it circles, a sullen-faced ruddy ogre, is nearing the end of its hydrogen reserves. Soon it will expand, engulfing the inner planets.

But events on a larger scale are going to spare the Earth this fate. For billions of years, the galaxy in which this star orbits has been converging with another large starswarm, the M-31 Andromeda galaxy. Now the spiraling clouds of stars are interpenetrating and falling through each other, and the sun is in for a bumpy ride as galaxies collide.

A binary system of red dwarfs is closing with the solar system at almost five hundred kilometers per second. They are going to pass within half a billion kilometers of the sun, a hairbreadth miss in cosmic terms: in the process they will wreak havoc on the tidy layout of the solar system. Jupiter, dragged a few million kilometers sunward, will enter an unstable elliptical orbit, and over the course of a few thousand years it will destabilize all the other planets. Luna departs first, catapulted out of the plane of the ecliptic; Earth, most massive of all, will spend almost five million years wobbling between the former orbits of Venus and Saturn before it finally caroms past Jupiter and drifts off into the eternal night, the tattered remnants of its atmosphere condensing and freezing in a shroud of dry ice.

Slow Recovery

Pierce was to remain on official convalescent leave for an entire year-subjective. His heart had been torn to shreds by a penetrator round; repairing the peripheral damage, growing a new organ in situ, and restoring him to physical condition was a nontrivial matter. Luckily for him, the fatal shooting had happened in the middle of a multiple-overwrite ambush that was finally shut down by Control Majeure using weapons of gross anachronism, and they'd whisked his bleeding wreckage out through a timegate before he'd finished drumming his heels.

Nevertheless, organ regeneration—not to mention psychological recovery from a violent fatal injury—took time. So, rather than shipping him straight to the infirmary in the alpine monastery in Training Zone 25, he was sent to recover in the Rebirth Wing of the Chrysanthemum Clinic, on the Avenue of the Immortals of Medicine, in the city of Leng, on the northeastern seaboard of the continent of Nova Zealantis, more than four billion years after the time into which he had been born.

The current Reseeding was Enlightened; not only were they aware of the existence of the Stasis, but they were a part of the greater transtemporal macroculture: speakers of Urem, obedient to the Stasis, even granted dispensation to petition for use of the timegate in extraordinary circumstances. In return, the Hegemony was altogether conscientious in observing their duties to the guardians of history, according Pierce honors that, in other ages, might have been accorded to a diplomat or minor scion of royalty. Unfortunately, this entailed rather more formality than Pierce was used to. The decor, for one thing: they'd clearly studied his epoch, but modeling his hospital suite on Louis XV's bedroom at Versailles suggested they had strange ideas about his status.

"If it pleases you, my lord, would you like to describe how you entered the celestial service?" The journalist, who his bowing and shuffling concierge explained had been sent by the city archive to document his life, was young, pretty, and shiny-eyed. She'd obviously studied his public records and the customs of his home civilization, and decided to go for the throat. Local fashion echoed the Minoan empire of antiquity, and her attire, though scholarly, was disconcerting: a flash of well-turned ankle, nipples rouged and ringed—Pierce realized he was staring and turned his face away, chagrined.

"Please?" she repeated, her plump lower lip quivering. Her cameras flittered below the ceiling like lazy bluebottles, iridescent in the afternoon sunlight, logging her life for posterity.

"I suppose so . . ." Pierce trailed off, staring through the open window at the lower slopes of the hillside on which the clinic nestled. "But there's no secret, really, none at all. You don't approach them—they approach you. A tap on the shoulder at the right time, an offer of a job, at first I didn't think it was anything unusual."

"Was there anything leading up to that? My lord? What was your life like before the service?"

Pierce frowned slightly as he forced his sullen memory to work. There were gaps. "I'm not sure; I think I was in a car crash, or maybe a war . . ."

His cardiac leech pulsed against his chest like a contented cat. Sunlight warmed the side of his face as he watched her sidelong, from the corner of his eye. *How far will she go for a story?* he wondered idly. *Play your cards right and . . . well, maybe.* His temporarily heartless condition had rendered amorous speculations—or anything else calculated to raise the blood pressure—purely academic for the time being.

"My lord?" He pretended to miss the moue of annoyance that flitted across her face, but the very deliberate indrawn breath that followed it was so transparent that he nearly gave the game away by laughing.

"I'm not your lord," he said gently. "I'm just a scholar-agent, halfway through my twenty years of training. What I know about the Guardians of Time"—that was what the Hegemonites called the Stasis, those in power who had polite words for them—"and can tell you is mere trivia. I'm sure your Archive already has it all."

This was a formally declared Science Epoch, in which a whole series of consecutive Reseedings were dedicated to collating the mountain-sized chunks of data returned by the Von Neumann probes that had been launched during the last Science Epoch, a billion years earlier. They and their descendants had quietly fanned out throughout the local group of galaxies, traveling at barely a hundredth of the speed of light, visiting and mapping every star system and extrasolar planet within ten million light-years. There was a lot of material to collate; The Zealantian Hegemony's army of elite astrocartographers, millions strong, would labor for tens of thousands of years to assemble just their one corner of the big picture. And their obsession with knowledge didn't stop at the edge of the solar system.

("A civilization of obsessive-compulsive stamp collectors," Wei had called them when he briefly visited his ex-student. "You've got to watch these Science Cults; sooner or later they'll turn all the carbon in the deep biosphere into memory diamond, then where will we be?")

"The Archive doesn't know everything, my lord. It's not like the Library of Time." There was a strangely reverent note in her voice, as if the Library was somehow different. "We don't have permission to read the forbidden diaries, my lord. We have to accept whatever crusts of wisdom our honored guests choose to let fall from their trenchers."

"I'm not your lord. You can call me Pierce, if you like."

"Yes, my, ah. Pierce? My lord."

"What should I call you?" he asked after a pause.

"Me? I am nobody, Lord Pierce! I am a humble journal-keeper—"

"Rubbish." He looked directly at her, taking in everything: her flounced scholar-lady's dress, the jeweled rings through her ears and nipples, her painstakingly knotted chignon. This was a high-energy civilization, but a very staid, conservative one with strict sumptuary laws: were she a commoner, she would risk a flogging for indecency, or worse, dressing above her station. "Who are you really? And why are you so interested in *me*?"

"Oh! If you *must* know, I am doctor-postulant Xiri, daughter of doctor doctor professor archivist His Excellency Dean Imad of the College of History, and Her Ladyship doctor professor emeritus Leila of the faculty of hot super-Jovian moons"—she smiled coyly—"and I have been charged, by my duty and my honor as a scholar, to study you in absolute detail by my tutors. They have assigned you to me as the topic of my first dissertation. On the hero-guardians of time."

"Your *first* dissertation—" Her parents were a professor and a dean; she might as well have said *sheikh* or *baron*. "Do I have any choice in the matter?"

"You can refuse, of course." She shivered and tugged her filmy shawl back into position. "But *I* can't."

"Why? What happens if you refuse?"

She shivered. "I would forfeit my doctorate. The shame! My parents"—for a moment the bright-eyed optimism cracked—"would blame themselves. It would cast doubt on my commitment."

Was failure to make tenure track justification for an honor killing? Pierce shook his head, staring at her. "I'm just a trainee!" He reached for the bed's control, stabbing the button to raise his back. The interview was out of control, heading for deep waters, and lying down gave him an unaccountable fear of drowning. "*I'm* the nobody around here!"

"How do you know that, my lord? For all you know, you might be destined for glory." She tugged at her shawl again and smiled, an ingenue trying to look mysterious.

"But I don't have any—" He switched off the bed lift once he was level with her, looked her in the eyes, and changed the subject in midsentence. "Have your people ever met me before?"

The hardest part of arguing with her, he found, was avoiding staring at her chest. She was really very pretty, but her pedigree suggested he'd be wise to abandon that line of thought; she'd be about as safe to seduce as a rattlesnake.

"No." Her smile widened. "A handsome man of mystery and a time hero to boot: yes, they told us why you were here." Her gaze briefly covered his chest.

For the first time in many months, Pierce resorted to his native language. "Oh, *hell*." He glanced at the window, then back at Xiri. "Everybody wants to study me," he confessed. "I don't know why, I really don't . . ." He crossed his arms, looked at her. "Study away. I am at your disposal." At least it promised to be a less harrowing experience than Kafka's cross-examination.

"Oh! Thank you, my lord!" She placed a proprietorial hand on the side of his bed. "I will do my utmost to make it an enjoyable experience."

"Really?" There was something about her tone of voice that took him aback, as if he'd answered a question that he didn't remember being asked. The idea of being studied struck Pierce as marginally more enjoyable than banging his head on the wall, but on the upside, Xiri was high-quality eye candy. On the downside—*Don't go there,* he reminded himself. "Where would you like to begin?"

"Right here, I think," she said, sliding her hand under the covers.

"Hey! I! Huh." Pierce found, to his mild alarm, that her busy hand was getting results. "Um. I don't want to sound ungrateful, but we really shouldn't—why are you—aren't you going to shut off your cameras—"

"I have read about your culture." She sat down on the bed beside him with a rustle of silk. "In some ways, it sounded very familiar. Did they not record everything that happened to them? Did they not talk about people marrying their work? Well, that is just how we do that here."

"But that's just a metaphor!" He tried to push her hand away, but his heart wasn't in it.

"Hush." She responded by making him shudder. "You're the subject of my dissertation! I'm going to find out *all* about you. It's to be my life's work! I'm so happy! Just relax, my lord, and everything will be wonderful. Don't worry, I have studied the customs of your time, and they are not so very alien. We can talk about the wedding tomorrow, after you've met my father."

Empty Mansions

Resistance was futile: nearly twenty years-subjective passed Pierce by with the eyeblink impact of another bullet, half of them shared with his new wife. Xiri, true to her word, wrapped her life around his twisted time line: at first as an adoring wife, and then, to his bemused and growing pride, mother to three small children and doctor-professor in her own right. Her dissertation was his life: merely glancing lightly off the skin of time was, it seemed, a passport to wealth and status in the Hegemony, and he found life as the consort of a beautiful noblewoman no less congenial than he might have expected.

Xiri did not complain at Pierce's eyeblink excursions from their family home (provided by the grace of her father the dean), which usually lasted only for seconds of subjective time. Nor did she complain about the inward-looking silences and moody introspection that followed, and were of altogether greater duration. On the contrary: they invariably provided additional data for her life's work, once she delicately untangled the story from his memories of unhistory. Sometimes he would age an entire year in an hour's working absence, but the medical privileges of the Stasis extended also to the Enlightened; there would be plenty of time to catch up, over the decades and centuries.

Pierce, for his part, found it oddly easier to deal with the second half of his training with a stable family life to fall back on. The Stasis were spread surprisingly thin across their multitrillion-year empire. The defining characteristic of his job seemed to be that he was only called for in turbulent, interesting times. Between peak oil and Spanish flu, from Carthage to the Cold War, his three-thousand-year beat sometimes seemed no more than a vale of tears—and a thin, poor, nightmare of a world at that, far from the mannered, drowsy contentment of the ten-thousand-year-long Hegemony. Most of his fellow students seemed to prefer the hedonistic abandon proffered by the Pleasure Empires, but Pierce held his own counsel and congratulated himself on his discovery of a more profound source of satisfaction.

On his first return to training after his convalescence, Pierce was surprised to be summoned to Superintendent-of-Scholars Manson's chambers.

"You have formed attachments while convalescing." Manson fixed him with a watery stare. "That is inadvisable, as you will no doubt learn for yourself. However, Operations have noted that there is no permanent Resident in place within a millennium either side of your, ah, domestic anchor-point. It is a tranquil society, but not *that* tranquil; you are therefore instructed and permitted to maintain your attachment and develop your ability to work there. Purely as a secondary specialty, you understand."

Pierce had almost fallen over with shock. Once he regained his self-control, he asked, "To whom shall I report, master?"

"To your wife, student. Tell her to write up everything. We read all such dissertations, in the end."

Manson looked away, dismissing him. Pierce nudged his phone, weak-kneed, not trusting his ability to make a dignified exit; after a brief routing delay, the timegate responded to his heartfelt wish, and the ground opened up and swallowed him.

One day very late in his training, with perhaps half a year-subjective remaining until his graduation as a full-fledged agent of the Stasis, Pierce returned home from a week sampling the plague-pits of fourteenth-century Constantinople. He found Xiri in an unusually excited state, the household all abuzz around her. "It's fantastic!" she exclaimed, hurrying to meet him across the atrium of their summer residence. "Did you know about it? Tell me you knew about it! *This* was why you came to our time, wasn't it?"

Pierce, greeting her with a fond smile, lifted young Magnus (who had been attempting to scale his back, with much snarling, presumably to slay the giant) and handed him to his nursemaid. "What's happened?" he asked mildly, trying to give no sign of the frisson he'd momentarily felt (for their youngest son could have no idea of how his father had just spent a week taking tissue samples, carving chunks of mortal flesh from the bubo-stricken bodies of boys of an age to be his playmates in another era). "What's got everyone so excited?"

"It's the probes! They've found something outrageous in Messier 33, six thousand light-years along the third arm!"

Pierce—who could not imagine finding anything outrageous in a galaxy over a million light-years away, even if mapping it *was* the holy raison d'être of this Civilization—decided to humor his wife. "Indeed. And tell me, what precisely is there that brings forth such outrage? As opposed to mere excitement, or curiosity, or perplexity?"

"Look!" Xiri gestured at the wall, which obligingly displayed a dizzying black void sprinkled with stars. "Let's see. Wall, show me the anomaly I was discussing with the honorable doctor-professor Zun about two hours ago. Set magnification level plus forty, pan left and up five—there! You see it!"

Pierce stared for a while. "Looks like just another rock to me," he said. Racking his brains for the correct form: "an honorable sub-Earth, airless, of the third degree, predominantly siliceous. Yes?"

"Oh!" Xiri, nobly raised, did nothing so undignified as to stamp her foot; nevertheless, Magnus's nursemaid swept up her four-year-old charge and beat a hasty retreat. (Xiri, when excited, could be as dangerously prone to eruption as a Wolf-Rayet star.) "Is that all you can see? Wall, magnification plus ten, repeat step, step, step. *There*. Look at that, my lord, look!"

The airless moon no longer filled the center of the wall; now it stretched across it from side to side, so close that there was barely any visible curvature to its horizon. Pierce squinted. Craters, rills, drab, irregular features and a scattering of straight-edged rectangular crystals. *Crystals?* He chewed on the thought, found it curiously lacking as an explanation for the agitation. Gradually, he began to feel a quiet echo of his wife's excitement. "What are they?"

"They're buildings! Or they were, sixty-six million years ago, when the probes were passing through. And we didn't put them there . . ."

○ THE LIBRARY AT THE END OF TIME

A Brief Alternate History of the Solar System: Part Two
. . . And then the Stasis happened:

SLIDE 7.

After two hundred and fifty million years, the continents of Earth, strobe-lit by the mayfly flicker of empires, will have converged on a single equatorial supercontinent, Pangea

Ultima. These will not be good times for humanity; the vast interior deserts are arid and the coastlines subject to vast hurricanes sweeping in from the world-ocean. As the sun brightens, so shall the verdant plains of the Earth; but the Stasis have long-laid plans to deflect the inevitable.

Deep in the asteroid belt, their swarming robot cockroaches have dismantled Ceres, used its mass to build a myriad of solar-sail-powered flyers. Now a river of steerable rocks with the mass of a dwarf planet loops down through the inner system, converting solar energy into momentum and transferring it to the Earth through millions of repeated flybys.

Already, Earth has migrated outward from the sun. Other adjustments are under way, subtle and far-reaching: the entire solar system is slowly changing shape, creaking and groaning, drifting toward a new and more useful configuration. Soon—in cosmological terms—it will be unrecognizable.

SLIDE 8.

A billion years later, the Earth lies frozen and fallow, its atmosphere packed down to snow and nitrogen vapor in the chilly wilderness beyond Neptune. *This* was never part of the natural destiny of the homeworld, but it is only a temporary state—for in another ten million years, the endlessly cycling momentum shuttles will crank Earth closer to the sun. Fifty million years after that, the Reseedings will recommence, from the prokaryotes and algae on up; but in this era, the Stasis want the Earth safely mothballed while their technicians from the Engineering Republics work their magic.

For thirty million years the Stasis will devote their timegate to lifting mass from the heart of a burning star, channeling vast streams of blazing plasma into massive, gravitationally bound bunkers, reserves against a chilly future. The sun will gutter and fade to red, raging and flaring in angry outbursts as its internal convection systems collapse. As it shrinks and dims, they will inflict the final murderous insult, and inject an embryonic black hole into the stellar core. Eating mass faster than it can reradiate it through Hawking radiation, the hole will grow, gutting the stellar core.

By the time the Earth drops back toward the frost line of

the solar system, the technicians will have roused the zombie necrosun from its grave. Its accretion disk—fed with mass steadily siphoned from the brown dwarfs orbiting on the edges of the system—will cast a strange, harsh glare across Earth's melting ice caps.

Replacing the fusion core of the sun with a mass-crushing singularity is one of the most important tasks facing the Stasis; annihilation is orders of magnitude more efficient than fusion, not to say more controllable, and the mass they have so carefully husbanded is sufficient to keep the closely orbiting Earth lit and warm not for billions, but for trillions of years to come.

But another, more difficult task remains . . .

SLIDE 9.

Four and a quarter billion years after the awakening of consciousness, and the Milky Way and Andromeda galaxies will collide. The view from Earth's crowded continents is magnificent, like a chaos of burning diamond dust strewn across the emptiness void. Shock waves thunder through the gas clouds, creating new stellar nurseries, igniting millions of massive, short-lived new stars; for a brief ten-million-year period, the nighttime sky will be lit by a monthly supernova fireworks display. The huge black holes at the heart of each galaxy have shed their robes of dust and gas and blaze naked in ghastly majesty as they streak past each other, ripping clusters of stars asunder and seeding more, in a starburst of cosmic fireworks that will be visible nearly halfway across the universe.

But Earth is safe. Earth is serene. Earth is no longer in the firing line.

The Long Burn is by far the largest program of the Stasis. Science Empires will rise and flourish, decay and gutter into extinction, to provide the numerical feedstock for the Navigators. The delicate task of ejecting a star system from its galaxy without setting the planets and moons adrift in their orbits is monstrously difficult. Planets are not bound to their stars by physical cords, and gravity is weak; innumerable adjustments to the orbits of all the significant planets will be required if they are to be carried along. The mass flow of Ceres alone will not suffice. Rocky Mercury has already been dismantled to provide the control mechanisms that keep the necrostar's accretion disk burning steadily; it's Venus's turn to supply the swarming light-sail-driven mass tugs. A brown dwarf ten times the size of Jupiter will fuel the rocket, an entire stellar embryo pumped down to the blazing maw in the course of a million years.

Galactic escape velocity is high, and escape velocity from the local group is even higher. The Long Burn will last ten thousand centuries. Each year that passes, the necrostar will be moving a meter per second faster. And when it comes to an end, the drastically redesigned solar system will be racing away from the local group of galaxies at almost a thousandth the speed of light—straight toward the Bootes Void.

SLIDE 10.

Over the next billion years, Starship Earth and its dead star will rendezvous with the other components of their lifeboat fleet; an even hundred brown dwarf stars, ten to fifty times as massive as Jupiter and every last one dislodged and sent tumbling from its home galaxy by the robot probes of the Engineering Empires.

Their mass will be gratefully received. For Earth is going on a voyage of discovery, where no star has gone before, into the heart of darkness.

Continent of Lies

Nothing in his earlier life had prepared Pierce for what came next. It beggared belief: a series of synthetic aperture radar scans transmitted by a probe millions of years ago in another galaxy had triggered a diplomatic crisis, threatening world war and civilizational autocide.

The Hegemony, despite being a Science Empire, was not the only nation in this age. (True world governments were rare, cumbersome dinosaurs notorious for their absolute topdown corruption and catastrophic-failure modes: the Stasis tended to discourage them.) The Hegemony shared their world with the Autonomous Directorate of Zan, a harshly abstemious land of puritanical library scientists (located on a continent which had once been attached to North America and Africa); sundry secular monarchies, republics, tyrannies, autarchies, and communes (who thought their superpower neighbors mildly insane for wasting so much of their wealth on academic institutions, rather than the usual aimless and undirected pursuit of human happiness); and the Kingdom of Blattaria (whose inhabitants obeyed the prehistoric prophet Haldane with fanatical zeal, studying the *arthropoda* in ecstatic devotional raptures).

The Hegemony was geographically the largest of the great powers, unified by a set of common filing and monitoring protocols; but it was not a monolithic entity. The authorities of the western principality of Stongu (special area of study: the rocky moons of Hot Jupiters in M-33) had reacted to the discovery of Civilization on the moon of a water giant with a spectacular display of sour grapes, accusing the northeastern Zealantians of *fabricating data* in a desperate attempt to justify a hit-and-run raid on the Hegemony's federal tax base. Quite what the academics of Leng were supposed to do with these funds was never specified, nor was it necessary to say any more in order to get the blood boiling in the seminaries and colleges. *Fabricating data* had a deadly ring to it in any Science Empire, much like the words *crusade* and *jihad* in the millennium prior to Pierce's birth. Once the accusation had been raised, it could not be ignored—and this presented the Hegemony with a major internal problem.

"Honored soldier of the Guardians of Time, our gratitude would be unbounded were you to choose to intercede for us," said the speaker for the delegation from the Dean's Lodge that called on his household barely two days after the discovery. "We would not normally dream of petitioning your eminence, but the geopolitical implications are alarming."

And indeed, they were; for the Hegemony supplied information to the Autonomous Directorate, in return for the boundless supplies of energy harvested by the solar collectors that blanketed the Directorate's inland deserts. Allegations of *fabricating data* could damage the value of the Hegemony's currency; indeed, the aggressive and intolerant Zanfolk might consider it grounds for war (and an excuse for yet another of their tiresome attempts to obtain the vineyards and breadbasket islands of the Outer Nesh archipelago).

"I will do what I can." Pierce bowed deeply to the delegates, who numbered no less than a round dozen deans and even a vice-chancellor or two: he studiously avoided making eye contact with his father-in-law, who stood at the back. "If you are absolutely sure of the merits of your case, I can consult the Library, then testify publicly, insofar as I am authorized to do so. Would that be acceptable?"

The vice-chancellor of the Old College of Leng—an institution with a history of over six thousand years at this point—bowed in return, his face stiff with gratitude. "We are certain of our case, and consequently willing to abide by the word of the Library of the Guardians of Time. Please permit me to express my gratitude once more—"

After half an hour of formalities, the delegation finally departed. Xiri reemerged from her seclusion to direct the servants and robots in setting the receiving room of their mansion aright; the boys also emerged, showing no sign of understanding what had just happened. "Xiri, I need to go to the Final Library," Pierce told her, taking her hands in his and watching for signs of understanding.

"Why, that's wonderful, is it not? My lord? Pierce?" She stared into his eyes. "Why are you worried?"

Pierce swallowed bitter saliva. "The Library is not a place, Xiri; it's a *time*. It contains the sum total of all recorded human knowledge, after the end of humanity. I'm near to graduation, I'm allowed to go there to use it, but it's not—it's not *safe*. Sometimes people who go to the Library disappear and don't come back. And sometimes they come back changed. It's not just a passive archive."

Xiri nodded, but looked skeptical. "But what kind of danger can it pose, given the question you're going to put to it? You're just asking for confirmation that we've been honoring our sources. That's not like asking for the place and time of your own death, is it?"

"I hope you're right, but I don't know for sure." Pierce paused. "That's the problem." He raised her hands to his lips and kissed the backs of her fingers. *If it must be done, best do it fast.* "I'll go and find out. I'll be back soon . . ."

He stepped back a pace and activated his phone. *"Agent-Trainee Pierce, requesting a Library slot."*

There was a brief pause while the relays stored his message, awaited a transmission slot, then fired them through the timegate to Control. Then he felt the telltale buzzing in the vicinity of his left kidney that warned of an incoming wormhole. It opened around him, spinning out and engulfing him in scant milliseconds, almost too fast to see: then he was no longer standing in the hall of his own mansion but on a dark plain of artificial limestone, facing a doorway set into the edge of a vast geodesic dome made from some translucent material: the Final Library.

A Brief Alternate History of the Solar System: Part Three

SLIDE 11.

One hundred billion years will pass.

Earth orbits a mere twenty million kilometers from its necrosun in this epoch, and the fires of the accretion disk are banked. Continents jostle and shudder, rising and falling, as the lights strobe around their edges (and occasionally in low equatorial orbit, whenever the Stasis permits a high-energy civilization to arise).

By the end of the first billion years of the voyage, the night skies are dark and starless. The naked eye can still—barely, if it knows where to look—see the Chaos galaxy formed by the collision of M-31 and the Milky Way; but it is a graveyard, its rocky planets mostly supernova-sterilized iceballs ripped from their parent stars by one close encounter too many. Unicellular life (once common in the Milky Way, at least) has taken a knock; multicellular life (much rarer) has received a mortal body blow. Only the Stasis's lifeboat remains.

Luna still floats in Terrestrial orbit—it is a useful tool to stir Earth's liquid core. Prone to a rocky sclerosis, the Earth's heart is a major problem for the Stasis. They can't let it harden, lest the subduction cycle and the deep carbon cycle on which the biosphere depends grind to a halt. But there are ways to stir it up again. They can afford to wait half a billion years for the Earth to cool, then reseed the reborn planet with archaea

and algae. After the first fraught experiment in reterraform-
ing, the Stasis find it sufficient to reboot the mantle and outer
core once every ten billion years or so.

The universe changes around them, slowly but surely.

At the end of a hundred billion years, uranium no longer
exists in useful quantities in the Earth's crust. Even uranium
238 decays eventually, and twenty one half-lives is more than
enough to render it an exotic memory, like the bright and early
dawn of the universe. Other isotopes will follow suit, leaving
only the most stable behind.

(The Stasis have sufficient for their needs, and might even
manufacture more—were it necessary—using the necrostar's
ergosphere as a forge. But the Stasis don't particularly want
their clients to possess the raw materials for nuclear weapons.
Better by far to leave those tools by the wayside.)

The sky is dark. The epoch of star formation has drawn to
a close in the galaxies the Earth has left. No bright new stellar
nurseries glitter in the void. All the bright, fast-burning suns
have exploded and faded. All the smaller main-sequence stars
have bloated into dyspeptic ruddy giants, then exhausted their
fuel and collapsed. Nothing bright remains save a scattering
of dim red and white dwarf stars.

Smaller bodies—planets, moons, and comets—are slowly
abandoning their galaxies, shed from stars as their orbits
become chaotic, then ejecting at high speed from the galaxy
itself in the wake of near encounters with neighboring stars.
Like gas molecules in the upper atmosphere of a planet warmed
by a star, the lightest leave first. But the process is inexorable.
The average number of planets per star is falling slowly.

(About those gas molecules: the Stasis have, after some
deliberation, taken remedial action. Water vapor is split by
ultraviolet light in the upper atmosphere, and the Earth can
ill afford to lose its hydrogen. A soletta now orbits between
Earth and the necrosun, filtering out the short-wavelength
radiation, and when they periodically remelt the planet to
churn the magma, they are at pains to season their new-made
hell with a thousand cometary hydrogen carriers. But eventually more extreme measures will be necessary.)

The sky is quiet and deathly cold. The universe is expanding, and the wavelength of the cosmic microwave background

radiation has stretched. The temperature of space itself is now only thousandths of a degree above absolute zero. The ripples in the background are no longer detectable, and the distant quasars have reddened into invisibility. Galactic clusters that were once at the far edge of detection are now beyond the cosmic event horizon, and though Earth has only traveled two hundred million light-years from the Local Group, the gulf behind it is nearly a billion light-years wide. This is no longer a suitable epoch for Science Empires, for the dynamic universe they were called upon to study is slipping out of sight.

SLIDE 12.

A trillion years will pass.

The universe beyond the necrosun's reach is black. Far behind it, the final stars of the Local Group have burned out. White dwarfs have cooled to the temperature of liquid water; red dwarfs have guttered into chilly darkness. Occasionally stellar remnants collide, then the void is illuminated by flashes of lightning, titanic blasts of radiation as the supernovae and gamma-ray bursters flare.

But the explosions are becoming rare. Now it isn't just planets that are migrating away from the chilly corpses of the galaxies. Stellar remnants are ejected into the void as the galaxies themselves fall apart with age.

Space is empty and cold, barely above absolute zero. The necrostar's course has passed through what was once the Bootes Void, but there is no end to the emptiness in sight: there are voids in all directions now. The Stasis and their clients have abandoned the practice of astronomy. They maintain a simple radar watch in the direction of travel, sending out a gigawatt ping every year against the tiny risk of a rogue asteroid, but they haven't encountered an extrasolar body larger than a grain of sand for billions of years.

As for the necrosun's planetary attendants . . .

One day they will burn Jupiter to keep themselves warm. And Saturn, and icy Neptune, water bunker for the oceans of Earth. These days have not yet come, for they are still working through the titans, through Rhea and Oceanus, Crius and Hyperion—the brown dwarfs built with Sol's stolen mass, and the other dwarfs stolen from the Milky Way during the Long Burn. Each brown dwarf burns for many times the age of the universe at the birth of humanity; black holes are nothing if not efficient. But one day they will be used up, the last titan reduced to a dwarfish cinder; and it will be time to start eating the planets.

Not long thereafter, it will be time for the final Reseeding.

Spin Control

Pierce stood uncertainly before the door in the dome. It glowed blue-green with an inner light, and when he looked around, his shadow stretched into the night behind him.

"Don't wait outside for too long," someone said waspishly. *"The air isn't safe."*

The air? Pierce wondered as he entered the doorway. The glassy slabs of an airlock slid aside and closed behind him, thrice in rapid succession. He found himself in a spacious vivarium, illuminated by a myriad of daylight-bright lamps shining from the vertices of the dome wall's triangular segments. There were plants everywhere, green and damp-smelling cycads and ferns and crawling, climbing vines. Insect life hidden in the undergrowth creaked and rattled loudly.

Then he noticed the Librarian, who stood in the clearing before the doors, as unnaturally still as a plastinated corpse.

"I haven't been here before," Pierce admitted as he approached the robed figure. "I've used outlying branches, but never the central Library itself."

"I know." The Librarian pushed back the hood of his robe to reveal a plump, bald head, jowly behind its neat goatee, and gimlet eyes that seemed to drill straight through him.

Pierce stopped, uncertain. "Do I know you?"

"Almost certainly not. Call me Torque. Or Librarian." Torque pointed to a path through the vegetation. "Come, walk with me. I'll show you to your reading room, and you can get started. You might want to bookmark this location in case you need to return."

Pierce nodded. "Is there anybody else here?"

"Not at present." Torque sniffed. "You and I are the only living human beings on the planet right now, although there may be more than one of you present. You have the exclusive use of the Library's resources this decade, within reason."

"Within reason?"

"Sometimes our supervisors—yours or mine—take an interest. They are not required to notify me of their presence." There was a fork in the path, around a large outcropping of some sort of rock crystal, like quartz; Torque turned left. "Ah, here we are. This is your reading room, Student-Agent Pierce."

A white-walled roofless cubicle sat in the middle of a clearing, through which ran a small brook, its banks overgrown with moss and ferns. The walls were only shoulder high, a formality and a signifier of privacy; they surrounded a plain wooden desk and a chair. "This is everything?" Pierce asked, startled.

"Not entirely. Look up." Torque gestured at the dome above them. "In here we maintain a human-compatible biosphere to reprocess your air and waste. We provide light, and heat, although the latter is less important than it will be in a few million years hereabouts. We've turned down the sun to conserve mass, but it's still radiating brightly in the infrared; the real problems will start when we work through the last bunker reserve in about eighteen million years. The dome should keep the Library accessible to readers for about thirty million years after that, well into Fimbulwinter."

Fimbulwinter: the winter at the end of the world, after the last fuel for the necrosun's accretion disk had been consumed, leaving Earth adrift in orbit around a cold black hole, billions of light-years from anything else. Pierce shivered slightly at the thought of it. "What's the problem with the outside air?"

"We were losing hydrogen too fast, and without hydrogen, there's no water, and without water, we can't maintain a biosphere, and without a biosphere the planet rapidly becomes less habitable—no free oxygen, for one thing. So about thirty billion years ago we deuterated the biosphere as a conservation measure. Of course, that necessitated major adjustments to the enzyme systems of all the life-forms from bacteria on up, and you—and I—are not equipped to run on heavy water; the stuff's toxic to us." Torque pointed at the stream. "You can drink from that, if you like, or order refreshments by phone. But don't drink outside the dome. Don't breathe too much, if you can help it."

Pierce looked around. "So this is basically just a reading

room, like a Branch Library. Where's the *real* Library? Where are the archives?"

"You're standing on them." Torque's expression was one of restrained impatience: *Weren't you paying attention in class the day they covered this?* "The plateau this reading room is built on—in fact, the entire upper crust—is riddled with storage cells of memory diamond, beneath a thin crust of sedimentary rock laid down to protect it. We switched the continental-drift cycle off for good about five billion years ago, after the last core cooling cycle. That's when we began accumulating the Library deposits.

"Oh." Pierce looked around. "Well, I suppose I'd better get started. Do you mind?"

"Not at all." Torque turned his back on Pierce and walked away. *"I'll be around if you call me,"* he sent.

Pierce sat down in front of the empty desk and laid his hands palm down on the blotter. *A* continent *of memory diamond?* The mere idea of that much data beggared the imagination. "It'll be in here somewhere," he muttered, and smiled.

Unhistory

One of the first things that any agent of the Stasis learns is patience. It's not as if they are short of time; their long lives extend beyond the easy reach of memory, and should they avoid death through violence or accident or suicide, they can pursue projects that would exceed the life expectancy of ordinary mortals. And that is how they live in the absence of the principal aspect of their employment, the ability to request access to the timegate.

Pierce thought at first that the vice-chancellor's request would be trivial, a matter of taking a few hours or days to dig down into the stacks and review the historical record. He'd return triumphant, a few minutes upstream of his departure, and present his findings before the council. Xiri would be appropriately adoring, and would doubtless write a series of sonnets about his Library visit (for poetics were in fashion as the densest rational format for sociological-academic case studies in Leng): and his adoptive home time would be spared the rigor and pity of a needless doctrinal war. That was his plan.

It came unglued roughly a week after his arrival, at the

point when he stopped flailing around in increasing panic and went for a long walk around the paths of the biome, brooding darkly, trying to quantify the task.

Memory diamond is an astonishingly dense and durable data substrate. It's a lattice of carbon nuclei, like any other diamond save that it is synthetic, and the position of atoms in the lattice represents data. By convention, an atom of carbon 12 represents a zero, and an atom of carbon 13 represents a one; and twelve-point-five grams of memory diamond—one molar weight, a little under half an old-style ounce—stores 6×10^{23} bits of data—or 10^{23} bytes, with compression.

The continent the reading room is situated on is fifteen kilometers thick and covers an area of just under forty million square kilometers, comparable to North and South America combined in the epoch of Pierce's birth. Half of it is memory diamond. There's well over 10^{18} *tons* of the stuff, roughly 10^{23} molar weights. One molar weight of memory diamond is sufficient to hold all the data ever created and stored by the human species prior to Pierce's birth, in what was known at the time as the twenty-first century.

The civilizations over which the Stasis held sway for a trillion years stored a *lot* more data. And when they collapsed, the Stasis looted their Alexandrian archives, binged on stolen data, and vomited it back up at the far end of time.

Pierce's problem was this: more than 90 percent of the Library consisted of lies.

He'd started out, naturally enough, with two pieces of information: the waypoint in his phone that identified the exact location of the porch of his home in Leng, and the designation of the planetary system in M-33 that had aroused such controversy. It was true, as Xiri had said, that the Hegemony was reveling in the feed from the robot exploration fleet that had swept through the Triangulum galaxy tens of millions of years ago. And he knew—he was certain!—that Xiri, and the Hegemony, and the city of Leng with its Mediterranean airs and absurdly scholastic customs existed. He had held her as his wife and lover for nearly two decades-subjective, dwelt there and followed their ways as an honored noble guest for more than ten of those years: he could smell the hot, damp summer evening breeze in his nostrils, the scent of the climbing blue rose vines on the trellis behind his house—

The first time he gave the Library his home address and the identities to search for, it took him to a set of war grave records in the Autonomous Directorate, two years before his first interview with Xiri. He was unamused to note the names of his father- and mother-in-law inscribed in the list of terrorist wreckers and resisters who had been liquidated by the Truth Police in the wake of the liberation of Leng by Directorate forces.

He tried again: this time he was relieved to home in on his return from the field trip to Constantinople—seen through the omnipresent eyes of Xiri's own cams—but was perplexed by her lack of excitement. He backtracked, his search widening out until he discovered to his surprise that according to the Library, the Hegemony was not, in fact, investigating the Triangulum galaxy at all, but focusing on Maffei 1, seven million light-years farther out.

That night he ordered up two bottles of a passable Syrah and drank himself into a solitary stupor for the first time in some years. It was a childish and shortsighted act, but the repeated failures were eating away at his patience. The day after, wiser but somewhat irritable, he tried again, entering his home coordinates into the desk and asking for a view of his hall.

There was no hall, and indeed no Leng, and no Hegemony either; but the angry spear-wielding raccoons had discovered woad.

Pierce stood up, shaking with frustration, and walked out of the reader's cubicle. He stood for a while on the damp green edge of the brook, staring at the play of light across the running water. It wasn't enough. He shed his scholar's robe heedlessly, turned to face the dirt trail that had led him to this dead end, and began to run. Arriving at the entrance airlock, he didn't stop: his legs pounded on, taking him out of the dome and then around it in a long loop, feet thumping on the bony limestone pavement, each plate like the scale of a monstrous fossilized lizard beneath his feet. He kept the glowing dome to his left as he circled it, once, then twice. By the end of the run he was flagging, his chest beginning to burn, the hot, heavy lassitude building in his legs as the sweat dripped down his face.

He slowed to a walk as the airlock came into view again. When he was ready to speak, he activated his phone. *"Torque. Your fucking Library is lying to me. Why is that?"*

"Ah, you've just noticed." Torque sounded amused. *"Come inside and we'll discuss it."*

I don't want to discuss it; I want it to work, Pierce fumed to himself as he trudged back to the airlock. Overhead, three planets twinkled redly across the blind vault of the nighttime sky.

Torque was waiting for him in the clearing, holding a bottle and a pair of shot glasses. "You're going to need this," he said, a twinkle in his eyes. "Everybody does, the first time around."

"Feh." Pierce shuffled stiffly past him, intending to return to the reading cubicle. "What use is a Library full of lies?"

"They're not lies." Torque's response was uncharacteristically mild. "They're unhistory."

"Un—" Pierce stopped dead in his tracks. "There was no unhistory in the Branch Libraries I used," he said tonelessly.

"There wouldn't be. Have you given thought to what happens every time you step through a timegate?"

"Not unduly. What does that have to do with—"

"Everything." Torque allowed a note of irritation to creep into his voice. "You need to pay more attention to theory, Agent. Not all problems can be solved with a knife."

"Huh. So the Library is contaminated with unhistory, because . . . ?"

"Students. When you use a timegate, you enter a wormhole, and when you exit from it—well, from the reference frame of your point of emergence, a singularity briefly appears and emits a large gobbet of information. *You.* The information isn't consistent with the time leading up to its sudden appearance—causality may be violated, for one thing, and for another, the information, the traveler, may remember or contain data that wasn't there before. You're just a bundle of data spewed out by a wormhole; you don't have to be consistent with the universe around you. That's how you remember your upbringing and your recruitment, even though nobody else does. Except for the Library."

They came to a clearing and instead of taking the track to the reading room, Torque took a different path.

"Let's suppose you visit a temporal sector—call it A-one—and while you're there, you do something that changes its historical pattern. You're now in sector A-two. A-one no longer exists; it's been overwritten. If there's a Branch Library in A-one, it's now in A-two, and it, too, has changed, because it is consistent with its own history. But the real Library—tell me, how does information enter the Library?"

Pierce floundered. "I thought that was an archival specialty? Every five seconds throughout eternity a listener slot opens for a millisecond, and anything of interest is sent forward to Control."

"Not exactly." Torque stopped on the edge of another clearing in the domed jungle. "The communication slots send data *backward* in time, not forward. There's an epoch almost a billion years long, sitting in the Archaean and Proterozoic eras, where we run the Library relays. The point is—back in the Cryptozoic-relay era, there are no palimpsests. There's no human history to contaminate, nothing there but a bunch of store-and-forward relays. So reports from sector A-one are relayed back to the Cryptozoic, as are reports from sector A-two. And when they're transmitted uptime to the Final Library for compilation, we have two conflicting reports from sector A."

Pierce boggled. "Are you telling me that we don't destroy time lines when we change things? That everything coexists? That's heretical!"

"I'm not preaching heresy." Torque turned to face him. "The sector is indeed overwritten with new history: the other events are unhistory now, stuff that never happened. *Plausible lies.* Raw data that pops out of a wormhole mediated by a naked singularity, if you ask the theorists: causally unconnected with reality. But all the lies end up in the Library. Not only does the Library document all of recorded human history—and there is a *lot* of it, for ubiquitous surveillance technology is both cheap and easy to develop, it's how we define civilization after all—it documents all the possible routes through history that end in the creation of the Final Library. That's why we have the Final Library as well as all the transient, palimpsest-affected Branch Libraries."

It was hard to conceive of. "All right. So the Library is full of internally contradictory time lines. Why can't I find what I'm looking for?"

"Well. If you're using your waypoints correctly, the usual reason why you get a random selection of incorrect views is that someone has rewritten that sector. It's a palimpsest. Not only is the information you came here to seek buried in a near-infinite stack of unhistories, it's unlikely you'll ever be able to return to it—unless you can find the point where that sector's history was altered and undo the alteration."

○ REPEATEDLY KILLING THE BUDDHA

Graduation Ceremony

You will awaken early on that day, and you will dress in the formal parade robes of a probationary agent of the Stasis for the last time ever. You have worn these robes many times over the past twenty years, and you are no longer the frightened teenager whose hands held the knife of the aspirant and whose ears accepted their ruthless first order. Had you declined the call, were you still in the era of your birth, you would already be approaching early middle age, the great plague of senescence digging its claws deep beneath your skin; and as it is, even though the medical treatments of the Stasis have given you the appearance of a twenty-five-year-old, your eyes are windows onto the soul of an ancient.

Your mind will be honed as sharp and purposeful as a razor blade, for you will have spent six months preparing for this morning; six months of lonesome despair following Torque's explanation of your predicament, spent in training on the roof of the world, obsessively focused on your final studies. You have completed your internship and your probationary assignments, worked alone and unsupervised in perilous times: now you will present yourself to the examiners to undergo their final and most severe examination, in hope of being accepted at last as an agent of Stasis. As a full agent, you will no longer be limited in your access to the Library: nor will your license to summon timegates be restricted. You will be a trustee, a key-holder in the jailhouse of history, able to rummage through lives on a whim, free to search for what you have lost (or have had taken from you: as yet you are unsure whether it was malice or negligence that destroyed your private life).

You will dress in a saffron robe bound with the black belt of your current rank, and place on your head the beret of an agent-aspirant. Elsewhere in the complex, a dozen other probationers are similarly preparing themselves. You will hang on your belt the dagger that you honed to lethal sharpness the night before, obsessively polishing the symbol of your calling. Before the sun reaches the day's zenith, it will have taken a life: it is your duty to ensure that the victim dies swiftly, painlessly.

Out on the time-weathered flagstones, beneath the deep blue dome of a sky bisected by a glittering torque of orbital-momentum-transfer bodies, you will stand in a row before your teachers and tyrants. Not for the first time, you will find yourself asking if it was all worth it. They will stare down at you and your classmates, ready to pronounce judgment—ready perhaps to admit you to their number as a peer, or to anathematize and cauterize, to unmake and consign into unhistory those who are unworthy. They outnumber your fellow trainees three to one, for they take the training of new eumortals very seriously indeed. They are the eternal guardians of historicity, the arbiters of what really happened. And for no reason you can clearly comprehend, they offered you, you in particular out of a field of a billion contenders, an opportunity.

And there will be speeches. And more speeches. And then Superintendent-of-Scholars Manson will utter a sermon, along exactly the lines one would expect on such an occasion. "This momentous and solemn occasion marks the end of your formal training, but not the end of your studies and your search for excellence. You entered this academy as orphans and strangers, and you shall leave it as agents of the Stasis, sworn to serve our great cause—the total history of the human species." He's going to go on in like vein for nearly an hour, you realize: one homily after another, orthodox ideology personified. Theory before praxis.

"We accept you as you are, human aspirants with human

weaknesses and human strengths. We are all human; that is *our* weakness and strength, for we are the agency of human destiny, charged with the holy duty of preserving our species from the triple threat of extinction, transcendental obsolescence, and a cosmos fated to unwind in darkness—notwithstanding your weaknesses, you, brother Chee Yun, with your obsessive exploration of the extremes of pain; you, sister Gretz, with your enthusiasm for the fruit of the dream poppy; you, brother Pierce, with your palimpsest family hobby—we understand all your little vices, and we accept you as you are, despite your weaknesses, despite knowing that only through service to the Stasis will you achieve all that you are destined for—"

You will not bridle angrily when Superintendent-of-Scholars Manson tramples on the grave of your family's unhistory, even though the scars are still raw and weeping, because you know that this is how the ritual unfolds. You will have reviewed the recording delivered in the internal post some days before, heard the breathy rasp of your own voice wavering on the razor edge of horror as he explains the graduation ritual to you-in-the-present. Your fingers will whiten on the sweat-stained leather hilt of your dagger as you await the signal. Though outwardly you remain at peace, inside you will be in turmoil, wondering if you can go through with it. Slaying your grandfather, cutting yourself free from the fabric of history, was one thing; this is something else.

"Stasis demands eternal vigilance, brothers and sisters. It is easier to shape by destruction than to force creation on the boughs of historicity, but we must stand vigilant and ready, if necessary, to intervene even against ourselves should our hands stray from the straightest of strokes. Every time we step from a timegate, we are born anew as information entering the universe from a singularity: we must not allow our hands to be stilled by fear of personal continuity—"

You will realize then that Manson is on track, that he really *is* going to give the order your older self described with shaking voice, and you tense in readiness as you call up a channel to Control, requesting the gate through which you must graduate.

"Weakness is forgivable in one's personal life, but not in the great work. We humans are weak, and sooner or later many of us stray, led into confusion and solipsism by our human grief and hubris. But it is our glory and our privilege that we can change *ourselves*. We do not have to accept a false version of ourselves which have fallen into the errors of wrong thought or despair! Shortly you will be called on to undertake the first of your autosurveillance duties, monitoring your own future self for signs of deviation. Keep a clear head, remember your principles, and be firm in your determination to destroy your own errors: that is all it takes to serve the Stasis well. We are our own best police force, for we can keep track of our own other selves far better than any eternal invigilator." Manson will clap his hands. And then, without further ado, he will add: "You have all been told what it is that you must do in order to graduate. Do it. Prove to me that you have what it takes to be a stalwart pillar of the Stasis. Do it *now*."

You will draw your dagger as your phone sends out the request for a timegate two seconds back in time and a meter behind you. Control acknowledges your request, and you begin to step toward the opening hole in front of you, but as you do so you will sense wrongness, and as you draw breath you will begin to turn, raising your knife to block with a scream forming in the back of your mind: *No! Not me!* But you will be too late. The stranger with your face stepping out of the singularity behind you will tighten his grip on your shoulders, and as you twist your neck to look around, he will use your momentum to aid the edge of the knife you so keenly sharpened. It will whisper through your carotid artery and your trachea, bringing your life to a gurgling, airless fadeout.

The graduation ceremony always concludes this way, with the newly created agents slaughtering their Buddha nature on the stony road beneath the aging stars. It is a pity that you won't be alive to see it in person; it is one of the most profoundly revealing rituals of the time travelers, cutting right to the heart of their existence. But you needn't worry about your imminent death—the other you, born bloody from the singularity that opened behind your back, will regret it as fervently as you ever could.

The Trial

The day after he murdered himself in cold blood, Agent Pierce received an urgent summons to attend a meeting in the late nineteenth century.

It was, he thought shakily, par for the course: pick an agent, any agent, as long as their home territory was within a millennium or so of the dateline. From Canada in the twenty-first to Germany in the nineteenth, what's the difference? If you were an inspector from the umpty-millionth, it might not look like a lot, he supposed: they were all exuberant egotists, these faceless teeming ur-people who had lived and died before the technologies of total history rudely dispelled the chaos and uncertainty of the pre-Stasis world. And Pierce was a *very* junior agent. Best to see what the inspector wanted.

Kaiserine Germany was not one of Pierce's areas of interest, so he took a subjective month to study for the meeting in advance—basic conversational German, European current events, and a sufficient grounding in late-Victorian London to support his cover as a more than usually adventuresome entrepreneur looking for new products to import—before he stepped out of a timegate in the back of a stall in a public toilet in Spittelmarkt.

Berlin before the century of bombs was no picturesque gingerbread confection: outside the slaughterhouse miasma of the market, the suburbs were dismal narrow-fronted apartment blocks as far as the eye could see, soot-stained by a million brown-coal stoves, the principal olfactory note one of horse shit rather than gasoline fumes (although Rudolf Diesel was even now at work on his engines in a more genteel neighborhood). Pierce departed the public toilet with some alacrity—the elderly attendant seemed to take his emergence as a personal insult—and hastily hailed a cab to the designated meeting place, a hotel in Charlottenberg.

The hotel lobby was close and humid in the summer heat; bluebottles droned around the dark wooden paneling as Pierce looked around for his contact. His phone tugged at his attention as he looked at the inner courtyard, where a cluster of cast-iron chairs and circular tables hinted at the availability of waiter service. Sure enough, a familiar face nodded affably at him.

Pierce approached the table with all the enthusiasm of a condemned man approaching the gallows. "You wanted to see me," he said. There were two goblets of something foamy and green on the table, and two chairs. "Who else?"

"The other drink's for you. Berliner Weiss with Waldmeistersirup. You'll like it. Guaranteed." Kafka gestured at the empty chair. "Sit down."

"How do you know—" *Silly question.* Pierce sat down. "You know this isn't my time?"

"Yes." Kafka picked up a tall, curved glass full of dark brown beer and took a mouthful. "Doesn't matter." He peered at Pierce. "You're a new graduate. Damn, I don't like this job." He took another mouthful of beer.

"What's happened now?" Pierce asked.

"I don't know. That's why I want you here."

"Is this to do with the time someone tried to assassinate me?"

"No." Kafka shook his head. "It's worse, I'm afraid. One of your tutors may have gone off the reservation. Observation indicated. I'm putting you on the case. You may need—you may need to terminate this one."

"A tutor." Despite himself, Pierce was intrigued. Kafka, the man from Internal Affairs (but his role was unclear, for was it not the case that the Stasis police their own past and future selves?) wanted him to investigate a senior agent and tutor? Ordering him to bug his future self would be understandable, but this—

"Yes." Kafka put his glass down with a curl of his lower lip that bespoke distaste. "We have reason to believe she may be working for the Opposition."

"Opposition." Pierce raised an eyebrow. "There is no opposition—"

"Come, now: don't be naive. *Every* ideology in every recorded history has an opposition. Why should we be any different?"

"But we're—" Pierce paused, the phrase *bigger than history* withering on the tip of his tongue. "Excuse me?"

"Work it through." Kafka was atwitch with barely concealed impatience. "You can't possibly *not* have thought about setting yourself up as a pervert god, can you? Everybody thinks about it, this we know; seed the universe with life, create your own Science Empires, establish a rival interstellar civilization in the deep Cryptozoic, and use it to invade or secede Earth before the Stasis notices—that sort of thing. It's not as if *thinking about it* is a crime: the problems start when an agent far gone in solipsism starts thinking they can do it for real. Or worse, when the Opposition raise their snouts."

"But I—" Pierce stopped, collected his thoughts, and continued. "I thought that never happened? That the self-policing thing was a . . . an adequate safeguard?"

"Lad." Kafka shook his head. "You clearly mean well. And self-policing does indeed work adequately most of the time. But don't let the security theater at your graduation deceive you: there are failure modes. We set you a large number of surveillance assignments to muddy the water—palimpsests all, of course, we overwrite them once they deliver their reports so that future-you retains no memory of them—but you can't watch yourself all the time. And there are administrative errors. You're not only the best monitor of your own behavior, but the best-placed individual to know how best to corrupt you. We are human and imperfect, which is why we need an external Internal Affairs department. Someone has to coordinate things, especially when the Opposition are involved."

"The Opposition?" Pierce picked up his glass and drank deeply, studying Kafka. "Who are they?" *Who do you want me to rat out?* he wondered. *Myself?* Surely Kafka couldn't have overlooked his history with Xiri, now buried beneath the dusty pages of a myriad of rewrites?

"You'll know them when you meet them." Kafka emitted a little mirthless chuckle and stood up. "Come upstairs to my office, and I'll show you why I requested you for this assignment."

Kafka's office occupied the entire top floor of the building and was reached by means of a creaking mesh-fronted elevator that rose laboriously through the well of a wide staircase. It was warm, but not obnoxiously so, as Pierce followed Kafka out of the elevator cage. "The door is reactive," Kafka warned, placing a protective hand on the knob. Hidden glands were waiting beneath a patina of simulated brass, ready to envenomate the palm of an unwary intruder. "Door: accept

Agent Pierce. General defenses: accept Agent Pierce with standard agent privilege set. You may follow me now."

Kafka opened the door wide. Beyond it, ranks of angled wooden writing desks spanned the room from wall to wall. A dark-suited iteration of Kafka perched atop a high stool behind each one of them, pens moving incessantly across their ledgers. A primitive visitor (one not slain on the spot by the door handle, or the floor, or the wallpaper) might have gaped at the ever-changing handwriting and spidery diagrams that flickered on the pages, mutating from moment to moment as the history books redrew themselves, and speculated about digital paper. Pierce, no longer a primitive, felt the hair under his collar rise as he polled his phone, pulling up the number of rewrites going on in the room. "You're really working Control hard," he said in the direction of Kafka's receding back.

"This is the main coordination node for prehistoric Germany." Kafka tucked his hands behind his back as he walked, stoop-shouldered, between desks. "We're close enough to the start of Stasis history to make meddling tricky—we have to keep track of continuity, we can't simply edit at will." Meddling with prehistory, before the establishment of the ubiquitous monitoring and recording technologies that ultimately fed the Library at the end of time, ought to be risk-free: if a Neolithic barbarian froze to death on a glacier, unrecorded, the implications for deep history were trivial. But the rules were fluid, and interference was risky: if a time traveler were to shoot the Kaiser, for example, or otherwise derail the ur-history line leading up to the Stasis, it could turn the entire future into a palimpsest. "The individual I am investigating is showing an unhealthy interest in the phase boundary between Stasis and prehistory."

One of the deskbound Kafkas looked up, his eyebrows furrowing with irritation. "Could you take this somewhere else?" he asked.

"I'm sorry," Pierce's Kafka replied with abrupt humility. "Agent Pierce, this way."

As Kafka led Pierce into an office furnished like an actuary's hermitage, Pierce asked, "Aren't you at risk of anachronism yourselves? Multitasking like that, so close to the real Kafka's datum?"

Kafka smiled sepulchrally as he sat down behind the heavy oak desk. "I take precautions. And the fewer individuals who know what's in those ledgers, the better." He gestured at a small, hard seat in front of it. "Be seated, Agent Pierce. Now, in your own words. Tell me about your relationship with Agent-Scholar Yarrow. *Everything*, if you please." He reached into his desk drawer and withdrew a smart pad. "I have a transcript of your written correspondence here. We'll go through it line by line next . . ."

Funeral in Berlin

The interrogation lasted three days. Kafka didn't even bother to erase it from Pierce's time line retroactively: clearly he was making a point about the unwisdom of crossing Internal Affairs.

Afterward, Pierce left the hotel and wandered the streets of Berlin in a neurasthenic daze.

Does Kafka trust me? Or not? On balance, probably not: the methodical, calm grilling he'd received, the interrogation about the precise meaning of Yarrow's love letters (faded memories from decades ago, to Pierce's mind), had been humiliating, an emotional strip search. Knowing that Kafka understood his dalliance with Yarrow as a youthful indiscretion, knowing that Kafka clearly knew of (and tolerated) his increasingly desperate search for the point at which his history with Xiri had been overwritten, only made it worse. *We can erase everything that gives meaning to your life if we feel like it.* Feeling powerless was a new and shocking experience for Pierce, who had known the freedom of the ages: a return to his pre-Stasis life, half-starved and skulking frightened in the shadows of interesting times.

And then there was the incipient paranoia that any encounter with Internal Affairs engendered. *Am I being watched right now?* he wondered as he walked. *A ghost-me surveillance officer working for Internal Affairs, or something else?* Kafka would be mad not to assign him a watcher, he decided. If Yarrow was under investigation, then he himself must be under suspicion. Guilt by association was the first rule of counterespionage, after all.

A soul-blighting sense of depression settled into his bones.

He'd had an inkling of it for months, ever since his increasingly frantic search in the Library, but Kafka's quietly pedantic examination had somehow catalyzed a growing certainty that he would never see Xiri, or Magnus and Liann, ever again—that if he could ever find them, shadows cast from his mind by the merciless inspection-lamp glare of Internal Affairs would banish them farther into unhistory.

Therefore, he wandered.

Civilization lay like a heavy blanket upon the land, rucked up in gray-faced five-story apartment blocks and pompous stone-faced business establishments, their pillars and porticoes and cornicework swollen with self-importance like so many amorous street pigeons. The city sweated in the summer heat, the stench and flies of horse manure in the streets contributing a sour pungency to the sharp stink of stove smoke.

Other people shared the Strasse with him; here a peddler selling apples from a handcart, there a couple taking the air together. Pierce walked slowly along the sidewalk of a broad street, sweating in his suit and taking what shelter he could from the merciless summer sun beneath the awnings of shops, letting his phone's navigation aid guide his footsteps even as he wondered despondently if he would ever find his way home. He could wander through the shadowy world of historicity forever, never finding his feet—for though the Stasis and their carefully cultivated tools of ubiquitous monitoring had nailed down the sequence of events that comprised history, history was a tangled weave, many threads superimposed and redyed and snipped out of the final pattern . . .

The scent was his first clue that he was not alone, floral and sweet and tickling the edge of his nostrils with a half-remembered sense of illicit excitement that made his heart hammer. The shifting sands of memory gave way: *I know that smell—*

His phone vibrated. *"Show no awareness,"* someone whispered inside his skull in Urem. *"They are watching you."* The voice was his own.

The strolling couple taking the air arm in arm were ahead of him. It was *her* scent, the familiar bouquet, but—*"Where are you?"* he sent. *"Show yourself."*

The phone buzzed again like an angry wasp trapped inside

his ribs. *"Not with watchers. Go to this location and wait,"* said the traitor voice, as a spatial tag nudged the corner of his mind. *"We'll pick you up."* The rendezvous was a couple of kilometers away, in a public park notorious by night: a French-letter drop for a dead-letter drop.

He tried not to stare. *It* might *be her,* he thought, trying to shake thirty-year-old jigsaw memories into something that matched a glimpse of a receding back in late-nineteenth-century dress and broad-brimmed hat. He turned a corner in his head even as they turned aside into a residential street: *"Internal Affairs just interrogated me about Yarrow."*

"You told us already. Go now. Leave the rest to us."

Pierce's phone fell silent. He glanced sideways out of the corners of his eyes, but the strolling couple were no longer visible. He sniffed, flaring his nostrils in search of an echo of that familiar scent, but it, too, was gone. Doubtless they'd never been here at all; they were Stasis, after all. Weren't they?

Guided by his phone's internal nudging, Pierce ambled slowly toward the park, shoulders relaxed and hands clasped behind his back as if enjoying a quiet afternoon stroll. But his heart was pounding and there was an unquiet sensation in the pit of his stomach, as if he harbored a live grenade in his belly. *You told us already. Go now. Leave the rest to us.* His own traitor voice implying lethally spiraling cynicism. *They are watching you.* The words of a self-crowned pervert god, hubris trying to dam the flow of history; or the mysterious Opposition that Kafka had warned him of? It was imponderable, intolerable. *I could be walking into a trap,* Pierce considered the idea, and immediately began to activate a library of macros in his phone that he'd written for such eventualities. As Superintendent-of-Scholars Manson had ceaselessly reminded him, a healthy paranoia was key to avoiding further encounters with cardiac leeches and less pleasant medical interventions.

Pierce crossed the street and walked beside a canal for a couple of blocks, then across a bridge and toward the tree-lined gates of a park. Possibilities hummed in the dappled shadows of the grass like a myriad of butterfly wings broken underfoot, whispering on the edge of actuality like distant thunder. This part of history, a century and more before the emergence of the first universal-surveillance society, before the beginning of the history to which the Stasis laid claim, was mutable in small but significant ways. Nobody could say for sure who might pass down any given street in any specified minute, and deem it disruptive: the lack of determinism lent a certain flexibility to his options.

Triggering one of his macros as he stepped through the gate to the park, between one step and the next Pierce walked through a storeroom in the basement of a Stasis station that had been dust and ruins a billion years before the ice sheets retreated from the North German plains. It had lain disused for a century or so when he entered it, and nobody else would use it for at least a decade thereafter—he'd set monitors, patient trip wires to secure his safe time. He tarried there for almost three hours, picking items from a well-stocked shelf and sending out messages to order them from a factory on a continent that didn't yet exist, eating a cold meal from a long-storage ration pack, and trying to regain his emotional balance in time for the meeting that lay ahead.

An observer close on his tail would have seen a flicker; when he completed the stride his suit was heavier, the fabric stiffer to the touch, and his shoulders slightly stooped beneath the weight concealed within. There were other changes, some of them internal. Perhaps the observers would see, but: *Leave the rest to us.* He slipped his hands into his pockets, blinked until the itching subsided and the heads-up display settled into place across the landscape, scanning and amplifying. He had summoned watchers, circling overland: invisible and silent, nerves connected to his center. *Fuck Kafka's little game,* he thought furiously. *Fuck them all.* Three hours in his unrecorded storeroom in the Cryptozoic had given him time for his depression to ferment into anger. *I want answers!*

It was a hot day, and the park was far from empty. There were young women, governesses or maids, pushing the prams of their bourgeois employers; clerks or office workers skipping work and some juvenile ne'er-do-wells playing truant from the gymnasium; here a street sweeper and there a dodgy character with a barrel organ and behind him a couple of vagrants sharing a bottle of schnapps. At the center of a well-manicured lawn, an ornate stone pedestal supported a clock with four brass faces. Pierce, letting his phone drive his feet, casually glanced around while his threat detector scanned through the chaff. *Nobody*— His phone buzzed again.

"What was the tavern where you fell for me called?" An achingly familiar voice whispered in his ear.

"Something to do with wildfowl, in Carnegra, the Red Goose or Red Duck or something like that—"

"Hard contact in three seconds," his own voice interrupted from nowhere. *"Button up and hit the ground on my word.* Now.*"*

Pierce dived toward the grassy strip beside the path as flaring crimson threat markers appeared all around him. As he fell, his suit bloated and darkened: rubbery cones expanded like a frightened hedgehog's quills as his collar expanded and rotated, hooding him. In the space of a second the park's population doubled, angular metallic figures flickering into being all around. Time flickered and strobed as timegates snapped open and shut, expelling sinister cargo. Pierce twitched ghost muscles convulsively, triggering camouflage routines as the incoming drones locked onto each other and spat missiles and laser fire.

"What's going on?"

"Palimpsest ambush! Hard . . ."

The signal stuttered into silence, hammered flat by jammers and raw, random interference. Pierce began to roll, rising to sit as his suit's countermeasures flared. *This is crazy,* he thought, shocked by the violence of the attack. *They can't hope to conceal—*

The sky turned violet-white, the color of lightning: the grass around him began to smoke.

The temperature rose rapidly. His suit was just beginning to char from the prompt radiation pulse as the ground opened under him, toppling him backward into darkness.

● REDUX

Army of You

When you see the ground swallow Pierce you will breathe a sigh of relief—you'll finally have the luxury of knowing that one of your iterations has made it out of death ground. But the situation will be too deadly to give you respite. If Internal Affairs are willing to *start* with combat drones and orbital X-ray lasers, then escalate from there, where will they stop? How badly do they want you?

Very badly, it seems.

There's going to be hell to pay when it's time for the cleanup; ur-history doesn't have room for a nuclear blitzkrieg on the capital of the Second Reich. The calcinated, rapidly skeletonizing remains of the governesses and the organ grinders contort and burst in the searing wind from the Hiroshima miscarriage, and the four faces of the clock glow cherry red and slump to the ground as a dozen more of you flicker into view, anonymous in their heat-flash-silvered battle armor. The echo-armies of your combat drones fan out all around, furiously dumping heat through transient timegates into the cryogenic depths of the far future as they exchange fire with the enemy's soldiers. *"Extraction complete. Prepare to move out,"* says your phone; the iteration tag of that version of you is astronomical, in the millions. This isn't just a palimpsest ambush: it's an entire talmud of rewrites and commentaries and attempted paradoxes piled up in a threatening tsunami of unhistory and dumped on your heads.

You'll grab your future self's metadata and jump toward a timegate to a dispersal zone drifting high in orbit above ruddy Jupiter's north pole, nearly a billion years in the future: the rocket motors at your suit's shoulders and ankles kick hard, and as you loft, you'll catch a flashing glimpse of the Mach wave from the first heat strike surging outward, lifting and crumpling schools and hospitals and churches and apartments and houses and shops in the iron name of Internal Affairs.

They won't find this dispersal zone. They won't uncover the truth about Control, either, or about the Opposition—you'll be sure of that for as long as you continue to live and breathe.

You will look down, between your feet, at the swirling orange-and-cream chaos of Jupiter's upper atmosphere. Your armor will ping and tick quietly as it cools, and you will wait while the star trackers get a fix on your position, your mind empty of everything but a quiet satisfaction, the reward for a job well-done: the extraction of your cardinal iterant from the grasp of Internal Affairs. Somewhere else in time—millions of years ago—the rewrite war is still going on, the virtual legions of you playing a desperate shell game with Kafka: but you've won. All that's left to do is to deftly insert the zombie ringer into ur-history on his way into Kafka's court, primed to tell Internal Affairs exactly what you want them to know, then to orchestrate a drawdown and withdrawal from the ruins of Berlin before Kafka overwrites the battle zone and restores the proper flow of history.

Your suit will beep quietly for attention. "Scan complete," it announces. "Acceleration commencing." The thrusters will push briefly, reorienting you, sliding Jupiter out of sight behind your back. And then the rockets will kick in again, pushing you toward the yard, and the fleet of thirty-kilometer-long starships abuilding, and Yarrow.

He Got Your Girl

I'm alive, thought Pierce, then did a double take. *I'm alive?* Everything was black, and he couldn't tell which way was up. There was a metallic taste in his mouth, and he ached everywhere.

"Where am I?" he asked.

"You'll have to wait while we cut you out of that," said a stranger. Their voice sounded oddly muffled, and he realized with surprise that it wasn't coming from inside him. "You took an EMP that fried your suit. You only just made it out in time—you took several sieverts. We've got a bed waiting for you."

Something pushed at his side, and he felt a strange tipping motion. "Am I in free fall?" he asked.

"Of course. Try not to move."

I'm not on Earth, he realized. It was strange; he'd effectively visited hundreds of planets with ever-shifting continents and biospheres, but he'd never been off Earth before. They were all aspects of Gaia, causally entangled slices through the set of all possible Earths that the Stasis called their own.

Someone tugged on his left foot, and he felt a chill of cold air against his skin. His toes twitched. "That's very good, keep doing that. Tell me if anything hurts." The voice was still muffled by the remains of his hood, but he could place it now. Kari, a quiet woman, one of the trainees from the class above him. He tensed, panic rising in a choking wave. "Hey— Yarrow! He's stressing out—"

"Hold still, Pierce." Yarrow's voice in his ears, also fuzzy. "Your phone's off-line; it took a hit too. Kari's with us. It's going to be all right."

You don't have any right to tell me that, he thought indignantly, but the sound of her voice had the desired effect. *So Kari's one of them too.* Was there no end to the internal rot within the Stasis? In all honesty, considering his own concupiscence—possibly not. He tried to slow his breathing, but it was slowly getting stuffy and hot inside the wreckage of his survival suit.

More parts detached themselves from his skin. He was beginning to itch furiously, and the lack of gravity seemed to be making him nauseous. Finally, the front of his hood cracked open and floated away. He blinked teary eyes against the glare, trying to make sense of what his eyes were telling him.

"Kari—"

The spherical drone floating before his face wore her face on its smartskin. A flock of gunmetal lampreys swam busily behind it, worrying at pieces of the dead and mildly radioactive suit. Some distance beyond, a wall of dull blue triangles curved around him, dishlike, holes piercing it in several places.

"Try not to speak," said Kari's drone. "You've taken a borderline-fatal dose, and we're going to have to get you to a sick bay right away."

His throat ached. "Is Yarrow there?"

Another spherical drone floated into view from somewhere behind him. It wore Xiri's face. "My love? I'll visit you as soon as you've cleared decontamination. The enemy are always trying to sneak bugs in: they wouldn't let me through to see you now. Be strong, my lord." She smiled, but the worry-wrinkles at the corners of her eyes betrayed her. "I'm very proud of you."

He tried to reply, but his stomach had other ideas and attempted to rebel. "Feel. Sick . . ."

Someone kissed the back of his neck with lips of silver, and the world faded out.

Pierce regained consciousness with an abrupt sense of rupture, as if no time at all had passed: someone had switched his sense of awareness off and on again, just as his parents might once have power-cycled a balky appliance.

"Love? Pierce?"

He opened his eyes and stared at her for a few seconds, then cleared his throat. It felt oddly normal: the aches had all evaporated. "We've got to stop meeting like this." The bed began to rise behind his back. "Xiri?"

Her clothing was outrageous to Hegemonic forms (not to say anachronistic or unrevealing), but she was definitely his Xiri; as she leaned forward and hugged him fiercely he felt something bend inside him, a dam of despair crumbling before a tidal wave of relief. "How did they find you?" he asked her shoulder, secure in her embrace. "*Why* did they reinstate—"

"Hush. Pierce. You were so ill—"

He hugged her back. "I was?"

"They kept me from you for half a moon! And the burns, when they cut that suit away from you. What did you *do*?"

Pierce pondered the question. "I changed my mind about . . . something I'd agreed to do . . ."

They lay together on the bed until curiosity got the better of him. "Where are we? When are we?" *Where did you get that jumpsuit?*

Xiri sighed, then snuggled closer to him. "It's a long story," she said quietly. "I'm still not sure it's true."

"It must be, now," he pointed out reasonably, "but perhaps it wasn't, for a while. But where are we?"

She eased back a little. "We're in orbit around Jupiter. But not for much longer."

"But I—" He stopped. "Really?"

"They disconnected your phone, or I could show you. The colony fleets, the shipyards."

He blinked at her, astonished. "How?"

"We all have phone implants, here." Her eyes sparkled with amusement. "This isn't the Stasis you know."

"I'd guessed." He swallowed. "How long has it been for you?"

"Since"—her breath caught, a little ragged—"two years. A little longer."

He gently trapped her right hand in his, ran his thumb across the smooth, plump skin on the back of her wrist. She let him. "Almost the same." He swallowed once more. "I thought I'd never see you again. Anyone would think they'd planned this."

"Oh, but they did." She gave a nervous little laugh. "He said they didn't want us to, to desynchronize. Get too far apart." Her fingers closed around his thumb, constricting and warm.

"Who is 'he'?" asked Pierce, although he thought he knew.

"He used to be you, once. That's what he told me." Her grip tightened suddenly. "He's not you, love. It's not the same. *At all.*"

"I must see him."

Pierce tried to sit up: Xiri clung to him, dragging him down. "No! Not yet," she hissed.

Pierce stopped struggling before he hurt her. His arms and his stomach muscles felt curiously strong, almost as if they'd never been damaged. "Why not?"

"Scholar Yarrow asked me to, to intercede. She said you'd want to confront him." She tensed when she spoke Yarrow's name. "She was right. About lots of things."

"What's her position here?"

"She's with him." Xiri hesitated. "It took much getting used to. I made a fool of myself once, early on."

He raised a hand to stroke her hair. "I can understand that." Pierce pondered his lack of reaction. "It's been years since I knew her, you know. And if he's who—what—I think he is, he was never married to you. Was he?"

"No." She lay against him in silence for a while. "What are you going to do?" she asked in a small voice.

Pierce smiled at the ceiling. (It was low, and bare of decoration: another sign, if he needed one, that he was not back in the Hegemony.) For the time being, the shock and joy of finding her again had left him giddy with relief. "Where are the children?" he asked, forcing himself: one last test.

"I left Liann with a nurse. Magnus is away, in the ship's

scholasticos." Concern slowly percolated across her expression. "They've grown a lot: do you think—"

He breathed out slowly, relieved. "There will be time to get to know them again, yes." She reached over his chest and hugged him tight. He stroked her hair, content for the moment but sadly aware that everything was about to change. "But tell me one thing. What is it that you're so desperate to keep from me?"

Nation of Me

"Good to see you, Pierce," said the man on the throne. He smiled pleasantly but distantly. "I gather you've been keeping well."

Pierce had already come to understand that the truly ancient were not like ordinary humans. "Do you remember being me?" he asked, staring.

The man on the throne raised an eyebrow. "Wouldn't you like to know?" He gestured at the bridge connecting his command dais to the far side of the room. "You may approach." Combat drones and uniformed retainers withdrew respectfully, giving Pierce a wide berth.

He tried not to look down as he walked across the bridge, with only partial success. The storms of Jupiter swirled madly beneath his feet. It had made him nauseous the first time he'd seen them, through a dumb-glass window aboard the low-gee shuttle that had brought him hence—evidently his captors wanted to leave him in no doubt that he was a long way from home. Occulting the view of the planet was the blue-tinged quicksilver disk of the largest timegate he'd ever seen, holding open in defiance of protocol with preposterous, scandalous persistence.

"Why am I here?" Pierce demanded.

A snort. "Why do you think?"

"You're me." Pierce shrugged. "Me with a whole lot more experience and age, and an attitude problem." They'd dressed him in the formal parade robes of a Stasis agent rather than the black jumpsuits that seemed to be de rigueur around this place. It was a petty move, to enforce his alienation: and besides, it had no pockets. To fight back, he focused on the absurd. Black jumpsuits and shiny boots, on a spaceship?

Someone around here clearly harbored thespian fantasies. "And now you've got me."

His older self stiffened. "We need to talk alone." His eyes scanned the throne room. "You lot: dismissed."

Pierce glanced round just in time to see the last of the human audience flicker into unhistory. He looked back toward the throne. "I was hoping we could keep this civilized," he said mildly. "You've got all the leverage you need. I'm in your power." *There*: it was out in the open. Not that there'd been any doubt about it, even from the beginning. This ruthless ancient with his well-known mirror-face and feigned bonhomie had made Pierce's position crystal clear with his choice of greeters. All that was left was for Pierce to politely bare his throat and hope for a favorable outcome.

"I didn't rescue you from those scum in order to throw you away again"—his older self seemed almost irritated— "though what you see in *her* . . ." He shook his head. "You're safe here."

Pierce rolled his eyes. "Oh, really. And I suppose if I decline to go along with whatever little proposition you're about to put to me, you'll just let me walk away, is that it? Rather than, oh, rewind the audience and try again with a clean-sheet me?" He met the even gaze of the man in the throne and suddenly felt finger high.

"No," said the man on the throne, after a momentary pause. "That won't be necessary. I'm not going to ask you to do anything you wouldn't ask me to let you do."

"Oh." Pierce considered this for a moment. "You're with the Opposition, though. Aren't you? And you know I'm not." Honesty made him add, "Yet."

"I told you he'd say that," said Yarrow, behind him. Pierce's head whipped round. She nodded at him, but kept her smile for the man on the throne. "He's young and naive. Go easy on him."

The man on the throne nodded. "He's not *that* naive, my lady." He frowned. "Pierce, you slit the throat of your own double, separated from you by seconds. You joined the Stasis, after all. But do you really imagine it gets easier with age, when you've had time to meditate on what you've done? There's a reason why armies send the flower of their youth to do the killing and dying, not the aged and cynical. We have a name for those who find murder gets easier with experience: 'monsters.'"

He raised a hand. "Chairs all around." A pair of seats appeared on the dais, facing him: ghosts of carved diamond, fit for the lords of creation. "I think you should be the one to tell him the news," he suggested to Yarrow. "I'm not sure he'd believe me. He hasn't had time to recover from the trauma yet."

"All right." Yarrow slid gratefully into her own chair, then glanced at Pierce. "You'd better sit down."

"Why?" Pierce lowered himself into his seat expectantly.

"Because"—she nodded at Pierce's elder self, who returned the nod with a drily amused smile—"he's not just a member of the Opposition: he's our leader. That's why Internal Affairs have been all over you like ants. And that's why we had to extract you and bring you here."

"Rubbish." Pierce crossed his arms. "That's not why you had to grab me. You've already got him: I assume I'm a palimpsest or leftover from an assassination attempt. So what do you want with *me*? In the here and now, I mean?"

Yarrow looked flustered. "Pierce—"

His older self placed a restraining hand on her knee as he leaned forward. "Allow me?" He looked Pierce in the eyes. "The Opposition is not—you probably already worked this out—external to the Stasis; we come from within. The Stasis is broken, Pierce. It's drifting rudderless toward the end of time. We've got a . . . an alternative plan for survival. Internal Affairs is tasked with maintaining internal standards; they're opposed to structural change at all costs. They overwrote your wife's epoch because they discovered possible evidence of our success."

The evidence of abandoned cities on an alien moon, the fleet of gigantic slower-than-light colony starships—was this all just internal politics within the Stasis hierarchy?

"Whatever would they want to do that for?" he asked. "They're not interested in deep space." Except insofar as there were threats to the survival of humanity that had to be dealt with.

Yarrow shook her head. "We disagree. They're *very* interested in deep space—specifically, in keeping us out of it." She inhaled deeply. "Did you notice, when you were consulting the Library, any sign of histories that touched on extraterrestrial settlement? Even though we have reterraformed the Earth thousands of times over, strip-mined the sun, rearranged gas giants, built black holes, and ripped an entire star system from its native galactic cluster?" Pierce shook his head, uncertain. "We've built and destroyed thousands of biospheres, sculpted continents, we outnumber the stars in the cosmos—but we've never spread to other solar systems! Doesn't that strike you as a little odd?"

"But we coevolved with our planet; we're not adapted to life elsewhere—" Pierce stopped. *We can do terraforming, and timegates,* he realized. *Even if we can only have one wormhole end open at any given time. We rebuilt the sun. We've mapped every planet within ten million light-years.* "Are we?" he asked, plaintively.

"There's a Science Empire running down on Earth right now," said the man on the throne. "They've been studying that question for twelve thousand years. We brought them the probe fleet reports. They say it can be done, and they've been building and launching a colony ship a year for the past six centuries." He frowned. "We've had that big gate in place ever since the dawn of civilization, to block Internal Affairs from detecting and overwriting our operation here. Officially we're in the middle of a fallow epoch, and the system should be uninhabited and uninhabitable: we moved in ahead of the first scheduled Reseeding. But they never give up. Sooner or later they'll notice us and start looking for the other side of our barricade, the static drop we funneled you through."

"What happens when they find it?" asked Pierce.

"Six hundred inhabited worlds die, and that's just for starters," Yarrow said quietly. "Call it unhistory if you like euphemisms—but did your graduation kill feel unreal to you? Unlike your"—her nose wrinkled in the ghost of a sniff—"wife and children, the inhabitants of the colony worlds won't be retrievable through the Library."

"And those six hundred planets are just the seed corn," his older self chimed in. "The start of something vast."

"But why?" he asked. "Why would they . . . ?" He stopped.

"The Stasis isn't about historicity," said Yarrow. "That

might be the organization's raison d'être, but the raw truth of the matter is that the Stasis is about *power*. Like any organization, it lives and grows for itself, not for the task with which it is charged. The governing committee—it's very sad. But it's been like this as long as there's been a Stasis."

"We rescued you because we specifically want you—my first iteration, or as near to it as we've been able to get, give or take the assassination ambush in Carnegra," said the man on the throne. "We need your help to cut us free from the dead hand of history."

"But what—" Pierce lowered his hands to touch his belly. "My phone," he said slowly. "It's damaged, but you could have repaired it. It's not there anymore, is it?"

Yarrow nodded slowly. "Can you tell me why?" she asked.

● RESEEDING

A Brief Alternate History of the Universe

SLIDE 1.

Our solar system under the Stasis, first epoch.

Continents slide and drift, scurrying and scraping across the surface of the mantle. Lights flicker around the coastlines, strobing on and off in kiloyear cycles as civilizations rise and fall. In space, the swarm of orbital-momentum-transfer robots built from the bones of Ceres begin to cycle in and out, slowly pumping energy downwell to the Earth to drag it farther from the slowly brightening sun.

SLIDE 2.

Snapshot: something unusual is happening.

We zoom in on a ten-thousand-year slice, an eyeblink flicker of geological time. For millions of years beforehand, the Earth was quiet, its continents fallen dark in the wake of a huge burping hiccup of magma that flooded from the junction of the Cocos and Nazca continental plates. But now the

lights are back, jewels sprinkled across the nighttime hemi-
spheres of unfamiliar continents. Unusually, they aren't con-
fined to the surface—three diamond necklaces ring the planet
in glory, girdling the equator in geosynchronous orbit. And
floating beyond them, at the L1 Lagrange point betwixt Earth
and Luna, sits the anomalous glowing maw of an unusually
large timegate.

The natives appear to be restless . . .

SLIDE 3.

A slow slide of viewpoint out to Jupiter orbit shows that
the anomaly is spreading. Already some of the smaller Jovian
moons are missing; Thebe and Amalthea have vanished, and
something appears to be eating Himalea. A metallic cloud of
smaller objects swarms in orbit around Europa, pinpricks of
light speckling their surface.

Meanwhile, the shoals of momentum-transfer bodies are
thinning, their simple design replaced by numerous perver-
sions of form and purpose. Still powered by light sails, the
new vehicles carry exotic machines for harvesting energy
from the solar wind and storing it as antimatter. Shuttles move
among them like ants amidst an aphid farm, harvesting and
storing their largesse as they swing out to Jupiter before dropping back in toward Mercury.

Some of the hundreds of metal moons that orbit Europa
are glowing at infrared wavelengths, their temperature suspiciously close to three hundred degrees Kelvin. Against the
planetary measure of the solar system they are tiny—little
bigger than the moons of Mars. But they're among the largest
engineered structures ever built by the dreaming apes; vaster
than cities and more massive than pyramids. And soon they
will start to move.

SLIDE 4.

Three thousand years pass.

Earth lies dark and unpopulated once more, for humanity—
as always—has gone extinct. Of the great works in Jupiter

orbit few traces remain. The great ships have gone, the shipyards have long since been deorbited into the swirling chaos of the gas giant's atmosphere, and the malformed, warped transfer bodies have been cannibalized and restored to their original purpose.

Five small moons have disappeared, and slowly healing gouges show the sites of huge mining works on Io and Europa, but by the time the Stasis reseed Earth (two-thirds of a million years hence) even the slow resurfacing of Europa's icy caul will have obscured the signs of industry. It may be thousands of years after that before anybody notices.

SLIDE 5.

Twenty million years pass, and the galaxy slowly lights up with a glare of coherent light, waste energy from the communications traffic between the inhabited worlds.

The first generation colonies have long since guttered into senescence and extinction; so have the third and fourth generations. Of the first generation, barely one in five prospered—but that was sufficient. Those that live spawn prolifically. Planets are common, rocky terrestrial bodies far from rare, and even some of the more exotic types (water giants, tidelocked rocky giants in orbit around red dwarfs, and others) are amenable to human purpose. Where no planets are available, life is harder, prone to sudden extinction events: nobody survives the collapse of civilization aboard a space colony. But the tools and technologies of terraforming are well-known, and best practice, of a kind, develops. Many of the dwellers have adapted to their new habitats so well that they're barely recognizable as primates anymore, or even mammals.

SLIDE 6.

Three billion years pass.

Two huge, glittering clouds of sentience fall through each other, a magnificently coordinated flypast of fleets of worlds meshing across the endless void. Shock waves thunder through the gas clouds, and millions of massive, short-lived new stars ignite and detonate like firecrackers. The starburst is indeed enormous. But for the most part, the inhabited worlds are safe: swarms of momentum-transfer robots, their numbers uncountable, work for millions of years ahead of and behind the event to direct the closest encounters. Emergent flocking rules and careful plans laid far in advance have steered colonies clear of the high-risk territories, marshaling brown dwarfs as dampers and buffers to redirect the tearaway suns—and both galaxies are talking to each other, for the expanding sphere of sentience now encompasses the entire Local Group.

Earth is no longer inhabited in this epoch; but the precious timegate remains, an oracular hub embedded in a cluster of exotic artificial worlds, conducting and orchestrating the dance of worlds.

There are now a hundred million civilizations within the expanding bubble of intelligence, each with an average population of billions. They are already within an order of magnitude of the Stasis's ultimate population, and they are barely a thousandth of its age. The universe, it appears, has started to wake up.

SLIDE 7.

The crystal ball is clouded . . .

The Kindest Lies

They walked along a twisting path between walls of shrubs and creepers, and a few short trees, growing from mounds of damp-smelling soil. The path appeared to be of old sandstone, shot through with seams of a milky rock like calcite: appearances were deceptive.

"You played me like a flute," said Pierce. He held his hands behind his back, as was his wont, keeping an arm's reach aside from her.

"I did not!" Her denial was more in hurt than in anger. "I didn't know about this until he—you—recruited me." Her boot scuffed a rock leaning like a rotten tooth from the side of a herbaceous border: tiny insects scuttled from her toes, unnoticed. "I was still in training. Like you, when you were tapped for, for other things."

They walked in silence for a minute, uphill and around a

winding corner, then down a flight of steps cut into the side of a low hill.

"If this is all simply an internal adjustment, why doesn't Internal Affairs shut everything down?" he asked. "They must know who is involved . . ."

"They don't." She shook her head. "When you call in a request for a timegate, your phone doesn't say, 'By the way, this iteration of Pierce is a member of the Opposition.' All of us were compliant—once. If they catch us, they can backtrack along our history and undo the circumstances that led to our descent into dissidence; and sometimes we can catch and isolate *them*, put them in an environment where doubt flourishes. If they started unmaking every agent suspected of harboring disloyal thoughts, it would trigger a witch hunt that would tear Stasis apart: we're not the kind who'd go quietly. Hence their insistence on control, alienation from family and other fixed reference points, complicity in shared atrocity. They aim to stifle disloyal thoughts before the first germination."

"Huh." They came to a fork in the path. A stone bench, stained gray and gently eroded by lichen, sat to one side. "Were you behind the assassination attempt, then?"

"No." She perched tentatively at one side of the bench. "That was definitely Internal Affairs. They were after him, not you."

"Him—"

"The iteration of you that never stayed in the Hegemony, never met Xiri, eventually drifted into different thoughts and met Yarrow again under favorable circumstances—"

Pierce slowly turned around as she was speaking, but in every direction he looked there was no horizon, just a neatly landscaped wall of mazes curving gently toward the zenith. "It seems to me that they're out of control."

"Yes." She became intent, focused, showing him her lecturer's face. "All organizations that are founded for a purpose rapidly fill with people who see their role as an end in itself. Internal Affairs are a secondary growth. If they ever succeed, there won't be anything left of the Stasis but Internal Affairs, everyone spying on themselves for eternity and a day, trying to preserve a single outcome without allowing anyone to ask why . . ."

Not everything added up. Still thinking, Pierce sat down gingerly at the other side of the bench. Not looking at her, he said: "I met Imad and Leila, Xiri's parents. How could they have survived? Everyone kills their own grandparents, it's the only way to get into the Stasis."

"How did you survive your graduation?" She turned and looked at him, her eyes glistening with unshed tears. "You can be very slow at times, Pierce."

"What—"

"You don't have to abide by what they made you do, my love. Corrupt practices, the use of complicity in shared atrocities to bind new recruits to a cause: it was a late addition to the training protocol, added at the request of Internal Affairs. It may even be what sparked the first muttering of Opposition. We've got the luxury of unmaking our mistakes—even to go back, unmake the mistake, and *not* enter the Stasis, despite having graduated. Agents do that, sometimes, when they're too profoundly burned-out to continue: they go underground, they run and cut themselves off. That's why there was no agent covering the Hegemony period you landed in. They'd erased their history with the Stasis, going into deep cover."

"You say 'they.' Are you by any chance trying to disown their action?" he asked gently.

"No!" *Now* she sounded irritated. "I regret nothing. *She* regrets nothing. Withholding the truth from you for all those years—well, what would you have done if you'd known that your adoring Xiri, the mother of your children, was a deep-cover agent of the Opposition? *What would you have done?*" She reached across and seized his elbow, staring at him, searching for some truth he couldn't articulate.

"I . . . don't . . . know." His shoulders slumped.

"All those years, you were under observation by other instances of yourself, sworn in service to Internal Affairs, reporting to Kafka," she pointed out. "Honesty wasn't an option. Not unless you can guarantee that *all* of those ghost-instances would be complicit in keeping the secret, from the moment you were recruited by the Stasis."

"That's why, back in college—" The moment of enlightenment was shocking. Yarrow's mouth, seen for the first time, wide and sensual, the pale lips, his reaction. He looked across the bench, saw the brightness in her eyes as she nodded. "I'd never betray her."

"It happened more than once, according to the Final Library. They can make you betray anyone if they get their claws into you early enough. The only way to prevent it is to make a palimpsest of your whole recruitment into the Stasis—to replace your conscript youth with a disloyal impostor from the outset, or to decline the invitation altogether, and go underground."

"But, I. Him. I'm not him, exactly."

She let go of his elbow. "Not unless you want to be, my love."

"*Am* I your love? Or is he?"

"That depends which version of you you want to be."

"You're telling me that essentially I can only be free of Internal Affairs if I undo what they made me do."

"There's a protocol," she said, looking away. "We can reactivate your phone. You don't have to reenlist in the Stasis if you don't want to. There are berths waiting for all of us on the colony ships . . ."

"But that's just exchanging one sort of reified destiny for another, isn't it? Expansion in space, instead of time. Why is that any better than, say, freeing the machines, turning over all the available temporal bandwidth to timelike computing to see if the wild-eyed prophets of artificial intelligence and ghosts uploaded in the machines were onto something after all?"

She looked at him oddly. "Do you have any idea how weird you can be at times?"

He snorted. "Don't worry, I'm not serious about that. I know my limits. If I don't do this thing we're discussing, him upstairs will be annoyed. Because Kafka will have all those naively loyal young potential me's to send on spy missions, won't he?" Pierce took a deep breath. "I don't see that there's any *alternative*, really. And that's what rankles. I had hoped that the Opposition would be willing to give me a little more freedom of action than Kafka, that's all." He felt the ghostly touch of a bunch of raisin-wrinkled grape joints holding his preteen wrists, showing him how to cast a line. He owed it to Grandpa, he felt: to leave his own children a universe with elbow room unconstrained by the thumbcuffs of absolute history. "Will you still be here when I get back?"

She regarded him gravely. "Will you still want to see me afterward?"

"Of course."

"See you later, then." She smiled as she stood up, then departed.

He stared at the spot where she'd been sitting for what seemed like a long, long time. But when he tried to remember her face all he could see was the two of them, Xiri and Yarrow, superimposed.

Saying Good-bye to Now

Twenty years in Stasis. Numerous deaths, many of them self-inflicted, ordered with the callous detachment of self-appointed gods. They feed into the unquiet conscience of a man who knows he could have been better, can *still* be better—if only he can untangle the Gordian knot of his destiny after it's been tied up and handed to him by people he's coming to despise.

That's you in a nutshell, Pierce.

You're at a bleak crossroads, surrounded by lovers and allies and oh, so isolated in your moment of destiny. Who are you going to be, really? Who do you *want* to be?

All the myriad ways will lie before you, all the roads not taken at your back: who do *you* want to be?

You have met your elder self, the man-machine at the center of an intrigue that might never exist if Kafka gets his way. And you'll have mapped out the scope of the rift with Xiri, itself rooted in her despair at Stasis. You can examine your life with merciless, refreshing clarity, and find it wanting if you wish. You can even unmake your mistakes: let Grandpa flower, prune back your frightened teenage nightmare of murder. You can step off the murderous infinite roundabout whenever you please, resign the game or rejoin and play to win—but the question you've only recently begun to ask is, who writes the rules?

Who do you want to *be*?

The snow falls silently around you as you stand in darkness, knee-deep in the frosted weeds lining the ditch by the railroad tracks. Alone in the night, a young man walks between islands of light. A headhunter stalks him unseen, another young man with a heart full of fears and ears stuffed with lies. There's a knife in his sleeve and a pebble-sized machine in his pocket, and you know what he means to do, and what will come of it. And you know what *you* need to do.

And now it's your turn to start making history . . .

Afterword—"Palimpsest"

"Palimpsest" wanted to be a novel. It really, *really* wanted to be a novel. Maybe it will be, someday. And maybe I could have gotten away with making it a short novel, just to round out this collection with an example of every format of fiction, if it wasn't for the imaginary voice of my editor nagging at the back of my head ("Do you know how much it costs to print a hardcover once it goes over five hundred pages?").

Part of the reason novels are the length they are is the cost of printing and binding. Binding a fat book is disproportionately more expensive than binding two thinner ones, and there is a downward pressure on the price of hardbacks, which makes it difficult for publishers to show a profit on a fat volume. No surprise, then, that many recent big fat fantasy novels have shown up split into two or more thinner volumes.

Perhaps once publishing moves wholesale onto the Internet, fashions in fiction length and the disappearance of printing and binding costs will lead to more and longer novels: but in the here and now, this short-story collection is pushing the limits of what I can get away with, without any need to add another hundred thousand words!

New in hardcover from
CHARLES STROSS

"Stross gives his readers a British superspy
with a long-term girlfriend, no fashion sense,
and an aversion to martinis."
—*San Francisco Chronicle*

THE FULLER MEMORANDUM
A Laundry Files Novel

When a top secret dossier known as the Fuller Memorandum vanishes—along with his boss—Bob Howard is determined to discover exactly what the memorandum contained (and perhaps clear his boss's name). But Bob runs afoul of Russian agents, ancient demons, and the apostles of a hideous faith who have plans to raise a very unpleasant undead entity known as the Eater of Souls.

Now Bob must use all of his skills to learn the secret of the Fuller Memorandum in order to save the world—and avoid becoming an item on the Eater of Souls' dinner menu . . .

M652T0310